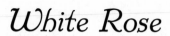

White Rose

FORGE BOOKS BY R. GARCIA Y ROBERTSON

American Woman
Knight Errant
Lady Robyn
White Rose

White Rose

R. GARCIA Y ROBERTSON

A TOM DOHERTY ASSOCIATES BOOK
NEW YORK

WHITE ROSE

This book is printed on acid-free paper.

Edited by David G. Hartwell

A Forge Book
Published by Tom Doherty Associates, LLC
175 Fifth Avenue
New York, NY 10010

www.tor.com

Forge® is a registered trademark of Tom Doherty Associates, LLC.

Library of Congress Cataloging-in-Publication Data

Garcia y Robertson, Rodrigo, 1949–
    White Rose / R. Garcia y Robertson—1st ed.
      p.   cm.
    "A Tom Doherty Associates book."
    ISBN 0-312-86994-0
    EAN 978-0312-86994-6
    1. Great Britain—History—Wars of the Roses, 1455–1485—Fiction. 2. Women motion picture producers and directors—Fiction. 3. Americans—England—Fiction. 4. Time travel—Fiction. I. Title.

    PS3557.A71125W47 2004
    813'.54—dc22

                                                        2004050081

First Edition: September 2004

Printed in the United States of America

0   9   8   7   6   5   4   3   2   1

For Allison, Steve, Allie, and Chanti

PART 1

Lady in Waiting

And ever, by the winter hearth
Old tales I heard of woe or mirth,
Of lovers' sleights, or ladies' charms
Of witches' spells, of warriors' arms.
—Sir Walter Scott

1

⊷⊜ Kenilworth Castle ⊜⊶

*L*ady *Robyn Stafford* sat on a grassy spot by the ruins of the great banquet hall at Kenilworth, eating a cucumber sandwich beneath soaring Gothic arches that enclosed empty October sky. She wore matte black French jeans and a scarlet riding jacket with MISS RODEO MONTANA sewn in gold on the breast. Red and gold were Lady Robyn's colors. Only her boots were British, fifteenth-century originals hand-stitched in medieval Northampton, but looking brand-new—not unlike Lady Robyn. Many medievals were maddeningly vague about their ages, and Robyn had picked up the habit. At twenty-something, she already felt centuries old.

Japanese tourists snapped photos of crumbling stonework while Robyn pictured the huge double-walled royal castle as she first saw it: basking under a hot summer sun, crammed with lords and ladies, knights and nuns, royal stewards and liveried washerwomen. She had ridden up from the south after spending the night in Stratford-on-Avon at a miserable inn with worse food. Smiling stable lads reeking of beer and manure had taken her white mare's reins, and a baron's son helped her dismount while minstrels strummed polished lutes and peddlers hawked snipe pies and fine Spanish lace to their betters. All that activity was ringed by towering walls and a vast hundred-acre lake dotted with swans.

Half a millennium had passed since those heady summer days in 1460, when Mad King Henry hid out here, avoiding the wrath of London. Walls were gone and the lake drained, leaving little but the shattered banquet hall and the tall stone keep alongside Elizabethan stables and a ruined gatehouse that were not even built when Robyn last saw the place. Of all those gallant lords and gay ladies, only Lady Robyn of Pontefract remained, relaxing in French-cut jeans with an electronic notebook on her lap.

"Is it true you ate here?" asked the nine-year-old next to her, a lively little girl with long black hair and wide eyes eager for wonder. Joy Grey was a godsend, happy to ditch school and tour ruins while listening to Lady Robyn stories—a witch child's notion of home schooling.

"Of course." Robyn flourished her cucumber sandwich, offering Joy some. "Here—you can, too."

Joy rolled bright gray eyes. "I mean with Mad King Henry."

"Several times." Robyn set down her sandwich and opened the borrowed electronic notepad in her lap. (Lady Robyn had left hers somewhere in 1461.) She typed:

Thursday, Kenilworth Castle, Warwickshire

Just the day, no date, since I am still badly in denial. (Wishing you were somewhere else is never a great place to be.) Back in the twenty-first century less than a week, and it already drives me nuts. Cars, roads, and buildings are everywhere, covering up the landscape, cold hard asphalt and concrete crowding out the farms, forests, and wild things. Where are the cottagers and hand weavers, the sheep and their shepherdesses, the forests and countryside, the wild wolves and the king's deer? I have not seen so much as a plow horse since coming back. Visiting familiar castles gone to seed is the sole thing keeping me sane and in touch with my "past life." Today it is Kenilworth, nearly obliterated by time and neglect, and inhabited by gawking tourists snapping Nikons and making rude comments in a king's hall. Amazing how the Brits put up with them.

Must keep reminding myself I am Lady Robyn Stafford of Pontefract, soon-to-be Duchess of York, and betrothed to the heir to the throne—otherwise I shall surely go mad. . . .

Robyn paused, summoning up a picture of the intact banquet hall, with its giant fireplaces and tall sculpted windows framed by banners and tapestires—all filled to overflowing, with ladies in long silk gowns and lords in gold-trimmed doublets arrayed around a high table draped in heraldic colors, a table so exalted that knights bused the dishes and lords served the meat. "They kept having me back," she boasted, "and King Henry himself fed me meat off his plate."

"Did His Majesty like you?" Joy thrilled to the hint of royal romance.

Robyn nodded. Even in those first amazing days at Kenilworth, when she was just a nobody from the future, Lady Robyn had already caught the royal eye. "And Henry knew I would not eat it any other way."

"Why not?" Joy demanded. At nine, the little witch wannabe took Robyn's tales for gospel, and her adoration made them fast friends. Joy wanted magic in her life, and Lady Robyn desperately needed someone to hear her story. She had lived through a fantastic adventure, spending months in the Middle Ages, meeting saints and sinners, princes and tavern maids, witnessing miracles and being fed offal off silver plate—only to return and find her own time disbelieving and indifferent. Joy Grey and her witchy mother were the only ones who listened.

Robyn made a wry face at royal tastes. "It was poorly cooked kidney with pickled lamprey."

Joy recoiled in horror. "Hideous!"

"And cokyntryce," Robyn added.

"What's that?" Joy was intrigued by the fairy-tale name.

"Roast pig with a chicken's butt sewn onto it." Medieval cuisine still made Lady Robyn shiver.

Joy grimaced. "You're making that up!"

"Wish I was. You should have seen the creature served on a silver plate, stuffed with peppered suet, painted with egg yolks, an apple in his mouth and the tail feathers stuck back into his butt." Robyn lost nearly twenty pounds in less than nine months, despite medieval attempts to force-feed her. "And folks call English cooking unimaginative."

"You sound American," announced a male voice in a London accent. Lady Robyn looked up to see a tall attractive Englishman standing beside her, wearing slate-gray jeans and a suede jacket over a classy print shirt and trendy shoes, smartly polished. He had clever eyes, elegant fingers, and an engaging grin, which made her think he was a graduate instructor, or maybe a musician—and good at whatever he did. He asked, "Am I right?"

"Sort of." Robyn nodded at the MISS RODEO MONTANA monogram on her pocket. She was born in Roundup, but had not been back since her parents died. Thanks to the generosity of King Henry VI, she had an adopted home with broad lands and a storybook castle—which, alas, no longer existed.

"She is Lady Robyn Stafford of Pontefract," Joy boasted, pronouncing it *Pomfret* like the cakes.

Robyn smiled up at the friendly, inquisitive Brit, knowing she hardly looked the part in her jeans and rodeo jacket—even though the boots were original, given to her by a young lord in love.

Saying his name was Brian, the good-looking Londoner asked, "You are just here visiting, right?"

"Certainly hope so." Trapped in this century, Robyn had urgent unfinished business back in 1461. She needed desperately to find the young lord in love who gave her the handmade boots and the white rose ring on her finger.

Handsome Brian had dark wavy hair neatly cut at his nape, framing a strong, clean jawline, full sensuous lips, and a candid smile. He asked, "But you do like Kenilworth?"

"Absolutely." Kenilworth had been an utter dream. From the moment Robyn rode down the walled causeway and into the outer ward, she felt she was in fairyland, cut off from the woes of the world, where fine ladies and gallant knights danced to the strumming of maiden harpers—but the rest of the Middles Ages was not nearly so garish and carefree. "Though it has gotten awfully run-down of late."

Brian nodded his agreement. "Henry Plantagenet would never recognize his banquet hall today."

"John of Gaunt." Robyn noted politely. "This hall was built by John of Gaunt, Duke of Lancaster, great-grandfather of King Henry the Sixth, the character in Shakespeare who says the "This scepter'd isle' speech." She quoted a snippet putting the ground with her hand, "This blessed plot, this earth—"

"—this realm, this England." Brian completed the line from *Richard II,* impressed she could correct him. "So you know something of our history."

"Not really." Until she found herself in the Middle Ages, Robyn had known next to nothing about English history—now she was intimately familiar with certain parts of it.

"You seem fairly knowledgeable about castles." Brian clearly did not care that some pretty American stranger might know more than he, displaying charming strength of character—confident yet unself-conscious.

Très attractive. Too bad she was already taken.

He cocked an admiring eye. "Or at least you know Kenilworth."

"A little." Robyn got up, brushing off her black jeans and sticking her half-eaten sandwich in her bag. Brian wanted company, and she liked Londoners, particularly bold charming ones undeterred by a ring on her finger and a child in tow—ones who decided she was worth whatever complications came with her. Quite a compliment, in its way. And smack on target. She was a genuine lady in distress, alone and nearly friendless in an age when most people thought her a mad liar. Thus far, only Joy and the girl's wayward mother believed her, making Lady Robyn oh-for-several-billion with the male half of the planet, an abnormal score. Some manly attention and support would be most welcome.

Even if she was spoken for circumstances demanded that she flirt a bit, confident it would swiftly end in disaster anyway. Despite his clear interest, this cute, daring Londoner only *thought* he was ready for her. Robyn, on the other hand, felt ready for anything. Living in the Middle Ages taught her to be totally unafraid of any man, no matter how suave and sexy, unless he at least carried a battle ax.

Strolling together toward the tall sandstone keep, with Joy running on ahead, Robyn recalled life at Kenilworth. "Henry the Sixth liked holding court here, to get away from London. He hated crowds and was always happiest when walled off from the world." She had some sympathy for the hapless king, who would have made a splendid monk.

Not at all monkish, Brian managed to edge the conversation around to her private life. "You seem awfully familiar with His Majesty."

Lady Robyn shrugged. "As familiar as you can get with a king who was grotesquely scared of women and has been dead for five hundred years."

"Does crimp the relationship." Young Brian was not afraid of women—not yet. The man plainly admired her tight jeans and tailored jacket, and Robyn could tell he was all set to see if American women were as loose as they say. Sorry lad, not a hope. Sometimes Robyn felt like *la belle dame sans merci.*

She shook her head, saying, "Pity this is all that's left. This keep was just a fortress and guardhouse. All the living space is gone, the galleried presence halls and grand apartments, where people lived and played." Lady Robyn still heard harp music in her head. She had celebrated Witches Night at Kennilworth, in a coven that included the Duchess of Bedford and a couple of the queen's ladies-in-waiting. Politics, sex, and spellcraft kept Mad King Henry's court in a constant whirl, leaving scant time for governing the country.

Brian reacted to the wistfulness in her voice. "You sound like you really miss it?"

"Very much," Robyn admitted. Not Kenilworth so much, but all of medieval England—its people, its problems, its mystery and magic. Kenilworth Castle was just a particularly amazing part, now much the worse for wear.

"Living in the past can be an addiction," Brian warned.

Robyn caught the hint: She might expect a marvelous future with someone new—maybe someone she just met. "Tell me about it." Robyn laughed. Did he think she was a widow? In a way she was, staying absurdly faithful to a boyfriend who had been dead for five centuries.

"Lady Robyn was here when there was a real court," Joy declared proudly, "with a king and queen, and princes and dukes."

Brian grinned at the talkative little girl, asking, "Which king and queen were they?"

"Mad King Henry and Margaret of Anjou," Joy replied, happy to get the names right.

"Charmingly imaginative." Brian turned his grin on Robyn, seeking adult rapport over the child's head.

Robyn hated to burst this guy's bubble when he seemed so nice and normal, and clearly liked her—but if brutally handsome Brian could not take the truth, he had no hope with her. When you have lain in a pitch-black cell in the Tower of London, trying to decide between being burned alive or tortured to death, you do not think twice about blowing off good-looking Londoners hoping to get into your jeans. Besides, she could not belittle Joy just to please some cute guy. "Actually, she is right."

"How so?" Brian waited for the catch.

Robyn shrugged, saying it as simply as possible: "I was here with Henry the Sixth and Margaret of Anjou. Hard to believe, but it happened. That's how I know Kenilworth so well. I saw the place in full swing, when it was King Henry's headquarters just before the battle of Northampton." Lady Robyn practically had to hold Mad King Henry's hand during that sharp brief battle, waiting for her lord Edward to fight his way to them.

"We're witches," Joy Grey announced smugly. "We can do anything."

"Is that so?" Brian looked taken aback, seeing the winsome young American he was chatting up suddenly transforming into a raving lunatic in a monogrammed riding jacket, French jeans, and old English leather.

"Well, not really *anything*," Joy admitted, coming back down to earth a bit, "but a whole lot."

Brian suddenly remembered he had somewhere to go, and said a hurried good-bye. Moments later he was as gone as Queen Margaret and Mad King Henry.

Sheesh. Robyn shook her head. Why should a little thing like being a medieval lady scare him so? Nobility was not AIDS or leprosy. Whatever became of English manhood? But young Master Brian, with his swank Estuary accent, had probably never swung a naked broadsword or faced spears and arrows wearing just a ball gown and an anxious grin. How could he ever hope to deal with her?

Lucky she had a boyfriend back in 1461. Medieval men were way more open-minded when it came to madwomen. No young knight-errant hitting her up would much care if Lady Robyn claimed to be from the moon. Lunacy in women was expected; otherwise, they would be men. Lord Fauconberg's wife, Joan, was insane since birth, but he married Lady Fauconberg for her lands and title, not for her mind. When Robyn's own true love first told her he was Edward Plantagenet, Earl of March, she thought he was nuts, too. But she heard him out and ended up having the adventure of her life—a gest Robyn hoped was not over yet.

Alas, not many folks wanted to hear you had a fabulously exciting life in a previous century. As soon as Robyn even hinted she was a medieval lady, betrothed to a royal prince, and stranded in the wrong century, eyes glazed over, or they widened in alarm. Potential dates suddenly remembered pressing engagements—though not to the heir apparent. Their loss. Being Lady Pontefract was incredibly exciting. She had been the belle of masked balls, starring in pageants, tournaments, and a few flat-out battles, living in castles and Greenwich Palace, and whipping up the Thames to Westminster in a galley flying her personal colors—with the handsomest young noble on the Royal Council at her side, and in her bed. Nice work if you could get it.

Bidding good-bye to King Henry's phantom court, Robyn headed back to the car, offering Joy the rest of her cucumber sandwich, which she no longer felt like eating. Robyn was hungry enough, but somehow white bread, cucumber slices, and homemade mayonnaise made her queasy. When she first returned to the world of fast food and health inspectors, Robyn wanted to gain back all the weight she lost in the Middle Ages in one sitting—only to find she had a sudden sensitivity to processed food. Even coffee tasted questionable, and a mere whiff of cigarette smoke made her gag. Now cucumber and mayo had turned on her, as well.

Jo Anne Grey, Joy's mother, had lent Robyn the family car. Called *Bouncing Bettie* or the *QE2*, the car was a big battleship-gray Bentley, 4.5-liter coupe, built sometime in the last century and reputed to have been through the blitz. As well as starring in an early Bond movie. Luckily, Lady Robyn learned to drive on a Montana farm truck, or she would never have managed the Bentley's locomotive transmission, not while driving without a license on the wrong side of the road.

"Did you like him?" Joy asked, leaning on the dash, which was decorated with the Grey family crest, a silver wyvern.

"Who? King Henry?" Robyn merged into fast traffic headed for Banbury, still wary of the way tons of metal whipped by without warning, missing her by inches at a mile a minute—a menace the Middle Ages never even imagined. "Henry was okay, for a neurotic lunatic. Pity he had to be king." Medieval politics made as much sense as today's.

"No, Brian." Joy nodded over her shoulder. "Back at Kenilworth, with the posh accent."

"Oh, he was nice enough." And his London accent had been utterly charming. "Too bad he did not stick around."

"Bit skittish, if you ask me," Joy decided. "And he did not take well to us being witches."

Not well at all. What was it with modern men? Deflating male egos was not nearly as fun as it sounds. Robyn had wanted Brian to believe her, and she would have dearly welcomed some manly sympathy. Ardent young Brian should have been thrilled to hear her betrothed lived in 1461, but instead he took off like a startled snipe. "You have to get used to that," Robyn warned, adding significantly, "if you want to be a witch."

"What did your Edward do?" asked Joy, who very much meant to be a witch, having taken in spellcraft with her mother's milk.

Robyn turned onto A452, crossing the Foss Way, an old Roman road transformed into two-lane blacktop. Edward was like a fresh stirring breeze compared to stuffy Master Brian. "When Edward found out I was born five hundred years off, he just wanted to know more. Everything about me fascinates him, and Edward listens attentively to my 'future fairy tales'—even if he does not like what he's hearing." She tried hard not to speak of Edward in past tense.

"What happened when Edward found out you were a witch?" That was the big question, the one that got women burned.

Robyn laughed. What her lord Edward did when he caught her doing Halloween spellcraft in the family castle was not for little girl's ears. "Just a spirited tongue lashing. Edward likes that I am a witch."

"You are so lucky." Joy enthused over Robyn's utterly romantic boyfriend, who at eighteen was already Earl of March, and Duke of York—ignoring the many practical problems of being betrothed to a historical figure.

Broughton Castle was much better maintained than Kenilworth, being a functioning manor owned by the Fiennes family since the Middle Ages. Sir William Fiennes, the second Lord Saye and Sele, and the first of his line to live here, had been a good friend of Robyn's, a gracious neighbor, and a fellow rebel against the crown. Robyn toured the older parts of the castle with Joy, including the much reduced great hall, and the stairs built by William of Wykeham. Joy asked excitedly, "Was I here?"

"We walked right up these stairs together." The reason the Greys believed Lady Robyn was because Joy's family were immortal witches themselves, repeatedly reborn throughout the centuries—something Robyn would never have believed if she had not seen it herself. When she arrived in the Middle Ages, Robyn had found medieval duplicates of Joy, her mother Jo, and her uncle Collin, living in the fifteenth-century Cotswolds—looking and acting much like their modern counterparts.

"We did?" Even though Joy was an exact twin of the medieval girl, the novice witch had little memory of her previous lives. In fact, the whole Grey family relied on Robyn to tell them about their medieval incarnations. Joy marveled at the worn stonework. "Up these very steps?"

"Hand in hand," Robyn recalled, running her fingers over the ancient rock, amazed that she herself had been there. Joy's medieval twin was her constant companion in that first horrifying month in the Middle Ages, acting as guide and mentor, sharing feather beds, shepherd's rests, and prison cells with Robyn. "Lord Saye and your uncle Collin had filled me with wine and brandy." One reason the Middle Ages got so messy was that the nobility rightly refused to drink the water, and went about half-swacked, making sober government impossible. "I was most glad for your help."

Their tour ended at Berkeley Castle, in the dungeon cell where Robyn spent her first night in the Middle Ages, along with Joy's medieval double—both of them charged with witchcraft. Being thrown unexpectedly and unwillingly into the past was horrific enough, but ending the day in a dungeon along with a child-witch totally topped it off. Dismal did not even start to describe her feelings. Her stay in the Tower was longer and more harrowing, but for sheer psychic shock, nothing matched that first day.

Joy asked solemnly, "This is where you met the medieval me?"

Robyn nodded. "You were sitting on that stone bench, with your magpie for company." The medieval Joy had a talking magpie familiar, a bird called Hela.

Joy's hand found hers, seeking security. Modern witch-girls did not have to worry about being tossed into Berkeley dungeon—for tourists to photograph and gawk at—but so far as Joy was concerned, that girl five centuries ago was also her. "Was I scared?"

"You had been crying, but you mostly looked bored." Robyn was continually amazed by how medieval children took on adult tasks. Medieval Joy had been a model prisoner, and Edward was still eighteen when he liberated London, won at Northampton, and convinced her to marry him. "You refused to give in to them, too, telling outrageous lies to your captors."

"And we got out," Joy added proudly. Thanks to help from the future. Joy had lifted the latch with Robyn's VISA card. Too bad Lady Robyn left that pricey bit of plastic in the Middle Ages, since it would be useful nowadays, as well. Together they said a hushed prayer to Hecate, the witch-goddess of death, who had them in her hands but did not take them—that time.

As they left the cell, they met a young guy on his way in. The gent smiled and shook his head, saying, "Gawd, what do you think it'd be like, ending up in this hole?"

"Do not even get me started," Robyn warned. She led Joy out into daylight, retracing the path she had used to escape.

They drove back through the ancient Saxon village of Winchcombe, now grown into a modern town, passing Sudeley Castle, where witch hunters caught up with Robyn and Joy after their escape from Berkeley. There, on Robyn's fourth morning in the Middle Ages, Sir Collingwood Grey fought a trial-by-combat on horse and foot against Gilbert FitzHolland to win her freedom. She had stood watching under the oaks of Sudeley park while two men in armor hacked away at each other, with her life as the prize. Another harrowing medieval moment she would never forget.

When she got to Joy's house, there was a message waiting for her from Heidi, Robyn's assistant back at the studio in L.A. "Hey, boss lady, what gives? Thought you had gone back to 1492?"

Jo Anne Grey, Joy's mother, made tea in her tiny kitchen, while Robyn sat with her elbows propped on a small linoleum table whose pattern exactly matched the linoleum floor. Jo's two-bedroom cottage had a shabby elegant air, with the Greys' wyvern crest on the silverware, and torn magazine pictures decorating the walls. Looking a lot like her offspring, Jo had straight black hair and a long strong face that seemed sterner on her than on her smiling, mischievous daughter. "Your assistant sounded concerned," Jo told her, "really worried about you. That's the second time she's called."

"Who? Heidi?" Robyn was trying to avoid thinking of her studio job and her life in Hollywood. Heidi was her spacey oversexed

~~production assistant, who read scripts, critiqued pitches, rolled~~
joints, and seduced reluctant costars, keeping Robyn clued in and
off the casting couch. "Yes, Heidi loves me a lot."

"Maybe you should ring her up," Jo suggested. "Just to say you
are okay."

"Wish I were." Robyn shook her head. She didn't have the heart
to return Heidi's call. "I said my good-byes to Hollywood, and I
desperately do not want to go back. This does not even feel like the
present to me. I look at the headlines and think, *Who cares?* Stock
fraud. Drug wars. Religious terrorism. Anthrax and no-cal snacks.
Makes the Middle Ages look absolutely enlightened." And worst of
all, there was no Edward nowadays.

"Our British papers are a bit of a fright," Jo Grey admitted
sadly, setting the teapot onto a hand-stitched coaster while her
daughter buttered homemade bread with a centuries-old knife
bearing the family crest.

"News from the States is just as pointless." Already Lady Robyn
felt like an expatriate. If she could not get back to the Middle Ages,
would the English let her stay here, at least? Probably not. She was a
titled lady, though she would have a devil of a time proving it—but
if the Brits could swallow "Sir" Mick Jagger, why not Lady Robyn
Stafford? "We have so much compared to medievals, yet we keep
making such a mess of things." Robyn thought of all the peasant
families that had taken her in, sharing their meager meals and giving her the best bed. Welsh even got down and washed her feet, and
then harped to her while she ate. "And the Middle East—please."
During her months in the Middle Ages, she had forgotten there
were parts of the "modern world" even more insane. "When you
have lobbied a papal legate against a new crusade, it is hard to take
car bombs seriously."

Jo arched an eyebrow. "You met a papal legate?"

"At a danse macabre," Robyn recalled. "In Bruges, a city criss-
crossed with beautiful canals." Women had all kinds of rights in the
more civilized parts of the third millennium, but back in the Dark
Ages, Robyn got to make really important political decisions, plotting coups and diplomatic missions, scuttling crusades, freeing
serfs, and baby-sitting Mad King Henry.

"Was I there?" asked Joy hopefully.

"At Bruges? Sorry." Robyn hated to disappoint the girl. "By then you were already in the Tower."

"Rats!" Joy wanted in on everything.

"Big black ones." Lady Robyn shuddered at the black rats in the Tower cells. She had slept curled atop the torture rack, just to be off the floor. Swiftly switching subjects, she told Jo, "Did you know I thought about starting a London tabloid?"

"In medieval London?" Jo grinned.

"Seemed totally natural." Robyn still liked the idea, hoping to do it someday. "London is the most gossipy town imaginable. And the medievals have printing, only it has not reached England yet."

"Sounds super." Jo poured her some Earl Grey tea ("some of ours" in Grey family slang). "So why didn't you?"

"I had to leave London a leap ahead of the law," Lady Robyn confessed.

"Accused of witchcraft?" Jo asked sympathetically.

Robyn nodded. "Necromancy, heresy, high treason, flouting the law, aiding and abetting a fugitive—"

"Oh, my." Jo was taken aback by Lady Robyn's list of offenses.

Robyn added honey to her tea. "—and attempting to murder the king's heir."

"Was I there?" Joy demanded.

"Absolutely." She smiled at the little witch wannabe. "We were indicted together."

Jo Grey shot her a quizzical look. "Sure you want to go back?"

"Afraid I have to." Robyn took a sip, finding the tea warm and comforting—she must be sure to take some back with her.

Friday, Witches Night, Cotswolds, Gloucestershire

It's witching hour—time to wake up and get to work. I do not even know the date, since my watch is still on medieval time. FRI 1-16-61. I haven't the heart to change it. That date on my wrist is electronic evidence, the only "proof" that I have actually been to the Middle Ages. How else did my digital clock get set for 1461? Right now I grasp at any prop to my insanity.

Speaking of psychos. Heidi called from L.A. Twice. How long can I keep my so-called life on hold? I certainly do not want to go back. I don't even want to talk to them. By now the studio must be wondering what the heck has happened to me—not a bad question, but one I prefer not to answer. I cannot think about a life in the present when I am still trying to get back to 1461. Tonight is Witches Night, and I must try to contact Edward. Holy Hecate, help me to get where I need to go. If I do not see Edward soon, I will end up as crazy as Lady Fauconberg. . . .

Setting the journal aside, Robyn cast her circle alone on the floor of Jo's spare bedroom, lighting a long green candle to remind her of her love, and of the spring they hoped to see together. She wore a winter-black silk slip, borrowed from Jo's Victoria's Secret collection, and the gold coronet and white rose ring Edward gave her. Jo and Joy had begged to join in the ritual—but Lady Robyn was far too harried and desperate to take on amateurs. When she first came to the Cotswolds, she was the helpless innocent, Miss Robyn Wide-Eyes from Roundup, Montana, hopelessly in love with Jo's bounder of a brother, while the Greys were the family of immortal English witches, with their manor house, dog pack, noble ancestors, and outrageous ways. Now she was witch, and they were the rich wannabes. Just because she was sent to the Dark Ages—much against her will—where she had to learn the Witches Flight or die.

Weirdest of all, she could not wait to get back. Centering her consciousness on the candle flame, she let her mind drift. By now she did not need chants or incantations, not when seeking Edward. All she had to do was open her heart, and her soul went to him. This was a special link between them, sealed by the miracle they had shared in snowy Sherwood, when Holy Mary opened a door into summer.

Sinking deeper into the candle flame, she felt the fire grow, pushing back the walls and filling her world with light, turning the dark fall bedroom into a bright spring day. Green trees on green hills, looked down on grassy pasture, broken by patches of bare gray heath. Blackbirds were out, and she spotted may blossoms on a bit of hawthorn. Bits of landscape seemed familiar, but all Lady Robyn could say was that she was somewhere in medieval England, most likely north of the Trent.

Her biggest hint that she was back in the Middle Ages was the horse between her legs. Somehow she was on horseback, wearing a red-and-gold riding dress and her ruby-studded coronet. Very medieval. And her mount was Lily, the white mare Edward had given her in the walled port city of Calais. Beneath Lily's dainty white fetlocks, Robyn saw green cropped pasture sprinkled with spring buttercups. In her first trip to the past, she had gone straight from fall to spring, leaving the third millennium in late October and arriving on April twenty-third, Saint George's Day—making this current hallucination seem encouraging, a sort of repeat arrival. Now all she needed was Edward.

"Happy to be home?" asked a bold familiar voice. Robyn looked around and saw her love sitting on his big black Friesian warhorse. Tall, brave, and handsome, Edward looked every bit the young feudal lord, from the white rose on his jaunty blue cap to the gold spurs on his big hip boots. He wore his own colors, a plush tunic—in a purplish black shade medievals called *murrey*—lined with royal blue that showed through the loose ragged-cut sleeves. At eighteen, Edward Plantagenet, Earl of March and Duke of York, outranked everyone in England, save only King Henry—yet he always treated Robyn as someone special, brightening whenever he saw her. "Or are you remembering the future?"

"What do you mean?" Even in a witch's dream, it was disconcerting to go from a dark October night to a bright spring day, especially one five hundred years away.

He leaned forward in the saddle, smiling, easily, sunlight shining on his long honey-brown hair, his gaze fixed on her. Edward had a mail T-shirt under his tunic and a sword at his hip, but for him, that was practically unarmed. Relaxed and happy, he acted like he had no cares, except what might be troubling his love. "Sometimes you get that faraway look, and I wonder if your mind is in the next millennium."

"At times it is," she admitted. Her mind and her body, as well. Right "now" she felt like a disembodied observer, able to ride and speak, but not daring to do anything that might break the spell. Push the spell too much, and she would be thrown back to the present.

"Do you wish you were back there?" he asked, turning solicitous. Lady Robyn had spent her first months in the Middle Ages frantically trying to get home to the twenty-first-century. Edward had to convince her to stay.

"Not at all." She shook her head, wanting horribly to be "here" in the Middle Ages with him, in flesh as well as in spirit. Reaching out, she had him bring his big black charger, Caesar, alongside her white mare so she could take his hand. Edward complied, interlacing his fingers with hers, riding with his leather hip boots and blue tights brushing her red-and-gold riding dress. Leaning over, he kissed her, and she kissed back, thrilling to the fresh clean taste of his mouth. God how she had missed this.

And not just the kissing either. She missed having a man who saw the world the way she did. Her very own knight in armor, devoted to justice, honor, and mercy, while holding them all second to her in his heart. Twice Edward had cheerfully put himself between her and witch hunters, defying law and religion for the woman he loved. And who loved him. Sometimes she thought the feeling between them was so strong that they could do anything together—right now they were triumphing over time and distance, keeping their love alive despite centuries of separation.

Closing her eyes, she gave in totally to the kiss, enjoying the fleshy contact, feeling his grip harden, his fingers thrust forcefully through hers. This bold boy was her feudal overlord, and he clearly wanted to do much more—like take her to some friendly manor or convenient castle, order the castellan out of bed, and then rip off her red-and-gold gown and do to her body what he was doing to her mouth. Her thighs tightened at the thought, hugging the saddle harder. Lady Robyn desperately wished to make this contact permanent, but at the same time she strove to enjoy the moment, doing nothing to break the tenuous spell.

Necking on horseback took practice, but luckily she had been doing it ever since she was a teen—being Miss Rodeo Montana was not all blue ribbons and barrel racing. Their horses ambled along side by side in the spring sunlight, unconcerned by the lewd goings-on upon their backs. Lily and Caesar had been through parades, battles, tournaments, and neck-or-nothing chases, so a little mounted lovemaking did not bother them in the least. Startled snipes took off from the grass in front of their hooves, zigzagging away into the blue overhead.

Cheers and laughter erupted around her. Opening her eyes, she saw little shepherdesses laughing at them from behind a hedge.

Their older brothers leaped up and gave Edward a hearty, "Aye-aye, ooray!"

And they did it in Yorkshire. Suddenly Lady Robyn knew where she was. This was her own Honour of Pontefract, north of Sherwood; in Barnsdale, not far from Wentbridge. She had never seen it in the spring before, free of snow and covered in green, and she had never seen her people looking so warm and well fed—but their West Riding accents were unmistakable. And these children knew her, too, crying, "Lady Pomfret. Lady Pomfret. Who is your lord?"

Then they collapsed in giggles. Ever since they helped Lady Robyn escape from her own castle—disguised as a dirty-faced stable boy on Holy Innocents' Day—the children of Pontefract had claimed her for their own, freely addressing their lady in the most atrocious Yorkshire accents.

How utterly astounding. Last time she saw her Honour of Pontefract it had been locked in winter, with snow on the ground and held fast by the enemy. The Duke of Somerset had made tall, white-towered Pontefract his military headquarters, defeating and killing Edward's father in front of Sandal castle. Now Robyn was seeing her Honour of Pontefract as it should be seen, covered in jade-green pasture, broken by bits of forest and fallow. Did this mean she and Edward had come together in the spring, when Pontefract was free and at peace?

"These people do like you." Edward eyed her happily, tickled to hear the children cheer her. Some of the shepherd lads were just a year or two younger than he, but Edward was the one with the sword and the horse, who got to kiss the lady of the manor. He was boy enough to thoroughly enjoy that, taking more pride in having her at his side than in all the honors heaped on him of late—like his murdered father's dukedom.

"It really amazes me," she confessed, unable to believe how popular Lady Robyn had become. When she left Roundup as Miss Rodeo Montana, headed for Hollywood, Robyn Stafford's life had been on an upward sweep, buoyed by cheers from the crowd—then during her years at the studio, applause had turned to canned laughter. How strange to find the cheers again, here in the fifteenth century.

"Why so? I like you." Edward assumed a royal duke's approval ought to be good enough for this rabble. By rights the children should have bowed to him, but if Edward had stood on his rank, he would never have had any fun. "Why should they not like you, too?"

"For one, I am still their landlord." Not to mention a weird witch from somewhere that did not exist.

"You mean the king is. You are just the pretty spendthrift who threw His Majesty's rents away." He kissed her again, getting more cheers from the children, who enjoyed seeing Her Ladyship in the hands of such a handsome stranger.

Her single attempt at medieval estate management had been a ruinous disaster, because she did not have the heart to take her revenues out of these children's mouths. Edward had gotten Mad King Henry to assign her the royal revenues of Pontefract—but as soon as she was faced with a bad winter, Lady Robyn renounced her feudal dues and forgave their rents, leaving herself horribly in debt to Venetian bankers. Only marriage to her rich young boyfriend would solve Lady Robyn's money problems, something the children probably sensed. "And you speak their language," Edward added. Though he was heir to the Duchy of York, Edward's "native" speech was Norman French—having been born in Rouen. Raised abroad and speaking Court English, Edward understood Latin better than he did upcountry Yorkshire. In contrast, Lady Robyn spoke easily with her tenants, since the Displacement spell that sent her to the medieval England let her speak whatever language was spoken to her. Just as in this Witches Night dream.

More boys came up, deserting their chores, followed by mothers and fathers, hastening to see what lord their lady was entertaining. Bowing to their betters, they wore homespun cloaks and gowns dyed with berry juice, or russet brown oxide, over soft tan linen mixed with hemp; muted, earthy colors that contrasted sharply with Edward's bright royal blue and her own scarlet silk and cloth-of-gold. The last time she saw these people, Lady Robyn was being led south by the Wydvilles, following the Duke of York's defeat at Wakefield. People had lined the road to see Lady Robyn safely away, after the Earl of Salisbury and other prominent Yorkists were executed at Pontefract. Then they had been grim and wary, standing bareheaded in the slush, women weeping and the men holding their bows and bills. Now they had hoes, shepherd's crooks, and wide happy smiles. Bold souls among them shouted greetings to Lady Robyn in West Riding accents.

Robyn translated for Edward, "They want to see who their lady is dallying with." Flattering, for sure, but a bit embarrassing, since they had first seen her come riding in with Duke Somerset, and now she was with Edward of March, the new Duke of York. Lady Robyn did not need any additional marks on her already dubious reputation.

Edward smiled at their impudence. "I did not know I needed their permission."

"They are most protective of me," Lady Robyn explained. Her Honour of Pontefract was Robin Hood country, and just south of them was Skelbrooke, with Robin Hood's Well and Robin Hood's Stone. From here to Sherwood, every cottage had its ax and bow, and the locals would stand up to the sheriffs' men, or even to a royal army—when the need arose. Right now they were just happy to see their lady with a stalwart young lord, even if he was a southerner.

Edward approved the sentiment. "My lady is well worth keeping safe."

How good to hear. Her "ladyship" was purely nominal, an insane king's extravagance, but coming to Yorkshire had made it real. She was now Lady Robyn of Pontefract, whether she liked it or not—since if she gave up the honor, it would only go to someone who would treat the people worse. She would not have them suffer because of her.

"And you gave them hope," Edward added. "You gave them hope during a terrible hard winter."

"Really?" She doubted it was that simple, though Edward was immensely popular among his own people, and should know whereof he spoke.

He nodded solemnly. "Just as you give me hope for the future." Edward did not think much of England's high-tech tomorrow, not wanting to see the land paved over and tilled by machines instead of by people, or to have horses replaced by metal monstrosities that fouled the air. In fact, the only thing he really liked about the far future was her. But Edward of March accepted that these commoners would one day run "his" England, and he was careful to win their respect and get their consent whenever he could. Even here in wild remote Yorkshire, among northerners who had cheered his father's death at Sandal. His willingness to look beyond north and south, Welsh and English, or noble and commons was most endearing.

One young shepherdess came hesitantly forward, holding a clay cider jug out to them. When the girl got to them, Robyn nodded for her to give the jug to Edward, saying, "He is my lord, and must be served first."

Bowing obediently, the girl handed the cider up to Edward, then turned back to her, saying, "My lady, you saved me when I was sick this winter."

"I did?" Robyn tried to remember the girl, who had auburn hair and big brown eyes. Tenants often brought their sick children to her, knowing she was a white witch, and Lady Robyn dispensed herbal remedies, antibiotics, and chocolate candy as the situation required—but she never took credit for cures. Life and death came from the Goddess. "More likely it was Mother Mary."

"Mayhap." This young shepherdess did not sound convinced, and she held out her dirty hand, which contained a tiny silver triangle. "But I know you gave me this on Holy Innocents' Day, and m'lady should have it back."

Reaching out, Robyn took the bit of silver, which felt cold and heavy in her hand.

Instantly, medieval Yorkshire disappeared, whisking away Edward, the little shepherdess, and the entire Honour of Pontefract, including the mare Robyn was riding. She found herself sitting on the floor of Jo's spare bedroom, feeling sick to her stomach and holding something hard and cold in her right hand. Her green candle had burned down and gone out, and she had to fumble for the light switch.

Lamp light flooded the room, confirming that she was indeed back in the twenty-first century. Opening her fingers, she saw she was holding a piece of silver, a triangle with one rounded edge. Printed along the rounded edge was the name HENRY. Robyn recognized it at once: it was a quarter of a silver groat.

Closing her palm, she pressed her fist against her forehead, feeling sad, ecstatic, and nauseated all at once. She had touched Edward, even kissed him. And she had brought back a bit of fifteenth-century silver. But when the candle was burned down and Witches Night was over, she was back in the twenty-first century, feeling sick to her stomach. What did it mean that she and Edward were together and happy in the springtime? And in her own Honour of Pontefract? Was it just a dream, a wish in her heart? Or did it mean they would have a beautiful future together, even if it was five hundred years in the past?

Life in the Middle Ages had taught her to be thankful for whatever was given. Pressing the quarter groat between her palms, she prayed to Mary, thanking the Goddess for this latest vision, for letting her see Edward and her people. All she asked for was to return to the Middle Ages, where her love was waiting, for she missed him terribly. When she was done, she crossed herself, then went into the bathroom to puke.

Jo was waiting in the hall when she got out, wearing a white lace nightgown and looking worried. Born and bred to witchcraft, Jo Anne Grey could sense when something was awry. "Feeling okay?"

"Just a little queasy," Robyn lied.

Jo did not press her, saying cheerfully, "Hope it's not my cooking."

"Wish it were," Robyn sighed. More likely her morning nausea came from not having had her period since the Middle Ages. She went back to bed, hoping to wake up in 1461.

2

☞ Heidi ☜

*H*ey, boss lady! Wakey, wakey." Someone banged loudly on the bedroom door, rousing her abruptly. Robyn fumbled about and found her watch, forgetting it was set on medieval time. Unable to work out the "real" time in her head, but guessing she was still in the third millennium, Robyn got out of bed and warily opened the door.

She was immediately grappled by a busty young blonde wearing dead black lipstick, with matching blouse and nails. Squealing in impish delight, Robyn's happy assailant wore formfitting jeans with laces up the sides, showing a half-inch strip of skin running from her ankles to her waist. Surprised and sleepy, all Robyn could say was, "Heidi? What the hell are you doing here?"

Hugging Robyn to her, the young woman swore, "Jesus, I never thought to see you again."

"Me, too." Robyn slowly realized that her hyperactive production assistant had flown in from Hollywood without warning. "Thought I had lost you for good."

Heidi scoffed. "You have to go way beyond the Dark Ages to do that."

Apparently. She had hoped her old life in L.A. would just die quietly without her. Fat chance. Her previous existence had taken on a life of its own, a very substantial life, with an excellent job, a neat car, nifty apartment, and stock options, all strong enough to reach across the Atlantic to try to drag her back. She had gleefully run up her credit cards, financing her last trip to the past, figuring she would be gone for good—by now the first bills were about due, along with the rent on her West Hollywood apartment, which she had no hope of paying without going back to work for the studio. Out of that entire mess in Hollywood, the only thing Robyn really missed was Heidi. Now the woman came banging on her bedroom door.

Wiping black lipstick off her cheek, Robyn led her enthusiastic assistant into the little kitchen, where Jo Grey sat next to the tea-kettle, amused by the raucous reunion. She told Jo, "This is Heidi, but I guess you already know that."

Jo nodded at the tea settings on the linoleum table. "We were getting acquainted."

"Lady Grey would not let me wake you before eight," Heidi explained, seating herself at the table. "Even if it's my job."

"Was your job," Robyn corrected Heidi, putting Hollywood securely behind her. Selecting a cup from the drying rack, she sat down next to Heidi and across from Jo.

"What a job it was." Heidi smirked, then reached into her skimpy top, pulling out a small plastic bag filled with a green leafy substance. "Nothing to do but throw parties and orgies, watch movies, put some laughs in lame scripts, and give head to household names—then try to be back to work before noon. Damned hard to believe we even got paid."

"Does seem rather amazing." Jo looked askance at the dime bag on her kitchen table.

"And I was perfect for it," Heidi proclaimed, opening the bag and starting to roll. "Amazing thing was that until Robyn came along, no one would hire me."

"Absolutely astonishing," Jo agreed, getting up to close the kitchen curtains and latch the front door.

Heidi shrugged. "Something about needing a high school diploma."

Sitting back down, Jo agreed. "Employers can be most particular."

"Not in Hollywood." Heidi scoffed at Jo's naïveté. "Patty Duke and Tatum O'Neal won Oscars before they were in high school. Shirley Temple was the world's biggest box office star in the fuckin' fifth grade."

Jo Grey tried to put a polite spin on these revelations. "American education must be very advanced."

"Not so you would notice." Heidi licked and sealed the joint, asking hopefully, "This stuff legal here?"

"Alas, not." Jo hated disappointing a guest.

"Good thing I brought it in my bra." Heidi produced a lighter from her pants, asking, "Okay if I break the law?"

"So long as Joy is not up." Jo happily exposed her daughter to witchcraft and necromancy, but not to illegal narcotics.

Heidi lit up, took a deep drag, and then looked at Robyn, asking, "Where did you get the ring."

She glanced down at the silver rose ring, saying, "Edward gave it to me."

Heidi grinned at her. "Your medieval earl?" Heidi was the only normal person who would truly believe her—though *normal* might be a stretch.

"He is more like a duke now." Robyn refused to think of Edward as dead, meaning to keep him as loving and alive as he was last night.

"Outstanding." Heidi took another drag on her joint, saluting Edward's elevation to a dukeship. "Kid's got taste. I knew he would treat you right." Heidi had always been a big fan of Edward, even from afar.

"Show her the coronet," Jo suggested.

Thrilled to have people here-and-now wanting to hear about her incredible life in the past, Robyn bounded up and went to the spare bedroom, returning with her gold-and-ruby coronet and the silver quarter-groat. Her coronet was a gold circlet set with six crimson rubies—Stafford colors. "Edward gave it to me, in Shrewsbury, when he announced our betrothal."

"Jeez." Heidi set down the joint and picked up the coronet, balancing it on her fingertips and admiring the bloodred rubies. "Why don't guys give me stuff like this?"

"Because you have not been to 1461," Jo pointed out.

"Figures." Heidi set the coronet back down on the kitchen table. "I have been with really big stars. Guys that millions and millions of people pay just to look at on the screen—all I got was herpes."

"Here is what's really amazing." Robyn showed them the quarter-groat, given to her that night by the brown-eyed Yorkshire girl she had cured. Her silver ring and a gold coronet were gifts from Edward, along with Lily, her white mare. *Très* generous—but having a good lord was like that, if you were lucky. This paltry bit of silver held out the hope that Lady Robyn might somehow return.

Heidi picked up the bit of hacked-up coin, puzzling over the inscription. Even Jo's teaspoon was more impressively medieval, with its silver wyvern crest, same as on Sir Collingwood Grey's shield. "What is it? And who's Henry?"

"Part of a groat," Robyn told her, "a silver coin minted by Henry the Sixth. A groat is worth four pence. On Holy Innocents' Day, I was down to my last handful of groats, so I cut them up into pennies with a chisel. Medievals literally *make* change. I gave this penny to a little shepherdess whose family fed me honey cakes when I was escaping from Pontefract Castle."

Heidi squinted at the quarter coin. "How do you know it is the same one?"

"Because that girl gave it back to me last night." Robyn knew that sounded fairly insane, but rational explanations would do her no good at all.

Heidi did a quick mental calculation. "Wouldn't that make her six hundred years old by now?"

"No." Robyn shook her head. "She was still under ten. She gave it to me in Barnsdale, below Wentbridge, just a few miles south of Pontefract Castle."

"You were in the Middle Ages last night?" Even Heidi had a hard time with this.

"Sort of." Robyn glanced at Jo, who was a witch descended from witches. Technically you were not supposed to tell witches' secrets to stoned and frivolous strangers from the States—but Heidi was clearly an exception. "Friday nights are Witches Nights, sacred to the Goddess. *Friday* means 'Goddess Day.'"

Heidi reached for her joint, which had gone out. "And I thought it just meant the weekend."

"That, too." Robyn agreed. Friday meant freedom, as well, and millions celebrated the witches' Sabbath without ever knowing it. "But last night I did a Witches Flight, an out-of-body trip to the past. Edward was there, and this little shepherdess, who gave me this penny back, because I cured her."

"Bo Peep's got a conscience." Heidi fished for her lighter. "So why didn't you stay there?"

"I am not that good a witch." So far Robyn had made only temporary out-of-body trips. That quarter-groat on the table was the first physical transfer through time she had ever made—an amazing bit of practical magic, but not nearly enough to get her where she needed to go. "Wish I were."

Relighting her joint, Heidi tried to make sense out of magic. "How did you get there in the first place?"

"A long story." Robyn gave her the abridged version of how she was first sent into the past by a local witch called Widow Wydville, with the aid of Collin's wife Bryn, Jo's sister-in-law.

"Would dear old Widow Wydville send you back again?" Heidi asked.

Robyn shook her head. "Not likely. Widow Wydville is the reincarnation of the Duchess of Bedford, the witch-priestess who returned

me to the present when I refused to betray Edward." She did not
expect Old Widow Weirdville would be nearly so helpful the second
time around. Though you could never be sure, since the modern
Widow Wydville knew things the medieval one did not. More than
one witch had ended up betraying herself.

Heidi took a long drag on her joint. "Do you truly want to go
back?"

Folks kept asking her that. "With all my heart." Kissing across
the centuries was fun and uplifting, but it was a mere shadow compared with really being there. "I will do anything to get back."

"Then it has to be Bryn," Heidi decided.

Robyn was shocked—Bryn despised her for sleeping with her
husband, Collin. Though the rotter had not told Robyn he was
married, Robyn felt royally bad for messing up Bryn's life. Had she
not blithely let Collin seduce her, none of this would have happened. "Bryn's the last person I want to see."

"Exactly!" Heidi exclaimed happily. "And the last person who
wants to see you here."

"But I do not even know if Bryn can do it," Robyn protested.
When she said she would do anything to get back, that had not
included confronting Bryn.

Heidi rolled her eyes. "Never hurts to ask."

Easy for Heidi to say. Robyn looked over at Bryn's sister-in-law.
"What do you think?"

Jo considered, then replied, "Bryn does have the best motive for
sending you back."

Too true. Robyn had seen Collin's wife twice in this century; the
first time Bryn threw her out of Greystone, and the second time
Bryn helped hurl her back to the Dark Ages. At worst, it would be
a painful scene, but even that was better than moping around, wishing she were with Edward. She asked Jo, "Will you go to Greystone
with us?"

"Certainly." Jo felt guilty about her part in the whole business,
being a member of Bryn's coven and the one who introduced
Robyn to Widow Wydville in the first place. Jo, Joy, Bryn, and the
good widow had all been at the ritual where Robyn was suddenly
catapulted into the Middle Ages. "I will gladly do what I can."

As soon as Joy was up, they all piled into the QE2 and headed down A46, taking the turnoff to Snowshill, an ancient abbey manor from the *Doomsday Book,* not much changed since it belonged to John Dudley, Earl of Warwick, who lost his head trying to put Lady Jane Grey on the throne of England. From there, they took the private tarmac road that led to the Greys' estate. Heidi's jaw dropped when she saw the stately manor sitting on Shenberrow Hill astride the Cotswold Way, framed by ancient burial mounds. "Some folks know how to live."

"This old place?" Jo laughed, saying, "Been in the family for ages. Hardly worth the upkeep, but we hang on to it out of sentiment."

"I'll bet." Heidi's eyes went wide as tall wrought-iron gates swung open on their own and the tarmac road turned into a gravel drive.

By now Robyn had seen Greystone at various times and conditions, as a modern mansion, and a medieval manor, and as a burnt ruin, partly rebuilt. Now it was back to being a glitzy twenty-first-century mansion with an ivy-walled porter's cottage, floodlit gardens, and two huge "new" wings built when Queen Victoria was a kid. (Hereabouts "modern" additions could be a couple of centuries old.) Leaving the Bentley in the gravel drive, Jo led them up the wide steps and through the French doors into the main hall. This had been the medieval keep, with a high wooden ceiling, and fire-scarred stone. Robyn had seen flames put those marks there during her first month in the Middle Ages, when witch hunters led by Gilbert FitzHolland sacked the manor and set fire to Greystone. Hopefully this visit would go better.

Collin Grey was there to greet them, a handsome male version of Jo—bigger, taller, and more rakish, with a spade beard and broad shoulders, but the same serious gray eyes and finely curved lip. Robyn had fallen for those dark good looks twice, once in Hollywood, and once again in the Middle Ages, where Collin's identical ancestor, Sir Collingwood Grey, fought that joust under the oaks of Sudeley park that saved her from the stake. How could she not feel thankful toward a brave strong fellow who risked life and limb to keep her from burning alive? That was the attraction of firemen. Thank goodness, she would not make that mistake a third time.

Heidi was the one with eyes for Collin, as she sashayed into the ornate grand hall, already totally at home. Half her reason for fly-

~~ing the Atlantic was~~ to get another chance at Collin, now that her boss had dropped him. "Some digs," Heidi declared. "It is thrilling to see you again."

Collin was not so sure, trying to hide behind feigned ignorance. "Heidi, is it?"

"*Enchanté.*" Heidi held out her hand for him to kiss.

He shook it awkwardly, attempting to keep Heidi at arm's length. Robyn wished him luck. Usually at ease with females, Collin was not at his best confronted by his sister, his nine-year-old niece, the woman he betrayed, plus her ardent young assistant. Looking to his sister for help, Collin asked, "What can I do for you?"

Before Heidi could suggest anything outrageous, Jo informed her brother, "We came to see Bryn."

Collin grimaced at the notion of dragging his estranged wife into this. Then every key female in Collin's adult life could be in the same great hall, all making demands on him. "I fear Bryn is not even seeing me."

Bryn must have taken his latest infidelity to heart. Jo asked, "Has she gone back to Wales?"

He nodded. "Taking the boys. To live with her old nurse, Agnes, last I heard." Collin was clearly rattled, having lost track of his wife and sons, left alone in this huge house, with only dogs and servants for company. Heidi practically had him to herself.

"Does Nest have a phone these days?" Jo asked. *Nest* was the Welsh name for Bryn's old nurse.

Collin shook his head. "Nest does not exactly live in this century."

Or the last one either. Nest was another immortal witch, reborn throughout the centuries. In fact, Robyn had first met Nest in the Middle Ages, far up the Afon Mynwy in the Golden Valley, when she and Sir Collingwood Grey were fleeing from the the sack of Greystone. Worming back into the conversation, Heidi asked, "Do we have an address?"

"Not even that." Collin sounded relieved not having to account for his witchy wife—there must have been scant peace in Greystone since Robyn first flew in from California. "Nest lives in a forest hut, far up the Eden on a nameless dirt road in Gwynedd."

"I know how to get there," Jo announced. Being coven members, they shared greater secrets than the location of Nest's cottage.

That meant they were through at Greystone. Much to Heidi's dismay, she was forced to settle for a second awkward handshake and a cheerful, "See you soon."

Not if Collin could help it. Robyn doubted the rotter had learned his lesson, but the last thing Collin Grey's shaky marriage needed was a new American girlfriend, no matter how pert and eager. During the brief interview he barely said a word to Robyn, which was just as well. She much preferred the medieval Sir Collin, who had seduced and betrayed her, too, but at least he'd saved her life first. Medieval bounders had more style.

Back at the cottage, Jo offered up the Bentley for an expedition into Wales. "Joy has lessons this afternoon, and you are not likely to be back before nightfall."

If at all. Hopefully Bryn would send her back in time right away. Robyn asked, "Do you trust Heidi to drive it home? If I get where I'm going . . ."

"Suppose I have to." Jo sighed. Thinking of Heidi bombing down the wrong side of the road, high and happy, was enough to give any responsible car owner pause. But having bested the blitz— not to mention a Bond movie—the Bentley could probably survive Heidi at the wheel.

"And, well . . ." Jo hesitated. "Parting is hard, for if all goes well, I shall surely miss you. By now it seems like we have known each other forever. . . . But most of all, I hope that you are happy. Whatever happens."

Whatever happens? Looking into her friend's eyes, Robyn saw that Jo knew what was coming. "You have read ahead, haven't you?"

Jo nodded soberly. Robyn had resolutely refused to read what happened to England in 1461—not wanting to know what her future might hold. Jo had clearly succumbed to temptation. That was one problem with being a witch: your future was never fully sealed, especially when it was in the past. You could know your fate—not that Robyn wanted to. She took Jo's hand, saying, "Thank you for being such a friend."

"You, too." Jo gave her hand a squeeze. Whatever Jo knew, Robyn would find out on her own. Jo Anne Grey had meddled far too deeply in Robyn's life already, having set Robyn on the path that led to Edward, and Medieval England—all in the name of cheering Robyn up. Which had worked wonderfully, though plunging a friend five hundred years into the past was a drastic way of putting her present problems in prospective.

Robyn arched an eyebrow, amazed at how circumspect Jo had become. Was 1461 that terrible? "Are you not even giving me a hint?"

What witch could resist the chance to prophesy? Jo laughed, thought for a moment, and then told her gravely, "Three things . . ."

Recognizing the magic number, symbolizing maiden, mother, and crone, Robyn listened intently—there might come a time when remembering Jo's precise words would be vital.

Jo began with the crone, saying, "Here is a gift from Hecate. If you see three suns in the sky, do not fear for Edward. He will not die that day."

"Three suns?" That was a bit much, even for the Middle Ages— but if it kept Edward safe, she was thankful.

Jo nodded, adding, "And when things seem most hopeless, trust in Mother London."

That went without saying. Jo finished with the maiden. "And if you and Edward have a daughter, name her Grace."

Robyn had not expected something so personal. "What makes you think I am pregnant?"

"I did not think you were." Jo sounded worried that she might have said too much. "I only meant if you two had a daughter, naming her Grace might help preserve her through the perils of youth and childhood."

Grace it is, then. If she was pregnant. And if it was a girl. Concern about the high childhood mortality was her biggest reason for not going back. Good sense and sanitation only got you so far—but Jo had given her added hope. By now Lady Robyn was medieval enough to know there was magic in a name. She thanked Jo for the three prophecies, and they kissed good-bye.

Then Robyn gave Joy a good-bye hug, and the little witch-in-training told her cheerfully, "See you in 1461."

"Hope so," Robyn replied heartily, slipping behind the wheel of the Bentley, with Heidi sitting in what should be the driver's seat, already starting to roll. Putting the Bentley in gear, Robyn pressed her accelerator foot to the floor, and the big two-inch exhaust boomed into life. They were off, headed west for M5, the major north–south motorway cutting through Hereford and Worcester. North of Birmingham, she turned west again, leaving the built-up area behind her, headed into Shropshire.

As the countryside got greener and the towns fewer, Heidi leaned against the passenger window, saying, "So tell me about Edward."

"What's to tell?" Now that Robyn was at the wheel, going somewhere, she felt like she might see Edward soon, maybe even tonight. She could easily be driving right to him. "He is wonderful. Suddenly I have this boyfriend who does everything right, who is strong and caring at the same time, charming and cute, but not utterly full of himself. Despite being a royal duke. He listens to me, even when he does not like what he hears."

"Sounds like the lady's in love." Heidi laughed. "So what's he like in the sack."

"His second favorite pastime is dancing," Robyn told her pointedly. "That and partying with me. But he sobers right up the next morning, and goes about running the country. Spending half the time in council, and half the time on horseback."

"Rescuing fair maidens and smiting evildoers?" Heidi got most of her information on the Middle Ages from Saturday-morning cartoons.

"That, too." Robyn smirked at the modern notion of medieval life. "He saved me a couple of times, but that was just a sideline. Edward fights only when he has to, though when he does, he is scary good at it."

"Really?" In Hollywood, Heidi got to sleep with "action heroes"—but Edward was the real thing. "So, have you seen, like, jousts, or sword fights?"

And more. "Edward killed two men in armor on the first day I met him."

"Jeesus!" Heidi shook her head in wonder. "That must have been something."

"You bet." That was when she started taking the Middle Ages seriously. "Edward had no choice. We were attacked by an armed mob—knights on horseback, armored bowmen, everything—only Edward's mace and warhorse saved us."

Heidi whistled softly. "Whew, just what you look for in a first date."

Hard to believe she wanted to go back. Having a teenage lord—as adept with a lance as he was on the dance floor—could be a real challenge. "At first I thought he was incredibly nuts, showing up in plate armor on a big black warhorse, claiming to be a medieval lord—"

"Makes total sense," Heidi agreed. "Only a bimbo would believe him."

"When I discovered he was telling the truth, I thought I would go crazy, trapped in the Middle Ages without so much as a toothbrush. Then Edward seemed too good to be true, a medieval warrior who was generous and compassionate, respecting women and forgiving his enemies." Robyn shook her head in amazement. "But he is really like that, courageous and honest, and determined to do right."

Heidi grinned at her friend's good fortune. "Add to that the thrill of having a brawny young warlord, who can snap baddies in half, bursting to show you a good time in bed."

"There is that, too," Robyn admitted. Edward's enthusiasm for her was astonishing at times.

Heidi arched an amused eyebrow. "But does he have a steady job?"

Robyn rattled off Edward's titles. "He is Earl of March, Earl of Ulster, Duke presumptive of York, and heir apparent to King Henry—"

"Quite a mouthful."

"So is Edward," Robyn replied smugly.

"And he brings out your lewd side." Heidi laughed, slapping Robyn on the knee. "I like that. I really do."

So did Robyn. She missed Edward mightily, and not just in bed—which was why she was headed hell-for-leather into Wales to see a witch who hated her. Robyn did not stop until she got to Shrewsbury, the county town of Shropshire, whose medieval core was enclosed by a big loop of the Severn. Standing guard over the "landward" approach to the peninsula was the much-rebuilt Shrewsbury castle—only the walls were truly medieval. Here Robyn halted and dug into her pack, getting out the ruby-studded coronet, saying, "I got this here."

"Really?" Heidi turned the coronet over in her hands and then tried it on, liking the way it felt. "So did you get this in the bedroom or at some big Court ceremony?"

"Lords and ladies were present," Robyn recalled demurely.

"Like in a throne room," Heidi asked, "with you on bended knee before him."

"Actually, it was during a game of strip backgammon."

Heidi handed back the coronet. "Now you are making the Middle Ages sound fun."

"Sometimes it was." And sometimes not.

Shrewsbury was fun. They went shopping using Heidi's credit cards, buying medieval essentials like tampons, toilet paper, cold pills, and instant coffee. This was the second such shopping spree Robyn had been on, and it was an incredible experience to see techno-industrial civilization reduced to what you could carry, finding out just what was absolutely needed. Fortunately Lady Robyn had already discovered there was a lot she could do without. The only downside was seeing how much Shrewsbury had changed. Heidi thought the place was unbelievably old, with its narrow crooked streets, black-and-white timber-framed houses, and Elizabethan market hall—but aside from the ancient walls, the city Robyn and Edward had shared was nearly gone.

"This was going to be our capital," Robyn recalled. "Edward and I were the Lord and Lady of the Welsh Marches, while Earl Warwick held London and King Henry. People cheered when I rode through the streets wearing that coronet, happy to have us ruling them, instead of being plundered by a mad king and a French queen. Now there is almost nothing left."

And no one was cheering her. Heidi was getting the looks, smiles, and occasional whistle, as Shropshire lads eyed the strips of bare laced flesh running up her thighs. Totally ignoring the attention, Heidi asked her, "So what is the same?"

"I'll show you." She took Heidi to Saint Mary's church, on the ground south of the castle, with its tall Norman tower and great stained-glass Jesse window. "This is where we came to pray for those who died at the battle of Wakefield, including Edward's father and brother."

"You make it sound so real," Heidi whispered.

"It was," Robyn told her, going down on her knees to give thanks to Mary. Heidi knelt beside her, and locals stared at the two pretty American tourists, praying in silence. When she was done, Robyn crossed herself, then rose and led Heidi out of the church.

"You did not used to be religious," Heidi observed.

Robyn smiled at her assistant. "You have to have been there."

Getting back into the Bentley, she drove west across the Welsh Bridge, headed deeper into the Marches. Crossing Offa's Dyke and then the Severn, she entered Wales, passing Powys Castle, an old Grey stronghold turned into a stately home and tourist attraction, surrounded by splendid grounds and terraced gardens, open noon to five on Saturdays. Robyn pointed it out to Heidi, who asked, "So did you sleep there, too?"

Robyn nodded. "In a bedroom decorated with silk hangings and Italian paintings, belonging to the Earl of Worcester."

Heidi looked impressed. "The guy who invented the steak sauce?"

"That was probably a relative." John Tiptoft, Earl of Worcester, was not called the Butcher of England for inventing Worcestershire sauce, but for cutting up and impaling his victims.

"So what was Lord Worcester like in the sack?" Heidi was delighted to be getting the bedroom tour of the Marches.

"Hard to say. He was in Italy at the time." Brushing up on torture techniques with the Borgias, no doubt. Robyn had never even met the man, just borrowed his bed. Many medievals spent their whole lives in their birth hovel, but not the nobility, who were descended from the horse nomads who overran the Roman empire, making aristocratic life one huge game of musical beds. Lady Robyn had slept in half the castles and keeps in the Welsh Marches—stop to revisit each of them, and they would never get anywhere.

Driving deeper into Wales, Robyn watched the land get wilder and less inhabited. Here was country she had never seen, not in this millennium or the last one. Past Welshpool, there were no built-up areas, just small towns, trailer parks, and campgrounds. Steep narrow roads wound through deep green valleys, first in Powys, then in Gwynedd. When they got to Dolgellau on the far side of Wales, Robyn turned north up the Vale of Eden, plunging into the Coed y Brenin, dense woods coming down to cover both sides of the road, crossed by foot trails and dotted with picnic sites.

Following Jo's instructions, Robyn turned left off the highway and onto a side road that crossed the Eden, then climbed the Rhinogs, ragged wooded hills between the Eden and the sea. The farther she went, the worse the roadway got, turning first into a gravel road, then shrinking to a rutted forest track. When the two-inch tailpipe banged against rocks and dirt, Robyn reminded herself that Jo had driven this road several times in this same battleship-gray coupe, so it could be done. Hopefully by her. Soon she was edging along in second gear, then in first.

Finally the "road" gave out in a leafy glade that ended in a footbridge that would never bear the Bentley. Robyn cut the engine and relaxed, working tension out of her shoulders. "Well, that's it."

"What now?" Heidi asked, staring into the green tangle around them.

Robyn heaved a sigh. "We walk."

"Sounds like a good medieval solution." Heidi pulled on a leather jacket, then helped Robyn get out the pack and a car blanket from the "boot," plus the food Jo packed them—in case they got lost. They hid the keys in the glove box, and then crossed the footbridge, finding a trail on the far side headed uphill. As they mounted the footpath, the flow of water faded, and they were surrounded by autumn silence, with just the soft squish of fallen leaves underfoot. Shadows crept out of the undergrowth, filling the darkening sky. Night was coming on.

"How much farther?" asked Heidi, unable to take the quiet.

"Not far," Robyn hazarded.

"How do you know?"

Robyn took a deep breath. "Smell the wood smoke?"

"Could be campers," Heidi suggested.

"Could be," Robyn admitted, "but it is not."

Just ahead, the trees opened up, and she saw another grassy glade.

This one contained a whitewashed half-timbered hut with a sagging thatch roof, looking for all the world like Snow White's cottage, minus the dwarves. Carved serpents twined around wooden pillars supporting a small thatched porch, framing a blue painted door. Heidi whistled, "Witchy and then some. What shall we do?"

Robyn smiled at Heidi's surprise. "Come on, Hansel, let's see who's home."

Stepping onto the hand-carved porch, Robyn knocked on the blue door, not sure what she would say to Nest, assuming this was not some other witch's hut. Nest was not the most talkative sort to begin with, and when she did speak, it would most likely be gibberish. Worse yet, Robyn no longer spoke Welsh. While in the Middle Ages, Robyn had been under a Displacement spell, which caused her to speak and understand, Welsh, Gaelic, Middle English and even medieval Danish. Speaking Cockney or Broad Northumberland like a native was an exhilarating experience—one more reason to go back to the past. Here and now, she could barely order a "cob and bangers" without sounding silly. Nest would be a real challenge.

But it was Bryn who answered, lovely as ever, her shining chestnut hair cut short in the Welsh fashion, showing off her elegantly curved neck and sculpted shoulders. Bryn was a witch born of witches, descended from Owen Glendower, the greatest Welsh wizard since Merlin, and the last native Prince of Wales. Ungodly proud and unfairly slender, Bryn never liked having Robyn around, not here or in the past, where Sir Collin was both Bryn's husband and Lady Robyn's personal champion—an unusual ménage, but Collin could not be happy without at least a couple of women feuding over him. Behind her, playing on the floor, was her youngest son, an impossibly cute combination of her and Collin.

Welsh hospitality called for Bryn to offer soap and water, so they could wash their feet. When Robyn first met the medieval Bryn in the Golden Valley, Bryn had gone down on her knees and washed them herself. Clearly her modern counterpart was not in the mood, curtly asking, "Why have you come here?"

Why, indeed? Suddenly the notion of going begging to Bryn did not seem so brilliant. She was perpetually showing up at Bryn's doorstep unannounced, crashing Collin's birthday party at Greystone, arriving on the run in the Golden Valley, and again at Delapre Abbey, and always to look for Collin, or worse yet, arriving with Collin in tow. But not now, this latest visit being totally Collin-free. "I was hoping to get your help."

That coaxed a cold smile out of Bryn. "What could I possibly do for you?"

Having slept with Bryn's husband on two continents and in different centuries, Robyn understood the hostility. Too bad, because when she first met Bryn, she thought they might be friends—showing what a shocking bad seeress she was. "Actually, I hoped you might send me away."

"How much farther away could you go?" Bryn eyed her evenly. "I put all of Wales between us, yet here you are at my door."

Nest's door, but Robyn saw her point. Until this moment, Bryn must have thought she was reasonably well hidden, living deep in the forest without fax or phone, at the end of an unmarked trail where even the Royal Mail could not find her. Robyn strove to reassure her rival, saying, "Far, far away."

"I tried that once," Bryn reminded her.

Too true. "Well, maybe this time it will stick."

Laughing outright, Bryn asked, "And your friend?"

"Heidi." Heidi held out her hand happily. Whatever carnal thoughts Heidi had about Collin, there had been no time to carry them out; entitling her to a reasonably clear conscience.

Bryn did not shake her hand, merely asking, "Are you going, too?"

"Nope, just came to see Robyn off." Used to being spurned, Heidi turned her gesture into an open-handed shrug. "Afraid I am here to stay, at least until my plane leaves Heathrow."

"Too bad," Bryn told her, but invited them in anyway. "This is not my home, but I am sure Nest would not mind."

Nest's house made Robyn feel instantly at home, with its rammed earth floor and smoky stone hearth; a small curtained hall separated the pantry and buttery from the main room and from a single back bedroom. Cast-iron cookware hung from the ceiling, and the sink was a brass tub and wooden bucket placed conveniently beneath the window. Water came from one of those weird Welsh wells, dug right in the floor, and the privy was at the downhill end of the clearing. By medieval Welsh standards, Nest lived in luxury, with a real hearth and smoke hole, and separate bedroom, instead of fire trenches and sleeping rushes piled along the wall—it did not take a lot of imagination to think you were in 1461. Heidi clapped her on the back, chuckling, "Halfway home already."

Bryn offered them sweet bannock and seaweed soup with mussels and onions, not having any herself. Welsh let beggars off the road eat before them, and had Bryn meant to be inhospitable, the woman would not have let them in. Sipping her seaweed soup, Robyn watched Bryn putter about, sorry there was no time to get on better terms. At least she had a truce of sorts with the medieval Bryn.

When her two older boys came home, Bryn ate with them by the light of oil lamps. Her walking and talking youngest was still nursing at will. Bryn did the dishes, as well, tossing the wash water out the window. There was no sign of Nest, and helping their host clean would have been against Welsh custom. As dusk deepened outside, Bryn asked the boys, "Where is Nest?"

Bryn's older boy shrugged, "In the woods. Won't likely be back till morning."

"Said she was searching for skulkers," the younger boy volunteered. "Three of them."

His older brother rolled his eyes, knowing better than to give adults too much information to chew on. Bryn shuttered the windows and bolted the door. No one questioned the wisdom of leaving the sixty-something Nest alone in the woods on a cold October night, or doubted the old woman's ability to deal with three night stalkers—whoever they were. Nest was notoriously able to defend herself, and if cold Welsh nights were going to kill her, they would have done so long ago.

Eventually the boys went to sleep in the bedroom, leaving the women awake and waiting. Bryn asked Robyn, "Do you really want to go back?" Even Bryn seemed to find that unbelievable.

Robyn nodded emphatically, "With all my being."

Bryn looked unconvinced, asking, "Do you know me in the past?"

Robyn nodded again. "Rather well."

"And Collin?" From the way Bryn said it, there was no good answer.

"He is not why I am going back," Robyn replied defensively. That was all Bryn needed to know.

Bryn sniffed. "He'd better not be."

"I have never lied to you," Robyn pointed out. She was not sure she could lie to Bryn, not successfully anyway.

"Very true," Bryn conceded. "You slept with my husband, crashed my party, and intruded on my solitude in the woods—all in straightforward American fashion."

"So if I am such a nuisance, why not send me away?" Robyn suggested coyly.

"Why not?" Bryn went to a small painted chest and produced a pair of black witch's shifts, handing one to Robyn, then began to strip off her dress.

"Don't I get one?" Heidi stood with one hand in her jeans pocket, watching them don the witch's shifts.

Bryn arched an eyebrow. "Are you an initiate?"

Heidi shook her blond head.

"Do you want to be a witch?" Bryn pulled the shift over her head, wearing nothing beneath the black fabric. Robyn did the same.

"Never thought of it that much." Heidi shot Robyn a questioning look.

"Maybe you should just watch," she suggested, not wanting to drag her assistant too far into this. With the keys to the Bentley waiting in the glove box, Heidi was free to duck out anytime.

"Whatever you say." Heidi sounded happy not to give up her leather jacket; Nest's hovel was colder than most Hollywood nights.

Bryn cast her circle between the hallway curtain and the hearth. All three of them were on their knees, their bodies centered on three corners of the circle, Robyn and Bryn in their black shifts, Heidi in her laced-up jeans and fur-trimmed jacket. Kneeling with her pack in her lap, Robyn looked over at Heidi, realizing that if this worked, she might never see her friend again. Sad, since Heidi was one old friend she would truly miss. There was certainly no one like her in the Middle Ages. She told her, "Have fun in L.A."

"When I am done here." Heidi was in no hurry to go home to

Hollywood, not with Collin sulking alone at Greystone urgently in need of TLC.

Bryn began to chant, slowly at first, gradually quickening the tempo. Letting go of Heidi, Robyn sank into the chant. Displacement rituals did not have to be done on Witches Night. When she first went to the Middle Ages, she left on a Saturday and arrived on a Wednesday. Any day would do, so long as Edward was there. Sinking deeper into herself, she concentrated on Edward. Her love for him could power a spell, and more than once it had brought them together. Magic was like anything else worth having, impossible to force, but miraculous when it worked.

Closing her eyes, chanting along with Bryn, and hugging her pack, she tried to think of nothing but her and Edward. Suspended in darkness, she reached out to him across the void, searching through empty blackness for him, opening her soul to the cosmos. In a twinkling, she was gone.

Opening her eyes, she found herself kneeling on the floor of her little tower room in Baynards Castle. She was back. Un-fucking-believable. Heidi was gone. And Bryn. And Nest's Iron Age cottage. She was back home in her own room, in Baynards Castle, the fortified London headquarters of the House of York, built into the southwest corner of the city wall. There was no need to pinch herself. This was not some Witches Night dream of riding the over lonely moors with her long-lost love; the carpeted floor felt firm and real, and the room was lit by a single tall taper. She wore the same black shift as at Bryn's, which felt no more or less tangible than the plush Persian carpet beneath her. Cold raised goose bumps on her skin, and she could smell the Thames wharves through the narrow arrow slits spaced along the wall. Night breeze made the candle flicker.

When was she? That was the real question. She had not been in this room since the first week in November, when she had to flee London one leap ahead of the law. It would be terribly awkward if there was still a warrant out for her, accusing her of high treason and plotting murder by witchcraft. This felt like a cold night, but not wintry, and there was no frost on the stone sills. Did that mean late fall? Early spring? Setting down her pack, Robyn stayed on her knees, thanking Hecate for bringing her home. Whatever month it might be, this was still a miracle.

Having given thanks, Robyn rose and lit a pair of lamps, then got a red-and-gold robe out of her cedar clothes chest, wrapping herself in her own colors. How wonderful to have all her things again, to no longer be dependent on handouts and hand-me-downs. Taking up the tall candle, she went to look for Edward.

If her love were here, he could make her legal difficulties go away. If Edward was not here, she had to get dressed and down to the stables, and light out for Shropshire to look for him. That was where she left him, on a frigid January Witches Night in the Welsh Marches—the second one of 1461. Her hope was that she had come down later in that year, with London back in Edward's hands. They had left London and King Henry in the care of Lord Warwick—not her first choice by any means—but Edward was needed on the Marches, to raise troops and fend off the Tudors. And for reasons Robyn could barely fathom, Warwick was ungodly popular in London, especially since he and Edward had returned Mad King Henry to his capital, freeing trade, and letting London get on with the kingdom's business. What most medievals wanted was good, sane entertaining government that did not cost them much.

Edward would gladly give them that, and more. But first she must find him. Lifting the latch on her door, she descended the stairs and headed for Edward's private quarters in the castle keep. Normally Edward used the main hall for state occasions and kept the castellan's quarters for personal use—he enjoyed being the greatest lord in the land, but not all the time. Edward insisted on being himself, as well, much to the despair of his noble family. Aside from attending secret conclaves and state dinners, their private life was a lot like that of a modern couple who lived together and planned to marry, but also happened to be running a medieval country.

Luckily, midnight was the perfect time for skulking about a castle, which had neither guards nor interior lights; everything was pitch black and empty, and everyone else was asleep. More castles were taken by someone sneaking in at night through the chapels and latrines than were ever carried by battering rams and armed assault. Stealing silently along, she missed Heidi, who was perfect at snooping—alert, imaginative, and wary when needed. Too bad the girl would not be born for several centuries. At least they'd gotten to see each other one last time. She whispered a prayer for her far-off friend: "Hecate help you, Heidi. And Diana defend you, for I cannot."

Happily, her big oak, copper-bottomed bathtub was in Edward's presence chamber. Excellent omen. Edward had the vat-shaped tub hauled into the chamber whenever he was in residence, to cater to her mania for cleanliness and increase his chances of seeing her naked. His bedroom door was unbarred, and she silently eased back the latch.

Edward's stuff lay strewn about—books, a lute, wool tights, odd bits of armor, his favorite mace. More good news. Anyone could have been using the room, and she did not mean to crawl in bed with some castellan and his wife. Or worse yet, Edward's mother, Proud Cis, dowager duchess of York. For all she knew, her future mother-in-law still wanted her hanged and quartered. Edward's white-and-gold canopy bed was closed, and the only light came from her candle. Walking cautiously across the carpet, she paused at the curtain, holding her breath. Nothing, not even breathing, just the cold musty smell of a castle at night. Parting the curtain, she peered inside.

Empty. Staring at his down comforter and bed linen, she considered her options. Strip naked, snuff out the candle, crawl in, and wait for him. That's what Heidi would do, and it had an edgy appeal. Certainly it was what Edward would most want.

Good sense prevailed. She did not know when or if Edward was coming to bed, and who he might bring with him. If she had been gone for months, he might well have given up on her. And London had plenty of comely lasses who would love to console the sad young Duke of York. Better to go looking for Edward. He might be right below her, carousing in the keep hall, or less likely, praying in the private chapel.

Candle in hand, she left the bedroom and crossed the presence chamber to where another door led to the stairs. She felt a queasy twinge as she drew the bolt—this was where she had been caught making Halloween magic. London constables, led by a prominent

Yorkist MP, had burst through this door, surprising her and Joanna Grey while they were holding a midnight séance with a couple of small girls and a serving woman. Not her finest Witching Hour. Hopefully she would do better this time.

Opening the door to the stairs, Robyn saw a glow in the light well below. Someone was moving in the darkened keep hall, carrying a lamp, and coming her way. This was right where she had fallen afoul of the law once before, since her Halloween bust for witchcraft led to the charges of treason and attempted murder. Watching through the crack in the door, she waited to see who was coming. So long as she kept her candle low, anyone mounting the stairs would not see her.

Boots rang on the stones. Peering past the cold stone doorjamb, she saw it was Edward, looking serious and sober, and handsome as ever, with a long brown lock falling over his furrowed brow. She had done it. He was here, alone and headed her way, carrying a single tall candle, its flame as stiff as a spear point.

Whatever Edward's worries, she knew how to put a smile on his face. Backing into the presence chamber, she shut the door, then retreated to the bedchamber, where she blew out the candle. Now she could greet him the way he would most enjoy. Finding the bed by feel, she burrowed into icy bed linen, not having the nerve to wait totally naked. Too bad. No medieval woman would have thought twice, since they slept naked as a matter of course, even when sharing a bed with girlfriends, something that had taken Lady Robyn much by surprise. Wearing clothes to bed was just another of Lady Robyn's manias, like daily baths and drinking boiled water. Luckily the English appreciated a pretty eccentric—except for the inhospitable few that wanted her burned at the stake. God, it felt good to be back.

Curled atop the feather mattress, she heard Edward enter the room and then remove his boots, followed by the soft sound of fabric falling on plush carpet. Heart hammering, she listened to his bare footfalls approaching, seeing the warm glow of his candle grow larger against the bed curtains. Then the candle abruptly went out, and her body tensed, tingling with night chill and pleasurable anticipation.

Curtains parted in the dark, and she felt the mattress sink

beneath his weight, pulling her down into warm contact with his bare flesh. She might not be naked, but Edward was, and not as surprised as she expected. Thrilling to the feel of skin on skin, she told him, "I missed you mightily."

"Me, too," he murmured happily. "That will never happen again." Strong insistent fingers gripped her bare shoulder, pulling her over to his mouth, which clamped down hard on hers. She kissed him back, enjoying the familiar sweet taste of mint and sugared wine on his tongue. His hand slid inside her shift to cup her breast, his thumb caressing her nipple. When their lips parted, he whispered, "From now on it is just the two of us."

"Truly?" She could barely believe it. Edward seemed incredibly sure of himself, nonchalantly reclaiming her after all their time apart.

"Who else is there?" Edward asked innocently, then kissed her again before she could answer. His hands felt their way down her bare back to the bottom of her spine, massaging as they went. She melted into his touch, molding her body to his, enjoying the minty sweet taste of his mouth, and the way his fingers pressed deep into her skin. This is what she had returned for, to feel Edward's arms around her, with all of medieval England laid out before them, confident that together they could do anything.

Then she was back, kneeling in Nest's hut with her pack at her side, staring across the witches' circle at Bryn. Edward was gone, along with his curtained bed, Baynards Castle, Old London Town, and all the rest of the Middle Ages. Even Heidi was gone. Robyn gaped at Bryn, asking, "What happened?"

No answer. Bryn was in her own witchy little world, but Robyn reached over and touched her, breaking the spell. "What happened?

Bryn replied with that enigmatic Welsh look reserved for insistent Saxon questions. "I thought you would know."

"Where's Heidi?" Nest's door was barred from within, as were the windows doors to the pantry and buttery. Heidi had simply vanished from her spot in the circle.

"Gone, I am glad to say." Bryn's face broke into a grin, looking pleased with how well her ritual went. "There's one at least who will not be bothering me and my family for a long, long while."

3

⊷≕ Nest ≕⊶

Robyn could hardly believe that she was here and Heidi was gone. How absurdly unfair! She had ached to be back there, while Heidi just came to lend a hand. Glaring at Bryn, Robyn demanded tersely, "How could you do this?"

Bryn looked blandly back, saying, "I did nothing. You and your friend came barging in on my solitude, demanding that I help you. Which I did."

Helped herself, actually. Robyn scoffed, "I was the one who was supposed to go back."

"Yes, I know." Bryn sounded equally disappointed. "In return for my aid, you promised to be gone. Yet here you are, sitting on my floor, berating me. Why did you come back? Did you not like what you saw?"

Bryn knew damn well she liked it. Edward had kept her thoroughly occupied, while Bryn disposed of Heidi. Powerful spells always required some willingness on the subject's part, and Bryn separated her from Heidi by showing her someone she wanted more. Heaven knew what Bryn had shown Heidi. Robyn asked angrily, "Where is my friend?"

Bryn smirked. "Where do you think?"

Robyn did not want to say, since to name a fear could make it real. Only half a witch, Robyn's words already had more power than she liked. Looking totally unconcerned, Bryn rose, picked up her candle, and headed for the bedchamber. Robyn's outburst had brought the ritual to an end. There would be no closing prayer.

Striding around the hearth after her hostess, Robyn caught Bryn at the bedroom door, saying, "I want her back."

"Then by all means, be after her," Bryn sniffed. "And stop hanging about here bothering me. Bad enough that you seduced my husband, without inviting your American friends to join in."

Robyn gaped at her, doubly offended. She had not *seduced*

Collin, or invited Heidi across the Atlantic—both of them were fully able to get into trouble on their own. Collin had done a smash-up job of seducing *her,* and Heidi's coming had been a complete surprise to everyone. "Holy Mary, I am not going to sleep with your husband."

"Good," Bryn declared grimly. "Now your friend won't either."

Bryn slammed the bedroom door in her face, leaving Robyn in total blackness. So much for Welsh hospitality. Like many a Saxon before her, Lady Robyn was left damning the lying, pagan, thieving Welsh. Bryn made it a point of honor to break her sworn word at whim, if it got her what she wanted. Generous and whimsical, the Welsh obeyed their own laws and would not let themselves be bound by Saxon oaths, no matter how sacred—nor did putting enemies up for the night stop them from setting ambushes the next day. Leaving Robyn neatly snared. What could she do? Call the bobbies? Accuse Bryn of kidnapping and witchcraft? These days, even British courts balked at magical evidence. Medievals would have heard her case, but in "modern" England curses, hexes, and murder-by-witchcraft were not even crimes. Witches never had it so well, except for Robyn, who had little to do but wait until daylight, dozing and fretting, curled up next to the warm hearth, hoping Heidi would show.

Of course Heidi did not. She might as well have expected Edward to come swaggering in. At first light, she woke up to a wave of nausea and gray day seeping through the shutters. Why not? She had a lot to be nauseated about. She had lost Edward. And Heidi. Bryn was as big a bitch as ever. . . .

She felt like banging on the bedroom door and giving Bryn and the boys a piece of her mind. Instead she collected her things and left. Unable to find the car blanket, she headed back down the footpath to the Bentley, cursing the cold. There had been a frost that night, and the frozen path felt slick beneath her handmade Northampton boots. She found her way easily downhill to the stream, and then to the footbridge that led to the clearing where she left Jo's car.

But the Bentley was not there. Her first thought was that this was impossible. How could she misplace a huge battleship-gray coupe, in the middle of the woods? Her second thought was Heidi. Common sense said that Heidi had gotten bored with the ritual, went back to the car, and roared off into the Welsh night, eager to get back to Collin at Greystone. That was the logical explanation. Though it did not fit well with Bryn's look of triumph. Would a Welsh witch be all that happy with a cute blond tart from L.A. speeding off to see her husband? Someone else could have come along, found that key in the glove box, and taken off with her wheels.

Either way, Robyn was walking out. It had taken forever to creep along the rutted road to the clearing, but that was because the road was so bad. It could not be more than three or so miles to the nearest phone; there had been one at the bridge over the Eden, near where the road first turned to gravel. Three miles over icy ground in riding boots? Miss Rodeo Montana did that every winter morning just to work up a taste for breakfast. Glad not to be asking too much of herself, she set out down the frozen dirt road.

Weird shapes peered at her in the half-light, skeletal trees and bits of frosty bracken, looking like gray snaky hydras, fearsome creatures reaching out to grab her. As the sun came up, shadows receded, and the ghouls became leafless brush and dead branches. Wales looked much grayer by morning light. And the dirt road was longer than she remembered, winding through the woods, doing a drunkard's walk along the wooded base of the Rhinogs. Twice the trail forked, and twice she took the downhill fork, headed for the bridge over the Eden.

By the time the sun was fully up, Robyn suspected she had missed a turning, and she stopped to consider. The morning had not gotten a lot warmer, but if she just kept going south, she had to strike a paved road, since the whole valley funneled into a scenic gorge and estuary.

Walking to keep warm, she headed off again, feeling better as sunlight filtered through the dead branches. She did not stop until she heard someone behind her call out, "Robyn!"

Wheeling about, she saw Heidi running happily toward her, the car blanket wrapped around her shoulders. "Hey, boss lady. Am I happy to see you."

"Me, too." She had worried she might never see Heidi again, but here the girl was, right when Robyn needed her most. "Where did you leave the Bentley?"

Heidi found the question ridiculously funny, laughing uncontrollably before finally saying, "Thought you had it."

"Still good to see you anyway, girl." Maybe Bryn had just sent Heidi around the block, having her spend a night in the woods, to teach her a lesson. But then where was the Bentley? Robyn asked, "How did you get here?"

Heidi looked embarrassed. "Sorry, but I got bored. I know it was really important to you, but the ritual left me cold, literally. You and Bryn were totally zoned out, absolutely into it, and I was not even getting a buzz. All I could feel was my cold butt on that frigid dirt floor."

"Let's walk while we talk," Robyn suggested, shouldering her pack. She had started to feel sick again, but movement still seemed the best way to stay warm. "I want to get somewhere."

"Sure thing." Heidi set out after her, plainly happy to have a direction. "So I was sitting there, freezing my ass off, and suddenly there was a knock on the door."

"Someone came during the ritual?" Robyn did not remember any of this, but then she had been wandering about Baynards Castle, searching for Edward.

"Yep." Heidi grinned at her surprise. "Neither of you were going to answer it, not from the twilight zone. So I got up, grabbed the car blanket, and went to the door." Her grin got wider. "You will never in a million years guess who was there."

"Collin." Robyn could tell just by looking at her.

Heidi was thunderstruck. "How'd you know?"

"I'm a witch, remember?" Robyn wished she were a better one.

Heidi smiled wryly. "Hard to think of you that way."

"You'll get used to it." She shook her head as she trudged along, seeing the dirt track get narrower as brush crowded in on both sides. Leafless limbs overhead turned the trail into a tunnel—not a good omen.

"Suppose so," Heidi agreed, and then went on. "Not wanting to disturb you two, I slipped outside and closed the door. Cool thing was, Collin was really happy to see me. Sort of stiff and formal, but nothing fatal, and plainly turned on. So I figured if I could just—"

"—get him into the Bentley." Robyn pictured that scene easily enough—crank up the heater, and turn on the radio. Bond had made do with way worse.

"You are a witch." Heidi sounded even more impressed. "You were not half this lewd in L.A."

"You forget dear, I had Collin in L.A." At least once in the back of a borrowed Mercedes.

"Too true," Heidi went on. "So I led him down the path to the footbridge—"

"But there was no Bentley." Robyn saw the road was rising even further, toward a low saddle where she might get a look at the land. As they mounted the incline, the road narrowed and her queasiness returned.

"Right!" Heidi agreed again. "And when I went looking for the car—"

"You lost Collin." Her nausea mounted. As the dirt trail rose to the saddle, a notch appeared in the trees. It was filled with white clouds and cold morning sky.

"Been freezing my tits off ever since," Heidi concluded, "wandering all alone in the woods—making me really happy to see you."

"Same here." Robyn stopped and bent over, pushing aside the bracken with one hand and holding her hair out of her face with the other. Taking careful aim, she puked between roots of a big gnarled oak, spewing last night's oat cakes and seaweed soup onto the cold ground, complete with currants and half-digested mollusks.

"Got an awfully odd way of showing it," Heidi observed.

Robyn wiped her mouth with her hand, then drank from the water bottle in her pack. "That feels way better."

Heidi cocked an eyebrow. "When did you have your last period?"

Robyn shrugged. "Sometime in the fifteenth century."

"That's what I thought." Heidi broke out her grin again. "Are we going to have a baby or an abortion?"

"Neither, I hope." One more crisis she did not need. She took another swig from the water bottle, getting all the vomit out of her mouth. There are few things as satisfying as a good puke, in fact Robyn found regurgitation great for clearing the head and putting your insides at ease—while taking inches off the waistline.

As Robyn bent down to wipe off her boot, Heidi asked, "Are there bears in Wales?"

"Doubt it." Still bent over, Robyn stopped to listen. Something big moved in the brush, snapping frozen branches.

"Look out," Heidi whispered urgently. "Here comes the result of some really careless inbreeding."

Glancing up the trail, Robyn was shocked to see two figures filling the gap at the top of the rise. Neither looked very Welsh. Lopsided clean-shaven faces leered out from beneath hooded cloaks worn over homespun smocks, wool leggings, and battered leather boots. Worse than the evil looks were their knives, big ugly bollock daggers dangling between their legs, the double-balled hilt and handle standing up like steel erections. Fairly grotesque, especially on a dark footpath deep in the Coed y Brenin.

"There's another one behind us," Heidi hissed.

Over Heidi's shoulder, Robyn could see another villain blocking the trail behind them, bigger and uglier than the other two combined. He, too, had a huge knife handle sticking out of his crotch. All of them looked incredibly unappealing, and enough alike to be brothers. Robyn could tell them apart only because one was missing two front teeth and another lacked an ear. Trying to maintain decorum, she told them, "Good day. Do any of you happen to know the way to Dolgellau?"

This simple inquiry produced gales of laughter from all three of them. As if Robyn's asking directions was the funniest thing they had ever heard. Stifling a gap-toothed guffaw, the man behind Heidi grabbed her arm and pushed her toward the others, saying, "Goo un, up."

"Hey, you let goo," Heidi told him, but went anyway, propelled to the top of the saddle, where the trail opened up, crossing a patch of bare frigid moor. Here Robyn had hoped to see a farmhouse, or better yet a police van, but all she saw was heather-covered tops ringed by more trees. Robyn strived to keep between Heidi and the other two, frantically searching though her pack for her can of bug spray.

As soon as they got to the top of the trail, the guy who had hold of Heidi tried to get a hand in her pants, but he could get only fingertips into her tight jeans. Heidi kept pushing him away, shouting, "Hey, how about buying me dinner first?"

Defeated by Heidi's tightly laced jeans, Gap-tooth let go and stepped back, saying, "Strip."

No-ear agreed. "Ya strip."

Heidi told them, "Go back to fuckin' your cousins."

Ignoring her, the men began dropping their knife belts, doffing cloaks, and rolling down their hose, but leaving on their big leather boots. Incredibly uncouth, though these louts couldn't have cared less. Grinning good-naturedly, they had stumbled on to something good, and they were ready to have a fine time with two pretty foreigners. They spread their cloaks out with their booted feet, making a little love nest on the moor. Seeing the women were not joining in the spirit of things, they insisted, "Goo ahn, strip."

"Goo ahn, yowself." Heidi was not having it. "Don't you know how cold it is?"

None of the men seemed to mind in the least. Robyn braced herself, left hand holding the can of bug spray—not much, but it was that or the scissors in her sewing kit. These guys were short and not in great shape, but they looked infernally strong and were all armed and confident, clearly assuming resistance was futile. She and Heidi were expected to provide naked entertainment on the frigid heath.

Gap-tooth seized Heidi, whom he seemed to like, grappling with her and trying to drag her out of her leather jacket. Here it comes, Robyn thought, as No-ear lunged at her, hampered by having his leggings down around his knees. She ducked under his one-handed grab, dropped down, reached between the startled man's legs, and seized the handle of his bollock knife, then sprang away with the blade in her hand.

Edward would have castrated the surprised fellow on the way out, as well, but she was proud just to have the knife. This was the first man she had ever disarmed, and on her first try, no less. Nor did No-ear believe what he has seeing, and he reached between his legs, groping at the empty scabbard. Only then did he realize where her knife had come from. His next mistake was thinking she would not use it. An attempt to snatch it back nearly cost him a finger.

Robyn had never been in this situation before, and she did not like it much. She had never had a knife between her and a man—at least not when she was holding the knife. No-ear turned to the other guy, who was laughing his head off, asking to borrow his bollock knife. "Gi'me, I say. Bey but a moment."

Instead of giving up the knife, the other fellow drew it and advanced on Robyn, smiling confidently. As well he might, being twice her weight and backed up by No-ear, eager to lay hands on her—both looked cut-up enough to have been in a dozen knife fights. She, on the other hand, had never used a blade on anything more dangerous than a peacock, which had screamed mightily, but otherwise not put up much of a fight. That bird's messy death made her never want to use a knife on anything bigger. He reached out to her with his free hand, grinning and saying, "Giv' it 'eer."

His knife hand stayed rock steady, and pointed at her. She kept her knife close to her breast, trying to hide behind it. Her best hope was the bug spray; a similar can once saved her from a boat full of men-at-arms on the Thames.

Seeing she would not give up the knife, the brigand took a swipe at her with his, then lunged with his free hand, trying to catch her wrist. Keeping the knife between them, Robyn jumped back to avoid his grasp.

And she landed right in the arms of No-ear, who wrapped himself around her, crowing in triumph. He had slipped up behind her while her gaze was riveted on the other man's knife point. Arms pinned, she kicked at the laughing lout, banging her heel against his heavy hip boot. Callused fingers closed around her wrist, wrenching hard, forcing the knife from her hands, hurting her hideously, which her captors found incredibly funny. Beery breath blew in her face, saying, "Gi' on now, strip."

Without waiting for her, No-ear wrenched open her jacket, pulling it back down around her arms, to get at the sweater beneath. His companion tore at her pants, which were not nearly so tight as Heidi's. Her struggles only aroused them. She felt No-ear's erection against her hip, as Beer-breath's big hard hand plunged into the front of her pants. Fingers dug between her legs, stopped by a thin layer of nylon.

Heaving herself sideways, she twisted away from Beer-breath's probing fingers and stamped as hard as she could on his booted toe. He responded by giving her a ringing clout alongside the head with the hand that held the bollock knife. Her vision blurred, and tears welled up.

He hit her again, and she thought she might throw up. Borne down by the weight of two foul sweaty bodies, both bigger than she, Robyn dropped to her knees, losing the can of bug spray. Tears blinded her. She felt catapulted back to her dark cell in the Tower, when Duke Holland's men had seized her and dragged her to the rack. She had struggled there, too, but it did her no good, and Duke Holland's men got her to confess to all kinds of lurid crimes—some true, some wild lies told to please her torturers. These two goons just meant to rape her.

Her head hurt terribly, and the men were not letting go of her. Despite her kicking and crying, they forced her to the ground, chuckling horribly. Unless she submitted to gross personal abuse, they meant to beat her senseless, then do as they pleased. Held down by cruel, indifferent hands, Robyn could only pray, "Holy Mary, help me. Please, please protect us—"

Suddenly she was free. Both men let go, leaving her on her knees, her head aching, pants undone, and jacket askew, about to puke on the frozen ground. That men could even think of sex at moments like this utterly amazed her. Making love on a frigid heath seemed marginal at best, not worth assaulting some unwilling stranger who just asked the way to Dolgellau.

Looking to see why her assailants had relented, she recognized a middle-aged woman in black standing at the head of the trail—a steel-haired giantess, nearly sixty years old and over six feet tall. The crone was leaning on an oak staff a head taller than she. This was Nest, Bryn's old nurse, and another immortal Welsh witch. Everyone had stopped to stare. Robyn's two attackers stood over her, holding their bollock knives. Gap-tooth got up off Heidi, who had ceased to struggle. Nest commanded instant respect, especially in her native hills.

Paying no heed to drawn bollock knives, the old woman in her black cloak and gown started to stride down the trail as if she did not see them. Wariness turned to wry amusement as the men started to wonder where this huge woman was headed and who she might be. "War ya off ta, grannie? Are ya deef as w'll as blind?"

Without warning, the old woman's staff leaped up, striking Gap-tooth hard between the legs. Giving a surprised shriek, the fellow doubled in agony, grabbing his crotch. Another swift rap with the staff, and he was on his knees, holding his bleeding head instead. With a grunt, Nest kicked Gap-tooth's fallen knife toward Heidi, who scooped it up. Alarmed, Robyn's two attackers separated, trying to tackle the white-haired giantess from two sides.

Stepping swiftly between them, Nest jerked her staff backward, hitting the man behind her with uncanny accuracy, smack in the right eye. Howling in pain, No-ear went down, taking another hit in the head on the way. Having disposed of him with her backhand, the old woman turned on her final attacker, cowering behind his knife. Her staff lashed out, and the knife went spinning into the brush, accompanied by a cry of pain. Disarmed and demoralized, Beer-breath staked everything on a mad rush, trying to overwhelm Nest through sheer momentum. Dodging his outstretched arms, the old woman swung her staff with both hands, hitting him across the face, then again on the back of the head as he stumbled past, landing ass up in the bracken.

All three attackers were groaning on the ground, and every blow had hit head, balls, or knife hand. Not a single blow had landed on Nest. One at a time, Nest prodded the disarmed men to their feet and sent them stumbling on their way. Watching in awe, Heidi asked Robyn, "You know her?"

Still on her knees, Robyn nodded. "That is Nest. You ate at her place last night."

"Nest?" Heidi's eyes went wide. "Bryn's old nurse?"

"Explains a lot, doesn't it." Byrn had nursed at those mammoth breasts, taking in spellcraft and nourishment. No wonder the girl grew into a witch with an attitude.

Reaching down to help her up, Heidi asked, "You okay?"

"Sort of." She accepted Heidi's hand, getting to her shaky feet, head throbbing and knees banged. Worse yet, she felt horribly shaken. She had been Miss Rodeo Montana, at home in any century, having her three-mile hike before breakfast—only to see her silly confidence slapped down by reality. Three strangers on a forest trail had shown her how fragile her well-being could be. One moment she was wiping vomit off her lips, grateful for having purged herself, feeling free and pure, and the next she was being forcefully violated by two misshapen guys she had never met. She told Heidi, "My head hurts."

"We'll fix that." Heidi found the fallen pack and rummaged through it, producing bottled water and pain pills. Popping a couple, Heidi knelt down beside her, saying, "Here, honey. This'll help."

It was a start at least. She took the pills and the water, which cut her headache some. Then Heidi gave her a hug, which helped more. Somehow Heidi seemed less of a flake, idly holding a bollock knife; in fact, her friend felt strong and comforting, and resourceful. Just who you would want with you in a world turned suddenly hostile. Letting go, Heidi nodded toward Nest. "So, is she dangerous?"

"Only if you cross her." Something Robyn tried never to do. When they first met in the Middle Ages, Nest carried a big Welsh bow that could put an arrow right through a man in chain mail.

"Will she help us get back to the Bentley," Heidi asked hopefully. "Wales is way wilder than I pictured it."

"Me, too." Way wilder. And it seemed a little late to worry about finding the Bentley. She surveyed the cold, barren heath and the surrounding fringe of forest. Nothing looked familiar, but she had never been this deep in Wales before, not in any century. Were these three guys with the bollock knives and bad accents the night stalkers Bryn mentioned? They had not been speaking Welsh, but whatever it was, she and Heidi had understood them perfectly—not a good sign. Moreover the day had gotten much colder. She scavenged the cloaks lying on the ground, knowing they would have lice, but even lice kept you warm, as medievals were eager to note.

"Shit, it is cold." Heidi shivered, gratefully accepting a cloak. "They could at least have offered to drag us back to the hovel. Any gentleman would have."

"*Absolument.*" Having been abducted by gentlemen, Robyn knew whereof she spoke. And she was starting to think in French, a sign of how far they had come.

"So do you think Nest knows the way back to the Bentley?"

Heidi had found a discarded belt and scabbard, and she was working at getting her new bollock knife to hang just right, acting a lot less traumatized by the attack. Though from what Robyn knew of Heidi's social life, being knocked down and fondled hardly even counted as a date.

"Maybe you should ask her?" Robyn suggested. Nest was notorious for noncommunication—able to say nothing in several different languages.

Heidi took a look at Nest and laughed. "Right, just ask. That woman would not say shit if her mouth was full of it."

Amen. Too bad, since their huge rescuer spoke Welsh, and one word out of Nest's mouth would let them know when they were. If they did not understand her Welsh, then they were still in the twenty-first century. When Nest started making sense, they were seriously Displaced, most likely to somewhere in the Middle Ages. But Nest was saying nothing, heading silently up the bit of rising moorland toward a flat ridge overlooking the saddle. Rescuing wayward Saxons was just a sideline with Nest, and no doubt she had witchy business of her own waiting. They could follow or not, as they liked.

Still jarred by the assault, Robyn was not about to wait for No-ear to return with heavily armed cousins—not when the nearest bobby might be centuries away. Nodding to Heidi, she shouldered her pack and set out uphill after Nest. "Heaven knows where we are going, but that's no excuse to be late."

White patches of snow lay along the windswept ridge, making it feel even less like October. Snow on Halloween was rare even in Wales. Robyn kept looking over her shoulder, making sure they were not followed, as Nest led them along a forest path and across a ford, before breaking out of the trees. No one seemed to be trailing them, as they climbed a broad heather-covered slope that skirted a narrow valley, then ascended to a pass. At the top of the pass, Robyn saw Snowdon rearing to the north and capped with snow, but she could not make out the cooling towers of the Trawsfynydd Nuclear Power Plant or the artificial lake to the south of it.

Suddenly feeling very hollow and hungry, Robyn dug into the pack, finding two of Jo's cucumber sandwiches. Starting on one, she handed the other to Heidi, who thanked her, asking, "Know where we are?"

"Sure." Robyn talked between bites. "This is the divide between the Vale of Eden and the sea. From here on, it is downhill all the way, until we hit the coast road—A496. I think . . ."

Heidi chewed happily on her cucumber sandwich. "Then we can hitch a ride back to the Bentley?"

"Hope so." If A496 were still there. Robyn saw no roads or power lines, no planes in the sky. No one to hitch a ride from.

"This cloak has bugs in it," Heidi complained. "Think it might be lice?"

"One more reason to keep moving." Done with her sandwich, Robyn picked up the pack and headed after Nest, who was already descending the far side of the pass. Here a long series of shallow paved steps led down into a little valley below. These were the Roman steps mentioned in the guide, showing they were nearing the sea. Having seen a fair amount of aged stonework by now, Robyn guessed the low narrow steps were medieval work, and not that old at all.

At the base of the steps, Nest followed a stream down the center of the narrow wooded valley, then turned and mounted the bare ridge to the right, which was topped by a line of standing stones. Heidi asked, "Who built these?"

"Most likely these were here when the Welsh arrived," Robyn guessed. This landscape was so incredibly old, it was almost timeless. Thousands of years ago, this was probably a processional way connecting the hills to the sea. And now two American women were walking down it, wondering what century they were in.

Beyond the last standing stone, the ridge ended in a small knoll, and from there the land fell away. Between them and the sea stood Harlech Castle, looking like a page out of a fairy story, with banners flying and smoke curling from the chimneys. Double curtain walls, with big round drum towers at the corners, surrounded an inner ward dominated by a tall towered gatehouse that guarded the only practical landward approach—an elegant economic design for a castle with a sad history. But what noble castle did not have its sad tale to tell? "Wow!" Heidi exclaimed. "Cool castle."

"Little too cool." Robyn set down her pack and stared at the castle, trying to make out the banners, seeing King Henry's white swan flying alongside the red dragon of Wales on a field of roses, a Tudor badge.

"What do you mean?" Heidi asked, rummaging through her pockets.

"This is Harlech Castle, and it should be an empty shell," Robyn explained, "half in ruins, with motor roads and a railway running past."

"But it is not," Heidi observed, taking a seat and starting to roll a joint in her lap. "Time to clear the air a bit."

Looking around, Robyn saw that Nest was gone. So much for their guide and guardian. Small surprise. Having two hapless Saxons on her hands, Nest had dumped them at the nearest castle, then disappeared, figuring she had done more than her duty.

Heidi licked the joint to seal it. "There is nothing, I mean nothing, that cannot be made better by a toke or two. Even making love."

"Maybe." Robyn was not so sure she wanted to face the Tudors stoned.

Lighting up, Heidi took a drag, saying between clenched teeth, "If it works for sex, it'll work for getting lost in the Middle Ages."

Heidi handed the joint up to her, and Robyn took it. They were not even breaking any laws, not anymore. Numerous things could not be legally consumed in King Henry's England, from meat on Fridays, to Communion wine and royal venison; Lady Robyn could safely bet Maui Wowie was not on the list. She took a long drag, hoping it would do something for her nausea.

No good. Giddiness just made it worse. Exhaling, she handed the joint back to Heidi, who was taking all this incredibly well. When Robyn first found herself in the Middle Ages, she had completely freaked, screaming, crying, and feeling sorry for herself, afraid to drink the water and terrified by the food. Heidi merely took another toke, saying again, "Cool castle. Are we going to visit it?"

"Could be." Robyn was not at all sure where they were going, since a lot depended on what part of the Middle Ages they had landed in. It was cold enough to be winter, maybe even the same month she left, January of 1461. If so, Edward was most likely in

Shrewsbury or Ludlow, on the far side of Wales. To get to him, she should turn about and go back the way they'd come, down the Eden to Dolgellau, then across the divide and down the Afon Banwy to the Severn—a pretty daunting prospect. Days of hiking in what looked like midwinter.

Heidi held up the joint again. "Think Nest wants some?"

"Nest is gone," Robyn noted, staring hard at the castle.

"So she is." Heidi glanced about, then took Nest's toke for her. What happened now was something among Saxons, and mattered not at all to Nest. But it mattered quite a bit to Robyn. Now that she was here, she must find Edward quick as possible. Three brainless thugs had seized and abused her, and they would have done more if Nest had not arrived. Easily the second worst thing that had happened to her in the Middle Ages, and she had only just got back. Edward was not only her love, but her safety, as well, with castles, retainers, men-at-arms, huntsmen, and hound packs at his command. He was what passed for law on the Welsh Marches, the popular alternative to chronic anarchy and Tudor tyranny. Both heart and head demanded she find him at once.

She started by giving Heidi a crash course in medieval politics. "All my friends, including Edward, are on the other side of Wales. Harlech Castle belongs to the Tudors, bastard relations of King Henry who are at war with Edward. Not my personal enemies—"

"But not your best buddies either." Heidi knew all about feuding dynasties and friendly backstabbing, having worked for a major Hollywood studio. "So what do we do?"

"We take our chances with the Welsh," Robyn decided. "They will feed and shelter us, and not ask our politics." With the Welsh, it would be enough that they were pretty and lost. "When we get to Powys Castle, they will probably take me in, maybe even arrange passage down the Severn to Shrewsbury, and Edward."

"What about the three stooges who jumped us?" Heidi asked. "Were they Welsh?"

"No, they spoke English." Sort of. "Displacement makes all languages understandable, but not the same. Welsh sounds like Welsh. You'll see."

"Seems like a plan." Heidi looked eager to try out her Welsh, offering up the joint. ~~When Robyn waved it away, her friend chuck~~led, standing up. "Forgot you were a preggy."

"We do not know for sure," Robyn replied tartly.

Heidi reached into her purse and pulled out a slim white package, handing it to her. "Here, boss lady, have one on me."

It was a pregnancy test. Robyn shook her head. "You carry these with you?"

"Only in romantic foreign countries, where a pharmacy might be hard to find." Heidi blew a cloud of marijuana smoke at Harlech Castle. "I think this qualifies."

And then some. Robyn apologized, "I am very, very sorry to have brought you here."

"Really?" Heidi looked puzzled. "You brought me here?"

"Not literally," Robyn admitted. It had been Bryn who sent both of them back. Or maybe Nest.

"Too bad." Heidi took another toke. "If you brought me here, you could always send me back."

"I'll try," Robyn promised lamely. Her latest attempt at time travel had landed Heidi at the wrong end of medieval Wales.

Heidi held up the joint. "So is this stuff legal?"

"As legal as church on Sunday." More so, actually, since you could get in real trouble going to the wrong church.

"These Middle Ages are looking better already." Heidi smiled as she got up, pinching out the half-smoked joint. "Too bad I am going to have to ration it."

"We are not going back the way we came," Robyn promised, heading south and east, keeping the knoll between them and the castle. At the base of the knoll, she came to a crossroads, with trails headed in several directions, back toward Harlech, down to the sea, or eastward into the hills. Robyn picked the main path heading south, following it until she saw a town ahead. Not wanting to make explanations to the locals, she turned off onto a smaller trail, climbing a bit of sparse bare pasture overlooking the sea.

There they stopped for lunch. Her "three-mile" hike before breakfast had turned into a ten-mile ordeal, one that included crossing the Rhinogs and attempted rape. Rummaging through the pack, she found two more cucumber sandwiches, some potato scones, a jar of homemade marmalade, and another jar of pickled herrings, plus a few staples like green tea, female toner, and instant coffee. Not much to show for her latest trip to the third millennium, but it would have to do—too bad they could not brew the tea.

Nonetheless, food made her feel better, even day-old potato scones slathered in marmalade. Looking down on the town, she saw a tall church and a cluster of warm homes, while she and Heidi were freezing their butts on a barren hillside. Yet another reason to get moving—if they could make Dolgellau by nightfall, she felt sure the Welsh would take her in. Lady Robyn kept telling herself that the three thugs who assaulted her were fellow Saxons. Welsh would know better or so she hoped.

Heidi nodded at the town, asking, "What is that place called?"

"Llanfair." Robyn had never been there before, but the name was on her tourist map of Wales.

"Llanfair." Heidi pronounced the medieval Welsh perfectly. "Does that mean 'the church of Mary'?"

Robyn smiled at her. "Your Welsh is improving."

"Shit!" Heidi shook her blond head in amazement. "This is unbelievable."

"What? That you can speak Welsh?"

Heidi nodded soberly. "I never really expected the magic to be in my head."

"Scary, isn't it?" Robyn stared down at the church, wishing she had time to give proper thanks to Mary.

"No lie." Until now their Displacement had a fairy-tale unreality to it, filled with standing stones and far-off castles. Heidi had "known" they would understand Welsh, but she was astonished when the words formed unbidden in her brain, as though she were born knowing them. Suddenly her amazement turned to concern, and Heidi whispered, "Someone's coming."

Robyn heard hoofbeats farther up the trail, from someone riding toward them, coming down out of the wooded hills. She tensed, hoping this would not mean trouble. After this morning, every new footfall had dire meaning. Her headache was gone, but her knees still hurt and were bound to be bruised.

Hoofbeats came closer. Then a horse topped the ridge, a clay-bank gelding with dark points, carrying a teenage girl riding bareback and barefoot and wearing a simple pleated dress of tan homespun, slit front and back for riding. For warmth, the girl had a tanned hide cloak from some hairy beast covering her from hip to shoulder. As the horse drew closer, Robyn could see the girl was blind, her white eyes showing under half-closed lids. When the horse got to them, he stopped, and the blind girl leaned forward, saying, "Who is there?"

Robyn got up, spreading marmalade on a scone, saying, "Good morrow. My name is Robyn."

"And Heidi," added her friend.

Smiling, the girl settled back on her horse, staring straight ahead. "Good morrow, Robyn and Heidi, my name is Gwyneth. Do you come from afar?"

Gwyneth seemed able to take the truth. "I am Lady Robyn of Pontefract."

"I'm from L.A. Actually, the Valley," Heidi volunteered.

"Lady Pomfret?" Gwyneth pronounced it like a native. "Is that so?"

"It is so." Robyn handed up the scone, saying, "Here, have this."

Reaching out of her hairy wrap, the girl took the scone, and when Gwyneth tasted the marmalade, her face lit up. "Oh! M'lady, this is marvelous."

"Thank you." Robyn watched the scone vanish into the hungry girl's mouth. "How did you know we were here?"

Gwyneth licked marmalade off her fingers. "The horse stopped, m'lady."

When she finished with her fingers, Gwyneth asked, "M'lady, is that Pomfret in Yorkshire."

"West Riding."

"Where they killed King Richard?" Gwyneth had heard the harpers, and King Richard II was a favorite in Wales, where he was once on the run himself.

"The very place." Every castle had it secret crimes. King Richard II was caught in Wales, then imprisoned and murdered at Pontefract.

"And where is the L.A. Valley?" Gwyneth was still staring straight ahead, seeing the places in her mind.

"California." Heidi handed up another scone.

Gwyneth squealed with delight at more marmalade. "What part of Wales is that?"

"A way faraway part," Heidi admitted, but Gwyneth was too busy with the scone to press her.

When she was done eating, Gwyneth merely asked, "Where is m'lady going?"

"Shrewsbury," Robyn replied, not wanting to be more specific. This far-off west coast of Wales was one of the last places in southern Britain holding out for Queen Margaret. Here, young Edward of March was the upstart villain who took London and King Henry away from them. Anxious to change the subject, Robyn asked, "Can I help you get where you are going?"

Gwyneth shook her head happily, marmalade still smeared on her cheek. "Oh, no, m'lady, the horse knows the way."

As Gwyneth rode away, headed north toward Harlech, Robyn called after her. "What day is this?"

" 'Tis Saint Anthony's Day," the blind girl replied, without looking back. "Saturday, the seventeenth of January."

Robyn did a swift mental calculation. Assuming this was 1461, she had been gone just over a week, having disappeared on Witches Night, Friday the ninth. Edward had been headed south for Ludlow Castle, and would most likely be there, or back at Shrewsbury, unless he went on to Hereford. Edward moved fast when there was work to be done, and right now he was raising knights and bowmen in the Marches for the defense of London. Her only way to catch him was to get across Wales as quickly as she could. Watching Gwyneth ride away, she told Heidi, "You have good hearing." Raised in the wilds, Robyn always thought she would be better than Heidi at woodsy stuff. "That's twice this morning that you have heard someone coming before I did."

"Yeah." Heidi laughed. "I'm a light sleeper, too. Comes from lying in the dark, listening for footsteps and creaking floorboads when you know Mom is dead drunk but her new boyfriend is up and restless." Picking up the pack, Heidi asked her in Welsh if they were going, "*Ydyn ni'n mynd?*"

"*Ydyn,*" Robyn agreed cheerfully, wanting to get to Dolgellau before dark.

Hiking south over sparse winter pasture, they passed an empty burial chamber with a huge sloping capstone, now used as a sheep pen. Past the burial chamber, the way narrowed, with wooded hills coming down to meet the coast road. Was it safer in the woods or by the sea? Robyn was wary of the coast road, where they could easily meet inquisitive strangers, but her last walk in the woods had been ghastly. Better to keep to the road, so they would at least not get lost. Farther south she could cut through the hills, crossing over to the Vale of Eden. She led Heidi down onto what would be A496 but was now a weedy bridle path curving along the edge of the Irish Sea. Wrapped in their lice-ridden cloaks, they drew curious looks from peddlers and drovers, but no one had the time or inclination to molest them. Plowing had started, and the locals were hard at work, tilling nearly vertical fields, while seabirds wheeled through the bleak winter sky, banking above wide mud flats and a sweeping blue estuary, then settling side by side in the surf.

Ahead, the coast road cut between a small wooded knoll and two standing stones. Drawing closer, Robyn saw that one of the stones was nearly ten feet tall, but the smaller one was Edward's size, looking solid and strong like him. It thrilled her to think that she was finally back here, and that each step brought them closer together. She could make it across Wales in a week. So by next Witches Night, she should be with Edward one way or another. Her only worry now was whether Heidi could keep up. So far, her production assistant had shown remarkable stamina striding along in this strange new world with her bollock knife between her legs, acting like this was one grand adventure. Hopefully Heidi would not find out different, not right away at least.

Without warning, armored riders issued casually from the woods ahead, where they had been lurking beneath the trees. These were not drovers or pack traders, but a dozen armed men wearing steel helms and leather knee boots, with bows slung across their backs and swords and bucklers hanging from their saddles. Some had lances, and their leaders wore red-and-blue hose, chain-mail shirts, and red livery jackets with gold trim—Stafford colors, though she doubted that would do Lady Robyn much good. Even Heidi knew immediately that they were dangerous, and Robyn saw her friend's cloak draw tighter and the hood go up to hide her blond hair. Welsh custom and King's Law held that women had the right to go where they willed, and could not be interfered with—but the Welsh were a conquered people, and King Henry was crazy, making every armed man a law unto himself. Running was worse than useless, and without a word between them, both women knew the best thing was to brazen it out, to keep walking down the coast road like they had business in the next town, putting one foot ahead of another, though each step brought them closer to peril.

Seabirds screeched angrily overhead as the horsemen approached, and Robyn turned off the road to let them pass. With a laugh, several of the men turned off, as well, blocking her path. When Heidi tried to go around them, they lowered their lances and blocked her way, too. Robyn heard her friend whisper, "Shit."

Raising her head to protest, Robyn recognized one of the men immediately—it was No-ear, wearing a pot helm to cover his deformity, but looking as ugly as ever. He was wearing a red-and-gold brigandine over the same ratty hose and boots, while Robyn was wrapped in his cloak. Leaning forward, he leered at her, and pointed with his lance, saying, "Gaht ya."

4

◆⇒ Harlech Castle ⇐◆

*R*obyn *wondered what* three Saxon felons were doing molesting women in West Wales; now she knew they were soldiers, wearing a lord's livery. Figured, since there was scant honest work for such men in Gwynedd. But what Saxon noble had his henchmen this deep in Wales? Some exiled court noble from Queen Margaret's faction, no doubt—but which one? Red-and-gold surcoats told her little. Those were Stafford colors, but also belonged to Audley, Drummond, Butler, and others—but they gave her an idea. Looking them straight in the eye, she told them, "I am Lady Robyn Stafford of Pontefract, and we are on King Henry's business. Pray do not interfere."

That got a good laugh all around. Her excuse for being in Gwynedd was even thinner than theirs. One of the happy miscreants called down to her, "What king's business?"

Lady Robyn was obliged to disappoint them. "That is a private matter between me and His Majesty."

More ribald laughter. At least she managed to amuse them. They were merely playing with her, enjoying her useless pleading, but she knew from past experience, she must pitch her appeal as high as possible. On her first day in the Middle Ages, she vainly claimed to be the Duke of Buckingham's daughter, figuring she would get better treatment. This time she was not even lying, since she was Lady Robyn of Pontefract, no matter how little she looked it. "Now, if you pray excuse me, we will be on our way."

She tried to steer Heidi past the horses, but the men were not having that. Lances came down to bar her way. "M'lady must go with us. Mad or not, there are charges you must face."

Welcome to the Middle Ages. Back only half a day, and already under arrest. She wished just once she could arrive as in her dreams, slipping safely into Edward's bed, warm, secure, and loved. No such luck. She feared from the first that Beer-breath and his buds would raise a hue and cry, and she'd been glancing over her shoulder all morning, hoping to put miles between them. Now it had happened—if not how she had expected. All these men and horses seemed like overkill. She looked them serenely in the eye, determined to play the lady, even in carbon-black jeans and a stolen cloak. "Go where?"

Their leader pointed up the road with his lance. "To Llanfair."

"Good," Lady Robyn declared, as if she had a choice. "I mean to give thanks there to Mary." She had tried to duck that this morning—hoping to stay out of sight and ahead of pursuit—this is what came of it.

Heidi nodded toward Llanfair. *"Ydyn ni'n mynd?"*

This was a situation when it was better to be Welsh than American. Robyn nodded in agreement. *"Ydyn."*

Turning about, they trudged the two miles or so back to Llanfair, each step taking her that much farther away from Edward—a most miserable way to end the day. Feeling incredibly defeated, Lady Robyn still kept her head up, looking at the green hills and sea, striving to ignore her captors. Men rode ahead and behind her, inordinately proud of their catch. No-ear in particular kept grinning back at them. What a ghastly defeat this was. Aside from some sympathetic priest, who would dare speak for them?

Welsh silently watched the small parade pass. These quiet watchers were unarmed plowmen and shepherdesses, but the hills of Gwynedd were infamous of old for their ferocious spearmen. Within living memory, this whole area had risen up under Owen Glendower, driving out the English and making Harlech the capital of a free Wales. If they wanted to, they could do it again, but right now they were treating this armed abduction as something among Saxons.

Halfway to Llanfair, more armed horsemen came riding up, headed south on the coast road, with Heidi's admirer, Gap-tooth, riding among them. They had dogs and must have tracked them down the west slope of the Rhinogs while No-ear went ahead to block the coast road south. This successful stratagem led to a lot of happy, mutual congratulations among these men in iron. No high-fives, just backslapping and some hip-hoorays, but Robyn found the scene a bit overdone, considering their quarry was two women armed with a single bollock knife and a can of bug spray. There was no sign of Beer-breath or of Nest, who seemed to have vanished completely, which the Welsh were adept at.

When the horsemen were done pounding their armored backs, they marched their prizes at lance point into Llanfair, which was no big place, just a church and twin rows of houses strung out along the coast road, smelling like a barnyard even at midwinter. Small as it was, the whole town turned out to see them, lining the single street with curious Welsh faces. Robyn got looks of sympathy from some of the women, and she saw grim scowls on many of the men. No one liked to have armed Saxons riding about, accosting women, but these horsemen were some powerful lord's retainers, and they would do as they willed.

Waiting by the church was another knot of riders, smaller and less heavily armed, some obviously Welsh with bushy beards and Celtic great cloaks. With them was Gwyneth, still sitting atop her claybank gelding, showing that the locals were not above listening to a blind girl. Beside her was a big, rugged clean-shaven fellow in his sixties, with a roguish look and a sword at his hip, dressed like an English gentleman, in a gold-collared scarlet doublet with puffed and slashed sleeves over green leggings and red leather boots. Graying hair worn long in the Welsh style was half-hidden by a fashionable cap hood with satin tassels. Greeting the sergeant in charge, the crimson gentleman asked, "What is this that you have found?"

Nodding out of deference, the sergeant answered, "Witches, my good sir. Two of them."

"That I can see," replied the dandy. "Why have you arrested them?"

How was it that every man with half a brain knew at once she was a witch? Sometimes Robyn thought it must be tattooed on her forehead in big red letters, leaving her able to fool only the illiterate. Her captor reached over and pulled her cloak aside, to show off her Northampton riding boots and French-cut jeans, saying, "Both were caught skulking about in men's attire."

She jerked her stolen cloak closed. True, her costume did not inspire confidence—but only the jeans and monogram jacket were strictly supernatural. And no one but a hopeless medieval would call Heidi's slit-and-laced jeans "male attire."

Showing off Heidi proved to be a tactical error, since the scarlet gentleman broke into a grin—obviously liking what he saw, slit jeans and all. Heidi knew that smile, and she immediately doffed her hood, shaking out her blond hair, making the male attire charge seem patently absurd. Straightening in the saddle, the sergeant added, "They attacked and robbed three of our bowmen, m'lord."

"Really? Robbed and assaulted three archers." The scarlet gentleman ran his gaze over Robyn, who did her best to look winsome. "These two. By themselves?"

As the translation spread through the assembled Welsh, wry smiles broke out, gloating over this latest Saxon defeat. Their distressed captor hastened to add, "Abetted by a notorious local witch named Old Anges."

"What? Old Nest, as well?" The Welsh dandy sadly shook his head. "I hope none of your men were harmed."

"Our men were unarmed, m'lord," replied the sergeant stiffly still trying to make them the victims.

"I should hope so. Using weapons on women can get a man

hanged." Satisfied to have tweaked this Saxon sergeant, the amused gentleman turned to Lady Robyn, asking, "Are you a witch?"

Never answer that question directly. "I am Lady Robyn Stafford of Pontefract, and a dear friend of His Highness King Henry."

That got another good laugh, but the scarlet gentleman merely doffed his cap hood, saying, "Owen ap Maredudd ap Tudor, at my lady's service."

Robyn recognized the name at once. Here was the head of the Tudor clan, old Owen ap Maredudd himself, who seduced a queen, fathered a pair of royal earls, and escaped from Newgate Prison—twice. He had no title, unless it was Keeper of King's Parks at Denbigh, and was not even a knight—yet he was King Henry's Welsh stepfather, and his two bastard sons became the Earls of Richmond and Pembroke. Some of Mad King Henry's relations were amazing, and none more so than the Tudors. "How delightful to meet you. When I last saw His Highness at Greenwich, he did speak highly of his hopes for his beloved brother, your noble son."

Bastard half brother actually, but she was bent on buttering up the proud dad. King Henry's hopes had been that Lord Pembroke would somehow rescue him from Parliament.

"When did you speak to His Majesty?" Owen Tudor sounded skeptical, but practically none of King Henry's extended family had seen His Highness of late, not since the battle of Northampton in July, where Robyn helped hand the king over to Edward and Warwick.

Smiling demurely, Lady Robyn told the head of clan Tudor, "I last saw His Majesty in October, just before Parliament, when I joined the royal hunt at Greenwich. There His Highness led a great slaughter of the king's deer, whose meat went to feed the royal household and the London poor." This winter was so hard, even Mad King Henry had to earn his keep.

"Amazing." Plainly liking what this diligent sergeant had turned up, Owen Tudor asked Heidi, "And who are you?"

"My name is Heidi, Your Majesty." Heidi did an enthusiastic bobbing bow. "I am from Hollywood, actually the Valley originally. And I am not a lady, and have never seen the king."

"Few in Gwynedd have." Owen grinned at her eagerness. "Are you, too, a witch?"

Heidi shook her head emphatically. "Not even close."

Robyn felt things swinging in their favor. Whatever Owen Tudor thought of them, he wanted to see more. Two pretty witches in designer jeans who went on hunts with the king were too huge a prize to leave in the hands of some officious Saxon sergeant. Owen Tudor turned back to the unfortunate horse soldier, saying, "I must take this matter under private advisement and lodge these women in Harlech until I make a judgment."

Stiffening further, the sergeant informed him, "They are the prisoners of my lord James Butler, Earl of Wiltshire and Ormond."

"Then I will gladly take them to Lord Wiltshire," Owen promised, "for I shall be seeing His Grace full soon."

Robyn shuddered, happy to be in the hands of Owen Tudor, and not those of James Butler, the vain, vicious, and cowardly earl of Wiltshire. Earl Butler was Mad King Henry's hated Anglo-Irish tax collector, who helped collect the Harvest of Heads after John-Amend-All's rebellion, notorious for twisting the law to his own ends, a trait his sergeant had learned, as well. Wiltshire, too, had seen the inside of prison, for breach of the peace and waging private war, but half the British nobility seemed to be out on parole, usually with good reason.

For once Lord Wiltshire's minions would not have their way, neither by force nor fraud. Though he had no Saxon title, Owen Tudor was whom the Welsh obeyed, and this deep in Gwynedd, his word was the nearest thing to law. Wiltshire's troopers had to give up whatever vicious amusement they hoped to get from their catch. Ordering two of his men down off their horses, Owen nodded at Robyn. "Now if my lady will be pleased to mount. And Mademoiselle Heidi, as well."

"May we first give thanks," Lady Robyn begged. Dragged to the very door of Mary's church, she dared not miss the chance a second time. Owen graciously obliged her, and while the men stood waiting outside, she and Heidi filed into Mary's house, fell to their knees, and thanked God's Mother most gratefully. Robyn had begged her aid that morning, and here they were, delivered to Mary's doorstep. As she crossed herself, Heidi whispered, "You have to show me how to do that."

She promised she would, but first had to get Heidi mounted.

Luckily they were given Welsh cobs to ride, friendly and sure-footed—far better than being saddled with a huge pair of spirited chargers. Back in L.A., she had taken Heidi riding on weekends, but this was the real thing.

Heidi seemed up to it, settling cheerfully into the role of horse-woman, enjoying the ribbing men gave her for wearing laced-up jeans and a bollock knife. "But, I thought this was how everyone dressed in Wales?"

Riding north toward Harlech, Robyn, too, relaxed. She was being led away from Edward, but she was not being force-marched to some dire fate, not right away at least. Heaven knew what would happen when they got to Harlech. Owen Tudor was Welsh, honor-bound to take them in, treating them as guests or conquests, rather than as criminals—but once they were behind the high thick castle walls, their genial host could do pretty much what he willed.

Not waiting till they got to Harlech to make friends, Heidi began flirting gaily with Owen in Welsh. Heidi under a Displacement spell had its harrowing aspects, knowing the woman could and would talk to anyone. Relighting her joint, Heidi took a drag, then offered it to their host. "Want a toke?"

Owen Tudor looked suspiciously at the little roll of burning paper. "What witchcraft is this?"

"No witchcraft," Heidi insisted, "just a magic herb from the tropics. Here, let me show you how. Breathe in hard, then hold the smoke inside."

Owen looked shocked. "Why would I ever do that?"

"It's fun, trust me," Heidi pleaded, giving the head Tudor a huge smile, then showing him again how it was done. "Here, now you try."

Owen Tudor had not gotten where he was by avoiding tempta-tion—or young women. After some coughing and amused com-plaint, he managed to get a taste, liking it at once, declaring the inhaled smoke to be "exhilarating and uplifting." Medievals had a lot to learn about intoxicants. "Where is this miracle herb from?"

"Maui," Heidi replied happily. "You would totally adore it—a jungle isle with warm beaches and sizzling hot luaus. Bake in the sun, then burn at night. I was there a week or so ago, and absolutely loving it—only flew here to give Robyn a hand."

He looked askance at her. "You flew here from this magic isle in a week, yet you are not a witch?"

"Nope," Heidi assured him, "just a frequent flier."

Cautiously, Owen Tudor inhaled more of Heidi's joint. "And there this herb grows wild?"

"You wish." Heidi laughed at Welsh innocence. "Let's just say the laws are not as progressive as here."

Thoroughly confused, Owen Tudor looked to Lady Robyn, asking, "Is this true, my lady?"

"Afraid so." She saw scant chance the stoned Welshman would make anything out of Heidi's chatter. "Maui is out of this world."

Owen Tudor could well believe it, since the Welsh coast already had to be taking on a different hue. Riding behind her stoned host, Robyn watched Harlech rear up ahead of them, dwarfing the trees and town around it, looking like the giant's home in "Jack and the Beanstalk." Harlech had indeed been built by an ogre, King Edward Longshanks, the Hammer of the Scots, the English king who first conquered Wales and ringed it with giant castles to pen in the Welsh. He also massacred the women and children of Berwick and drove all the Jews from the kingdom. Fee-fi-foe and then some. Heidi rose in the saddle, asking her host, "Is this lovely castle yours?"

"Harlech belongs to King Henry," Owen Tudor explained. "I but hold it for him."

"Wow! Castle-sitting." Heidi marveled at the great towered gatehouse, with its wide moat and fortified double-drawbridge. "Cool gig."

Harlech had an awesome entrance, including an outer barbican, tall stone towers and twin drawbridges, followed by fifty feet of entranceway enclosed by a huge double-gate house. Emerging from this mass of stone, Robyn dismounted by the stables, between the kitchen and the granary. Owen helped Heidi down, and then ordered servants to install his new guests in second-floor quarters, adjoining the great hall. Serving women met them at the bedchamber door with a basin of warm water, for the traditional Welsh footbath greeting, giggling and asking, "Where did m'lady get such fine boots?"

Lady Robyn passed them around, saying, "They are Northampton made. I had them resoled there last summer, but they have been through the wars since then." Literally.

Heidi's Doc Martens were the real hit, eliciting cries of amazement. Yet another wonder from the Saxons, like plate armor and cheese crepes. Lady Robyn asked the women for a pot of boiled water for tea, giving out two of the gold rings Heidi bought in Shrewsbury. Pretty cheap lodgings, considering the carpeted bedchamber had a stone fireplace, wood-beam ceiling, cedar chest and wardrobe, a tall curtained bed, and a private garderobe. An ivory harp hung on one wall, and in the back of the chamber, narrow stairs descended into blackness. Heidi peered down them, asking, "Where do these go?"

Lady Robyn found the clothes chest full of neatly folded silk and velvet gowns, fumigated with incense to keep them free of vermin. "Probably straight down to the master suite."

"Very convenient." Heidi grinned, then went to study the harp on the wall. "Wonder whose room this is."

Robyn held up a gown from the chest, a striking V-neck white-satin dress decorated with large crimson roses. "Some woman's, from the look of it."

Heidi *ooh*ed at the handsewn red flowers, then reached into the chest, pulling out a green silk gown trimmed with gold leaves. "And now it is ours."

Lady Robyn held the white satin dress up against her, seeing how much it needed to be taken in. "I think that's the general idea."

By the time the boiled water arrived, they had traded their "male attire" for silk robes smelling of aromatic herbs, and Lady Robyn made mint tea for her production assistant, afraid dinner would be a drinking bout over dubious meat, followed by lord knows what. At least it did not look like they would land in a Welsh communal bed. Taking the tea mug, Heidi told her, "Don't act so worried. This is where you wanted to be, right?"

"Close," Robyn conceded. She had not pictured landing at the wrong end of Wales, drinking tea and trying on Tudor gowns. "But I did not want to bring you with me."

"So you keep saying." Heidi sipped her tea, sitting on a clothes chest, since the room had no chairs. "Makes me feel like a third wheel, when I thought I was a big help this morning."

"You were a huge help," Robyn assured her. "I am just sorry I got you into this to begin with."

"Not totally your fault," Heidi pointed out. "Who flew here from LAX uninvited?"

"You did."

"And who dragged you into Wales, insisting we must see Bryn?"

"That would be you again," Lady Robyn admitted.

Heidi took a smug sip from her clay mug. "Which makes it awfully silly for me to blame you."

"Guess so." Heidi had certainly done a lot to hurry her fate, though without Robyn's help, the girl would have gotten no farther than the twenty-first-century Cotswolds.

"Right." Heidi gave her a triumphant grin. "So quit blaming yourself."

"I'll try." Still feeling guilty, Robyn stared at her friend, who sat on the clothes chest wearing a red silk robe, backed by a huge tapestry decorated with scenes from the life of the Virgin. "What about you? How do you feel about being here?"

Heidi laughed lightly. "When we first met, I was working for a temp agency, with no benefits and no future. Sleeping on my mom's couch to hide from my ex-boyfriend-turned-stalker." Getting up off the handcarved chest, Heidi walked over to where Robyn sat on the canopy bed. "You jerked me out of that, giving me a cool job working for rich people, and that came with a sporty car and a poolside apartment. Studio security even scared off my stalker boyfriend, claiming they would beat the crap out of him. You absolutely changed my life."

"And now I've gone and done it again," Robyn added, ruefully.

"That's the spirit, boss lady. Let's show these Welsh a good time." Heidi selected the white satin dress with the huge red roses, while Lady Robyn wore her own colors, a shining gold creation trimmed in crimson. While they worked to take in the outfits, Heidi asked, "So what is Owen's story? Is he married?"

"Not that I know." All Lady Robyn knew was the oft-told tale of Owen Tudor and Catherine of Valois. "Long ago, in a kingdom not so far away, the King of France went crazy, absolutely berserk, killing several of his knights before he could be subdued. This being the Middle Ages, he stayed on as king even though his attacks grew more bizarre, including fits of thinking he was made of glass and would break if touched. And he kept fathering children, including a daughter named Catherine, who grew up in a Paris hotel, living with her mad dad and dressed in rags. While her mom took a long string of noble lovers and got immensely fat on French pastries."

"Every sane woman's dream," Heidi declared, tightening the gold waist on Robyn's gown. "Too bad you have to be Queen of France to do it."

How true. "Alas, that left no one governing France, while England had a bold young king called Henry of Monmouth, Mad King Henry's father, who easily trounced the leaderless French and demanded that debauched Queen Mother give him one of her daughters to wed. So the French hauled Catherine out of the hotel, dressed her like a princess, and married her to the young English king."

"And they lived happily ever after," Heidi declared, stepping back to get a look at the hang of the dress.

"Not a chance." By now Robyn knew that real fairy tales seldom had happy endings. "Turns out that the French royal family suffered from hereditary male insanity, so by marrying Catherine, Henry the Fifth brought it into his family. The current king, Henry the Sixth, is mad as a bedbug, and his son, the infant Prince of Wales, does not inspire hope. Ironically, thanks to the queen mother's many infidelities, the current French royal family is no nuttier than most."

Poetic justice. Heidi asked, "But how does Owen fit in?"

"Just getting to him." Robyn went down on one knee, to fix the hem on Heidi's gown. "When Henry the Fifth died, he left behind an insane baby and a young widow. With typical foresight, the King's Council put the brain-damaged kid in charge of the country, while refusing to let Mom remarry, or even go home to France. Fortunately Catherine had a handsome Welsh footman, who began as one of her husband's bodyguards and ended up as her Master of the Wardrobe—"

"That's our Owen," Heidi declared gleefully. "Must have mastered more than her wardrobe."

"Apparently." Robyn rose, to work on the sleeves. Harp music welled up from below, a sign dinner was on its way. "Owen and

Catherine had half a dozen children over the next ten years—but all the boys are suspect for the same male insanity, and the girls could be carriers."

"Too bad." Heidi shook her head at the shaky foundations of this would-be royal family. "But that applies only to children by Catherine of Valois—"

"Who died years ago." Robyn stepped back and admired her work. "In childbirth."

"Go figure." Heidi grimaced, then looked down at the big red roses on her gown. "So whose clothes are we wearing?"

Lady Robyn rearranged the wide gold pleats on her own gown, getting them to trail properly onto the floor behind her. "These are court gowns, but the harp on the wall makes me think she was Welsh."

Heidi eyed the ivory harp hanging forlornly by the bed. "Hope she has not been sent back to the hovel because Owen thinks two birds are better than one." Robyn agreed, knowing that Owen Tudor was totally unpredictable, especially toward women, a Welsh bandit turned courtier, and Edward's sworn enemy, but he was also a friend to her friends, like King Henry and the Duke of Somerset. Wishing Edward were here, she fished the pregnancy test out of her pants pocket and put it on the candle ledge in the loo; then she led Heidi down the stairs to dinner, stepping lightly in time to the harping.

Whatever Owen Tudor had in mind, they were greeted like royal guests in his black-timbered hall, seated at the the head of the high table on either side of Owen, and next to a pair of knights, Sir Richard and Sir Dafydd, one Saxon and one Welsh. This melding of Welsh and Saxon ran throughout the meal, which was served in a royal castle, with Welsh touches. As guests, Robyn and Heidi were served first, a mixed blessing since the main course was heron stewed in sweet wine, with sea bream aspic, followed by boar's meat and fried monkfish, causing Lady Robyn to miss Jo's cucumber sandwiches.

While picking through this mess for parts that seemed edible, Lady Robyn told Owen and the two knights the latest scandals at court, half of which involved her. In the Middle Ages less than a day, and she was already telling the locals what was happening, but that was the way things went in a world without CNN, where most news went by word of mouth. Clearly this was the same year and month as when she left, and while the Tudors were stuck here at the wrong end of Wales, Lady Robyn had been right there in King Henry's tent at Northampton, while Lords Buckingham, Beaumont, Shrewsbury, and Egremont were killed outside. "His Highness bore defeat with dignity," she assured them, "never showing the least fear, except for me." Losing was the one thing Mad King Henry did well.

"And was m'lady afraid?" asked Owen, filling her cup with fortified wine.

"Terrified," she confessed, "but I hid it well. King Henry made me Lady Pontefract for facing his enemies without fear."

"I did assume there was a good reason." Owen Tudor had seen two of his own sons ennobled by the same insane king, whose mania for giving things away included not just titles of nobility, but also lands and offices to his relatives, provinces to the French, colleges for boys, and coins to beggars. Unable to govern the country, His Majesty felt compelled give it away piecemeal. "And did m'lady meet Edward of March face-to-face?"

Lifting her goblet, Lady Robyn hid behind a drink, finding it was honey wine, fortified with "medicinal" brandy, sweet and heady. Owen Tudor's wry look said he knew all about her and Edward, but she could only brazen it out and hope for the best. "More than once," she admitted, setting down her cup. "At Northampton I saw him kneel and pledge fealty to His Highness."

"Which pledge he broke on Halloween," Owen added pointedly, "by disinheriting the Prince of Wales."

"Halloween was hard on all of us." Lady Robyn took another sip, wishing she could turn the talk away from Edward.

"Really? Did m'lady dare oppose the Act of Accord?" Owen seemed surprised that Edward's lady would defy the disastrous Act of Accord, which split the country by disinheriting the infant Prince of Wales and making Edward's father heir to the throne.

"*Absolument.*" She opposed the act because it put Edward directly in the line for the throne.

"Is that why m'lady is so far from London?" Sir Richard asked. "Exiled for defying the Act of Accord?"

Men all around her were ready to believe the worst of the Yorkists, who took London and the king from them. But much as these
Welsh might like to place a possibly crazed infant on the English
throne, Lady Robyn saw scant hope of that happening. Parliament
had voted for the Act of Accord, and while feudal England was
hardly a democracy, Parliament represented a fair cross section of
the most powerful men in the land. Being a woman and a royal pen-
sioner, Robyn was not even asked to vote, so she could hardly be
blamed for men's mistakes. Shaking her head, she told them, "No,
I left London because I was wrongly accused of a crime."

"What crime was that?" Owen sounded intrigued by the twists
in her story.

Lady Robyn decided to skip over the accusations of witchcraft
and high treason, which would only cloud the issue. "Attempted
murder."

Men's eyes went wide all around the high table; plainly they had
expected something more tame and titillating from a wayward London lady. Owen asked politely, "Whom did my Lady Pontefract
attempt to kill?"

"No one," Robyn protested. She was absolutely innocent, but
aside from Edward, hardly any man immediately believed her. Half
of them wanted her to be guilty. Somehow, men found a pretty mur-
deress sexy, especially one on the run—making her bad, desperate,
and disposable all at the same time.

"It is true," Heidi seconded her, though her friend had been
nowhere near the scene of the crime. "I have known Robyn for
ages, and she would not harm a fly."

Maybe so, but she was death to fleas, having passed her time in
the Tower learning to kill them in the dark. She pressed Heidi's foot
under the table, thanking her for speaking up.

"Forgive me, Lady Pontefract." Owen apologized to his maligned
guest. "Whom was my sweet lady most slanderously accused of
wishing ill."

She sighed, knowing by now what the reaction would be.
"Richard Plantagenet, the late Duke of York."

"Hip hooray, m'lady." Owen and his fellows raised their cups in
a spontaneous toast. Until his death a few weeks ago at Wakefield,
Richard of York was the Tudors' most dire enemy, who had

stripped them of lands and castles and then disinherited their royal nephew. "No one will hold that charge against you."

Hopefully not, but "medieval justice" was pretty much an oxymoron. People had been hanged, drawn, and quartered on far flimsier charges. Nonetheless, she tried to look encouraged.

Thankfully, Heidi leapt in with her own story of coming through London on her way here from "Holy Wood" and the Isle of Maui—though the London Heidi described was nothing like the one Owen knew. "Super shopping, all those theaters, and you can get wherever you want on the Underground. Food is not near as bad as they claim, and there is always McDonald's." From there it was but a short hop to the magic Isle of Maui, which the men found even more fascinating, with its white beaches and wildly partying natives. "First morning I was there, I woke up on the sand, having passed out next to the luau pit, with only a beach towel and a brawny surfer to keep me warm. Looking over the surfer's shoulder, I saw a woman fly-casting bare-assed in the surf, wearing nothing but sunblock and a backwards Mets cap. I said, girl, this is where you need to be—"

"Me, too," declared Sir Richard, topping off Heidi's goblet so they could toast this naked Mets fan, wishing Wales had such fisherwomen. "Here's to the mermaids of Maui."

Welsh, Saxon, or in between, the men all thought Heidi was delightfully crazy, and did not care a whit what century she came from; all that mattered was that she was blond, bubbly, and getting drunker by the minute, looking flushed and lovely in her white satin gown. They kept plying her with wine and laughing at her stories. Robyn was having a hard time staying half-sober herself, since a bit of bad sea bream put her off the meat, but she still had to drink the toasts. By the time they brought out the glazed pig, in honor of Saint Anthony, she gave up on the main courses, sticking to nuts and pastries.

When dinner was done, she was drawn into several rounds of giddy good-night kisses, which meant being felt up by a Welsh knight twice her age. Owen also had a bad attack of wandering hands. Smiling Welsh children then sung her and Heidi up the stairs to their bedroom, where a warm fire awaited. As soon as they staggered inside, Robyn shot the bolt, and Heidi flopped down on the feather bed, struggling to get out of her gown. "Damn, what an amazing party!" the drunken girl declared. "Did you see that food? You were not lying about the Middle Ages."

Robyn nodded grimly. "No one could make this up."

Heidi fumbled with her ties and buttons, fighting a losing struggle with her satin dress. "Hope we do not have to do this every day."

Amen. Lady Robyn was in no hurry to get undressed, suspecting the party was not over yet. Welsh dinners began at dusk, leaving a long winter's night for making mischief. Overwhelmed by the need to pee, Robyn retreated into the garderobe, taking a lit candle with her.

Still dizzy from dinner, Robyn balanced the candle on the little yellow ledge put there for that purpose. This was one of the "modern" privies, basically a gaily painted outhouse attached to the second-floor bedchamber, a light, airy odor-free toilet with a cushioned seat, and one big disadvantage: there was still absolutely no plumbing, so the lavatory discharged onto whatever, or whoever lurked below. In London, these new toilets made the narrower streets impassable, but the hanging toilets at Harlech had masonry screens enclosing deep ventilated cess pits. Which did not stop the open-air seat from getting horribly cold. Sitting there, freezing her fanny, and straining to pee, she saw the pregnancy test lying next to the candle. She must do it now. No more putting it off. This was one of those nights when you better know ahead of time if you were pregnant.

Of course as soon as she decided to do the test, she really had to go, making it a race between the pregnancy test packaging and a bladder full of fortified wine, seeing which broke first. Not the easiest thing to manage in a small outhouse, half-drunk and wearing a gold ball gown. Cinderella in the loo, trying to see if Prince Charming had knocked her up. She just managed to get the test stick into position without peeing on herself, or dropping it. When she was done, she closed the padded trap and held the stick next to the candle flame. Positive. There was no mistaking the blue cross. Holy Mary, she was already a mother.

What a way to find out, half-swaked in a hanging outhouse attached to Harlech Castle, on Saint Anthony's Day, January 1461.

Mary was told by flights of angels—but being a virgin, Mary probably needed more convincing. Robyn had thought it possible, ever since that snowy night in Sherwood. Good thing they were due to get married in a couple of weeks, on Groundhog Day. Called Candlemas hereabouts.

Bowing her head, she prayed to Mary, God's Mother, begging her protection for the child inside her, promising if it was a girl to name her Grace. By now she was medieval enough to see nothing wrong with praying in the privy. Mary came for sinners in far worse places.

Compline bells rang in the chapel, as if in answer to her prayer. Not angels singing on high, but nonetheless a sign.

Too bad Heidi was blotto, since she could really use someone to talk this over with. Getting up, Lady Robyn opened the trap and dropped her positive pregnancy test down the hole, leaving it as a puzzle to future archaeologists, searching through the remains of the Harlech Castle ladies' loo. Serves them right. Some things were not supposed to be studied.

Opening the door, she saw Owen Tudor standing in crimson doublet and green-white hose at the head of the narrow back stairs, which did lead down to the master suite. He had a sly grin on his face and a gold goblet in his hand, along with a fresh flagon of fortified honey wine. As she suspected, the party was not near over, but had just moved to her bedchamber. Owen made a deep bow, then straightened gracefully, saying, "Tell me more about this Holy Wood, where you and Heidi lived."

"You would love it." This spirited Welshman was made for Hollywood, seducing young widowed queens and willing to try his hand with wayward time travelers, as well. Not to mention mothers-to-be. Pregnant for the first time, and who is here to share the moment? King Henry's drunk and horny Welsh stepfather. That's what came of putting off the test until she absolutely had to know.

Glancing at the bed, she saw Heidi lying passed out, looking very fetching, half in and half out of her white satin gown. Golden hair spilled serenely over the pillow and a soft breast and pink nipple showed among the big red-silk roses. No help there.

"Your friend is incredibly lovely." Owen ambled over and sat down on the clothes chest to get a closer look, treasuring the sight as only an older man might. Heidi's left leg hung half off the bed, bared all the way to her thigh. He asked, "Have you known her long?"

"Years." Robyn stepped closer, not wanting Owen Tudor to get too friendly with her unconscious companion. She could hardly order him out of the room, since this was his room, in his castle, in his corner of Wales—giving her nowhere to run to, except downstairs to the master suite. Owen had craftily seized the only seat, leaving Lady Robyn swaying on her feet, forced to chose between the bed and the floor, neither of which matched her mood. She warned him, "And we always look out for each other."

"That I do believe." Owen Tudor smiled at her, expertly opening the flagon with one hand, then pouring as he spoke. "I saw that in the way you stood together against Wiltshire's men and spoke up for each other at dinner. Is this Holy Wood truly across the sea?"

"And then some," Robyn agreed, seeing how Catherine of Valois could fall wildly in love with this man, defying law and custom to die bearing his illegitimate children. Forceful and persuasive, even at sixty-something Owen had the same animal magnetism as Edward, the confident masculinity that said, what other men only promised, he would do—and damn the consequences. Just the man to inject some Welsh stamina in a royal line that was dying out from lack of interest.

"They say that in Owen Gwynedd's time, his son Madoc sailed into the west and found a sunny garden isle of perpetual love and music, called the Isle of Ely—"

"It is pronounced L.A. But that is definitely the place." Too drunk to be inventive, she went with whatever Owen said, figuring he was smart enough to fill in the gaps.

Handing her the heavy gold goblet, he asked, "Do you really fly there?"

"Figure of speech." She took a polite sip to cover her embarrassment, determined not to drink more. She did not do well on fortified wine. Last May Day, it landed her in bed with Sir Collingwood Grey, a mistake she vowed not to repeat. And now she had a baby to consider.

"Yet you are a witch." Drunk or sober, Owen was a hard man to fool. "A fair and lovely white witch, and this Holy Wood sounds to be a dangerous place."

She nodded grimly. "I knew girls who died there."

"Well, you are safe here in Harlech." To show her how safe, Owen Tudor took hold of her gold dress, pulling her next to him, letting her feel the tense strong body standing between her and danger. Feudal lords exercised power "in person" whether in judgment, or in battle, and the earl of Wiltshire was roundly despised for letting professional thugs do his fighting. Lords like Owen and Edward led from in front in both love and war, caring more for the woman than for titles and honors, daring to love outside their station. Reaching down, she found Owen's hand felt strong and warm, and hard to budge, older and surer than Edward's.

Unable to defeat his grip, Lady Robyn asked coyly, "Whose clothes are these?" And would she approve of what he was doing?

"Mine." Owen set the flagon on the floor and suddenly had a free hand while both hers were occupied, one with the gold goblet, and the other with his hand on her dress. Owen swiftly undid buttons on her bodice, working with the effortless ease of someone who had done this often, both drunk and sober.

"I did think it seemed large on me." Robyn let go of the hand on her thigh, trying to hold her bodice closed. "You must look dreadfully silly."

Owen laughed at the suggestion, reaching around and undoing the ties at the back of her gown. "I was Keeper of the Queen's Wardrobe. And I find women's gowns fascinating, with all their fastenings and unfastenings." He pulled out a last tie, and the gown sagged loose at the waist, held up by a single sleeve and shoulder. She felt ridiculous, still holding the wine goblet while clutching the remains of her limp gold ball gown, when the silk chemise beneath was much more comfortable. When she tried to secure the sleeve, Owen reached up and deftly undid the shoulder laces, saying, "Here, m'lady, let me help you."

Her gown fell away from her, leaving her standing barefoot in her long chemise amid a pile of gold fabric that barely hid her ankles. Owen was a master of women's wardrobes, and his jovial good humor came off like restraint, as though he would not dream of violating her, and was merely helping her out of an uncomfortable gown that she certainly could not sleep in. She warned him sternly, "I am lady to another."

Owen stood up, not as tall as Edward, but still taller than she, his hands resting easily on her shoulders, making the chemise feel awfully thin. He told her with tolerant affection, like a grown-up indulging a little girl's fancy, "Yes. I know, Lord Edward of March, a condemned traitor sentenced to death."

Her teenage boyfriend was at best a minor impediment soon to be eliminated by the law. Clearly she needed a better protector, or who knew what would happen? "When a man is my age, he no longer cares who else a lovely lady is with, or even if she is a witch. All that matters is that you are wickedly beautiful, and so is your friend. I could well believe you were both fairies from the happy Isle of Ely."

"L.A." She braced herself, having been in this same situation with Duke Somerset. But Somerset was a young knight-errant, flushed with victory, and when she would not give in, Somerset quickly decided he had better ways to celebrate his victory than forcefully raping a lady under his protection. Owen would not be so easy to duck.

His grip tightened, massaging her shoulders through the silk. Which did feel good. His broad strong fingers stroked and kneaded her flesh through the fabric, expertly seeking out knots of tension. This a.m. had been the morning from hell. Her body had been hit, grabbed, grappled, and banged hard against frozen ground, then force-marched over the Rhinogs to the sea. What she could really use was a full body massage, followed by a wake-up call for noon.

In line with that last thought, Owen settled down onto the bed, dropping his particolored tights as he slid her onto his lap, his hands still massaging her back, and at the same time pressing her against him. What began as a neck rub was now a near-naked embrace. She tried to resist, but her struggles only aroused him further, and he whispered to her in Welsh, "Do not make me wish I left you with Wiltshire's men."

Feeling him pressing against her through the thin silk, she hissed back, "Do not make me wish that we were with them."

Owen laughed at that. "You would not be lodged this well, believe me." His hands began dragging up her chemise as they went, sending cool fabric gliding over her thigh. "Here you get a feather bed to go with my protection."

"At what price?" she asked, staying his hand.

"Why, for love, m'lady." He gave her a swift kiss. "For love alone." Well, not exactly alone, with the sleeping Heidi sprawled across the foot of the feather bed. "Lord Wiltshire's men will not be so gentle about it," Owen warned. "Would you prefer putting your case to them? The earl himself is quite handsome."

And notoriously cruel. Her body still ached from the beating his men gave her that morning, while this Welsh bandit would be more than satisfied with a simple good time. Albeit at her expense. Why did men have to be the way they were? Most men anyway. Edward had risked life and limb for her, then asked for naught but a kiss and fond remembrance. Of course by being the shining exception, Edward got it all anyway—so maybe he made a bad example. By now Lady Robyn had seen the back side of British chivalry. Welsh custom, Saxon law, and Church dogma agreed that women had an absolute right to say no to men, and all women, from little girls to aged crones, were afforded protection. Gwynedd was a place where a blind girl could go riding on a valuable horse, greeting everyone she met with a smile. But protection did not come free, being paid for by pretty wayward young women—like herself and Heidi. When she refused young Somerset, the duke simply removed his protection, turning her over to Wydvilles and witch hunters, taking pious revenge on the sorceress who spurned him. Now Owen Tudor was making her the same offer.

Which she would be an idiot not to take. Owen was powerful and charming, and good-looking for his years, which clearly had not slowed him in battle or bed. And in this innocent age, before AIDS or syphilis, the costs of giving in were less. Plus she was already pregnant—the gravest danger in medieval sex was a done thing.

Sensing weakness, Owen slid the silk chemise out from between them, letting her feel his stiff warm erection against her skin. So much for saving Heidi from date rape. At least Owen knew what he was doing, exposing her belly and breasts, then bending close to kiss and caress, his tongue flicking lightly around her nipple, which stiffened with an impersonal sort of desire. She was not "interested" in Owen Tudor, having just met the man this morning, but his thumb still gave her an unexpected thrill as he ran his fingernail down the front of her panties. This would not be rape, unless she insisted.

Deftly, Owen twisted about, and suddenly his bare excited male body was pinning her to the pillows. She began to panic. Much as he meant to make this fun for both of them, her body hurt, bringing up horrible memories of that morning. Kissing and caressing were tolerable, but she did not want some older guy she just met shoving himself inside her. That was way more personal than she could take on her first day back in the Middle Ages.

As her panties came down, panic turned to terrible flashbacks of being forced onto the freezing ground and hit when she resisted. Robyn tried not to tense up completely, at the same time wishing she were somewhere far away. Fortified wine and a soft feather bed had removed her right to say no, forcing her to take the least objectionable man. Delighted to have her on her back, Owen tossed her underwear aside and pushed her legs open, making room for him.

"Hey, you guys are forgetting me," said a sleepy voice as a slim hand and a bare white arm came between them, gently prying them apart. Owen started to object, but Heidi's blond head appeared, kissing him, stopping his protests with her tongue.

Robyn rolled to the edge of the fluffy feather matress, gladly giving her friend room to work. Somehow Heidi had shed the remains of her gown, rising up naked behind Owen's back and greedily reaching down to grab his aroused member. When their lips parted, Heidi whispered in Welsh, "Here, let me make up for being late."

Sliding easily in between them, Heidi knelt over Owen's crotch, giving the head Tudor treatment generally reserved for reluctant co-stars and famous-name producers. Drunk or sober, Heidi knew just what to do, having turned going down into a science. Mouth gaping, Owen sank back in astonished delight, falling into the stupefied state that helped peddle several dubious studio projects to otherwise clear-thinking businessmen, or their theatrical agents. Leaving Heidi to her task, Lady Robyn slipped out of bed and went down the back stairs in the master bedchamber, hoping to get some rest.

5

⋆⟜⟝ East of the Sun and West of the Moon ⟞⟜⋆

Lady Robyn woke up sleepy and hungover in a strange dark bed, wondering where in the world she had landed. Staring into blackness, her head throbbing and her stomach queasy, she slowly remembered. She was back in medieval Wales, in Harlech Castle, after a harrowing day that began before dawn with her stalking out of Nest's hovel in search of Jo's Bentley, only to be twice assaulted by the Earl of Wiltshire's goons, then subjected to an outrageous feast and amiable attempted rape by Owen Tudor. How great to be home, and so easily, too. Her last two trips to the 1400s had landed her immediately in jail—both times she woke up the next morning in a dungeon cell, first in Berkeley Castle, then in the Tower of London. She must be getting better at time travel.

Curled beneath several blankets and a comforter, Robyn felt cautiously about the dark curtained bed, confirming she was indeed alone, a luxury for Wales, where most folks slept in family beds, when they had one. Lady Robyn reveled in this unexpected bit of solitude after an incredibly crowded first day back.

Not for long. Footsteps sounded on the narrow stairs at the back of the master bedchamber. Her body tensed, as she recalled whose bed this was, not wanting to begin again where she and Owen left off last night. It was Sunday morning, the Lord's day. Why could not guys just give it rest? With six days a week to rape and fornicate, Sunday ought to be a break—this was the Middle Ages, for Christ's sake.

Curtains spread in the dark, and a warm naked body slid into the bed and snuggled up against her, whispering, "Shit. Are the Dark Ages always this cold?"

Thank heavens it was Heidi. Robyn relaxed into her friend's embrace, finding Heidi was freezing. Medieval England could certainly use central heating. Giving a good-morning kiss on shivering lips, Robyn remembered where Heidi's mouth had been. "Thanks for last night," she whispered. "Sorry I deserted you, but I really, really needed the rest."

"Deserted?" Heidi giggled. "Not to worry—Owen and I got on famously. He's pretty neat in an older guy sort of way, and he really likes me, kept it up until the church bells rang, and I thought I would go insane. We set a couple of records that will stand until the sixties, so naturally, he's completely crashed."

"Do not go falling for this Welsh godfather," Robyn warned. "These people can be incredibly dangerous."

"So I noticed." Heidi snuggled closer, trying to warm her naked body. "No need to be jealous. You are the one I really love. And Collin, of course."

Of course. Robyn was not the least jealous, just fearful of dragging her friend in too deeply. "You love me, yet you sleep with Owen?"

"Best of both worlds," Heidi boasted. "Besides, someone had to pay for the room, and you already have a boyfriend."

How noble. Heidi had her own code of honor, forged during the girlhood from hell, growing up in the dark heart of the San Fernando Valley, skipping school to care for her alcoholic mom, but getting a thorough hands-on education from guys she met in the mall. Robyn whispered happily, "Not just a boyfriend."

"You took the test!" Heidi threw her arms around her, hugging her ecstatically. "So are we having a baby?"

Robyn laughed. "I am, at least. Unless you and Owen got careless."

"Hey." Heidi sounded indignant. "I've had my shots."

Robyn hoped so. "Then why tote around a pregnancy test?"

Heidi kissed her again. "Came in handy, didn't it?"

Very handy. Robyn was thrilled to know for sure that she and Edward were having a child, more excited than she had ever expected to be. Before she had "worried" about being pregnant, and now the worries were gone—she was there. Finally free to revel in motherhood, Robyn realized she had always loved babies, doting on her friends' tiny siblings because she had no small brothers and sisters. And not just babies either; as Lady of Pontefract, she took in orphans and treated her tenants' children—who returned the favor by helping free her on Holy Innocents' Day. In fact, she got on famously with all kinds of kids, big and small—being currently pregnant by a teenager.

Which made it even more utterly unbelievable to have a baby inside her. She wished she could tell Edward at once, thinking how proud and delighted he would be. Alas, medieval England did not have a single working phone or fax, and the totally private mail system was marginal at best, especially on the far side of Wales. She would have to find Edward on her own.

Just as well, since she wanted to be in his arms when she told him. Instead of having Edward's arms around her, she had Heidi's. Happy and awed at the same time, Robyn shook her head, sighing, "So much is happening."

"You said it, sister." Heidi laughed at their predicament, lying in the bed of a Welsh bandit lord who was sleeping off his latest debauch in the room above—just the place to plan for a family. "Scared?"

"Some." How could she not be? "Prenatal care is pretty primitive nowadays."

Heidi giggled. "Positively medieval."

"Weirdly enough, I am not that worried." Childbirth and childhood were dangerous times here and now. As dangerous as battle. But most women faced them with a joyous confidence, steadfastly defying the odds. Mad King Henry had gone catatonic when his wife became pregnant, but Queen Margaret bore her baby and would have governed the country, as well, only the men would not let her. They would gladly be ruled by a madman, but not by a woman. "I have this absurd feeling that everything will be okay—at least for the baby. Jo sort of predicted that if I have a girl and named her Grace, everything will come out all right."

"And you trust her predictions?" Heidi sounded encouraged.

"Most days." Showing how medieval she had gotten—though Jo's latest prediction had doubtless come from some twenty-first-century history of the Wars of the Roses. "I will have to find a midwife I can trust and who is willing to be antiseptic. But people here are not as stupid as the future thinks, just dirt poor and ignorant. Half the women I talk to instinctively believe in germ theory, and keeping things clean—its men that need convincing."

Heidi's hold on her tightened. "I'll be there for you."

Robyn smiled at her blond bedmate. "You will?"

"Have I got a choice?" Heidi inquired innocently.

"Guess not." She stroked Heidi's fine gold hair, feeling like she had brought two new lives into this world. "We'll just make the best of it. I was born at home in the middle of a Montana spring blizzard. If Mom could do it, so can I."

"I'm an ER baby myself," Heidi declared, "but it'll be a blast. Can't wait to be Auntie Heidi."

"I can." She had a thousand things to do before she could even think of giving birth. She had to escape from the Tudors, hunt down Edward, then find some secure spot to be with him, and have the baby. Baynards Castle sprang to mind, the London headquarters of the House of York, where they first made love and where they were betrothed. And where she had been denounced as a witch and traitor—before she went back to London she'd better get those charges lifted. Right now her main worry was getting dressed for Sunday Mass.

Prime sounded outside, and presently heavy feet hit the ceiling above. Owen was up. Footsteps sounded, followed by bootsteps, but no one came down the narrow back stairs. Instead the chamber door opened, and men were in the room, lighting candles and moving quietly about. Lying inside the curtained bed, Robyn listened intently while Heidi giggled naked at her side. Having royally pleased the master of the castle, Heidi no longer feared his men.

Soon as they departed, Heidi stuck her head out, saying, "Look what they have left." Two high-waisted gowns were laid out for them, long trailing dresses in Tudor white-and-green, sprinkled with red roses. Owen Tudor wanted his conquests dressed in his own colors. When they had gotten their dresses to fit, she showed Heidi how to wear a white butterfly headdress. "Jesus," Heidi exclaimed, eyeing herself in a polished steel mirror. "Every day is going to be Halloween."

"Pretty much," Lady Robyn admitted, adding, "these are Tudor colors. Putting them on means we are in Owen's household and under his orders." Which they were anyway, but wearing Tudor white-and-green just made it official.

"Leave Owen to me," Heidi laughed mischievously. Gangs and colors were familiar territory to a Valley girl. Boys and blades had merely gotten bigger, and Owen was not just the gang leader but the local law, as well. Heidi's only complaint was the lack of plumbing. "Who do you have to screw to get a hot bath around here?"

"That would be Owen, too," Robyn replied, "but after Mass. Godliness comes before cleanliness." At Sunday Mass they knelt together, brazenly sporting Owen's livery, giving thanks and begging forgiveness. A mere day into the Middle Ages, and they already had much to be thankful for, plus numerous sins to absolve.

When they rose and crossed themselves, shy Welsh serving women came up, offering to bring warm water to wash with and anything else they needed. Speaking Welsh meant more to the locals than any dubious Saxon titles—in fact, the women went to Heidi first, already having heard this was Lord Owen's "especial" friend. After breakfast and two warm baths, before a roaring fire, Robyn took the new Lady of Harlech on a tour of her castle, ending up on the seaward wall walk, gazing out at Cardigan Bay. Heidi asked, "What's on the other side?"

"Ireland." Robyn had made the crossing, a mad magical weekend on the Emerald Isle that began with a wild Witches Night, followed by a fight with Irish pirates, a fortuitous mutiny at sea, and whirlwind shopping tour of Waterford and Wexford, in which she picked up several new outfits and a Welsh-Irish maid before setting sail for France. "Had a wonderful visit there, which I barely escaped alive."

Heidi smiled. "Always sounded like that sort of place. Whose ships are those in the bay?"

Two big carracks were anchored by the sea gate, along with a small carvel, all flying Tudor green pennants. "Owen's, I guess." Robyn could not make out any badges or ship names. "Word is that he goes south to Pembroke soon."

"Will he take us?" Heidi wondered.

"Hope not." Pembroke was at the far southwest tip of Wales, even farther away from Edward.

Heidi turned to face the castle, looking over high rooftops at the busy inner ward, with its kitchens, stables, and well, and the great gatehouse-keep rearing above everything, defiantly facing the rumpled green line of the Rhinogs. "Unbelievable digs. Does Owen really own all this?"

"For the moment." Robyn hated to deflate Heidi's new boyfriend, but Owen Tudor was living far beyond his means. "Harlech is a royal castle," she explained, "built by Edward Longshanks, the evil king in *Braveheart*. And like most castles, she has a sad history."

"Sad and romantic?" Heidi suggested.

"Heartbreaking," Robyn assured her. Being both noble homes and fortresses made castles doubly tragic. "When Owen was a boy, Wales rebelled against Mad King Henry's grandfather, who had murdered the rightful king at Pontefract Castle. Owen Glendower led the rising, declaring himself Prince of Wales and seizing Harlech for his capital, holding Parliament here and receiving foreign embassies. Glendower even captured one of the heirs to the English throne, Sir Edmund Mortimer, and married him to his daughter Katherine. Then Mad Henry's father, the heroic Henry the Fifth, defeated Glendower and laid siege to Harlech—with Sir Edmund, Katherine, and their children inside—slowly starving the castle into submission. Nest, Owen, and guys like Sir Dafydd all saw it happen as kids, watching in the hills with Glendower while his daughter and grandchildren starved. Edmund Mortimer died defending his family—then Katherine and her daughters were hauled off to die in the Tower." Having done time in the Tower herself, Robyn felt for that poor doomed family, who were Edward's relatives. And Bryn's.

Now there was another Mortimer heir growing inside her. Her child carried the same claim to the throne that doomed Glendower's granddaughters and split England in half. Fairly sobering, if you thought about it.

"The kids, too?" Heidi shivered. "No wonder the Welsh hate us Saxons so much."

"Not all of them," Robyn protested. "Owen likes you well enough."

"Should hope so." Her friend's grin returned.

"And Bryn's marrying one."

Heidi rolled her eyes. "Well, it's Collin. Who wouldn't?"

"Me." They both laughed at that. "Not anymore anyway."

Heidi soberly surveyed the castle. "So now, thanks to Owen, the Welsh have got it back." Anarchy in England had set the Welsh free, and they were quite happy about it, treating the two of them like visiting royalty and tolerating other Saxons so long as they behaved. Earl Wiltshire's men lodged in town and never got past the gatehouse. Heidi turned back to her. "Will Edward come and take it away from them?"

"Not personally." Edward was not the type to troop off to some remote part of Wales just to make the locals bow to him. His ego was not that thin, and he had way more important matters on his mind. "But if the Tudors do not submit, Edward will send someone to make them do it." Edward and Warwick had Parliament behind them, making continued Tudor resistance treason.

"Well, when you get back with your boyfriend, please put in a word for Owen." Heidi was already worried for her new lord.

"Of course." Robyn had already gotten Edward's promise to spare the Duke of Somerset—though Somerset had plotted the defeat and death of Edward's father at Wakefield. Owen Tudor ought to be an easier sell.

Owen himself did not act at all worried for his future, doting on Heidi by day, showing her off to clan chiefs at dinner, and making the master bed creak at night. Far from being embarrassed by Heidi, Owen wanted her always at his side, tickled by her outlandish notions. Beautiful women from Faerie were expected to be shameless in speech and action, and Heidi was born for the role. Which left Owen with hardly any time to molest Lady Robyn, aside from the odd squeeze on the tit, and his tongue thrust between her lips when they kissed good night. Robyn felt both relieved and insulted. What was wrong? Did she not tempt an oversexed reprobate like Owen Tudor? Heidi could not be that great in bed. Any old reprobate worth his salt ought to be trying to bed them both, just to maintain his reputation.

When she complained to Heidi while dressing for Mass, her girlfriend laughed. "Not to worry—Owen thinks you are totally hot. He keeps hinting pathetically that we would make an outstanding threesome."

"And what do you say?" She knew Heidi had been in ménages before, once with a name actress infamous for her "family" roles.

Heidi put on her most pious expression. "I pretend like I cannot comprehend what he is saying. Like two women making love is something only the depraved male mind could picture."

Robyn smirked at the image of Heidi as the blushing ingenue, with her baby-sweet smile, all puzzled confusion and blue-eyed innocence. Heidi had megawatts of raw acting talent, which the studio never tapped. Holding up a green slinky gown, Heidi admired herself in the steel mirror. "Besides, if we do it together, it will not be with Owen Tudor."

"Why so?" Never having made love with another woman, Robyn had no idea what the rules were. Or that there were any.

"Because you are too special to me, boss lady." Heidi looked back at her, grinning above the borrowed gown. "I would not share you with some random Welshman that I am fucking for room and board."

Très sensible. It took more than being made Lady of Harlech to turn Heidi's head. After Mass that morning, Owen surprised everyone by ordering his traveling household aboard the two big carracks waiting in the bay. Word was that they were headed for Pembroke Castle, and the place was already full to bursting, with every bed taken, so Robyn had their curtained bed dismantled and stowed in the hold, along with the clothes chests. Earl Wiltshire's men came along, plus two boatloads of Gwynedd spearmen and the usual butlers, harpers, seamstresses, jugglers, and pastry chefs. Half of Harlech seemed to be coming south, leaving only the washerwomen and a lean garrison commanded by a pair of knights, one Welsh and one Saxon.

For the second time, Lady Robyn crossed Cardigan Bay and entered Saint George's Channel, sans the howling gale that accompanied her first trip. This time a fair north wind swept her past Saint David's Head, and through the gap between Ramsey Island and the Bishops, then Owen Tudor's little flotilla did not turn east until they had rounded Saint Ann's Head and entered Milford Haven, where they dropped anchor to wait on the evening tide. Night had fallen when they docked at Pembroke, separated from the mainland by a deep moat that made William the Marshal's great castle into an island fortress.

It took hours to get the bed unloaded and hauled to a warm inner ward bedroom with thick leaded windows facing the river. Flemish hangings on the wall showed how close they were to the continent, here at the southern tip of Wales. Waiting for them was a round-faced Welsh teenager with short brown hair who offered them warm wash water and fresh baked bread, acting more like a hostess than a servant, moving furniture to make room for the big curtained bed and checking the gowns for water damage. Her name was Gwyndolen, and she had a one-year-old son who stared wide-eyed at the two young women from the future when he was not nursing. While Gwyndolen worked, Robyn played with the toddler, showing him her watch, letting him change the glowing numbers on her wrist. "What is his name?"

"Owen, after his father," Gwyndolen replied brightly. "Owen Dafydd."

"His father?" Robyn looked at Heidi, who rolled her eyes and reached for the bag inside her blouse.

Nodding proudly, barefoot Gwyndolen announced, "He is lord Owen Tudor's natural son."

Half brother to the Earl of Pembroke and uncle to the infant Earl of Richmond. Heidi sighed and began to roll. Clearly this was going to be one of those evenings. "And a beautiful boy he is," Robyn declared in Welsh, letting Owen Dafydd up onto her lap, doubly glad now that she had not given in to Owen Tudor's advances. "Well worthy of his father."

"Amen," Heidi agreed, sealing the joint with her tongue. "And as good at getting around."

"Better even," Robyn pointed out, holding Owen Dafydd in the one lap his father had not been in.

Gwyndolen's eyes lit up, glad the two grand Saxon ladies had taken such a shine to her little bastard son. "Will you watch him, please? M'lord Owen will be wanting me."

With her guests at ease, sweet young Gwyndolen could not wait to run upstairs and properly greet her returning lord and master— who had what nearly every woman wanted. Robyn grinned back at her over the boy's head. "Of course, we would love to watch him." Time she started honing her maternal skills.

"Here, take this with you." Heidi held out the joint.

Gwyndolen took it, looking puzzled. "What is this?"

"Peace offering," Heidi explained. "Owen will know what to do with it."

Thanking them both, Gwyndolen gathered her skirts had bounded happily upstairs, having plainly missed her master's company. Robyn and Heidi grimaced at each other. Just when you think medieval men are maybe half-civilized, something like this happens. Heidi shook her head, saying, "So now we know where all the gowns and dresses came from."

Bouncing little Owen Dafydd on her knee, Robyn found the boy's weight just right, and she felt her smile returning. "At least your new boyfriend's got balls the size of California."

"Hell yes," Heidi agreed. "How many guys do you know, with a whole goddamn castle to pick from, who would put all his girlfriends—past, present, and prospective—in the same room?"

Lady Robyn cocked a doubting eye. "All his girlfriends?"

Heidi grimaced again. "Sorry, that was an unwarranted assumption." Women in all corners of Wales could be caring for Owen's kids.

"Relax," Robyn advised. "Same thing happened to me on May Day. Nothing like being surprised in bed to make you realize that medieval men are not nearly as backward as they seem."

Slowly the distinctive odor of marijuana smoke drifted down from the bedchamber above, followed by a familiar creaking. "Better break out the kids' games," Heidi advised, "Owen's gonna be up all night."

And into the morning. Gwyndolen did not come back downstairs until after the matins bell rang, thanking Lady Robyn profusely and then taking the groggy toddler to a straw mattress by the door, muttering, "Thank you, m'lady, thank you."

While Gwyndolen nursed the Earl of Richmond's uncle to sleep, Robyn lay on the dark feather bed with Heidi's warm sleeping body beside her. Little Owen Dafydd had been no burden at all, boding well for her own impending motherhood. Gwyndolen's boy had felt great in her arms, a wonderful little weight, especially when he slept. Bright and inquisitive, he was a welcome diversion after a long day, perfectly glad to bounce around on the bed with two young women from the future, keeping it up until he wore himself out. Like father, like son.

Morning revealed another Lady Stafford in residence, Margaret Stafford, wife to Sir Henry Stafford, but more important, the mother of the Earl of Richmond and a Beaufort by birth. Since neither Owen nor his son, the Earl of Pembroke, were even married, the whole Tudor future rested on Lady Margaret's lone son, a quiet slender lad of three. At seventeen, the thrice-married dowager Countess of Richmond looked pretty tiny herself, though she was the hereditary head of the Beaufort clan, senior cousin to Duke Somerset and the Earl of Devon. Seeing little Margaret with her small son at morning Mass reminded Robyn of the whole tortured sexual history of the Tudors and Beauforts, Mad King Henry's bastard relations. Owen Tudor thought nothing of seducing the widowed Queen Catherine and keeping her pregnant until she died in childbirth. And Owen's oldest son, Edmund, had not hesitated to get his tiny twelve-year-old bride pregnant. Then he died, leaving a teenage widow behind. All this enthusiastic procreating with widows and children had produced a legitimate next generation of one. Hard to believe these Franco-Welsh hillbillies would one day own the English throne.

Tudor morals were too much even for Heidi. "Owen's daft if he thinks I'll troop up the stairs to give him a bang good night while the wife and kid sleep on a straw mattress below." Heidi had her standards, being raised by an unmarried mom herself, and she would not screw Gwyn's man in Gwyn's house—even if the castle actually belonged to the Earl of Pembroke. "My days of playing baby-sitter-cum-concubine are way behind me."

Or well ahead of her, depending on how you looked at it.

Lady Robyn found an unexpected ally in little Lady Margaret, who was devout to a fault and disapproved of her stepfather's dalliances. Lady Margaret heard several Masses before breakfast, and she personally fed the poor and tended the sick, often with the infant Earl of Richmond at her side. Seeing a seventeen-year-old lady in furred silk and a three-year-old earl washing sores on the feet of a lame old Welshman gave a whole new meaning to *medieval.* Even the hint that Heidi was ready to turn away from sin had Lady Margaret eager to take her in, which would have been way too much for Heidi, but attending Lady Margaret gave both of them a place to "be" that was not right beneath Owen's bedroom.

And something to do, too. You could not be around the former Margaret Tudor without being put to immediate use. Pembroke castle bulged with sinners, many of whom fell under the purview of Lady Margaret—pregnant whores, seasick Irish, and dying sailors. No matter where they came from, Lady Robyn spoke their language, which made her and Heidi a godsend. Lady Margaret could hear exactly what the trouble was and give clear concise instructions to the patient. For a religious fanatic, little Lady Margaret proved remarkably broad-minded, and she took to germ theory like a convert, instantly seeing the sense in having clean, boiled bandages— blaming herself for not have come up with the concept sooner. Margaret would have swabbed down Pembroke Castle with germicide, if it had only been invented.

This strong-minded teenager had already been married three times, having divorced her first husband at age nine. Margaret had been married as a child to the boy Duke of Suffolk, but the girl learned that Edmund Tudor, Earl of Richmond, a man in his twenties was interested in her. Her mother being dead, an old nurse advised her to pray to Santa Claus, who watched over young virgins. Margaret prayed all night, and Santa appeared to her dressed as a bishop, telling her to give herself to the Earl of Richmond. Under Church law, child brides could dissolve their marriages and marry whoever they pleased once they turned thirteen—by which time Lady Margaret was already a pregnant widow. All that remained from her first two marriages was Edmund Tudor's son— but Margaret was more than happy with the boy, telling Robyn, "I expect great things of him."

What mother did not? Robyn said a silent prayer to Saint Nick for her own baby, who was conceived in his season.

Lady Robyn had her own special spiritual needs. This was the Dead Month, following the Christmas season, the two weeks before and after Candlemas that were the deepest part of winter. Friday, January twenty-third, was her first Witches Night since returning from the future, and also marked nine months in the Middle Ages—minus a couple of detours into the future. She had first arrived in this world on Saint George's Day, the twenty-third of April, and now after nine long months she was being reborn in Edward's century. And not alone. For the next nine months she would have a little accomplice in all her magic, accompanying her on every Witches Flight. She must make all her spells loving ones.

Easy enough tonight. Robyn cast her circle by candlelight, kneeling at the foot of the bed. Gwyndolen was upstairs entertaining her lord, and Heidi slept on the curtained bed with little Owen Dafydd. Keening softly, Robyn reached out to her own lord, opening herself up to love. She already felt near to Edward, in his own time and not a hundred miles away—a day by boat, four days on horseback even over Welsh cattle trails. After being centuries apart, that was practically in his lap.

Sinking into the chant, she called to Edward on the far side of Wales. At the same time, she sank down into herself, keeping in touch with the child inside her, the life that quickened even in the Dead Month, the darkest days of winter, when Hecate took the young and the frail. Edward's child was finally in the same millennium as its father, and she prayed for all three of them to be together this Witches Night.

There was a whoosh of air, followed by blackness. Thinking the candle had gone out, she kept on keening, while feeling around for her lighter. Unable to find it, Robyn slowly realized that she was in a different bedchamber, one without either candle or lighter. She stopped fumbling about, ending her chant and listening intently.

Breathing came from behind her, strong and rhythmic, muffled by a curtained bed. With the breathing came a whiff of mint. Thank heavens, she had found him. She said a silent prayer to Diana, who presided over the new year, virgin goddess of children and childbirth. When she first became a witch, nine months ago, the Duchess of Bedford gave her the coven name Diana. Now she began to see why.

Rising, Robyn felt her way through the blackness to the bed. She parted the curtains and sat down on the mattress, reaching under the covers, feeling for his warm weight. Moments like this made her think of "East of the Sun and West of the Moon," her favorite fairy story as a girl, where the heroine dares not wake her phantom lover, or even look on him by the light of the lamp, for fear of losing him. Only in the secret blackness of night can the sacred marriage take place, the wedding of Cupid and Psyche, body and spirit, love and soul, the blind renouncing of the vast differences between the sexes.

Women and men were always separate creatures, yet through this plunge into dark mystery, they could for a moment become one— or sometimes three, or more.

Luckily Lady Robyn was no lovestruck girl straight from her mother's hearth. She had already pierced the mystery and was a mother-to-be, facing the trials set for her by Hecate. Finding Edward's sleeping form, she leaned through the blackness, following his breathing, until their lips touched.

Her kiss started out askew, with mouths crossways, but she quickly corrected, fitting her lips to his. First came the thrill of contact, then the warm flood of tingling sensation as his lips awoke against hers, followed by his tongue.

Edward's hand closed around her wrist, warm and hard against her flesh. Without breaking the kiss, he brought another arm around, lifting her witch's shift and pulling her up against him, breasts to chest, and hips to groin. When their lips parted, he asked, "Who are you, dream girl?"

"Who do you think?" She giggled, glad to have his hands back on her. His strong, sure grip encircling her wrist felt incredibly reassuring, despite the miles of dark lawless country and two contending armies that still lay between them. Love and spirit had come together, even if body and soul could not.

"Mary save me, what a miracle," Edward gasped, pulling her tighter to him. "I have not even heard of you for a fortnight."

"Not a miracle." She grinned at his enthusiasm for her naked form. "Just me."

He ran his hand along her leg and side, pulling up her black witch's shift higher, checking to see she was all there. "I can barely believe it."

Yet he had immediately kissed back and dragged her closer, his hand on her bare rump. "At least you did not call me Meg or Kate."

"Oh, no," he laughed. "As you see, 'tis the serving girl's night off."

"Her loss." Robyn rubbed playfully against him, seeing he was not disappointed by his unexpected bedmate.

He gripped her rear tighter, making sure she did not wiggle away. "Where have you been? I missed you terribly. I thought I would die when Deirdre and Cybelle came back without you. Wherever did you go?"

"Hither and yon." Telling him the whole story would violate witches' secrets. Being betrothed to a sorceress must be as hard on him as being betrothed to a royal heir was on her. "I never wanted to go, and I have spent the whole time trying to get back to you."

"How happy that you have succeeded." Edward pressed his fingertips deeper into her flesh, pushing her against his bare hips, letting her feel how immensely pleased he was.

"Even now I am not really here," she warned, not wanting to get his hopes up, as well.

Edward immediately tested her word, sliding her around until she straddled him, bringing them into intimate contact. Grinding his groin hard into hers, he asked huskily, "So am I dreaming?"

"Sort of." She certainly was, thoroughly enjoying this Witches Flight, riding Edward instead of a broom, feeling his naked flanks pressed against her inner thighs. What went on during Witches Night was a women's secret, and just by being here, she was bending the rules. Good witches did not use the Witches Flight to seduce sleeping teenagers, no matter how much the debauched boys might enjoy it. This bordered on wicked witchcraft, but she made an exception for Edward, whispering softly to her willing victim, "Where are we?"

"Gloucester Castle," Edward replied, sliding his arms firmly around her, meaning to keep her in his naked lap by main force if need be. "How did you get here?"

That was a ridiculous long story, and another witches' secret. "I am not really here," she reminded him. "I am in Pembroke Castle."

He stroked her longingly, running his hands along the whole length of her body, determined to get as much as he could from this Witches Night visit. "Yet you feel real enough."

Shivering at his touch, she enjoyed how his fingers strained to claim her, making Lady Robyn wish her young lord had her in the flesh. "Trust me, I am in Pembroke."

"Pembroke?" Edward sounded unconvinced, not wanting to hear that she was on the other side of Wales, though by now he had seen enough women's secrets to know that such things happened.

"Yes, Pembroke." And not alone. "Owen Tudor is here, too. And

~~also my friend Heidi from America." And an unborn baby, his~~
baby, but she did not say it.

"What force does Tudor have?" Edward meant to get her at
once, needing only to know how many men to bring.

"Only a few hundred." She had not done a head count, but there
was just the castle garrison, Owen's household knights, plus some
of Wiltshire's exiled retainers, and several hundred Gwynedd spearmen. "But enough to hold Pembroke Castle against all of Christendom."

"Not when my love is inside." Edward's hands gripped her
harder. When she was a prisoner in the Tower of London, he
marched straight there from Northhampton with every man he
could muster, opening the fortress prison in a matter of days. "I have
gathered thousands here at Gloucester for the relief of London—"

"Worry not," she put her finger to his lips, to stop him from saying too much. "I am leaving here quick as I can." She had no reason
to linger in Pembroke, and she certainly did not want Edward to
come marching to her rescue, invading Wales and laying siege to the
castle. "To go to where we hoped to get chocolate and granola."

He laughed in the dark, starting to rock gently, slowly rubbing
his stiff member against just the right spot. "And soy lecithin. We
went to find them in the vale—"

Again she stopped his lips, this time with a kiss, her hips moving
with his, while wet warmth spread between her thighs. No matter
how excited she got, she could not let him say Llanthony, or the
Vale of Ewyas. When their lips parted, she whispered, "Do not say
the name aloud."

"Why not?" Edward was always curious about witchcraft, especially when aroused. Sex and magic went so naturally together.

"Someone might be listening," she warned. To name names
would invite more trouble. Llanthony was a holy sanctuary in the
Vale of Ewyas, a long day's ride west of Gloucester, and she must
get there without arousing suspicion. Though the valley itself was
sacred and sheltered, they had both fallen into a magical ambush
nearby, on the very first day they met. "I will be there within the
week," she sighed. "Send for me if you can."

"Worry not," he whispered, creating more wet friction between
them. "I will come for you."

To show her what he meant, Edward slid slowly into her, inch by slippery inch. Oh, Mary help me, she thought to herself, how heavenly this feels, even at a distance. Sex was every bit as incredible as magic, able to send you on impossible flights to unbelievable places, without ever leaving your bed. With mouth open and eyes closed, she sank down onto him, giving herself completely to the sensation of having her man inside her. Forgetting everything but how good it felt.

Which instantly broke the spell. Too bad. Especially for Edward. He had been having a midnight visit that most teenage boys only dreamed about, when she suddenly evaporated. Being a witch, Lady Robyn could try to do better next time, but Edward was left nursing his cheated libido in the dark, wishing to heaven she would return. If only she could—but so far, she was a once-a-night witch, still learning her craft. Just getting this far had been hard enough. Six days "ago" she had been sitting at Kenilworth, eating cucumber sandwiches, and missing Edward.

As soon as Lady Robyn came to bed, Heidi wanted to know everything that had happened, asking in the dark, "Did you find him?"

Her friend had not been sleeping, and she instinctively knew whom Lady Robyn was seeking. Robyn could tell it was hopeless to keep witches' secrets from Heidi, who was already known as "the sorceress" among the men of Harlech. "Edward is in Gloucester Castle, about ninety miles away."

"As the spirit flies." Heidi liked the sound of this sort of spellcraft. "So what did you do?"

"Nothing that you would not have done," she replied primly.

"Good job!" Heidi laughed happily. "The boy does bring out your lewd side. How does witchcraft compare to cybersex?"

"More like the real thing, I am afraid." Robyn could still feel Edward between her thighs. "Only without AIDS, herpes, or having him falling asleep on you."

"And they call this place medieval." Heidi shook her head in wonder. "How did Edward like it?"

"He's wishing I was still there." Right now, Edward of March, Duke of York and heir apparent to the English throne, with thousands of armored bowmen at his back, was languishing in the night like any other teenage lad.

"Paradise interruptus." Heidi sympathized, being pretty permanently in touch with her male side. "Always leave 'em wanting more."

All the more galling, since he originally just wanted a good night's sleep—alone. Tricks like that were what got women burnt, but luckily her love was more broad-minded. What Robyn really needed was to be with Edward during daylight, so she could have a "normal" Witches Night, with a coven of women, exploring their link to the cosmos, doing the sort of Witches Flights that did not leave wet spots on the carpet.

Heidi asked, "Did you tell him about the baby?"

"Seeing me was surprise aplenty. Fatherhood on top of that would have been too much." For that they must be together in the flesh. Nor was there any need to advertise her pregnancy, when any witch might listen in. Bad enough she told the world she was in Pembroke Castle. Wake up, all you wicked witches, evil sprites, and would-be warlocks, Lady Robyn was back.

Her euphoria over being with Edward was punctured the next morning when she awoke to find more ships anchored in the roadstead, big carracks flying the banners of the Earls of Pembroke and Wiltshire. Dawn broke on an inner ward jammed with armed men and the women that came with them, including whole field battalion of French whores. Robyn watched in horror as French and Breton men-at-arms disembarked, along with Irish mercenaries, filling both the inner and outer wards with troops. She had underestimated Tudor strength and speed, being accustomed to the leisurely way Lancastrians usually made war. Queen Margaret and Duke Somerset had won a crushing victory at Wakefield a month ago, and no one had heard from them since.

Knights and mercenary captains sat at the high table, and the prime dinner topic was invading England, something Lady Robyn urged against in the strongest terms, saying, "I have seen the army Edward of March is raising, full of big brawny Shropshire bowmen and veteran men-at-arms."

Sir John Throckmorton doubted Lady Robyn's military judgment. "To my lady, all men clad in steel must look fierce."

Plainly Sir John had never seen Mad King Henry cowering in plate armor. Lady Robyn knew quite a lot about invading England, having done it successfully herself that summer with Edward, taking both London and the king. To make it work, the English had to "want" to be invaded—and it had better be done politely. When Edward landed at Sandwich that summer, he and Warwick swore to restore justice and curb an insane king who had lost France and bankrupted the country. They paid their way to London, giving silver for food and lodging and praying at every church, asking only for volunteers to the cause. Naturally folks flocked to their banners.

Doing the reverse would not be so easy. Few would fight to put the French queen and corrupt Court back in charge of the country they looted. Sitting around Lady Robyn were men who had profited tremendously off the king's insanity, which turned rebellious Welsh gentry into royal dukes and earls. Robyn owed her own ladyship to a similar fit of royal insanity, but Mad King Henry could have her title back anytime. She was not about to fight anyone for it. Lady Robyn became immediately popular at Pontefract because she worked to keep her tenants out of trouble, while other lords were dragging theirs into battle. Earl Pembroke leaned across the table to ask, "Have you really seen the army Edward of March is gathering?"

"Heavens, yes." Lady Robyn had found it was best to be honest in politics, and she did not much mind telling Edward's plans to his enemies, since his methods were so sure and straightforward that they were virtually unstoppable. "I watched him recruit, in Staffordshire and at Shrewsbury."

"How many were there?" asked Owen, who had held her and Heidi for days without giving any thought to getting useful military information from them.

She shrugged. "Not terribly many, for when I left, the Marches were at peace, and every household was happy for that. War was something happening way off in the north, or at worst around London, and few were willing to go so far away just to fight."

Her hosts were heartened to hear of the war weariness in the Welsh Marches. Sometimes the Lancastrians acted like they meant to win the civil war by sheer persistence, continuing to fight when every sensible person had gone home. That might work with her, but not with Edward's earldom of March. Lady Robyn looked levelly at the lords across the table, who were eating minced peacock off gold plates with silver-handled knives. "But bring war to their hearths and homes, and the Marches will rally to Edward, and he will be there to meet you—most likely at the border. Yorkist knights, civic militia, Shropshire men-at-arms, Powys spearmen, and Gwent bowmen will be waiting with arrows nocked and axes bright." With Edward Plantagenet at their head—over six feet of shinning steel wielding a double-bladed ax.

"Is that a witch's prophecy?" asked handsome Earl of Wiltshire, famously unwilling to risk his pretty face in battle.

"Just common sense." Which often amounted to the same thing. She had seen the Welsh Marches and its people, who had borne most of the early fighting in the current civil wars—from Shrewsbury to Blore Heath—leaving them accustomed to battle and wary of outsiders. Some parts of medieval England were not safe to invade. "You need no foresight to guess how Edward of March will react, but I will gladly roll my eyes and chant in Gaelic, if it will convince Your Grace."

"Now that sounds like fun!" Talking politics with professional hooligans bored Heidi. "We could put on some really medieval music and douse the candles to make it spooky."

No one took her up on it. Wiltshire sneered, "What lords have come out for him?"

"Hardly any," Robyn admitted. "Audley for sure. And Lord de Wilton. It is lesser men who will come out for him, Vaughans, Baskervilles, Herberts, Morgans, Powels, and Greys." Some of the Greys anyway. Edward's strength lay with the commons, whom these men knew they would never win over—at best they hoped to kill Edward and seize the king, installing an unpopular government by force. Not a strategy Lady Robyn favored.

Nor Heidi either, who had seen enough dangerous stupidity as a kid. In private, as they packed to go, Heidi asked, "How could Owen be so crazy? Tramping off through the cold and wet to attack heavily armed neighbors."

Silly way to start the new year. "When Queen Margaret ran things, the Tudors got a slew of Yorkist estates and royal castles," Robyn explained. "Now they must give them back."

Heidi snorted. "Seems a thin excuse for suicide."

"None of this was well thought out," Robyn observed. By now

the Tudors had little choice, being unable to feed thousands of men through the winter in this isolated bit of Wales. They must plunge on into England or send the mercenaries home. One mistake led neatly to the next.

When the little Tudor army left Pembroke Castle, Lady Robyn rode at the head with Owen's household, behind the earl's banners. She got a gray gelding to ride, which she promptly named Plunket after one of the first horses she had ridden in the Middle Ages. Heidi got a beautiful buckskin mare with a blond mane, which she named, Britney. French and Breton men-at-arms rode behind them, followed by squires and mistresses, then came mailed mercenaries, and mounted bowmen, followed by Welsh spearmen and wild Irish, with their women and children. Thousands of people in a long column tramped through a frigid treeless landscape dotted with white farmsteads and black cattle. Ahead of them reared dark wooded Welsh hills, shielding them from Saxon eyes.

And at every hamlet, Welsh joined the line of march, prosperous squires in full armor backed by spearmen out of the hills and archers up from Glamorgan. Tudors made much of the Act of Accord, which disinherited the Prince of Wales, as if that were some insult to the Welsh, though the infant prince was three-quarters French and one-quarter English. It depressed Robyn to see them choosing sides in what should be a Saxon civil war, which hardly needed the Welsh joining in, not to mention French and Bretons.

On the Roman road north of the Afon Tywi, she and Heidi stopped to rest and water the horses, watching the cavalcade file past. Banners hung limp, and men-at-arms wore furred cloaks in place of plate armor, which clattered along behind them aboard pack ponies and donkeys, led by mounted valets. Some Breton pikemen had brought their wives, and no force of French men-at-arms could move without its train of mistresses and courtesans, if only to save them from English cooking. Teenage French girls wrapped in furred cloaks called out to Lady Robyn from atop the pack saddles, trying to attract the attention of a fine lady who rated her own palfrey. Robyn waved back, which produced delighted squeals, and shouts of, "*Bonjour!* What pretty horses."

For the young, even war could be fun, seeing foreign lands with well-paying, hard-partying men-at-arms. Giving a shriek, a dark-

haired young woman in a green-and-gold dress swung down off her
pack pony and raced over, throwing her arms around Robyn, saying, "My Lady Stafford, how spectacular!"

Shocked by this enthused camp follower, it took Robyn a second
to realize it was Cybelle, Lord Audley's French mistress—who had
been with her on that Witches Night when she disappeared south of
Shrewsbury. "What in heavens are you doing here?"

Cybelle whispered coyly in French, "Spying for Edward."

Robyn stared at the smiling woman in her arms. "Really?"

Cybelle rolled her eyes toward the bleak Welsh hills and fog-
shrouded mountain passes ahead, cut from great masses of Jurassic
rock topped by black pines. "Why else would I be here?"

Of course. Cybelle was a poetess and would-be-witch, with a
milk-white complexion, big dark eyes, a wry wit, and a titled boyfriend. Why go trolling for guys in a Tudor army?

"And looking for you, as well," Cybelle added, proud to have
found her.

"For me?" Who would have thought to look for her here? "What
do you mean?"

"You vanished into the fog, gone to God knows where." Cybelle
made it sound as if she had deserted them. "Lord Edward searched
everywhere, sending men to scour the countryside. Pembroke was
one place his men could not go—so Edward said I was to especially
listen for any word of you. Privately, I thought that if you were
nowhere else, you would be in Wales."

And here she was. Edward would have someone checking on the
Tudors; she had just not imagined Cybelle. All Lady Robyn said
was, "We must talk."

Cybelle nodded eagerly. "Tonight."

That beat exchanging confidences in front of whistling bowmen
on the march. So Cybelle got back on her pack pony and caught up
with her girlfriends, while Lady Robyn went back to watering her
palfrey. Heidi asked significantly, "Who's your friend?"

"Someone you must meet." She made the formal introduction
that night at Dynevor Castle, on a bluff above the Tywi. Dynevor
had never fully recovered from a sack by Owen Glendower, and
parts were already in ruin, but Cybelle had a dry apartment, with a
valet to tend the fire, thanks to a "special friend" among Pem-

broke's household knights, "a most chivalrous gentleman who was my admirer, before my Lord Audley went over to side with York." Now her "knight" and "my Lord Audley" were on different sides, so Cybelle could have both of them, all for the sake of king and country. England was the land of opportunity for talented young Frenchwomen—from Queen Margaret on down.

"How did you get here?" Cybelle asked casually.

"Witchcraft." Heidi had no trouble answering that one. "One moment I was visiting a weird friend of Robyn's in the Welsh woods, next thing I know, *wham!* Welcome to the Middle Ages."

"Middle when?" No one here and now knew they were in the Middle Ages, least of all Cybelle.

"Between the past and future," Robyn explained. "When that Witches Night fog enveloped us, I was drawn centuries into the future—no doubt by the Duchess of Bedford." Better people than Duchess Wydville had tried to be rid of her, yet here she was, freezing her butt off in Wales.

"We called and called for you," Cybelle complained, pouring wine for her guests, "but got no answer. By the time Deirdre and I got back to Edward's manor, I was so cold, I cried."

"You wanted to be a witch," Robyn observed. Cybelle insisted on going with them that Witches Night, having a talent for insinuating herself into the lives of the rich and powerful—witness her latest appearance in Wales, gleefully adding spy to her current career as a witch-poetess-courtesan.

"I did indeed, though now I wonder." Cybelle handed her a warm wine cup, then passed another to Heidi.

Robyn sipped her mulled wine, feeling the heat flow through her. "How were you to get word to Edward?"

"By boat," Cybelle replied brightly. "Seamen out of Swansea and Bristol love your Lord Edward, and will do anything for a pretty woman who serves him."

How true—she once saw Edward talk a whole shipload of sailors into mutiny, with nothing but a wink and a smile—though that did them small good this deep in the Welsh hills. Robyn started boiling water for the trip, spreading out her tourist map of Wales. "With Carreg Cennen in his hands, Owen will head straight up the Tywi Valley, at least as far as Llandovery." She traced the line of the Tywi on the tourist map, which was six hundred years out of date, but infinitely better than any made here-and-now. "From there they will swing north through central Powys, to keep well clear of the Herberts, but we can cut straight southeast through Herbert country, without much fear of being followed."

Heidi spotted the obvious flaw. "Why are Owen's people so wary of the Herberts?"

"Everyone is. Herberts are quarrelsome, ruthless, treacherous, and untrustworthy—known for making their own law, then breaking it, too." William Herbert and his father-in-law, Walter Devereux, were the twin terrors of the southern marches, courted by both York and Lancaster. At the moment they sided with Edward, for whatever that was worth.

"Both treacherous and untrustworthy?" Heidi made it sound redundant.

"They betrayed their fellow traitors." It helped that the Herberts never took Saxon oaths seriously.

"Just the guys you want to meet on a cold dark moor."

"We have not got much choice." Owen Tudor, with two earls and thousands of spearmen at his back, was skirting Herbert country, so should Lady Robyn be taking them on, with just her production assistant? Probably not, but that was the way to get to Edward first. "I am hoping we can just clip the corner of Herbert country and find shelter with the Vaughans at Tretower, who have hidden me before. Once I even had dinner with William Herbert, the head of the clan." Of course, that had been at Kenilworth under Mad King Henry's watchful eye, where Welsh bandits were on best behavior. She looked straight at Heidi. "I do not deny the danger. Are you up for doing this?"

Heidi grinned at her. "Do the Welsh shit in the woods?"

Anything to get safely away from Owen's mad midwinter invasion—which they did the next morning, kissing Cybelle goodbye and stepping quietly over the sleeping valet. Clutching a thermos of coffee for the road, Lady Robyn mounted one-handed, and they headed upriver, crossing the Afon Tywi at Llandovery, the "Church over the water"—one tributary ran right down the main street, carrying away trash and sewage. Which was why Lady Robyn refused to drink out of the river like the rest of the army.

Bad water regularly killed more knights than the broadsword. Mad King Henry's heroic father died of dysentery while on campaign in France, leaving a baby king and a widowed queen to be seduced by Owen Tudor.

Beyond the town, Robyn found the Roman road headed east, worn stretches of stone running straight across the moor, and she set off into the sunrise with Heidi at her side, glad to be free of the growing Tudor army. What Tudors saw as a crisis of kingship, most people called peace. Plowing had begun, along with the pruning and hedging, and ordinary folks had families to feed and firewood to gather, with no time to attack their neighbors. Gingerly unscrewing the coffee thermos, she felt sorry for Cybelle, who was caught in a moving box of armed men headed blindly into battle.

"Cybelle seems a bit of a trip." Heidi had years of experience at reading Robyn's morning moods.

"I hardly know her," Robyn confessed, pouring coffee into the thermos top, which she used as a cup. The young Frenchwoman had thrust herself into things, reading poetry to rebel troops, sleeping with lords, crashing magic rituals, and now spying for Edward. Handing over the coffee cup, she told Heidi, "Do you know she has two kids in France?"

Heidi nodded, taking a sip. "Had that medieval mom-on-the-run edge to her."

"She's not the only one." Robyn touched her own belly, thinking of the child inside. On the far side of the wooded top was Y Pigwn, seamed by the square slumped contours of a Roman camp, with its ramparts and ditches. Knowing that Italians once ruled these parts made the current conflict seem more transitory.

Descending into the Usk Valley, passing from Dyfed into southern Powys, they stopped for noon rest at a prosperous farmstead. Bearded men in long shirts and baggy leggings came out to greet them, followed by women in gay dresses and wool cloaks, who offered water to wash their feet. Robyn politely refused, since they were wearing boots and not planning to spend the night. While they ate cheese and onions on thin slabs of oat bread, women harped to them, and the whole family sang songs—men, women, and children—all taking different parts, each voice distinct, but joined together in sweet B-flat harmony—just to please a pair of

Saxon "ladies" who happened to wander by, speaking excellent Welsh. This deep in Powys, the Welsh lived the way they always had, before the Saxons curbed their "barbarous ways." Robyn gave her hosts gold rings as parting gifts, then she and Heidi set off into the cold crisp day.

Two lads with gold inlaid harps went ahead of them, playing to show them the way. Two more brought up the rear, carrying spears and trailed by silent greyhounds, seeing them safely off. Heidi pulled her cloak tight, saying, "Shit, this is like out of a fairy tale. Gold harps and all."

"That is the Welsh. They put you in another place." Wales had no beggars, just guests. She had counted on Welsh hospitality to get them safely to Tretower—"But I did not expect a harp escort."

"How far to Tretower?" Heidi asked, huddled in her cloak. Snow was coming down, small white flakes falling from gray sky.

"Halfway there already," Robyn assured her freezing companion. "We will sleep warm tonight." Hopefully not in a Welsh communal bed. Avoiding Brecon itself, their escorts led them to a safe crossing over the Afon Ysgir, leading to a line of Welsh hamlets spaced every couple of miles, marking the ridge trail to Tretower. Roman roads ran straight across the flats and along the valley floors, but Celts favored high, dry trails running along low ridgelines. She tried to buck up Heidi, saying, "Ten, fifteen more miles more at most."

"Who are they?" Heidi pointed to a half-dozen armored riders issuing from the grassy ramparts of Pen y Crug wearing sallet helmets, blue-red livery jackets, steel sleeves, and knee-length leather boots. Their ensign bore a banner with a green Welsh dragon, making them look like Arthur's knights emerging from the triple-banked hill fort.

"Herberts from the look of them." The green dragon was a Herbert badge. As the riders approached, one of them peeled off, galloping head down to the east. Whatever message he bore most likely concerned her, since few folks hereabouts had even heard of Heidi.

Ignoring the harpers and spearmen, their leader rode straight up to Lady Robyn and doffed his steel cap, saying, "Ralph of Raglan, at m'lady's service."

Without his sallet helm, Ralph of Raglan was not bad-looking, with short brown hair, a strong broad nose, and thin tense lips. Robyn held out her hand for Ralph to kiss. "Lady Stafford of Pontefract."

He happily complied, saying, "Where is m'lady headed?"

"We are going to visit the Vaughans at Tretower," Robyn replied firmly, lest this Herbert get any ideas of diverting them for his own ends.

His men chuckled at her plans, and Ralph wagged his head dolefully, saying, "Vaughans are a rough breed, brought up in these wild hills, far away from houses and people."

"Thoroughly uncouth." His men agreed, cheerfully blackguarding their Vaughan cousins. "M'lady is far better off in our hands."

"Doubtless." These were Edward's allies, but that did not make her trust them. "However, my business is in Tretower."

Ralph of Raglan waved his grinning accomplices to silence, then made a polite, nodding bow to her. "Alas, m'lady, it is not so simple. Pembroke's harbingers have been in Brecon, and they are watching the ridge road to Tretower."

"Then what am I to do?" Pembroke's men were not going to let her through to Tretower, since their main job was to see that Edward got no word of Tudor movements. Owen meant to burst out of Powys unannounced and either fall on Edward from behind or march to join Somerset in the Midlands.

"Well if m'lady goes harping and singing into their hands, then there is no hope." Ralph had an armed horseman's contempt for folks who went witlessly about with peace in their hearts and a song on their lips. His own men were armed with swords, lances, and bollock daggers, along with little round shields for defense. "However, my riders and I will get m'lady safely through to Tretower, if m'lady will have it."

"How do I know you will?" Herberts were like the Nevilles, now on one side, now on the other. If these even were Herberts.

"If you did doubt me, I was told to show you this." Ralph of Raglan reached into his purse—you knew you were in the Middle Ages when armed ruffians carried hand-stitched purses, sometimes more than one. His gloved hand came out, and he turned back to her, proudly displaying its contents.

Lying on its leather palm was a blue plastic cigarette lighter.

After all the harping and King Arthur fantasy, it was a shock to see that little bit of chrome and see-through plastic. Heidi gave a hushed, "Holy shit! Where did he get that?"

It was hers, of course—Robyn recognized it immediately. And the man could only have gotten it from Edward. Ralph of Raglan smiled at the women's surprise. "If you flick the wheel, it makes fire. How is that?"

"A very tiny flint," Robyn told him, her mind racing. That lighter was a sure sign Edward was close at hand. She had given him a couple in Shrewsbury, one blue, one purple, to match his colors. "Where did you get it?"

"Amazing." Ralph peered at the lighter mechanism, then looked back at her with a grin. "I received it in Llathony, from someone you will know, and whom I must not name."

Enough said, literally. Lady Robyn turned to her escort, thanking them for bringing her so far in safety, giving each a gold ring and a good-bye kiss. She had kissed more men she did not know since coming to the Middle Ages than in all her years in Hollywood. And women, as well. Everything was more intimate in a kingdom with the population of Fresno.

Instead of following the ridge trail, Ralph led them past Tal-y-llyn, skirting the north shore of the Lake Llangorse, the largest lake in Wales. Past the lake, they mounted the bare tops, crossing a low pass in the Mynydd Llangorse to descend into the valley beyond, a narrow notch in the Black Mountains that led straight to Tretower Castle. Ralph of Raglan boasted, "Pembroke's men do not know the ways on this side of Wales."

By now the winter sun had sunk low in the sky, taking what warmth there was with it. Keeping to the eastern heights, they approached Tretower from uphill through broken woods and pasture, riding in the last of the light. Ralph pointed out a standing stone below them, marking the trail, and a mile or so beyond lay the castle itself, barely visible in the twilight. "My lady shall be there by vespers."

Determined to prove him wrong, a dozen riders burst from cover, lancers in half-armor wearing Tudor green-and-white. With the advantage of ground and numbers, Pembroke's cheering riders swept over the surprised Herberts, driving them downslope. Riding at the head, Robyn just had time to grab Heidi's reins, urging her forward, dashing straight down the cow path they were on. Ralph of Raglan was right behind them, sword in hand and swearing in Welsh. Pembroke's men had surprised him on his own turf, springing an ambush within sight of Tretower.

Steel rang out, followed by shouts and oaths. Ralph of Raglan went down, swinging wildly, his mount buckling beneath him and rolling downslope, a Tudor lance tangled in the horse's legs. Seeing their final defender disappear in a flurry of flailing hooves and flying turf, Robyn resisted the urge to flee blindly downhill, striving not to give up height, galloping down the cow path as fast as her tired gray gelding could go, with Heidi's spirited mare pounding at her heels. Up close, she saw some of their pursuers wore white hunting hounds on their surcoats—a Tudor badge.

Suddenly the trail dipped down, and she splashed through a stream, then mounted the far bank, hugging the high ground. Having driven the Herberts downhill, the Tudors now had to climb back up after her. Which they did. Hoofbeats sounded behind them, coming closer, followed by shouts and a mounted struggle. Heidi shrieked, "Hands off, asshole!"

All that got was laughter, and an admonition, "Be careful with her. That one belongs to Owen."

Lady Robyn was still up for grabs. There was nothing she could do for Heidi, and should she so much as falter, she would swiftly join her friend. Having been hotly pursued before, Lady Robyn knew only blind never-look-back panic would save her; show any hesitation, and she would end up in these horsemen's hands, wishing to hell she were free. Throwing strategy aside, Robyn broke straight downhill, frantic to put distance between her and pursuit. Heather slashed at her skirts, and black limbs swung at her as she dodged between dark trees, expecting all the time to feel a Tudor lance point prodding her butt.

She came crashing out of the bracken and onto a wider trail, headed east over bare tops toward Llanthony. Hardly any roads ran through the Black Mountains, so Robyn immediately took this one, and her tired mount picked up speed on the packed earth. Hopefully, Pembroke's horsemen would not know which way she had gone. Head down, Lady Robyn listened for hoofbeats that were not from her frightened gelding, hearing nothing. If true, it meant she was on her own, without Heidi. Without anyone. Absolutely alone, for the first time since returning to the Middle Ages, a feeling as refreshing as it was frightening.

PART 2

Candlemas

Dazzle mine eyes, or do I see three suns?
—Shakespeare, *Henry VI, Part III*

6

⋙ Knight of the Black Plumes ⋘

Lady Robyn slowed her horse to a trot, giving poor Plunket a rest, with no sign of pursuit and a long way still to go. By now she was well past Tretower, deep in Herbert country, with the last Tudor stronghold, Carreg Cennen, a long day's ride behind her. Llanthony lay in a hidden valley a dozen miles ahead, and finding it in the dark would be a feat. Fortunately the big waxing moon was already up, bathing the frigid heath in pale wintry light.

Her cattle path curved around the bare flank of a peak that might have been Pen Cerrig-calch, and there was a cook fire somewhere below her, because she smelled the wood smoke. If she followed the path far enough, she would come on a Welsh village, and Lady Robyn was not afraid to ask directions. That felt like a plan, though she wished Heidi were here to help carry it out, or better yet, Edward.

After more than a mile of feeling her way through the gathering gloom, she came on a smaller height, capped by a ring fort that had to be Crug Hywell. Ahead and below her lay the village of Llanbedr, at least on her tourist map, heaven knew what was there here and now. She pushed on past the hill fort, continuing to follow the path until it turned down toward the village; then she paused to check her bearings.

And heard hoofbeats. Not loud—in fact barely there—but slowly growing more distinct, and unnerving. Unable to be sure, she looked back.

Damn! She was instantly sorry, seeing she was no longer alone. Silhouetted against the western twilight was a lone rider, armed with a lance and headed her way. Robyn spurred her weary horse down toward Llanbedr, passing a dark farmstead, where dogs barked at her.

As the path turned up again, she looked back and saw the armed rider was still coming on, easily closing the gap. Urging her exhausted gelding forward, Robyn found her mount totally run out, barely managing a trot. Her relentless pursuer cut the lead from two hundred paces to one hundred, then seventy, then fifty.

At twenty paces, she could tell he was not a Tudor at all, but wore a scarlet surcoat, glinting with gold trim—one of Earl Wiltshire's men. Turning to urge on her tired mount, her heart sank even further, seeing another armored rider galloping up out of the gloom ahead of her, blocking further flight.

Lady Robyn wanted to cry, but it would do her no good. Seeing no escape, she reined in, trying to collect herself. In seconds, she was going to be in the hands of steel-clad horsemen, and she had to make that less ghastly than it sounded, reminding herself she had yet to break any major laws on this latest trip to the Middle Ages. She had merely run off with Owen Tudor's estranged girlfriend, which ought not to be a crime. And happily she was in female attire.

Confident the law at least was on her side, Lady Robyn waited for pursuit to catch up. Maintain decorum, and at worst they would drag her and Heidi back to confront an angry Owen, who would sentence both of them to bed, something Heidi claimed was not too horrible. First to rein in beside her was Wiltshire's man, a grim armored lout, who snatched her reins with a steel-gloved hand. His sallet was tipped back, and Robyn recognized an old friend—Gap-tooth, who held Heidi while his buddies beat her into submission on her first day back. He knew her, too, leering happily. "How splendid ta see m'lady. Lost yer way again?"

"Not at all." Now she wanted to scream and snatch back her reins, but getting loud or physical would hardly help. Gap-tooth and his buds taught her that last time. Holding hard to her reins, she decided her best defense was not to give an inch, which meant an immediate test of wills with the brute. "Now, if you will excuse me, I have a ways to go, and the hour is late—"

Wiltshire's henchman pulled hard on her reins, growling, "Let go, ya daft whore." Lady Robyn tightened her grip. Life in the Middle Ages had taken the sting out of *whore* but *daft* did hurt a bit—coming as it did from a certified loon. The result was a silent tug-of-war over her reins, while Plunket shook with cold and fatigue beneath her, too exhausted to care who won.

Before either of them could get control of the weary beast, a third contender came trotting up, the horseman who had loomed ahead of her, cutting off her escape to Llanthony. Clearly Welsh, he wore old-fashioned half-armor, showing gaps of mail, and sallet-helm with a red dragon crest—a Tudor badge. His helmet half hid his face, but Robyn could tell he was young, and excited. He had a huge two-handed sword hanging from his saddle bow, as well as a lance, but no leg armor, just stout leather boots. "Good eve," the Welsh man-at-arms called out cheerfully, reining in a few feet away. "What need have thee?"

"Gaw' way, yew Welsh ape," her would-be captor warned. "Our needs are none of yer affair."

"Beware, Saxon!" replied the newcomer in a fluid Powys accent. "You have the honor of addressing Alan ap Gruffydd ap Rhys, and whatever happens hereabouts is my affair."

Another Welsh busybody. First Nest, now this Alan ap Gruffydd; the locals were not letting Wiltshire's men molest vagabond women in peace. Her accoster protested stiffly, "I am the most trusted servant to His Grace, James Butler, Earl of Wiltshire and Ormond, lord of Abergavenny, and councilor to the Prince of Wales, who is here in these hills with ten thousand men."

"Well then, you will well know whom to complain to." Alan ap Gruffydd had his sallet visor up, showing a bold smirk on his young clean-shaven face, pleased to take on any number of Anglo-Irish hooligans. He was more her age than Edward's, but had not lost that devil-may-care certainty of youth. "For unless this lady objects, she is coming with me."

"No objections whatsoever, good sir," Lady Robyn hastened to declare. "So long as we go to Llanthony."

"Llanthony it is, m'lady." Alan added a pert nod, as if he often picked up pretty damsels at odd hours, and needed only to know where this one would go.

"Blast yew, harp-assed, interfering fool!" Gap-tooth struggled to swing his lance around while keeping hold of her reins. Alan ap Gruffydd unslung a small round shield that had hung across his back, bearing his red dragon badge. Alarmed at her futile attempt to grab a few medieval minutes alone, Welsh and Saxon were set to do battle for her by moonlight.

Even in the shimmering glow of a nearly full moon, having men fight over you was never so fun as it sounded. In fact, Robyn could barely believe her ill luck. Mere minutes ago, she and Heidi had been home free, exhausted but happy, within sight of Tretower, cheerfully anticipating hot food and warm beds. Then *wham!* Heidi was gone. And now she was in the hands of armed men with small concern for her cares or wishes. How incredibly infuriating that total strangers could casually quarrel over "her"—squaring off like stags in rut. Such thinking angered every woman in England, and it made Edward's promise of simple justice immensely popular. Summoning up her strength, Robyn reached deep into her abdomen, where new life lay growing, and shrieked, "Stop! Cease this madness!"

And they did stop. Wiltshire's man looked back at her in blank astonishment, while the Welsh rider halted with his lance halfcouched. Thanking them with a firm, *"Merci, messieurs,"* she gave a swift jerk that freed her reins, adding a polite, *"Merci beaucoup."*

Praying the trance would hold, Lady Robyn prodded her tired mount down the path toward Llanthony. Hopefully they would see that, thrilling as it had been, this evening's spirited jaunt across the Welsh moors was at an end. It was well past time from them to find warm—but separate—beds.

"Stop, strumpet!" Gap-tooth shouted over his steel shoulder. That broke the spell. Without waiting to see if she obeyed, Alan ap Gruffydd spurred his mount and leveled his lance. Lowering his own lance, Wiltshire's man sent his stallion thundering to meet his Welsh rival. Suddenly she went from center of attention to solitary spectator, watching mayhem by moonlight.

Her claimants met with a ringing crash that resounded over the dark frozen heather, sounding like the crack of doom. Taking the Saxon lance on his dragon shield, Alan ap Gruffydd aimed high, spearing his opponent's helmet. Gap-tooth's lance shattered against the Welsh knight's shield, while the Saxon's sallet went sailing off into the night, accompanied by an anguished howl.

Disarmed and bloodied, Wiltshire's man tottered in his saddle, while his horse bolted in terror beneath him, spiriting the stunned Saxon back down the path toward Tretower. Another victim of Welsh hospitality, lucky to escape with his head.

Suddenly it was just the two of them, alone in the cold moonlit moor. An awkward moment. Alan ap Gruffydd had fought for her, making her to some extent "his." Sir Galahad was just a story, and the Crusades were long over. There were no more saints in armor, and nowadays knights planned to be paid in full by their feudal lord, or any wayward young ladies they saved. Had she a husband, even a clan enemy, he would make good—but all she had was a secret betrothal. Being out of her teens and unmarried, "chivalry" practically demanded that she put out. Under Welsh law, she might even have to marry him.

Determined to start out friends, Robyn rose in the saddle, giving him a cheerful, "Many thanks, noble sir. I am Lady Robyn Stafford of Pontefract, and dearly in your debt."

Alan ap Gruffydd looked her over, liking what he saw. "No thanks are needed, Lady Stafford. I was merely paying the debt that valor owes to beauty."

He certainly said the right things. Did beating Gap-tooth make him trustworthy, or merely good with his lance? She widened her smile. *"Merci beaucoup."*

Happy they were getting on so famously, Alan looked down the cow path after his Saxon opponent, already lost in the gloom. "Who was that felon?"

"I do not even know his name," Robyn admitted, ashamed that she could not bother to acquaint herself with someone who accosted her twice; since Gap-tooth had certainly kept track of her, running her down across country, both here and in Gwynedd. But getting to know every guy who showed unwanted interest only encouraged them. "He does serve Earl Butler."

"Not well, it seems." Alan ap Gruffydd laughed, sounding very cavalier about angering an earl. Which side was he on? Robyn had never seen war up close until coming to the Middle Ages, but right away she saw the crying need for standardized uniforms—if only to separate the combatants from civilians, like her. Her newfound champion turned back to her, asking cheerfully, "Whom does m'lady serve?"

That was the polite way of saying, Is there a Lord Stafford? Now was the moment for her to claim some man's protection. Unlike some, she had a choice, Edward of March? Sir Collin Grey, her champion? Owen Tudor, whose colors she wore last. Lady Robyn stuck with the safe choice, "His Majesty, King Henry."

Alan ap Gruffydd laughed at that evasion. "We all hope to serve His Majesty."

Absolute loyalty to an insane king led to the current civil war—but Lady Robyn meant kingship in its truest sense, with every woman protected by King's Law. As in theory, any woman was, though theory and fact were leagues apart in Mad King Henry's England. Luckily she had specific proof of Henry's concern, saying, "Pontefract is a royal honour, making me His Majesty's personal dependent."

"Pontefract is a long way off," Alan pointed out. Anyone could claim vast holdings in Yorkshire. Half the families in Powys had tales of ancient British lordships, lost to the Saxons.

"Luckily, I need only go as far as Llanthony this evening." She had to make this man take her to Edward, without giving in too far to him.

"Even Llanthony is a long ride on a cold night." His tone implied there were way better ways to get warm. "Must you be there this evening?"

"I must." Grateful as she was, she would not let him wear her down. Having a friendly, handsome Welshman willing to do her favors was another big reason to get to Edward quick. "They say Llanthony is a most refreshing place, and I have much to recover from."

"My lady could find rest and refreshment closer," Alan suggested, ready to start her recovery on some convenient straw mattress as soon as he evicted the owners.

"And holy," Robyn hurried to add. "Llanthony is totally free of sin and carnal desire, a vale of incredible purity—"

"So I have heard," Alan ap Gruffydd admitted, showing scant enthusiasm for a sin-free evening.

She sought to console her amorous benefactor. "Birds come down and eat from your palm."

"You should worry more for your poor mount," Alan noted, "who is fully ridden out. That tired gelding will never get you to Llanthony."

Probably true, since Plunket did not have someone waiting for him. "Then I will walk."

Alan ap Gruffydd laughed at that notion, swinging out of his saddle and offering up his charger. "No, I will."

He knew the way to a horsewoman's heart, and Lady Robyn thanked him, glad to give her gelding a rest, even letting Alan "help" her board his charger, a tall Welsh-Arabian breed much favored by the local gentry, who were great horse fanciers, rustlers, and importers. His hands felt sure and strong, lifting her easily and not wandering far from their purpose, except for a squeeze on the thigh, once he had her secure in the saddle. Ignoring the squeeze, she inquired innocently, "Do you have no one you must return to?" Was there a Mrs. Alan ap Gruffydd?

"None but my aged parents," protested Alan, "who will easily pass the night without me." Another knight who lived with mom and dad. How terribly sweet, much more homey than she originally pictured the Middle Ages.

Relaxing into her seat, she asked, "What is his name?"

"My father?" Alan sounded puzzled. "Gruffydd ap Rhys ap Owain?"

"Actually, I meant your steed." She patted the charger's graceful Arab neck. "What is his name?"

"Gwynt." Alan sounded justly proud.

"Good name." It meant "wind" in Welsh. True to his word, Alan ap Gruffydd led them away from a warm mattress in some Powys hovel, walking ahead of her around the cold flank of Crug Mawr, toward the steep sacred valley of the Afon Honddu. Letting Alan lead the horses, she flipped on the purple lighter, studying the tourist map.

He peered back at her, asking, "What witchcraft is that?"

"Flint, steel, and burning oil." She held it up for him to see.

"I have never seen the like." Welsh men were wary of women's magic, just as happy that it did not involve them.

"Got it in London." This deep in Powys, London was no more real than L.A. By the tiny light, Llanthony looked to be almost due north, beyond a wooded ridgeline. If she kept her eye on the northern star, she could tell if Alan led her astray. In Sherwood, she had been fooled by Black Dick Nixon into going the wrong way, but that was in snowy woods, not a clear stark night like tonight. Flicking off the lighter, she let the stars be her guide, closing her eyes for long stretches, lulled by the sway of her horse.

After a hugely long day in the saddle that started before dawn and still had not ended, she drifted into fitful sleep. High-back knight's saddles, built to keep a big rider from keeling over on impact, were perfect for napping, and Lady Robyn did not wake until the steady hoofbeats stopped and Alan ap Gruffydd shook her to say, "My lady, if you will, I need my charger back."

Jerked alert, she looked frantically about, finding that the wooded ridgeline was behind them, and they were on a bare top above the Afon Honddu. Ahead of her, an ancient British ridge trail curved through the frozen heather. She asked, "What is it?"

"Someone is coming." Alan helped her down, and she heard the hoofbeats, too, coming up the ridge trail from below, growing louder. Just across the narrow valley, on the eastern ridgeline, she and Edward had been ambushed on her first attempt to find Llanthony. Then black riders had appeared, backed by foot bowmen, who chased her halfway to Pandy. Llanthony was a holy place, but here on the lip of the valley, anything could happen.

She took Plunket's reins, climbing atop the weary gelding while the young Welshman mounted his charger and unshipped his lance. Staring down the dark path toward Llanthony, Lady Robyn spied a single rider trotting toward them, lance in hand, wearing plain black armor. As he drew closer, she saw that his small jousting shield was adorned with the Prince of Wales's badge—three black ostrich plumes—worn to protest the Act of Accord. His old-fashioned helmet had a hound-skull visor and was topped by triple ostrich plumes. Tudors had been giving out black-plumed badges to anyone supporting their royal nephew.

Which made this black knight Edward's outright enemy. Robyn had thought it best not to question Alan's politics, though like most sensible Welsh, he treated the civil war as something between Saxons—not fearing Lord Wiltshire's anger, or questioning her claim to King Henry's protection. Which gave Robyn every reason to favor Alan ap Gruffydd, who was bold, handsome, and had risked his neck to save her from a brigand on horseback—while she knew absolutely nothing about the other fellow, except that he was

Edward's foe, though not necessarily hers. Lady Robyn also opposed the Act of Accord. Perhaps they could come to some political understanding, assuming he survived the next couple of minutes.

With her mount firmly on the trail to Llanthony, she waited to see what happened, hoping it would not be homicide. How absurd—yet another fight over her. This was the moment to cry, "Good sir knights, hold your swords, lances, and lesser edged weapons. It is silly to kill yourselves over me. Idiotic, really." Sure she was pretty, talented, astonishingly good with languages, and sometimes able to see the future—but nothing to die for.

Neither of them saw it that way, facing each other across the heather, lances cocked, their steel points twinkling in the moonlight. Men bent on mayhem could look strangely beautiful, especially in the Middle Ages. Alan ap Gruffydd explained that he was taking this lady into Llanthony, and if the black knight wanted women to molest, the Welshman pointed east with his lance. "Offa's Dyke is that way."

Bachelor number three was having none of that, and he spurred his big bay mount, black ostrich plumes nodding ominously atop his helm. Lady Robyn felt like the prize idiot, waiting on horseback upon a dark moor, watching two men ride right into each other over her—again. She did not even know both their names, which should have shown their idiocy, but instead made the fight all that much more elemental. She went with whoever won, sight unseen. There would be no saying no.

Her claimants came together on the ancient ridge path with a resounding crash. Alan aimed at the helmet again, but his lance point skidded off the black knight's hound-skull visor, clipping feathers from the plumes. At the same instant, the sable knight's lance struck the Welshman's dragon shield, slicing through the metal and slamming into Alan ap Gruffydd's armored shoulder, flipping him from the saddle. Gwynt kept going, galloping off down the path toward Llanthony, while his rider tumbled through the night air, hitting with a horrid clang on the frigid heath.

Without even looking to see how his foe had landed, the black knight wheeled about, urging his big bay charger toward her. He had a calm economy about his movements, having leveled his lance as soon as he arrived on the scene, then disposed of Alan ap Gruffydd

~~in a single pass. Now he turned immediately to her and came trot-~~
ting over, his plumes half-shorn by the Welshman's lance. Alan ap
Gruffydd moaned a bit and rolled over onto his back, showing he
was still alive, if barely.

This was a delicate moment, since whoever was inside that black
armor was not her knight, and she had never promised to be anyone's prize—but he had fought for her, and won handily. Under the
rules of chivalry, that made her his for the night, unless she was
married, a nun, or hopelessly disfigured, none of which applied.
Reining in before her, he reached up, lifting his scarred houndskull
visor, revealing his handsome, grinning clean-shaven face. Dark
eyes twinkled with delight above the wide confident smile—it was
Edward.

"My lord!" she breathed in happy surprise, her love's face being
the last one Lady Robyn expected to see beneath the Prince of
Wales's plumes.

Stripping off his steel gloves, Edward leaned over and took her
startled face in his hands, kissing her hard on the lips. Shock turned
to surprised relief as she returned the kiss. Here he was in the flesh,
just the way she wanted him, holding her in his warm firm hands
and thrilling her with his cunning French-born tongue. When their
lips parted, Edward replied softly, "My lady."

Still in shock, she asked, "How did you find me? How did you
get here?"

Edward beamed at his own cleverness, saying, "Herberts sent
word straight to Llanthony when they found you above Brecon. I
set out to meet you at Tretower—all else was happenstance." He
had the knack for correctly reading a situation, then responding
speedily, regularly surprising both friends and enemies. Happily he
was not nearly so swift in bed as he was in battle.

"When I saw you ride up, I did not know what to think." His
Prince of Wales ostrich plumes had totally thrown her.

"Pray forgive me." Edward's smile turned into concern. "We
heard that Pembroke's riders were on the road, and I wanted to find
you, not a fight." As it was, he found both. "So I set out in disguise,
then dared not raise my visor and show who I was, for fear that
would bring harm to you."

And he figured he could upend Alan easily, then have everything his way. Which he did—for the moment. She reminded him, "You should have let me know it was you."

"Why so?" Far as Edward could see, things had come out famously.

"Because now I must see how my previous protector is doing." Disengaging from Edward, she handed him Plunket's reins and hastily dismounted.

"What previous protector?" Edward demanded, but she did not answer. Lifting her skirt hem, she hurried over to where Alan ap Gruffydd lay groaning on the ground. Heartrending as the groans were, they at least showed he was alive, and Lady Robyn's worst fear was that she might have killed this man by insisting on going to Llanthony. Without much questioning her destination, Alan ap Gruffydd had fought for her twice, assuming she was well worth whatever trouble came of it.

Sorry. Gallant young Alan ap Gruffydd was about to find he had risked life and limb for awfully little. Robyn felt both relieved and mortified, bending over her would-be champion, who had a great dent in his shoulder armor, which meant at best a broken collarbone and possibly worse internal injuries. Kneeling at his side, she asked, "Are you hurt?"

Alan nodded painfully. "My shoulder is." And his pride.

Edward steered his charger over to where she knelt, leading Plunket by the reins. He halted next to her, leaning down to peer at Alan. "Did this man come to your aid?"

"He was doing a decent job of getting me to Llanthony." Until her love knocked him for a loop.

"Luckily we are near to the vale," Edward noted, "for the monks of Llanthony are astoundingly adept at healing."

Luck had little to do with this. "Had you not been so quick to upend him, we would not be needing healing monks."

"It was he who challenged me," Edward replied easily. For a king's heir, Edward could be deliberately casual about his own dignity, wearing plain armor and his enemy's badge if need be; but he was quick to act when it came to her. Some Welsh busybody coming between him and his lady was a situation that begged to be settled with a lance.

"You need not have accepted nearly so readily," she replied, turning back to her ex-champion, untying his shoulder armor to see how badly Alan was hurt. There was no blood pouring out, and his chain mail seemed intact, but it was hard to diagnose an armored patient in the dark, especially for an amateur nurse.

"Seeing you, I had naught else to do," Edward answered airily, making it sound like her fault.

"Do you know this knight?" Alan asked, looking painfully up at Edward, who had not only beaten him to the ground, but to the lady, as well.

"This is my lord, Edward, Earl of March," Robyn admitted, sorry they had to meet this way.

Alan grimaced at that news, making her even more ashamed, wishing Edward were not so eager to fight for her. "Please forgive me, had I known it was him, I would have spoken up."

Alan managed a weak smile. "M'lady is not at fault. I issued the challenge and must pay the price." Alan ap Gruffydd's gallantry did not make her feel a whit better. She and Edward had nearly killed a man, who meant only to see her safely to Llanthony.

Torches appeared, a long line of them coming up the path from the valley below, borne by monks and lay brothers wanting to see what the fight was about. Gwynt was with them, being led by a stable boy. As soon as they saw Alan was hurt, the monks took charge, not asking what the Welshman had done to merit his drubbing. In God's eyes, all that mattered was the injury. Lashing cloaks to the knight's lances, they made a simple stretcher and gingerly lifted Alan onto it, being careful not to shift his broken shoulder.

When the monks had made him comfortable, Robyn knelt down beside the stranger who had come so boldly to her aid, and now suffered for it. She took the wounded knight's hand in hers saying, "You have done me a great good service, and I will forever be in your debt. Please, if I can ever do anything to repay you, call on Lady Robyn Stafford of Pontefract. To me, you will always be a brave and generous knight." Then she leaned in and kissed him tenderly on the lips.

Seeing this was all the reward he was likely to get, her fallen hero kissed back hard, almost coming up off the stretcher. Nothing brings a stricken Welshman back to life like a Saxon lady's loving kiss. His good hand found her shoulder, and though Alan did not manage to pull her down onto the makeshift bed, the kiss did go on longer than her Lord of March would have liked. Too bad. Edward had to learn to be less ready with his lance, and mayhap this liplock would help.

When the kiss subsided, monks lifted up the stretcher and started down the steep slope, bearing away the beaten knight. Lady Robyn remounted Plunket and took her place beside her lord, who looked askance at her, saying, "You seem very warm toward this Welshman."

"Why not?" she asked airily. "He came gladly to my aid and fought valiantly for me. Twice."

"Rather foolishly the second time," Edward declared. His head still had to be ringing from the Welshman's blow, and she bet that her kissing Alan had hurt even worse.

"Foolish or not, he did it all for me," Robyn reminded him. "If you had shown yourself at once, this senseless combat could have been avoided."

Edward was not used to being reprimanded, especially by a woman that he had ridden all the way from Gloucester to rescue. "If my lady had not vanished in Shropshire, and then reappeared in Powys with some bold Welshman, none of this would have happened."

"I had little choice in the matter," Robyn protested.

"As did I," Edward retorted. He had found her with another man-at-arms, a pushy foreigner who treated her as his own, and to Edward that was reason enough to act.

Seeing she could not sway her lord, Lady Robyn fell silent, and they headed downhill into the Vale of Ewyas. After all she had been through, coming over five hundred years to see him, dodging armed rapists and Tudor ambushes, Edward should have gotten down on his knees and thanked Alan for bringing her safely home, instead of insisting on riding a high horse that was not even his. Had he been atop his beautiful black Friesian stallion, she would have known him at once, even by moonlight. She asked, "Where is Caesar?"

"Waiting for me in Llanthony," Edward replied. "I rode him out from Gloucester, and he needed the rest. This is Brutus, a gift from the Herberts, who helped with my disguise."

"Certainly fooled me." And she should have known him best of all. Though if he had been aboard Caesar, no amount of armor and ostrich feathers would have deceived her.

"Black is for my father, whom I am still mourning," Edward explained. "And as for the ostrich feathers, the king's heir is traditionally Prince of Wales, as well—"

"Don't remind me," she replied tartly, having yet to tell him about the baby. Right now she was not at all in the mood. She had brought herself and her unborn child to this ungodly age, just to be with Edward, who was now acting like a total idiot, playing the arrogant man-at-arms with his brains in his broadsword. Robyn felt like an even bigger idiot for coming back.

She and Edward had argued before, but always over matters of statecraft, never over someone else. Alan had challenged him for possession of her, and so far as Edward saw it, that was reason enough to flatten the poor fellow. He was not just her lord, but the local law, as well, a power he exercised "in person"—without restraint or appeal, except to Mad King Henry in London. Not a realistic option, even in the best of times. However she had a piece of news that should puncture his proud composure. "Did you know that Pembroke and Wiltshire are back?"

Edward nodded. "So the Herberts say. Some of Pembroke's riders have been seen in Brecon, threatening Tretower."

"Not just Tretower. They brought thousands of mercenaries over from the Continent." From the shocked look on his face, she could tell Edward had not heard this. "And now they are marching on Builth, with Owen Tudor's Welsh followers flocking to their banners."

She could see Edward gauging distances in his head. His own men had to be spread out between Hereford and Gloucester, headed for London, while the Tudors were falling on his rear, with only the mountains of Powys in between. "How many thousands?" he asked. "And what nationality?"

"French and Bretons mostly. And Irish." She tried to remember what the Tudor army had looked like on the march. "Several thousand for sure, but not so many that they cannot get through Powys in a matter of days. Cybelle is with them."

Edward grinned at the mention of Cybelle in the Tudor camp. "Good for her."

And hopefully Heidi was there, as well; together the two of them could constitute a whole second front. Descending through dead grass and heather into the Vale of Ewyas, she saw Llanthony laid out before her, lit by cold stars and a three-quarter moon. Ewyas was a sort of Welsh Shangri-la, a holy valley deep within the Black Mountains, where the air was magically healthful and animals lived at peace with men. The lead-roofed priory, with its abbey church, hospital, and cloisters, was built of squared native stones on the spot where Saint David had a small monk's cell nearly a thousand years before. The name Llanthony was a Saxon contraction of Llanddewi Nant Honddu, "Church of David on the River Honddu." This was where Edward had been headed when he and she first met, and now many months later, they had finally arrived, though not at all the way she had expected—with monks bearing the beaten knight who had befriended her, and her carrying a baby that she had so far kept secret.

Dismounting, Edward stripped off his helmet and armor out of deference to the vale's holiness while she went to check on Alan. Her would-be rescuer was lying under a blanket, still in his armor, which could not be safely removed until he was in the hospital. She got down off Plunket and knelt beside the injured Welshman, wishing she could do more for him. "These monks are marvelously good at mending," she told him, "and they will take wonderful care of you." Or so she hoped.

Alan smiled back at her, saying, "Thank you, m'lady, though I would mend even more quickly with a woman's loving touch."

No doubt. Even flat on his back, with his collar broken, Alan ap Gruffydd could not resist making another pass at her. Quite a compliment really, and totally understandable. He had been there when she needed him, taking her side at once, not caring what the dispute was about, wanting only to see her safe. And naked. That was not going to happen, not here in this holy valley, with Edward looking on. She did, however, give him another tender kiss, hoping it would do him some good, and Edward, too.

More monks and lay brothers met them at the abbey gate, inviting them in and taking their horses, while Alan ap Gruffydd was hauled off to the hospital on his lance and cloak stretcher. Though it was past midnight, the monks sat them down in the empty main hall, feeding them a late supper—not granola and chocolate as Edward had originally hoped, just bread and beer, with some goat cheese and dried figs. Stripped almost to the bare walls by their English "daughter" house, the monks had little else to offer. Robyn found the simplicity soothing, and the plain fare refreshing after a truly horrendous day on the road.

After supper, she was given a room in the cloisters, a simple monk's cell lit by a single lamp, with a crucifix on the wall and a straw mattress in one corner that Edward clearly hoped to share. She curtly reminded him that they were in a house of God, adding, "I thought you had to get back to Gloucester?"

Reaching down, Edward slid a deft hand inside the slit of her riding dress, searching for her thigh. "Not tonight, thank God."

Plainly he had other plans for the evening. Stopping his hand with hers, she asked, "Don't you have a Tudor invasion to deal with?"

Edward grimaced. "Yes, and we must get to Gloucester. That will happen all too swiftly, but we have been separated for weeks— surely our Lord Jesus will understand."

Jesus might, but Edward certainly did not. Were all men this dense, or just the ones she fell for? Could his lordship not see that he had angered her by almost spitting Alan with his lance? She firmly removed his hand from the folds of her dress, saying, "If we are indeed leaving on the morrow, then I really need some sleep."

Edward looked crushed. "I only hoped to steal a little time together. And give thanks."

"Thanks are surely in order," she agreed. "You should start by thanking the knight who brought me here." And whom he put in the hospital. Edward stared at her in disbelief, and he was still searching for a proper reply when she shut the door on his handsome puzzled face.

Frazzled and exhausted, she still took time to pray, giving thanks for having gotten to Llanthony alive and whole. Usually her prayers were to Mary, who taught her humility and saved her in Sherwood; tonight she prayed to Jesus. Here was a man who would listen to her, Mary's son, and who cared for her soul, not her body. Seeing him hanging there, nailed to the cross above her simple bed, reminded her of his sacrifice, and of his willingness to speak for women, no matter how wayward and sinful. In his own hour of need, Jesus was deserted by all twelve disciples, then mocked, scourged, and humiliated by everyone from high priests to simple centurions. He chose women to be with him at the end and to witness his greatest miracle, to receive his body from the cross, to wash and anoint him, and to find his empty tomb. Without these women's faith and testimony, Jesus would have just been another victim of Roman justice, since it was the men who claimed not to know him and who cried out to Pilate, "Give us Barabas."

She begged her Lord above to take especial care of Heidi, who was as wayward and sinful as they came. Then she gave her poor exhausted body the rest it craved.

Bedbugs woke her in the morning, reminding Lady Robyn that she had not had a proper bath since leaving Pembroke. Nor did she foresee one in her near future. Another long day of riding lay ahead, and her best hope for finding a tub of hot water was Gloucester Castle, more than forty miles away. Too bad.

By day, Ewyas was as beautiful as she had imagined, with wooded tops overlooking steep grassy slopes that plunged straight down to water meadows on a valley floor that was barely three bow-shots wide. Sheep searched for green shoots in the sparse winter pasture, and goats grazed in dark thickets. Birds called to her from leafless branches set against a steely sky, chirping away as if it were already spring. She felt the same sense of awe as she had in Sherwood, when Mary opened a door into summer. Going straight to the hospital, to see how Alan was doing, she found him alive and awake, his shoulder swathed in none-too-clean bandages. He greeted her with a smile, "My lovely Lady Pontefract, how good of you to come see me again."

His easy good humor was mortifying, since this had to be a case of hit and run. "I fear it is only to say good-bye."

Alan did not hide his disappointment. "Must m'lady be going?"

"My lady must." Lady Robyn was part of the working nobility. There were Saxon ladies aplenty who were waking up this morning on their family estates, with serving women waiting to pass them warm clothes and take away the chamber pot. Widowed grandes dames and dowager duchesses could spend the day as they willed, but most ladies had manors or households to manage and, at times, to defend. Nouveau nobility like Lady Robyn had no family estates to support them—her only income was from the Honour of Pontefract, currently in enemy hands so she must make herself useful here and now. No matter how badly things stood with Edward, there was still a Tudor invasion to turn back and Heidi to be rescued. "But I am still sorry and grateful. If ever you need my aid, send word to me at Baynards Castle in London."

His smile returned. "Your lord has already extended a similar invitation."

"Really? Edward did?" Mayhap there was hope for him yet.

Alan nodded. "Last night. He thanked me for saving you and promised a suitable reward. Very decent for a Saxon."

Robyn wondered what was "suitable" payment for having rescued her, more than she could afford, that was for sure. Since this was holy ground, she gave him a chaste parting kiss on the cheek. Then she politely scolded the monks for the dirty bandages, pleading with them to boil Alan's bandages and use only clean utensils. They vowed to do their best, though Lady Robyn could tell the holy fathers merely meant to get rid of her, being famous throughout the Marches for their healing ability. Ill and dying monks from the prosperous daughter house by the Severn were regularly brought back to plain simple Llanthony to recover. Maybe it was magic.

Edward's restless energy—and the coming Tudor onslaught—dictated that they leave Llanthony at once. Monks brought them beer and bread for breakfast, while Lady Robyn made up a thermos of instant coffee and broke out the last of her trail supplies, jam pastries she had baked before leaving Pembroke—from here on, she would be living off the land. Even the animals said their good-byes. As Robyn got ready to go, birds flew down to eat pastry crumbs out of her hand, and a deer came up to lick her fingers for salt, something that had happened to her only once before, during a Witches Night in Sherwood Forest. By the time they mounted up, she was feeling better about Edward, and she gave him the same chaste kiss that Alan got, saying, "This place seems truly magical."

He smiled at the kiss. "Some compliment, coming from a witch. I will pass it on to the monks." Edward was always glad to be drawn deeper into the witches' circle. For him, witchcraft was all thrilling miracles and nocturnal romance. Men made magic, casting iffy horoscopes and turning lead into fool's gold, but any young warlord who wanted something really useful—like a sneak peek at tomorrow's battle or a shapely succubus to warm his bed—needed to find a woman. "Remember how I vowed to take you to Llanthony?"

"Too bad it took so long." She still could not bring herself to tell him about the baby.

As they mounted the steep slope, Robyn saw the narrow valley seem to close up behind her, like a fairy-tale cleft in the earth, leading to the Land Under the Hill. And this was the same path on which she and Edward first met—some five hundred years in the future. She saw the same slanting stone wall sprinkled with lichens, where Duchess Wydville's men had lain in ambush, and the grassy ridge running south toward Hatterrall Hill. Here was where Wales ended. On the far side of the frozen footpath was England. Unable to let the moment pass, she made Edward dismount and kneel with her in that last little bit of Wales and give thanks to Mary for bringing them full circle, back to where their journey together had begun.

When they first met here, she thought he was nuts, claiming to come from another century. None of this seemed remotely possible. Yet here she was, for better or worse. Taking his hand, she gave silent thanks to Diana, her secret namesake, virgin goddess of boundaries and beginnings, of children and childbirth. No matter what happened next, they had fulfilled the promise of that first meeting.

Oh, dear Diana, give me the strength for all I must do.

She crossed herself, then started searching about in the dead frozen grass, not sure if what she was looking for was ever even here. It could just as easily be five hundred years in the future—in fact, she used to be absolutely sure it was not here.

Suddenly, there it was, lying pressed into the earth. Rain had dissolved the glue and washed away the feathers, but the cracked black shaft still had the tarnished point attached—it was a black arrow, with faded white writing on the shaft. She picked up the arrow and turned it over in her hand, seeing that the letters were nearly gone, but she already knew what they said. JUSTICE.

"John-Amend-All's arrow." Edward immediately recognized the black arrow, which had been fired by a red-suited archer named John-Amend-All, warning them of the Wydville ambush.

Robyn nodded solemnly. "Until this moment, I was sure I was in the twenty-first century when this arrow landed at my feet."

"Now you know better." Edward had always contended that they met in his time.

So far as she could tell, he was only half right, her walk had started in the third millennium, but when she met Edward—and decided to "show him the way to Llanthony"—she started to enter the Middle Ages. "I began in my own time, but when I met you, I stood at a choice point."

"A choice point?" Edward took the black shaft, turning it over in his hand.

"When I saw you, I had a choice, either dismiss you as merely another armed lunatic, or take you seriously, and start to get sucked into your world." Any man presented that choice; Edward just happened to be more man than most.

He handed the arrow back to her. "If I was in my world, and you were in yours, why did we ever meet?"

Good question, even for a farseeing witch. "Partly it was a ploy by the Wydvilles, to get you to come willingly to this spot."

"Willingly?" Edward looked about. Last time he was here, two dozen armed men had been lying in wait for him.

She nodded. "In magic, intent matters. It is impossible to make people do what goes against their very natures. Saints and pious nuns are notoriously immune to magic. Even death curses usually work on some defect on the person's character or depend on an action of the victim."

Edward smiled at her. "Curiosity can kill a cat, but do not try it on a turnip."

"Exactly." Some witches called her a traitor, for telling so much to a man, but in this case, Edward was a victim himself, and he needed to know what was done to him. "You were drawn into my time because there you were unprotected. John-Amend-All was looking out for you, so they moved you to another time, when he did not exist." John-Amend-All was a sort of spirit of rebellion, the embodiment of a national wish for just and honest lordship.

"And I had to come willingly." Edward smiled ruefully at how well his enemies knew him. Only one thing would draw Edward here, alone and against his better judgment. "But why were you there?"

Aside from the obvious reasons. "I do not think the Wydvilles meant me to be here."

"Why not?" he asked. "You are the perfect bait to trap me."

Too true, but the Wydvilles could not have known that. "I was here because Jo Grey suggested I take the walk, and even planned my itinerary. Jo wanted me back in the past for totally different reasons—since I rescued her daughter Joy from witch hunters. Twice."

Edward saw where this was headed. "So if Jo had not sent you on that walk—"

"Another woman would have been there." Nothing else made sense. It explained why the Wydvilles turned against Jo as soon as Robyn appeared in the Middle Ages. "In fact, a woman probably was waiting, or headed your way, maybe just a bit behind me on the trail."

"What woman?" Edward sounded intrigued by the one that got away.

"We may never know for sure." And so far as she cared, this other woman could remain a mystery forever. "We know only two things about her."

"What two things?" He was plainly trying to picture this femme fatale in his head.

"That she was very beautiful." Robyn had to give him that, for the Wydvilles had a bevy of unmarried daughters to choose from— like the innumerable Nevilles, there seemed to be no end to them. "And she would take you straight into a Wydville trap." Lady Robyn left the black arrow lying in the frosty heather, and they rode over the ridge together, down into Herefordshire.

As they rode out from under the cloud cover hanging over the Black Mountains, warm winter sun glistened on Edward's armor. Passing through tiny hamlets, she returned greetings in Welsh, delighting surprised inhabitants, thrilled to get a proper good morning from a Saxon lady. Soon they would be back in the thick of things. By medieval standards, Edward moved at lightning speed—last Friday night he had been in Gloucester, and she was in Pembroke on the far side of Wales. In less than a week, Edward had found her and brought her to Ewyas, nothing shy of amazing in an age that ran on sundials. Yet getting to Gloucester would take all day, at least, and Lady Robyn did not know if she could stomach another long winter day in the saddle.

Past Ewyas Harold, the land leveled even more, and they entered Saxon country, passing through villages with names like Howton, Kilpeck, and Much Dewchurch. On the far side of Wormelow Tump, a wave of nausea forced her off her horse, and she threw up into a frozen ditch. Edward asked anxiously, "Are you ill?"

"Not really," she replied, wiping her mouth. Barfing had actually made her feel better.

Edward was not taking her word on that, clearly worried that she was starting to slow him down, keeping him from getting to Gloucester in time to turn his army around. Without bothering to get out of the saddle, he told her, "Hoarwithy is just ahead. I could leave you there for the night and go on to Gloucester—then be back for you tomorrow or the next day."

She shook her head. After being hustled out of Llanthony, and away from Alan ap Gruffydd, she did not want to be dropped off in some Saxon hovel like a mare who had thrown a shoe. If he was worried for her well-being, he should have left her in that magically healthful valley with her would-be Welsh champion. "I do not want to be left behind."

Edward would not let it be, saying, "I must get to Gloucester, but if you are sick—"

"I am not sick," she blurted out, angered at seeing her dashing young lord preparing to dash off, putting politics ahead of her. "I am having your bloody baby."

He stared down at her in stunned silence, finally asking, "Are you sure?"

"Who else's baby would it be?" She had not slept with anyone else since last May Day, despite Duke Somerset's attempted seduction and Owen Tudor's genial stab at rape.

With a rattle of armor, Edward swung slowly out of the saddle to stand beside her. Stripping off his gauntlets, he took her hands in his, saying, "I mean, are you sure you are with child?"

Her love's hands felt warm and inviting, and she could feel her anger fading. "As sure as science can be."

Edward's face lit up, and he gave her a long loving kiss, then added, "This is utterly magnificent."

"And just in time for the wedding," Robyn observed dryly. They were supposed to be married that coming Monday, Groundhog's Day, when Edward's month of mourning his father and brother ended.

He looked aghast. Naturally with no bride, nothing had been done, and there was no wedding planned. For once in his pampered young life, the warrior prince who was everywhere at once was caught totally unprepared—and for his own wedding, no less. "My lady, you know I will marry you right now, in Hoarwithy if you like, or at Ross-on-Wye."

Seeing that astonished look and hearing his fervent protests made the whole horrible, madcap trip here worthwhile. He did truly love her. "Relax," she told her worried teenage warlord, "I do not want to get married in the middle of a Tudor invasion."

"Are you sure?" Edward grinned at her with witless delight. He was the sort who wanted children, lots of children, coming from a big Catholic family himself, with an army of cousins and in-laws— literally. He looked forward to a castle crawling with kids and filled with music and dance. So did she, though she meant to take the children one at a time.

"Yes, I am sure." Despite yesterday's armed mayhem and the war madness going on all about her—plus the baby turning her body upside down—she felt strangely at peace. Not just at peace, but in her place, where she ought to be.

She, Edward, and the baby, were all together at last. "Now let us get going; it is still a long ways to Gloucester."

They mounted up and set out again, with Edward grinning triumphantly. Such enthusiasm was infectious, cheering her even further. Not so long ago, Lady Robyn had been a tourist in her own time, visiting decaying castles while forcing cucumber sandwiches onto her queasy stomach, desperately ignoring the first signs of motherhood; now she was back in the saddle, the Lady of the March, with her armored love at her side fearing nothing: not the future, not pregnancy, or even a Tudor invasion. Too bad tall and handsome Brian from Kenilworth, with his tony London accent, could not see her. Who was the crazy one now?

After twenty-some miles on horseback, they reached the Wye at Hoarwithy—"white willow"—an ancient Saxon village that made its living by shipping oak bark down the Wye to tanneries in Gloucester. They stopped at a farmstead to eat and rest, dismounting amid barking dogs and bleating sheep. Children ran up and took their reins, grinning boys and giggling girls, already picturing themselves as squires and ladies-in-waiting. Several of the oldest went ahead of them, grandly announcing, "Lady Robyn Stafford of Pontefract, and Lord Edward of March."

Surprised adults fell to their knees when they realized that the king's heir had truly arrived. Edward waved them to their feet, saying he was not standing on ceremony; indeed, he was wearing his enemy's badge. "We are on our way to Gloucester to give warning of a French invasion."

"The French?" These good folks could barely believe it. "Here in Herefordshire?"

"And wild Irish, too." For folks in Hoarwithy, Edward's exploits were stories out of legend, like tales of Arthur, or of Owen Glendower. Now they were part of the saga, and so was she. "My Lady Stafford saw them land at Pembroke and rode through Wales to warn us."

Lady Robyn said it was all too true, real French men-at-arms were slogging through the frozen Welsh hills, headed for Herefordshire. "Soon they will have us all eating snails with a fork."

Children grimaced, and their parents waxed indignant that foreigners should invade their native isle while hastening to put pease porridge before their Norman lord and his Hollywood lady. Robyn found pregnancy was giving her new appreciation for medieval cuisine. With salt to season it and enough firewood to keep it sanitary, days-old pease porridge is one of the great treats of medieval cooking—beans, oats, carrots, onions, garlic, and any other available vegetables, spiced with bits of meat or sausage, all blended together during days of slow cooking. Eaten with fresh home-baked bread, it was the most delicious and nourishing meal imaginable—all the products of a peasant holding put in a wooden bowl.

And way ahead of minced quail, buttered snails, or boiled nightingale tongues.

When they were done, the whole family saw them off, helping them mount and cheering them on their way. Edward gave a silver groat for their trouble, but they were not doing it for the money. They were thrilled to entertain their lord and lady, and the children would tell this tale to their grandchildren, how the Lord of the March and his ladylove stopped in for dinner.

And why not? Edward was these people's hero, already starring in songs and stories. They were not his tenants, so they owed him no rent. And being copyholders they neither voted nor paid taxes. Edward Plantagenet, Earl of March and Ulster, Duke of York, and heir to the English throne was going to put his fine young body on the line for them, to save Herefordshire from the frog-eating French and the heathen Irish. All he asked for risking his royal neck was their good wishes and two bowls of porridge, for which he overpaid extravagantly. Edward gave a whole new meaning to "popular government."

Riding side by side down the willow-shaded west bank of the Wye, Edward was extra solicitous to her saying, "We can rest if you wish, and make Gloucester on the morrow."

She knew Edward wanted to go on, while she barely cared if they made Gloucester or not. After several days in the saddle, she had pains between her thighs that had little to do with pregnancy—but now that they were back together, she could feel herself giving in to her boyfriend. "As you wish, just so we are together."

"My aim exactly," Edward declared happily. When the Wye swung westward, they turned south, making for the Gloucester road near Saint Owen's Cross, their time alone together rapidly coming to an end. By this time tomorrow they would be back, trying to solve the myriad problems of medieval England. How to best stop the coming Tudor invasion? How to keep London safe from the French Queen? And what in heaven had happened to Heidi? All worthy questions that cried out for answers. Already civilization loomed in the form of the major market town of Ross-on-Wye, where they could expect semi-clean lodging and a leisurely ride to Gloucester in the morning. Edward touted the New Inn in Gloucester, on Northgate Street, saying, "It has grand rooms framed by tremendous chestnut beams, with tiered galleries, and two squared courts. Better by far than a drafty castle. We could have adjoining balcony apartments."

Just like Romeo and Juliet, but by now Lady Robyn knew that *new* could mean fifty years old. Medievals happily trimmed the truth if it earned a groat or two. Edward still wanted to get to Gloucester and turn his army around—but was that worth the saddle sores it would take to get there tonight? She was still pondering the problem when it was taken out of her hands.

As they reached the Gloucester road, riders appeared, coming from the direction of Saint Owen's Cross. Most were mounted bowmen, more than a score, wearing red-and-black brigandines and white hound badges—not a good sign. Those were Talbot colors and a Talbot badge, meaning these men were loyal to the Earl of Shrewsbury, currently in rebellion, along with Queen Margaret. Of course, Edward was wearing the feathered badge of Margaret's son, but how long would it take to see through that Lancastrian plumage?

Not long. When Lady Robyn saw their leader, she thought she was hallucinating. He wore a cloth-of-gold gown with angel-wing sleeves and white silk scallops that she had last seen on the late Lord Scales, but instead of old Lord Scales's white-haired death's-head, she saw the handsome cultured face of Sir Anthony Wydville, bareheaded and clean-shaved, with brown bangs, a sharp nose, and full red lips. Last year, Sir Anthony had married Lord Scales's daughter, but this was the first time she saw the brave young troubadour wearing the chief witch hunter's colors.

Technically, the new Lord Scales was still on parole for opposing Edward and Warwick, and he was indeed unarmed, aside from the customary broadsword. In fact, the one comforting thing about this scene was that only Edward wore plate armor—so if he had to cut himself free, he probably could. But that would mean leaving her with the Wydvilles, something Edward would not do. Instead of drawing his battle ax, he gave Sir Anthony a cheery greeting, saying, "My good Lord Scales, how grand it is to see you."

"Yes." Sir Anthony grinned back, saying, "This is a most happy chance."

Chance had nothing to do with this. When Robyn had picked Llanthony as her safe haven, her sole worry was that the Wydvilles would find out, since not much happened on Witches Night that Duchess Wydville did not know about. When they made it in and out of Llanathony so easily, Robyn had relaxed, thinking the duchess must have missed them. No such luck.

"And my Lady Stafford." Sir Anthony nodded to her. "How splendid to see you, as well. Come join us for the night. It is nigh on dusk already, and the day grows chill."

Near to freezing, but that was no reason to accept Wydville hospitality. Edward declared, "We had just been debating the merits of the Saracen's Head, or the New Inn in Gloucester."

"Neither can match the table we have waiting." As Sir Anthony gave his lordly invitation, archers fanned out on both sides of the road, cutting off any escape. Sir Anthony himself was pious to a fault, and bound by his parole, but the real power lay in the Wydville witches. He was just the sturdy sword arm that did the women's bidding. "Pray pass the night with us at Goodrich, and spare yourselves further riding. We shall gladly provide a proper escort to Gloucester on the morrow."

Fat chance of that, but Edward turned to her, still smiling, saying, "There seems to be no choice." Clearly they were trapped.

"Who wants to stay in an inn anyway?" Robyn replied. Flat beer, boiled beef, and a flea-ridden feather bed that hundreds of medievals had slept in—Lady Robyn knew that roadside lodging in Herefordshire was one-star at best. If you wanted fine wines, high cuisine, and talented maid service, go to France.

"Goodrich will be much more to my Lady Stafford's liking," Sir Anthony promised. "I will send ahead for them to boil water and draw a proper bath." Young Lord Scales knew all about Lady Pontefract's mania for cleanliness and herb teas; coming from a family of witches, he was used to accommodating strange female demands.

Vespers bells sounded over the furrowed earth, as they turned southward, riding past plowed fields where seeds lay germinating under the frost. Edward and Sir Anthony began to talk jousting, to which they were both addicted. Had they not been enemies, they would have made excellent drinking buddies, both being teenage

lords whose main interests were music, women, and politics—but
civil wars were like that.

Goodrich Castle stood on a high rock above the wandering Wye,
its tall walls of old red sandstone resting on corner towers braced
by great triangular buttresses. This ancient brooding Talbot fortress
looked squat and sinister in the winter twilight. Nor was the great
gatehouse very reassuring, reminding her uncomfortably of the
main gate to the Tower of London, with its deep rock-cut ditch, and
outer half-moon barbican, shielding two drawbridges and twin
drum towers. When the second portcullis rang down behind her,
Robyn felt firmly hemmed in. The Wydvilles had finally gotten
what they always wanted, both her and Edward in their hands.

7

⊶⇒ The Red Knight of the Red Lawns ⇐⊷

Far from being tossed into the keep dungeon, Robyn was once again
back in the bright rich world of the English aristocracy. After
her tramp through Wales followed by the humble poverty of Llanthony and pease porridge in Hoarwithy, she was back in what
passed for luxury, with hot rose water waiting for her, along with
mint tea and her favorite sugar pastries. Courtesy of the Wydvilles,
no less. Reminders of the happier times she had with Sir Anthony,
at Greystone when she first arrived, and during the "peace" tourna-
ment at Smithfield, before the Act of Accord came between them.
Of all the medieval Wydvilles, she had met Sir Anthony first, and
liked him best.

And even trusted him somewhat. Sir Anthony was not the type to
murder Edward outright—but he was the type to turn Edward over
to his witchy mother, or to Queen Margaret, for future execution.
Raised by his sisters, Sir Anthony had been obeying women for so
long, it must have seemed like second nature.

Lord Scales gave commands to the Talbot stable hands, and to
the castellan who greeted them, treating Goodrich like his own. The
Earl of Shrewsbury and his household were in rebellion in the

north, but Sir Anthony was out on parole, free to use his ally's castle. Women in Wydville white-and-red met them at the main hall, curtsying low to Edward, then offering to take her to her bath. She was loath to leave Edward alone, but she could not very well haul him off to the bath with her. Lady Robyn's reputation for excessive cleanliness was cheerfully indulged, but she would not get away with washing Edward, no matter how badly he needed it.

So they had to part. Robyn realized they had been together nearly twenty-four hours, but now it seemed like no time at all. Whether she ever saw him again would be up to the Wydvilles. Rather than admit their power, she went down on one knee to Edward, begging his permission to go. Edward acted totally unconcerned by his predicament, saying in mock seriousness, "My lady may go, and do not come back until you are clean."

She hated leaving her love in enemy hands, but among Edward's many foes, she trusted Sir Anthony the most, never knowing him to do anything unchivalrous, since he had more scruples than the rest of his family combined. Women closed in around her, smiling and curtsying, addressing her in Court accents, showing the Wydvilles had arrived in force. Sir Anthony alone would have made do with local washerwomen and whatever Talbot retainers resided at Goodrich. These women chattered together in French as if they could not be overheard. "My God, that was Edward of March. He is as beautiful as they say, so tall and friendly—did you see how he smiled at me?"

"At you?" One of them giggled. "And I thought it was me."

"Hush," whispered a shocked friend. "She will hear."

"Why?" Her companion snorted. "She knows what he is like. Far better than you or me." They all laughed at that.

Happily her reputation preceded her; being notorious saved on countless embarrassing explanations. They led her down the length of the great hall, through a door behind the high table and into a vestibule, separating the hall from private apartments. So many women meant several Wydville ladies were in residence, but which ones? Lady Robyn pretended not to care. Beyond the vestibule was a private audience room, what might be called a solar, but it was on the ground floor, below the chapel. Waiting for her, in a white satin gown and a red jacket trimmed with white ermine, was the lady of the castle, Duchess Wydville's eldest daughter and Sir Anthony's older sister, Lady Elizabeth Grey, wife to Sir John Grey. That explained all the women.

Fair and golden-haired, Lady Elizabeth was not your ordinary knight's wife, being both lady-in-waiting to the queen, and a senior priestess in her mother's coven. Crafty, self-centered, Elizabeth Grey, née Wydville, was the witch who initiated Lady Robyn into the Wydville coven, easily as dangerous and ambitious as her mother. Lady Elizabeth had already fooled Robyn once, by promising to protect her at Pontefract and then scheming to turn her over to witch hunters. Still, Lady Robyn had to find friends wherever she could, and she curtsied low, knowing such things mattered a lot to Elizabeth. Treat Lady Elizabeth royally, and the woman might let down her guard. Robyn very much needed this senior witch's sympathy, if not for herself, then for Edward.

Pleased, Lady Elizabeth told her, "Arise, Lady Stafford. You do me much honor."

Robyn rose, sucking up solemnly, saying, "My Lady Grey got me out of Pontefract, when I was alone and friendless, and I will always be in her debt." Gilbert FitzHolland began executing Yorkist prisoners after the battle of Wakefield, and Lady Elizabeth had spirited her safely away—aiming to hand her over later—but Robyn pretended not to know that part, acting like the Wydvilles were responsible for her escape, letting Lady Elizabeth wonder how much faith to put in such fulsome thanks.

Duchess Wydville would have seen the lie at once, but her daughter was unsure, trying to read Robyn's intent. "But you missed the full moon ritual with my mother at Codnor?"

Missed was not the word. When she discovered Duchess Wydville was at Codnor Castle, Robyn had run blindly off into the night with a stock thief named Black Dick Nixon, figuring chances were better with a border bandit than with the Duchess of Bedford. "I had pressing business in Sherwood."

Elizabeth Grey arched an eyebrow in disbelief. "In the midst of a blizzard?"

Robyn shrugged her naked shoulders. "Some things just cannot be put off."

Goodrich Castle had its own heated bathhouse, adjacent to the living quarters, and as soon as Robyn stepped in, she was surrounded by a steamy rose-scented mist rising from tall wooden copper-bottomed tubs, warmed from below. By now she was used to bathing being a group experience. Her hostess turned out to be a natural blonde, who showed no sign of the two children from her teens. Lady Elizabeth merely smiled and said, "I see why Edward of March is so fond of you."

Robyn took it as a compliment. Medievals were great believers in man's baser instincts, and from dukes to serving girls, they thought they all knew why Edward was so fond of her. Only King Henry blandly assumed that she and Edward had a chaste relationship, a virtuous union of spirit, but not of flesh—another sign of His Majesty's insanity. Mayhap they just knew Edward better than she did, though so far as Robyn knew, Edward and Elizabeth had never even met.

Serving women helped her into the high tub, offering to scrub her. Lady Robyn said she would manage, knowing the women just wanted to speed her bath and use the water after her. Alas, they would have to wait. Warm, soothing water dissolved the knots in her neck and shoulders, washing away dirt and worry. Clearly the Wydvilles knew how to treat prisoners. Closing her eyes, she floated in warm dark water, thinking this was how her baby saw the world—dim, quiet, and far removed from the woes of medieval England. Hopefully those woes would be gone by the time her child arrived. Lady Elizabeth must have sensed her silent pleas, and while they were drying off, Duchess Wydville's daughter whispered, "Worry not, your young Edward of March has naught to fear from me."

So you say. Robyn dearly wished it were true. Being witches, the Wydvilles were careful with their karma, to keep the magic from turning on them. Even when Duchess Wydville sent her into almost certain death in the Tower, the duchess gave her a flip warning they knew Robyn would ignore—"Do not come back."

But if Edward need not fear Lord Scales and his sister, the same could not be said for their allies. Pembroke, Wiltshire, and Owen Tudor were tramping through the Powys hills, headed this way.

When they got to Goodrich, they would haul Edward out and kill him, whether the Wydvilles willed it or no—she had heard them promise to do it over dinner, less than a week ago.

So it was weird to arrive at a formal supper accompanied by Lady Elizabeth, treated as a guest of honor by her most persistent enemies. Edward sat at the head of the high table, with Sir Anthony on his right, and she was seated on Edward's left, while Lady Elizabeth sat beside her brother. Her two small boys were at the table, as well, Thomas and Richard, and Edward and Sir Anthony entertained them with tales of last summer's Smithfield tourney. Five-year-old Thomas wanted to know, "Is it true you were my Lord of March's squire at Smithfield?"

"Absolutely," she assured the boy. "And your aunts were squires to Lord Scales." Their mother had a bevy of unmarried younger sisters, in their teens and twenties—three of them had served as Sir Anthony's squires, wearing boy's doublets, red-and-white Wydville tights, and ballock daggers. Both boys grinned at the thought of titled lords slamming into one another on horseback while attended by pretty ladies in drag. Life in London was as wild and wicked as advertised.

Edward leaned over to say, "Lord Scales says there is going to be a disguising."

That meant a play. All theatrics were amateur, aside from a few paid players who performed in lord's halls and religious pageants. Some were quite good, but those were not likely to play a neglected castle on the Welsh side of the Severn.

"And I shall be in it," Thomas announced, sitting up in his oversize seat.

"Yes, he will." Lady Elizabeth smiled proudly. "But the parts must remain secret, or it will spoil the disguise." Thomas took the hint and said nothing about his role.

"Lady Robyn was an actress, as well," Edward told the boy, proud to have a talented girlfriend.

"Wanted to be," she corrected him. Most of her screen time ended up on the cutting-room floor, and she mainly appeared among those countless names in the credits—but try to explain that to folks in 1461.

"Nonsense." Edward grinned at her. "I have seen you play everything but the Fool." Right—everything from knight's squire to wanton witch and lady-in-waiting.

Sir Anthony added, "This disguising was written by an unfortunate knight named Sir Thomas Malory, now in prison for rape, sacrilege, blackmail, and attempted murder."

"Giving him time to write," Edward noted dryly, and Lady Elizabeth laughed at his remark, the light knowing laugh of a well-married woman who could really please a man—if she were so inclined.

"Hardly sounds like child's play." Robyn recognized the author of *Le Morte d'Arthur,* but had not realized Malory had such a rap sheet.

"Oh, no, the man is not near as bad as his enemies make him," Sir Anthony declared.

"No one is," Edward observed, sitting amiably in his enemy's seat of honor, having just had his treason conviction lifted by Parliament. Sir Anthony was on parole, and Robyn still had charges of treason and heresy hanging over her. It was hard to be politically active in an absolute monarchy without running afoul of the law. Lady Elizabeth was the only one of them never under legal restraint, unless you counted marriage.

Trumpets sounded and a herald appeared, announcing that this was Caerleon Castle, the Home of the Legions, and Good King Arthur has decreed that his knights "shall eat no meat until adventure came his way."

People groaned to hear this. With Lent a couple of weeks away, the table at Goodrich was piled with meat—boiled beef and capons, stewed heron with pickled cabbage, French beans and kidney pie, minced peacock aspic. Too bad she was not having bizarre cravings. What she pictured was a cheeseburger, which was not on the menu.

Hearing the catcalls, the herald hastened to add, "But two leagues down the road, a damsel cometh, with a tale that is passing strange. So good sirs, go to your meat."

That was greeted by cheers, as people fell to eating. Jugglers entertained while Talbot retainers tore into the meat, happy to eat with lords in the midst of a hard, cold winter. Young energetic lords like Edward and Anthony were genuinely popular, since they usually brought excitement, good food, and pretty women along with them, not to mention music and song. When the meal was over, Lord Scales himself took up a lute and sang a song in honor of Lady Robyn of Pontefract:

> Lyth and listen, gentlemen,
> All that now be here;
> Of Robyn Hood that was the king's man,
> Good mirth you shall hear.
> But always went good Robin
> By hideout and hill
> And always slew the king's deer
> And delt them at his will. . . .

His song went on to tell of Robin Hood's adventures in Barnsdale, Wentbridge, and Ferrybridge, all in Lady Robyn's Honour of Pontefract. Music loosened her up and let her relax enough to try the buttered French beans and cabbage, then demolish most of a capon. Stewards thought she was mad to turn down more wine, asking instead for fennel tea—pregnancy was giving her an appetite and cutting into her drinking. No more getting blotto at medieval drinking bouts, then begging forgiveness at Mass the next morning. Motherhood was already making her more responsible.

Lord Scales retuned his lute, and when he started to play again, it was an old Welsh melody, harking back to the days of Arthur. As he did, the doors swung open and a sad young maiden robed in green entered the hall, wearing silk flowers in her blond hair. Robyn recognized the golden-haired girl at once, it was Jacquetta Wydville, the winsome teenage sister of Lady Elizabeth. Staying admirably in character, Jacquetta ignored the applause that greeted her entrance, staggered up to the high table, to fall weeping at Edward's feet, saying, "Good sir knight, pray have pity on a helpless damsel."

Jacquetta Wydville was a witch-in-training about as helpless as a young tigress, and even more cuddly. The girl had danced naked before the bonfire at Robyn's initiation, but now played the innocent supplicant quite well, weeping and refusing to rise until Edward had promised her succor, asking earnestly, "What misadventure has befallen you?"

Edward was no mean actor himself, unless he was totally taken in by the teen witch. Jacquetta looked up at him with just the right mix of hope and desolation, as though she might have finally found a man who took some small pity on her. Happy to shield her frail beauty from the horrors of the world, while giving her blond body a royal going over. "Good sir knight," Jacquetta beseeched him, "pray help me. My mistress is a lady of great worship and renown, but she is held captive by an evil tyrant. Since King Arthur's knights are the noblest in the land, I came here for aid."

"Who is your lady?" Edward asked. "And who is the rogue who has betrayed her?" He gave her plight the same serious attention he would to any shapely, distressed teenager who threw herself at his feet, Wydville or not.

"My mistress's name is Lady Lionesse," Jacquetta explained, "and the tyrant holding her is the Red Knight of the Red Lawns, one of the most perilous knights in the world, an unmanly villain in blood-red armor with the power to lay any good knight on the ground. Please give me a champion to free my sister from this unnatural monster."

What knight could resist? Apparently none. Before Edward could respond, a champion appeared. A knight in full armor entered the hall, wearing a great helm and a black surcoat with three white hands. Walking ahead of him was young Thomas, dressed like a dwarf in a green leprechaun suit. Thomas led the knight up to the high table, where the boy bowed to Edward, saying, "My master is Beaumains, the Knight of the Fair Hands, and he begs the boon of going on this quest."

Jacquetta objected, "Please do not heed this dwarf and leave me to some unknown knight, when what I crave is a true champion."

Plainly the champion she wanted was Edward. By now the purpose of this "disguising" was plain, they wanted to draw Edward into the play, getting him to champion one of the Wydville daughters, either Jacquetta, or Lady Lionesse, who was bound to be another underage blonde. The easiest way to win Edward over was to have him marry one of the Wydville daughters, a much smarter match than Lady Robyn—whose Honour of Pontefract would revert to the king if she married. But Edward was not buying, telling Jacquetta, "Sir Beaumains has begged this boon, and has the will to see it through."

Having put her case to the highest lord on hand, the young Wydville had to accept Edward's judgment, since no one could overrule him. Jacquetta did not pretend to like it, berating her champion, calling the silent knight a "cowardly kitchen knave" and worse, while young Thomas thanked Edward, promising that Sir Beaumains would do his best. Despite this vow Jacquetta continued to chide her silent knight, wishing aloud that Lord Edward had given her a "real man-at-arms."

These teenage histrionics delighted the diners, who raised tankards in salute, cheering the quiet champion who took the woman's tirade without a word of protest. At the same time squires wheeled out a wooden prop painted to look like a gated castle tower. Just as Robyn had expected, atop the tower was Lady Lionesse, another blond Wydville daughter, whose real name was Mary—not as winsome as Jacquetta, but nearer Edward's age at seventeen or so. She, too, had danced naked at Robyn's initiation. "Lady" Lionesse began to sing a sad lament, accompanied by her uncle on the lute, pitying the fate of a lonesome maiden trapped in a tower by a jealous brute, awaiting some handsome champion to slay her oppressor. Silly as it was, everyone was swept up into the drama, even Robyn, who watched two young Wydville sisters making a blatant appeal for Edward as their champion. Not funny, even in jest. From personal experience, she knew that a knight could go from champion to paramour at the drop of a panty.

Alongside the castle was a tree made from logs and evergreen boughs, with shields hanging from it, indicating the knights Lady Lionesse's captor had defeated. Of course, the beaten knights were all Yorkist. Robyn saw Edward's white lion of March, hanging above Warwick's red-and-white saltire cross, and Sir Collingwood Grey's silver wyvern shield hanging between his uncle's black ragged staff, and Audley's gold fret on a red shield. All the traitors to Queen and Court were vanquished for the night, if only in fun. Dangling beneath the shields was a big brass hunting horn.

Sir Beaumains strode up to the shield tree, with Jacquetta still roundly berating her knight. Seizing the horn, Sir Beaumains blew a stout blast, barely lifting the great helm's visor, and facing away from the tables, still not showing his face.

In answer to the horn, the tower gate flew open, and out stepped the Red Knight of the Red Lawns, wearing full armor and a crimson surcoat. Silently the two knights faced each other, there being no need for taunts or challenges, since the purpose of their meeting was plain. Servants scurried about, setting up a foot-combat barrier, a long plank running waist high between the two knights. Then the herald measured their swords, finding they were both hand-and-a-half broadswords. Robyn had seen such battles at barriers before, fought by bored knights at Pontefract trying to endure the Christmas truce that proceeded the battle of Wakefield. Each knight got three blows with the sword, with one point for striking the opponent's armor, two for a blow on the helmet, and three for bearing him to the ground. When the herald was satisfied, he told Sir Beaumains to take the first blow, which the knight did, aiming a roundhouse swing at the Red Knight's helmet, which was easily parried. People jeered the feebleness of the blow.

As soon as the herald gave leave, the Red Knight answered with a tremendous clout, that Sir Beaumains was barely able to parry. No points, but Fair Hands seemed shaken by the near miss. Sir Beaumains's follow-up blow was even weaker than the first, and just as easily turned aside, while the Red Knight's overhand return drove Sir Beaumains's blade back almost to the helmet. Still no points on either side. Jacquetta continued to boo her champion.

Sir Beaumains took a final swing, which the Red Knight deftly parried. This wasted effort provoked not just jeers but laughter, as well. No points at all for Fair Hands.

Now came the final blow, and the Red Knight had saved the best for last. With another full overhand swing, the Red Knight knocked Sir Beaumains's blade aside and landed a ringing blow on the knight's great helm. Two points.

Make that three, or maybe five. Sir Beaumains's armored legs buckled, and the armored knight collapsed in a clattering heap. Point, set, and match. Cheers erupted from the tables as the fallen contestant failed to get up.

Jacquetta walked over to her downed champion, saying, "Sir scullery knight, it is safe to arise, the contest is over."

Getting no response, Jacquetta kicked the steel-plated body, shouting, "Up you lazy oaf!" Still no response from the prone suit of armor.

Servants carried out Sir Beaumains to a chorus of boos and yells of, "Back to your pots and pans." While at the same time, a shield with three white hands went up alongside the Neville saltire. Yet another knight had fallen to the Red Knight of the Red Lawns, and all in pantomime, since so far neither knight had said a word.

Without breaking silence, the Red Knight stripped off one gauntlet, then threw it contemptuously down at the foot of the high table. In case anyone could miss his meaning, Jacquetta dropped to her knees and begged for a "real" champion to take up the challenge. From the top of the tower, Lady Lionesse added her pleas to those of her sister, imploring some brave knight to take up the gauntlet and defeat her captor.

All eyes turned to the high table. Robyn realized this was a trap for Edward. Everyone wanted the show to go on, and Edward was just the boy to oblige. But once the Wydvilles got him into armor, anything could happen. Edward could get killed, and the Wydvilles would be able to say it was an "accident" during a friendly bout after supper—while still winning the heartfelt thanks of Queen Margaret, for whatever that was worth.

Or if Edward won, the two young Wydville daughters would be all over their "champion," sitting with him at the table and trying to entice him into bed. If she objected, she would look like a shrew and killjoy. For all she knew, they would lock her in some tower or dungeon, while closeting Edward with their young daughters. Edward started to rise, and if she tried to stop him from fighting, she would just look silly.

Why look silly, when you can act flat-out ridiculous? Robyn rose up herself, startling everyone. Being a seat closer to the foot of the table, she easily beat Edward to the gauntlet, snatching up the armored glove, saying, "I claim the challenge."

Cheers and laughter broke out. Women applauded, while men shouted lewd suggestions, and Wydvilles cried foul. Sir Anthony objected that the challenge was meant for the knights at the table. "Ladies are the object of battle, not participants."

Lady Robyn held tight to the gauntlet. Edward would not take it from her, and any man who did would then have to fight the Red Knight. Going down on her knee before Sir Anthony, she told him, "Good Lord Scales, I would be these women's champion."

"It is unnatural," Sir Anthony insisted, surprised at her stubbornness.

"Why so? What is more natural than that I should champion women who are held in thrall?"

"It is natural that you should champion them," Sir Anthony admitted. "It is unnatural for you to do it by combat."

"My Lord Scales, the previous holder of your title was beaten by women, twice. Once by Joan of Arc at Patay, and again by me in his escape from the Tower." This last fatal defeat put Sir Anthony in the House of Lords, something the Wydville had never properly thanked her for. "That was in battle, while this is mere play."

Sir Anthony had naught to say to that, so Robyn rose and turned to Edward, the senior lord and guest of honor, asking, "Do I have your permission to champion them?"

Jacquetta and Lady Lionesse shouted no, while the lower tables applauded wildly. Lady Elizabeth sat staring at her, wondering when Lady Robyn went off her rocker. War was in the air, with a Tudor army headed for Herefordshire, and these bored, wary Talbot retainers were desperate for diversion, in a perfect mood to get smashing drunk on Wydville wine, while watching Lord Edward's pretty strumpet put on armor and fight the Red Knight at barriers. Why have nobles about except to entertain you?

Edward shook his head ruefully, saying, "You know I can deny you nothing. Only please let me assist you."

"Of course." She would very much need Edward's help, if they were to get through the evening in one piece. Just when she thought that she might sup safely with the Wydvilles, she found herself plunged into a deranged psychodrama, with Edward as the prize. All scripted by a genteel felon in jail for rape and blasphemy. Only in merry old England.

Men scrambled to find armor that would fit her, while Lady Eliz-

abeth took her back in the vestibule to improvise an arming doublet. Elizabeth found a boy's padded jousting jacket, studded with
"points" for tying on armor, helping her try it on, saying, "It might
work, but you are absolutely mad."

"Apparently." She held her nose while she pulled on the jacket,
sure it was crawling with lice. That jacket alone should have convinced her this was crazy.

Elizabeth helped her out of her gown and into the boy's jacket,
then pulled it tight, bringing the lice into secure contact with her
undergarments. "Why are you doing this?"

Why, indeed? "Because I do not want Edward to fight."

Fortunately medieval men ran to smalls, and Lady Elizabeth was
able to find a chain-mail shirt that fit perfectly over the doublet.
When the shirt was on, Elizabeth used her nails to pull the point ties
through the chain mail, saying, "There are easier ways of keeping
your man out of combat."

"God, I wish there were," Robyn complained, adding a private
prayer for at least a year of peace—so she would not be taking the
Lord's name in vain. "Your man will be leading Queen Margaret's
vanguard."

"At least he will be leading, not me." They both laughed at that,
breaking some of the tension.

"Are you not afraid of getting hurt?" Elizabeth asked, pulling
another point through the mail.

Or killed. "Yes, but the Red Knight is much less likely to kill me
than Edward." And that was the object, to get out of this party alive.

"Mayhap." From the deft way Elizabeth did the points, Robyn
knew she had done this many times, probably on her husband, or
on her jousting brother. "But when he beats you, he will just go on
to challenge Edward."

Too true, but there was always the hope. Mail was not near as
heavy as she feared, in fact it felt comforting, a steel jacket between
her and any mayhem. "Mayhap, I will win."

Lady Elizabeth grimaced at that suggestion, but Robyn could see
the Wydville's initial horror had faded, replaced by wry resignation.
Lady Robyn really was going to do this ridiculous thing. Looking at
the nylon support hose Robyn was wearing under her mail skirt,
Elizabeth asked. "What are you going to do about leg armor?"

"Nothing, I hope." Robyn glanced at her nearly bare legs. "Can you get me some leather breeches and big hip boots to go over them? I mean he is not supposed to hit me there." That was what the barrier was for. The Red Knight would get only three swings at her, all above the waist, where she would be well armored. It would be a lot like mock combat at a Renaissance fair, only the swords would be honed steel, and wicked sharp. She would mainly have to protect her head, trying to keep it on her shoulders.

Elizabeth went in search of breeches and boots. Edward came in as Lady Elizabeth left, carrying plate armor under his arm and giving her a warm smile. Robyn was pleased to see that smile grow even wider when he saw her standing in chain mail and support hose. Pronouncing the combination fetching, he asked, "Why are you doing this?"

Exactly what Elizabeth had said. In some ways, the two of them thought a lot alike, neither being typical medievals, but instead sharp freethinkers who listened to their own hearts and were not at all awed by royalty. They would probably get on famously, and she would have to take care to keep them apart. She shrugged, saying, "It seemed the only way."

"I could fight him." Edward had been through real combat the night before, and was not frightened by a fight at barriers in Goodrich Castle.

"Doubtless, but that is what the Wydvilles want. I know them better than you."

"Really?" He reached under her mail, stroking the curve of her butt through the pantyhose. This time the mail between them was on her. "You do? Which of us was born in this century?"

She kissed him long and lovingly on the lips, to show he was not going to miss out on all the fun. "Which of us has seen the Wydville sisters naked?"

Picturing that stopped Edward in his tracks, his hand on her rear tightening involuntarily, fingers gripping her flesh through the pantyhose. "Really, all four of them?"

"Five." Six, if you counted Lady Elizabeth. "Dancing round a May night bonfire in Northamptonshire."

Edward had no answer for that arresting image, except to say, "What if you get hurt?"

"I won't." She said it with way more conviction than she felt, but it was easy to be brave with Edward's arms around her and his hand on her ass.

Edward held tight to the body he did not want damaged. "You do not know how dangerous this is."

"Would that were true." By now Lady Robyn was thoroughly familiar with the dangers of mock combat. "Who pulled you out of the mud at Smithfield, when you needed CPR?"

"Would that be you?" he asked, making light of the mishap. "I do remember an angel bending over me, bringing me back to life, but it is all rather vague."

"Comes from having your head banged," she reminded him.

His look turned serious. "But what if you are harmed?"

"Then I am counting on you to kill the brute." She frantically hoped it would not come to that. Having seen blows delivered in anger, she knew she could easily be hurt, maimed, or killed, yet she would not let Edward play into whatever the Wydvilles had planned—not when they were so desperately outnumbered. Looking straight into her love's eyes, she begged, "Please do not be angry. You know you would do just what I am doing—"

"Of course." He wanted to be the one wearing the armor.

"What would you do if you were faced with overwhelming force that cannot be met head-on?"

"Something unexpected," Edward admitted ruefully.

"Well, I hope this qualifies?" She held up the steel gauntlet, which she still had not let go of, even while changing.

Edward conceded that it did, letting go of her so they could tie on her armor. Her armored sleeves fit fine, but the molded plate back-and-breast was oversize, coming down too far in front. Just as well, since she was not wearing leg armor. Her womb was well covered, safe behind two layers of steel. As he tied the points Lady Elizabeth had poked through the chain mail, Edward gave her quick advice on sword play. "Remember what I told you in Calais: Pivot from the hips, with your weight on the balls of your feet and your whole body behind the blow."

She nodded, tying points along the armored waistline, happy she did not have to do this every day.

Down on one knee Edward tied the last point. When he was

done, he looked up at her and smiled, his hand going back up her thigh, finding bare flesh between her armor and support hose. "I suppose this is what I get for insisting to ride at Smithfield."

"Absolument," she whispered, liking the feel of his hand under her armor, wishing it did not have to go away. Too bad they could not do this together. At Smithfield, she had been furious with him for risking his neck in a tourney and nearly ending up with a concussion. Now he would be the one to sit and suffer, watching someone taking hacks at his love.

"Just remember one thing," he warned her, standing up, his hand sliding deep inside her hose, fingers tickling her pubic hairs.

"What is that?" She leaned into his hand, pressing it hard against her, wishing he could safely take her place.

He kissed her and whispered, "Swing through the man."

Right. Through the man, she thought, kissing him back. How the hell did they get into this? They were supposed to be in the New Inn in Gloucester by now, lying together by the fire—not in a do-or-die struggle with the Wydvilles over a late dinner of boiled beef.

Lady Elizabeth came back into the vestibule with short leather pants and hip boots. *Très chic.* Medievals were very modern when it came to chains and leather. Edward slipped his hand out from under her mail skirt, and he retired, smiling at Elizabeth on the way out. When he was gone, Lady Elizabeth observed evenly, "Lord Edward is most delightfully familiar."

"Yes." Robyn pulled on the sweat-stained breeches, glad to have her hose between her and the leather. "Delightfully so."

When the boots were on, she was encased in steel and leather from chin to heels, with only her head protruding from between curving pieces of shoulder armor. Steel plate was far more wearable than she ever imagined, cool and comforting, weighing less than a backpacker's rig, and so evenly distributed, she barely felt the weight. She felt the same rush of excitement that Joan must have felt the first time she put on armor. Suddenly she was protected, invulnerable, and invincible. Blows could not hurt her, not even when struck with a sword. Nothing could get through this armor but heavy axes and armor-piercing arrows, neither of which were allowed in tonight's match.

"How does it feel?" Lady Elizabeth retied a couple of loose points.

"Now I know why men fight in these suits." She had been through two full-out battles, not counting minor skirmishes and fights at sea, and this was the first time she had even tried on armor. What a fool! From now on, she was never going into battle without it. "I feel as if I cannot be hurt."

Elizabeth smiled and shook her head. By now both of them had seen enough corpses in armor to know the folly of that.

As soon as she emerged from the vestibule, men burst into wild applause for the new champion, absolutely thrilled to see pretty women playing their games.

Jacquetta Wydville immediately began to howl, "Is this what you call a real man?" Robyn could sympathize; men perpetually trivialized women's needs. This pretty blond teenager had gone down on her knees before two lords, begging for a champion to give the Red Knight a decent whacking, and what does she get—Lady Robyn in steel drag.

Applause drowned out Jacquetta's pleas. Men wanted to see Robyn fight the Red Knight, and they paid no heed to the girl's complaints, leaving Jacquetta to abuse Robyn the same way she had berated Beaumains. "Get back to cooking, you kitchen knight. You are made for mopping floors and scrubbing pots. Better fitted for an apron than armor."

And pregnant to boot. Robyn absolutely agreed with the enraged Wydville, but she could not help being who she was. Right now she was much more frightened by the Red Knight's big hand-and-half broadsword than by anything Jaquetta Wydville might say behind her back.

Her opponent stood nonchalantly behind the barrier, looking six feet tall in the red-plumed great helm, the only one in the room with nothing to say about Robyn's entrance. Completely covered in steel, the powerful menacing presence had just one unarmored spot, the hand that lacked a gauntlet, and it, too, was tucked in a red leather glove. Such total anonymity was doubly unnerving. Having disposed of Beaumains with three hard strokes, the Red Knight looked ready to do the same to her, all without saying a word.

As she stepped up, returning the gauntlet, she was relieved to see that they were about the same size; the Red Knight just looked bigger, wearing wooden pattens and a plumed helmet. While she was bareheaded and wearing flats—leather boots without heels. A lot of medieval men were no taller than she, and this one was no fencer, either, relying on a single overhand blow to batter down Beaumains. He no doubt meant to do the same to her.

Edward was waiting by the barrier with her helmet and gauntlets, playing her squire this time. As he put the steel gauntlets over her gloved hands, Edward whispered, "He swings overhand, so—"

"Shush," she told him, sliding her hands into steel. "I saw, and you are not supposed to give advice." She knew the squire's role better than he did by now.

"Pardon, my lady," Edward apologized, and since she had no sword of her own, he offered her his, but she shook her head, not wanting to see him disarmed. Instead she selected one from a basket sitting beside the barrier, the lightest and longest she could find, then saw it measured against the Red Knight's, and pronounced acceptable. Trying to recoup, Edward had the helmet ready, first pulling the leather coif over her hair and then trying the laces under her chin. That brought their faces almost together, with the whole hall watching—the Lord and Lady of the March, alone in their enemy's hall, ringed by the foe's blades.

Next came the helmet, which had straps and padding inside, to cushion her skull. As Edward brought it down over her head, he leaned in and kissed her. With the helmet half on and the visor up, her head was hemmed in by steel plate. For a brief instant, Edward filled the only open side, his lips pressed to hers as he kissed and she kissed back.

Cheers erupted from the tables, and diners lifted their goblets in salute. It was not very often that you got to see knight and squire necking, not in a crowded banquet hall, at least. Tonight's entertainment had gone far beyond anything the Talbots—or even the Wydvilles—had intended.

Then Edward buckled her helmet's chin strap and lowered the visor. Suddenly she was seeing the world through two steel slits at eye level, and rows of small breathing holes on the lower half of the visor. Weird and then some. She had no idea what was going on behind her, or to the side, and had a very poor view forward. There was a metaphysical lesson: The price of absolute protection was blindness. Men in armor always seemed so blind toward other people's needs, but now Lady Robyn realized they could hardly even see where they were going.

Luckily she was already facing the barrier, so she was saved the embarrassment of having to search for her opponent. This was not good. How could she dodge blows she could barely see? She used to laugh at the old movies, where knights fought with visors up, so you could see the stars' faces. Now it seemed totally practical, except that the Red Knight of the Red Lawns would see how scared she was.

Standing sword-in-hand before the barrier, quaking in her armor, she heard the herald's instructions echoing in her helmet. As "challenger" she would take the first hack, but aside from the single fencing lesson Edward gave her in Calais, she could not remember having swung a sword. Certainly not *at* someone, especially a heavily armed stranger at a supper party. She settled on a modified softball stance with the sword held high above her shoulder. Rearing back, she copied the Red Knight's swing, aiming a terrific overhand cut at a spot between her opponent's knees—like Edward said, "Swing through the man."

Her blade came to a jarring halt in midswing, clashing against the Red Knight's sword. She felt the shock through her arm and shoulder, all the way down to her booted feet. Her foe had blocked her blow easily. So much for the direct approach.

Now it was her turn to receive a blow. Even with her upper body encased in steel, she shrank from the idea of letting this crimson villain slash at her with a heavy honed blade. She went back to her softball stance, hoping it would be the same overhand blow that the Red Knight had used three times before.

It was, and she swung to meet it. Blades clanged off each other in another jarring collision. Sharp steel whizzed past her head. Had her helmet come with plumes, she would have lost them. As it was, the Red Knight's blow went wide, and the benches cheered Lady Robyn's parry. Despite the rules against coaching, bystanders called out, "Well parried, m'lady. Whack him back."

Emboldened, she went back into her stance. She had taken her first hack to set up this one, betting the Red Knight of the Red Lawns had never seen a baseball game. Seeing the Red Knight standing with blade aloft, Robyn took a swift, hard swing at the knight's armored belly button, pretending it was a fast underhand ball right in the zone.

Her crimson foe never saw it coming. Before the Red Knight could get the big hand-and-half sword down, Robyn's blade banged off the knight's side armor. One point.

She felt a wave of elation, hardly believing she had gotten a hit. That will teach you to meddle with Miss Rodeo Montana. And the crowd agreed, applauding the first point scored against the Red Knight of the Red Lawns. If Edward had been the one in armor, the Talbot retainers would have instinctively cheered the Red Knight, hoping to see Edward beaten to his knees, or worse. As it was, half the men and most of the women were rooting for Lady Robyn.

Now came the return blow. She braced herself, and the Red Knight swung even harder. This time sparks flew, and Robyn's softball swing barely beat the blade aside. She had to duck and weave to keep from being hit—but that, too, drew a roar from the Talbots, now solidly on her side.

Last swing. She tried the trick that had scored for her before, but this time the Red Knight was ready, blocking her blow with a quick parry. Shouts and groans came from the tables, disappointment for her miss mixed with appreciation for the Red Knight's parry. With only one point scored so far, it all came down to the last blow.

Lady Robyn could hear the hall grow silent behind her, and she felt tension through her armor, though all she could see between steel slits was the gold-striped barrier and the upper half of the crimson knight. The rest of the world was reduced to a pattern of bright dots next to her cheeks, showing patches of floor and the Red Knight's wood and metal footwear.

Slowly the Red Knight raised the long hand-and-a-half sword, preparing a blow that would not be blocked. A hit on the body would tie the contest, a hit on the helmet would win—the Red Knight meant to have one or the other. Without warning, the sword came down.

Robyn twisted away from the blow, as if she were dodging an inside pitch, while blindly striking at his blade with hers. Swords met again in midair, colliding with a fearful clash that she felt in her toes. This time her foe's blade did not bounce off, but slid down her own, a blur of steel screeching straight for her, scaring her horribly, then coming to a startling halt against her hilt.

Shouts rang out, turning to applause that echoed off the rafters. It took a moment to realize the rejoicing was for her. She had won—one to nothing. Incredible. Her first sword fight, and she had beaten a fellow with a tree full of shields. Truly outstanding, and totally unexpected. She had hoped she might somehow avoid being hit, and manage to tie the man. Now she had won outright.

Edward was there to congratulate her, acting as judge as well as squire, lifting off her helmet and declaring her the winner. Then he rewarded the victor with a kiss. Sweat dripped from under her leather coif, and she swayed on her feet. As the adrenaline drained from her system, she felt weary and relieved, horrified by the risk she had taken. Edward asked her, "Will m'lady claim her prize?"

"My prize?" She hoped it was something useful.

"Yes, my lady." Edward indicated the lofty wooden castle tower, saying, "Lady Lionesse awaits."

So much for something useful. Totally intent on dodging the Red Knight's cleaver, Robyn had forgotten what the fight was over. Lady Lionesse, aka Mary Wydville, awaited her rescuer atop the tower. Stripping off her leather coif, Robyn shook out her short hair, drawing more applause—a lordless castle in the depth of winter was an easy house to work.

Sword in hand, she entered the tower and ascended the short staircase, bringing blond young Lady Lionesse down to a chorus of hip-hoorays from the men, who thought it amusing to have one lady save another. Robyn could tell that Mary Wydville wished Edward were her rescuer, leading her out of the tower and into bed. Both Jacquetta and Lady Lionesse were barely civil to their savior, forced to play along as their intended victim became the heroine of the hour. Showing superb training, the blond teenagers threw themselves at Edward's feet, giving him a look down their plunging necklines. Together they thanked Edward for giving them such a splendid champion, vowing, "My lord may have whatever he wishes in recompense. His Grace need but ask."

Standing in half-armor, leaning on her sword, she could not help but feel pretty butch, compared with these two teenage virgins freshly rescued from villainy—which was the effect intended. She felt tempted to use the flat of her sword on their privileged fannies, but refrained. A moment's hilarity was not worth the recriminations later. Besides, it was Edward's life they were playing for, and anything she did would rebound on him. Instead she asked Edward, "What about my other prize?"

He looked up from the pair of blondes at his feet. "Which is?"

She nodded at the Red Knight, still standing in mortified silence by the barrier. "My opponent's armor."

Technically she might not be entitled to it, but it looked to be a fit, and red was one of her colors. Edward as always was eager to stretch a point for her, and he strode over to the scarlet villain, saying, "For now the helmet will do."

Without moving or saying a word, the Red Knight managed to look reluctant, but Edward was not only the Lord of the Marches, he now had the crowd behind him, too. Everyone but the Wydvilles wanted to see the Red Knight's face, especially after being beaten by Lady "Pomfret." Slowly stripping off a gauntlet, the knight undid the red helmet's chin strap, then lifted the visor and doffed the helm.

Another blonde. Robyn recognized Margaret Wydville, Lady Elizabeth's strapping twenty-something sister. Her overstuffed coif came off with the helmet, and golden hair tumbled out, glistening with sweat in the torchlight. "Here"—Margaret held it out by the chinstrap—"my lord may have the helmet."

That brought down the house. Talbot retainers stood and toasted the defeated knight, happier even than if it were a man. What a story to tell in winters to come! Having seen the Earl of March's lady fight the Duchess of Bedford's daughter at barriers with broadswords, while dining on beef and capons and drinking Lord Scales's wine.

Relieved to have survived this bit of dinner theater, Lady Robyn realized she had lost some of the men's esteem, having "only" beaten a woman—but Margaret's surprise appearance was proof she chose right. Had Edward picked up the gauntlet, there would have been no good outcome. He would have ended up beaten by a woman or playing a brute. Both would have ensnared him with the Wydville daughters, either as their conqueror or as their prize. She would have gotten shuffled off for the evening, to be used against Edward at a later date.

But not tonight, for Lady Robyn Stafford was now the darling of Goodrich, and could have anything she wished—except her freedom. What she most wanted was Edward, for the night at least, so whatever the Wydville women had in mind must wait. When she had exchanged her armor for evening wear and then returned to the hall, Talbot retainers serenaded her victory and drank more toasts to the Lady of Pontefract; then they formed a double line of torchbearers between the great hall and Goodrich's ancient Norman keep, a square tombstone of a tower, dating back to the days of Henry I. Harpers went ahead of them, and women sang sweetly in the still night air, turning their going to bed into a triumphal march. A year ago in Calais, Sir Anthony had been Edward's prisoner, and he was subjected to a torchlit dressing down by Warwick, Salisbury, and Edward—now that the tables were turned, the new Lord Scales wanted to go him one better.

When the singing stopped, she entered the dark windowless first floor of the keep. As harping faded behind stone, it felt like *Aida,* where after the triumphal march the lovers are entombed alive. They were taken to a windowless upper room, which had thick carpets and a fire in the hearth, but only a stone firing slit for ventilation. When the door was barred behind them, they were locked in for the night—if not longer. None of Edward's people knew they were there, and the Talbots would not tell. Her saddlebags and belongings were piled neatly atop an oak chest, and the room had a big curtained bed, a table and chair, a washstand, and a garderobe in one corner. Wine and bread were laid out on the table, along with lit candles and an oil lamp. Thanks to her, they were at least locked up together. Edward looked about with satisfaction, saying, "That was most exciting, but what are we going to do now?"

"This." She took Edward's elbow and pulled him to her, sliding a hand into his doublet, laying claim to what she had won. If they were lovers entombed alive, Lady Robyn meant to make the most of it. In her various incarcerations, from Berkeley dungeon to her dismal days in the Tower, she had always taken heart from the fact that Edward was free and might possibly even save her. Now she knew she had that all wrong—it felt far better having Edward behind bars with her. No wonder unisex prisons never caught on—too much fun.

Edward responded at once, forcing a hand inside her bodice, feeling for her breast. Medievals were way too practical to let a moment like this pass, and his fingers felt strong and reassuring on her bare flesh, making her forget their current plight. Still, she stopped him, staying his hand and saying, "At ease, young squire. I am the one who won you."

Her lord and master looked surprised. "What do you mean?"

"You are mine for the night," she reminded him, "and must obey without question, or I will have to summon the guard."

First the Wydvilles, and now her. Edward Plantagenet, Earl of March and Ulster, Duke of York, and heir to the throne, had become a woman's plaything, to be fought over, kept under lock and key, then strictly ordered about, and from the look on his handsome face, he was loving it. Her young lord grinned and bowed, saying, "As m'lady bids."

"Very good," she declared, pleased he knew his place. "You may start by readying me for bed."

Edward dutifully obeyed, first removing her butterfly headdress, then dropping to one knee to slip off her crimson slippers and reach under her skirts to loosen her garters and roll down her hose. Not the usual order of things, but she enjoyed his impatience to get at the good stuff. Fingers slid down her thighs and calves, caressing her flesh in a most unservile fashion. Then he rose and went to work on her bodice, unbuttoning her sleeves, undoing the laces, and finally sliding her out of the evening gown, her fourth or fifth costume change today—Lady Robyn had lost count after doffing her armor. When she stood before her lord in just her silk chemise and panties, she told him, "It is not seemly for a liveried servant to see his lady naked."

"Not seemly?" Edward looked surprised and disappointed.

"Not at all," she informed him. "So you must remove your livery." Terribly eager to please, Edward immediately stripped off his shoes, hose, and doublet, then threw off his shirt. Six feet of naked, young nobleman, rippling with muscles and hugely aroused, made a delightful sight by candlelight. Lady Robyn wanted him right now, but she also meant to savor this moment, so she took her time, looking him over thoroughly, then adding nonchalantly, "Now you may put me to bed."

She did not have to demand twice. Forgetting decorum—and who was in charge of whom—Edward lifted her silk chemise over her head and tossed it aside, then stripped off her panties, leaving her naked in his hands. Without letting go of her, he opened the bed curtains and pulled back the coverlet; then he picked her up, pressing her against his hard sweaty chest, which had not been properly bathed since Lady Robyn last left the Middle Ages. Usually she liked her men fresh and washed, but medievals had taught her to appreciate the hot frenzied coupling that came after a chase, or a battle. By now Lady Robyn felt like she had been through both. She cocked an eye at him, saying, "For a serving boy, you are being awfully familiar."

"As my lady desires." Her impudent squire let go, dropping her onto the bed, then climbing in atop her. Bed linen felt cool against her naked back, while he ran hard strong hands over her bare skin, slowly and deliberately at first, getting rougher and surer as he reached her breast. She felt a shiver of pleasure as her nipples got hard, anticipating his touch. Leaning down, he kissed her tenderly on one breast, then the other, whispering, "Soon I will have Madame right where she needs to be."

"Where is that?" Lady Robyn asked warily, wondering what her mad young lord would come up with next.

"Back home in Baynards Castle, naturally." Edward sounded like he could not wait.

She was glad her fellow prisoner could be so confident. Taking his hand from her breast, she placed it firmly on her abdomen, putting first things first. "Is that where we will have the baby?"

"Why, of course." He gently massaged her belly, glorying in the feel of fatherhood. "Pontefract is in enemy hands."

"So are we," she reminded him. Mother, father, and child, all securely behind bars—as was apt to happen when you fell for good-looking fugitives.

Edward laughed lightly, as if their capture were a minor reversal, a sort of forced vacation, to be thoroughly enjoyed and then easily rectified. "Imagine—you, me, and our babies living together in Baynards Castle."

"Babies?" She touched her bare belly, which had hardly started to swell. "It is way too early to be talking twins."

He looked shocked. "Surely we will not stop with one."

Spoken like a true Catholic. "One baby at a time," she warned. "If this one works out, then we can try for another."

"And another, and another." He artfully spread her legs, as if to show how it was done—determined to give her a thorough preview of married bliss. Then he was inside her, starting slowly at first, then rocking harder and harder, making her hips arch, while her body buckled and beat against the bed. She could not believe how long it had been, and how fantastic it felt. This was what she had missed most from the Middle Ages, more than masked balls, Court etiquette, and well-tuned lutes—that raw naked passion that drove heaving sinful bodies together in defiance of God and law. Something truly worthy of atonement, a thrilling dangerous coupling that turned confession into boasting. Small wonder that priests in London lined up to help Lady Robyn cleanse her soul.

When they were done thrashing, Edward stared at her for a long time, like he was amazed to find something so utterly lovely in his bed. Finally, he blew out the candle, slid next to her, and nuzzled her neck, very pleased with how the night's "disguising" had gone. "This Malory is not so bad."

Lying in the dark, feeling his arousal returning, she agreed, "He tells an amusing tale."

Edward was certainly enjoying the ending, running his hands over her, producing pangs of renewed desire when he paused to massage favorite parts. "Maybe we should see he is set free?"

"Maybe." Robyn was less sympathetic to a knight accused of rape. "Once we are free ourselves."

"Of course." They had to get out before they pardoned anyone, though right now Edward was thoroughly pleased with imprisonment. "But only if he promises to write; otherwise, he might be better off in jail."

Until she came to the Middle Ages, she had never truly realized how productive prison could be, and that night was the best she had ever spent behind bars. For once she was neither worried, nor frightened, for Edward had her tight in his arms. Always before she had been alone, or with some child she had to watch over. Now she was the one being watched over and held close. And was it not about time? Edward's grip on her tightened, and he began to move in the

180 ◆ R. GARCIA Y ROBERTSON

dark. That she was already with child did not dampen Edward's enthusiasm for the act of love and there was something uniquely tender about making love with your cellmate. Who better could ever understand you? This was the purest act of love imaginable, two people totally cut off from the world, not knowing if they would ever see daylight again. With only each other to hold on to, and everything else against them.

8

⊷⟹ Herefordshire Beacon ⟸⊷

Robyn awoke in the pitch darkness, the solid inky blackness found behind layers of stone. She could feel the cold draft through the narrow firing slit, and knew immediately where she was, the ancient keep of Goodrich Castle. The fire had gone out in the fireplace, and the little stone room was freezing cold, but all that mattered was that her love lay beside her, still asleep and breathing deeply. Ignoring the fleas and bedbugs, she luxuriated in being next to Edward, mildly aroused by his warm weight and the musky odor of male sex. His long hard body fit perfectly against hers, a warm comforting promise that somehow they would get through this together.

Lying in the dark, with eyes closed, she ran through the things she had to do today, which were fairly monumental. Today was Friday, and tonight was Witches Night, and she definitely did not want to spend it with the Wydvilles. Which meant she had to start by somehow getting out of this room—no easy task, since the door was barred on the outside, the stone firing slit was only a few inches wide, and the garderobe emptied into a narrow smelly shaft. Nonetheless they had to somehow escape Goodrich Castle and get thee to Gloucester in time to turn Edward's army around—for if Owen and Pembroke got here first, they would immediately execute Edward. The Tudors were the family that converted the Tower of London from a royal dwelling into death row, and in the next century they would be running the whole show. When did their reign start? Hopefully not anytime soon.

Before her thoughts went any further, Edward moved in the darkness, waking slowly, but as soon as he was fully up, he had immediate inventive uses for her. Without a word, the Lord of the Marches reached around, taking his lady into his arms, enfolding her with his warm powerful body. Almost without volition she opened her thighs and let him slide inside, his silent impatience reviving last night's primal urgency. Long strong loving strokes sent waves of pleasure pulsing through her, rocking her gently back to sleep. Being betrothed to a teenager could be exhausting, even before you got out of bed.

Next time she awoke, dawn light fell through the firing slit, filling the room with cold gray illumination. She still had all those things to do today, and now she had to pee, as well. Lady Robyn lay nerving herself for a half-naked dash to the garderobe, when she heard the bar scrape. Someone was coming in. She grabbed Edward's shoulder and shook him hard. His sword leaned against the wall by the bed, within reach but still in its scabbard. Slowly the door swung open.

Edward was up immediately, stark naked and drawing his sword. Instead of Talbot retainers with bared blades, the two younger Wydville blondes came in, Mary and Jacquetta, bearing beer and fresh warm linens. Getting themselves a good eyeful, the girls bowed at the foot of the bed, feigning awe at the sight of Edward's sword, though Robyn was the one who won them. Mary, the older teen, looked up at her, saying, "M'lady, we have come to dress you for Mass."

And to sneak a look at Edward naked—if she had not won last night, they would be attending to him alone. Making the most of her victory, she sat up in bed, holding the coverlet against her breast, thanking them for such diligent service. "Please put the beer by the bed and show us what you have brought."

Jacquetta came boldly over to Edward, who set aside his sword but did nothing to cover himself. Bowing low, the blond girl gravely offered up the beer—and anything else Edward might want. This was these teenager's big chance to thrust their tits before an unmarried heir to the throne, and the Wydvilles were not going to waste a second.

Edward was up to the challenge. Out the corner of her eye,

Robyn could see him graciously taking the beer from the girl, thanking her easily. No matter how many females they threw at him, Edward would work to win their hearts. Like Edward's arch-foe, Lord Clifford, observed, there were no "enemy" women.

Mary produced clean linens warmed by the fire, silk drawers for Edward, and a fresh chemise for m'lady. As soon as she was enveloped by warm layers of silk, Robyn ran over to the freezing garderobe while Edward entertained the two blondes by donning his drawers. When she emerged, she got a rather old-fashioned long-sleeved black tunic, topped by a short crimson surcoat, Talbot colors. Edward was given a trimly tailored short tunic with gathered sleeves and a matching jacket done in his own murrey and blue. Clearly Edward's visit had been eagerly anticipated and prepared for, while she was an afterthought, best left to the Talbots.

After morning Mass, Sir Anthony took Edward hawking, along with two dozen Talbot retainers and a couple of Wydville daughters, Mary and Anne, who had played Beaumains in last night's "disguising." Lady Robyn was definitely not invited—in fact, she was being kept at Goodrich to ensure Edward's return. So long as Edward had a sword and a horse, she was the only way to hold him against his will. So she kissed her knight good-bye at the castle gate, then watched him ride off under armed guard with a gay young lady on either side. Carrying merlins on their leather-gloved wrists, the two young women were determined to teach Edward the joys of falconry, making coy comments like, "We must be tender with these birds, for it is near to the mating season."

"Truly?" Edward acted like he knew nothing about the sex life of birds, though he had grown up amid his mother's hawks.

"When that happens, they go absolutely wild." Sitting sidesaddle, Mary leaned forward to show off her crimson low-cut gown sprinkled with white Wydville magpies. "Becoming utterly uncontrollable."

"Females especially," Anne assured him, carefully preening the bird-of-prey on her wrist. Her riding gown was the reverse of her sister's, white satin with scarlet magpies.

Seeing Edward ride away with two curvy young Wydvilles competing for his attention was not easy. She trusted Edward—to a point. But right now, his enemies had him neatly trapped, since all the Wydvilles needed to do was to spin out this "visit" until the Tudors arrived, which would likely be early next week. Until then, the Wydvilles were free to try any means to win him over, and pretty young females were their weapons of choice.

Hating to see him go, and knowing she might easily never see him again, Lady Robyn retreated into the dark, smelly stables. Even the familiar tangy odor of horse piss failed to cheer her, and the former Miss Rodeo Montana sat down on a low stool, sobbing quietly. Heaven only knew how they could get out of this. With Edward gone and no Wydvilles about, she no longer had to be brave. Tears poured down her cheeks as she gave in to grief and anger. Just being able to cry could be a blessing in the truest sense, a chance to be alone with God, holding nothing back and admitting fear and frailty.

She kept crying until a tall, freckle-faced stable boy in Talbot livery appeared, asking, "How may I help, m'lady?"

Dabbing her eyes, she looked him over. Medieval England might not have much, but it never lacked for broad-shouldered lads ready to hear a lady's troubles. "You could get me a good strong coil of rope."

"Rope?" He looked taken aback.

"Yes." She nodded brightly. "Rope that is easy to knot, but will bear my weight."

Giving her a wary look, the boy obeyed, returning with the rope looped around his arm, asking, "Will this do?"

"Looks perfect." Lady Robyn reached out to take the rope.

He hesitated, asking, "M'lady, is anything amiss?"

She saw he did not know who she was and that he took her Talbot colors as genuine. "Nothing that coil of rope will not cure."

Dirty fingers tightened around the rope. "Please, m'lady, I cannot give it to you."

"I will pay," she promised, working a gold ring off her white finger.

He shook his head stubbornly. "Not if m'lady means to hang herself."

"Hang myself?" There was a solution she had not thought of. "Heavens why?"

Flustered, he pointed to a tear streak on her cheek. "M'lady was crying most miserably."

"To get your attention." Not totally true, but she gave him a convincing kiss of gratitude. One great advantage of the Middle Ages was that teenage boys were totally fair game. The age of consent was thirteen, and beyond that, boys were as big as they wanted to be. Lady Robyn was currently sleeping with an eighteen-year-old on the Royal Council. "All I need is a rope for my mistress, to replace one I have lost."

What English boy could resist a lady in distress? "Then here it is."

Taking the rope, she told him, "Please, tell no one you gave it to me."

"Oh, never fear that, m'lady." There was no one in authority that he wanted knowing about this adventure.

She kissed him again, saying, "Sometimes women just need to cry. It does not always mean we are going to kill ourselves."

He grinned happily back at her. " 'Tis most heartening to hear that, m'lady."

She handed him the ring, and he went off, happily clutching his prize. Lady Robyn was the sort of noblewoman stable boys dreamed about, and her old-fashioned tunic dress had a loose waist, so as soon as she was alone, she raised her skirts and wrapped the rope around her middle. With the rope concealed under her tunic, she headed for their keep bedroom.

And ran right into Lady Elizabeth, who had come to console her, saying, "You must not sulk about this dreary old keep. Come, let us have some fun. Even if my sisters are after your man, I am not, so we at least may be friends."

By all means, but first she was desperate to get rid of the incriminating rope around her waist. Excusing herself, she ducked into the garderobe and unwound the rope, stashing it under the seat. Then she straightened her Talbot livery and stepped out to face Lady Elizabeth, who wore her husband's colors, a fashionable tight-waisted blue satin gown, trimmed with cloth-of-silver. Robyn looked like a serving woman by contrast, which was the Wydville intent; so far they had managed to totally fool a Goodrich stable boy. When she emerged, Lady Elizabeth said she looked much better. "No longer slumping about the middle like a milkmaid in her seventh month. I appreciate your fondness for young Edward of March, and I would hate to see harm come to him, for he seems a most wonderful boy."

"Really?" She always wanted to believe the Wydville women had a shred of conscience—but so far she had been bitterly disappointed. Only Sir Anthony had treated her decently, until this most recent kidnapping.

"My yes, he is most handsome and charming, and so marvelously condescending." Elizabeth smiled like a woman in love, adding, "What a shame it would be to lose him."

Robyn solemnly agreed, "I, too, would see him safe."

Lady Elizabeth's smile widened. "That is most easily done."

"How?" None of this would be easy, but one could still hope.

"Use your wiles, my dear, maybe even some spellcraft." Love spells were a Wydville specialty. "Get him to renounce the Act of Accord."

Robyn rolled her eyes in reply. Lady Elizabeth knew she had tried, since Lady Robyn's opposition to the act was notorious, making her practically the only sane young woman in London who did not think Edward would make a wonderful king.

"Then you could marry him," Lady Elizabeth pointed out, piously intent on making an honest woman out of her.

Lady Elizabeth invited her into the solar, where her sisters were sewing on spring dresses, long trailing gowns with tight formfitting tops, for Queen Margaret's triumphal march into London—which now seemed quite possible. With Edward trapped at Goodrich, the defense of London would be in the unsteady hands of Richard Neville, Earl of Warwick. Robyn very much doubted that Warwick could hold London on his own. These Wydville sisters plainly agreed, gleefully planning a grand return to the capital, this time as attendants to the queen.

Life was going to be one long string of parties once London gave in to Queen Margaret. All they talked of were dances, games, masquerades, and tournaments in their honor. There was a quaint appeal to their notions, if Lady Robyn had not already seen the ruinous effects of such self-indulgent government. Margaret, whom she had beaten at barriers last night, boasted, "We are all going to marry the best men in the land, the richest and most powerful around."

"Sight unseen?" That was like saying your husband had to come from the Texas congressional delegation. "Even aging widowers or little boys?"

Wydvilles laughed at her scruples. "Look at your lord," Jacquetta scoffed.

Touché. She was bedding the cream of the bachelor crop, and could hardly blame them for taking second best. That was the Wydville women's plan for world domination: they would all get noble husbands—the higher, the better. That was how mother got to be Duchess of Bedford, and the king's aunt.

Lady Elizabeth smiled sardonically at her younger sisters' ambitions, being married to a mere knight herself, actually a squire whose elevation had yet to be confirmed by the king. Though no one said it, Edward was the ideal prey. A quickie marriage in the Goodrich chapel, and Edward need not fear being turned over to the Tudors. Wydvilles would instantly become his allies, with private connections to Queen Margaret's inner circle. Warwick and the Nevilles would go ballistic over a Wydville marriage, but everyone would agree it made more sense than marrying Lady Robyn Stafford, pregnant witch on the lam. If Edward kept acting coy, they need hold him only until the Tudors arrived. Each day would make the case for a Wydville marriage that much stronger.

Even the threat of forced matrimony did not dampen Edward's spirits. He came back enthused by his day of hawking, not the least put off by it being a "woman's" sport, not with two pretty young women to extol its delights. It was a wonder they got back at all. He told her, "I have always loved hawks, but never had time to raise them right. It takes diligence, you know, and sympathetic attention—"

"Plus the heartlessness to feed your hand-raised hawks live doves," Robyn noted. Her idea of birding was to feed pine nuts to the redpolls and siskins.

Everyone laughed at her squeamishness, which was further displayed at dinner, as she passed up the gingered boar's meat and some suspect sea bream—not even pregnancy could make her eat everything medievals put on her plate. Finding some fresh bread and onion soup more to her liking, she talked to Sir Anthony about publishing, telling him about her plan to open a print shop in London. Sir Anthony confided that he had a printed book on Latin grammar, and was looking for a printed Bible. "Seeing God's words written without the hand of man has a certain mystic appeal.

We live in an age when things are happening faster than hands can write. Novel experiments and mechanical marvels are devised, even as ancient truths are rediscovered, and strange lands arise beyond the sea. How will people hear of them if they must wait for monks and clerks to make copies?"

Lady Robyn agreed, "A new age needs a new voice." Too bad she and charming Sir Anthony had to be enemies, since they got along so famously. Of course, the last Lord Scales could not get enough of her either, and that had landed her in the Tower of London.

When dinner was done, Lady Elizabeth whispered in passing, "My apartments, at midnight. Jacquetta will come for you."

Witches Night was tonight, one more reason to escape. But she could not get Edward alone, since Wydville women were all over him, begging him to play the lute or tell about his adventures in exile. Last year at this time, Edward had held their parents and brother prisoner in Calais; now they talked like turnabout was fair play, inventing "penalties" for him to pay. When the music started, he had to dance with each of them in turn.

Leaving Robyn to dance with Lord Scales and several energetic Talbots, while trying not to look at Edward. Finally she took refuge with the small knot of married gentlewomen seated by an ice sculpture of Hymen, goddess of marriage, used to cool refreshments in the hot, torchlit hall. Lady Elizabeth asked, "Are you having fun?"

"Almost as much as when I was tortured in the Tower." Then at least she had been the center of attention.

Lady Elizabeth smiled, amused by circumstances—or by the thought of Robyn under torture. "You are a determined woman, and brave, as well. I am sorry to add to your suffering, but word has come that Wiltshire's men will be here on the morrow to take charge of Lord Edward."

More torture. She thought they had days before the Tudors could arrive; now that was reduced to hours. "Will Lord Scales turn Edward over to them?"

"Shrewsbury's steward will be with them, and the Talbot retainers will obey him." Wydvilles meant to wash their hands of Edward, letting Wiltshire and the Talbots take the blame.

"What will they do with him?" Robyn demanded.

Elizabeth shrugged. "That will depend on whatever orders Lord Wiltshire gave them."

Most likely that meant execution on the spot. "And will you do nothing?"

Lady Elizabeth looked insulted. "I am warning you, am I not?"

"But you won't save him?" She knew the Wydvilles could if they wanted to, Talbot steward or no.

Elizabeth laughed at that suggestion. "Marriage to any of my sisters would save him. You are pleading with the one lady in this castle who can do nothing for handsome Lord Edward."

So she had to give up Edward, either to death or the Wydvilles. "Then there is no other way to save him?"

"Ask my mother," Elizabeth replied airily. "When you see her tonight."

Duchess Wydville was going to be here, at least in spirit. More bad news. Robyn begged, "Let me be alone with Edward, to at least give him this warning. I vow to care only for his life. If he desires to wed one of your sisters, I will do nothing to dissuade him."

Lady Elizabeth softened, saying, "I am sorry to see you forced to make this choice, for I know how you feel. I married a squire, for love alone."

"And now he is a knight," Robyn noted. Thanks to Queen Margaret, since King Henry had yet to dub him. These were trying times, and Edward was not able to pledge fealty for his earldom of March until he captured King Henry at Northampton.

Lady Elizabeth was true to her word, and Robyn got to see Edward alone, in the same keep bedroom where they had spent the night. His White Lion of March shield hung above the hearth, in honor of Lady Robyn's victory, but there was no late supper spectacle planned for this evening. Wydville women were getting ready for Witches Night, and their noble captives were left to amuse themselves with a butt of hard cider and a light supper of cheese pastries, fried smelts, and dried figs. As soon as the door shut behind them and the bar dropped in place, Edward took her in his arms, saying, "We must get out of here."

Sometimes their minds seemed totally in sync. Wydvilles had bombarded Edward with curvy young blondes, and all he wanted was to get away. She kissed him, saying, "My feelings exactly."

Her young lord liked the kiss a lot, though it got them not a whit closer to Gloucester. "They have been pushing fair young women onto me, when all I want is a kiss from you."

What a hard life. Handsome young heir to their throne, and he still could not kiss the lips he desired. Condemned instead to spend his days with a bevy of available young virgins, hawking, dancing, flirting, and diverting himself. She kissed him again, saying, "Worse yet, Wiltshire's men will be here on the morrow to take you into custody."

Edward shook his head ruefully. "Why is it one of us is always wanted for something?"

"Just lucky, I guess." Being hounded by the law had certainly brought them together.

His Grace, the Earl of March and Ulster, smiled wide, glad to have a girlfriend adept at dodging the authorities. "It will be a cold moonlit night, and we could easily make our way north."

She grinned at Edward's eagerness to get away from the Wydvilles. "If we could get out of this room?"

He granted her point. "That first, of course."

"And then over the wall beyond," she added.

Edward looked askance at her. "You make it sound passing difficult."

"Not at all." She had been bursting all afternoon to tell him about the rope, but had not had him alone until now. "I think we could do it tonight."

That took him aback even further. "How?"

"I'll show you." Slipping out of his arms, she went to the garderobe and got the rope, flourishing it over her head like a lariat.

"Most excellent." He applauded. "Though we still must get free first, since we cannot climb out of this bolted room."

"Wanna bet?" She stripped off her gown and hose, much to Edward's delight. Their escape might have ended right there, but she managed to fend him off, while putting on a tight tunic and wool hose, cinched at the waist with a length of rope. When she was done, she struck a pose. "What do you think?"

He smirked at her ensemble. "I liked you better naked."

"Not likely. I will be dirty enough as is." She went over to the fireplace, which had not yet been lit for the night, and kicked aside the kindling in the hearth. Then she leaned in and looked up the flue, a flashlight in hand. Flicking on the light, she searched for handholds, seeing only blackened stone. "Here, help me up."

He walked over and put his hands on her waist, enjoying the tightness of her tunic. "You are going up the chimney?"

She pressed her hands against his, thankful for the support and for the firm strong feel of him against her back. "Just like Santa Claus."

Only half believing she could do it, he hoisted her up into the flue, a black stone slot just wider than her shoulders. She braced her back against the cold stones while her toes found footholds on the opposite wall. Collin used to take her climbing in Malibu and Yosemite, and she had gone up rock chimneys far harder than this one—though a lot cleaner. The sooty flue ended in a narrow ledge beneath a round brick chimney. Looking straight up the shaft, she saw winter stars overhead. Hallelujah. She sat for a moment on the ledge, tasting clean open air coming down from above, then she started back up. Her hips and shoulders almost did not go in, and she had to worm her way up, twisting from side to side, her frozen feet feeling for toeholds between the frigid bricks.

Finally she reached the top, sticking her head out into the cold starlight. She had done it. She was out, and alone, atop the keep battlements. Everything was bathed in bright bluish moonlight, broken by deep black shadows. Squirming all the way out, she perched on the edge of the old-fashioned open chimney crown, her dirty feet dangling down into the shaft. No one stood watch on the battlements, which were completely surrounded by Goodrich Castle. Most likely the only guard was on the first floor, keeping watch on the outer door.

Swinging her legs out of the chimney, she dropped onto the roof of the keep, flicked on her light, and found the stairs leading back down into the tower. Barefoot and freezing, she descended the dark stairs to the landing outside their bedroom. Shaking from the cold, she lifted the bar from the door and slid back the bolt. Edward was still kneeling by the fireplace, looking up the flue. He leaped up and applauded her entrance. "Now that indeed is magic."

Her most physically challenging Witches Flight, for sure, and her dirtiest, leaving her freezing cold and covered head to foot in soot, which did not stop Edward from throwing his arms around her. His warm earnest hug stopped her shaking, reminding her of how he held her after her Halloween bust at Baynards Castle—then she had just been cold and frightened, not filthy, as well. Too bad there was not time for him to thank her properly—as it was, he just got dirty, too.

Besides, they were out of the room, but not the keep, or the surrounding castle, so sweaty congratulations had to wait. Instead she stripped again, washing as best she could in wincing cold water. Then came the inevitable question of what to wear while making her escape. Her days of fleeing in a ball gown were long gone, and she dug down into the bottom of her saddlebag and found her French jeans, perfect for the occasion. She put them on, followed by loose wool hose and glove-leather boots, all topped by a fur-lined jacket that Owen had given to Heidi. Lady Robyn prayed that the jacket's owner was alive and well. She had not seen Heidi since Tudor riders ambushed them at Llangorse Lake, two days ago.

Though they had not seen it, both she and Edward knew the main floor of the keep would be guarded. With Edward locked above, the Wydvilles would not take any chances—someone would be keeping watch. Though not anyone important or vigilant, since this was a fortified keep surrounded by a stoutly defended castle, and medievals did not waste time guarding against the impossible, or even the highly unlikely. Edward took his White Lion of March shield off the wall, drew his sword, and went down to talk to their jailers.

Four guards were on duty that night, lounging about in Talbot livery with their swords sheathed and their knife belts unbuckled, not even wearing chain mail. Two open pots of beer sat on the floor, one empty and the other half full. When Edward surprised them by appearing, sword in hand, none of them showed much enthusiasm for a losing fight. He told them, "I am Edward Plantagenet, Earl of March, and I command you to obey in the name of King Henry."

Half-drunk bowmen gaped at him, astonished to have their Friday-night beer bash crashed by a six-foot, sword-wielding young nobleman who had been safely locked away with his beautiful strumpet and a butt of cider. Any sane fellow would have been enjoying himself immensely, but England was cursed with an eccentric aristocracy, and instead the teenage heir to the Duchy of York was standing over them, saying with a smile, "To touch your blades is treason."

The guards looked questioningly at one another, unsure what to do. Having the nobility at each other's throats was hard on the commons, who could be doing their duty one moment and committing high crimes the next, all over a friendly pot of beer. Nor was there anyone to call to, since the window was shuttered tight and the floor below them was a windowless stone box, used for basement storage. Edward reminded his would-be jailers, "These Wydvilles will soon be gone, and you will be the ones explaining your actions to a royal judge."

Slowly the sergeant of the guard rose and bowed, asking, "What are your orders, m'lord?"

Edward turned jovial, lowering his blade and saying, "Only that you be my guests. We have a butt of cider upstairs that we can never finish on our own."

"Also fried smelt and cheese pastries," Robyn added cheerfully, hoping to set them at ease. Shamefaced, her former guards filed past, climbing the stairs to her bedchamber, where her boyfriend locked them in. Part of the wonder of being with Edward was that she was always with the best man in the room. On their second date, he talked a whole shipload of sailors into surrendering.

She had packaged up some cheese and dried figs to go, and had her saddlebags slung over her shoulder. Edward brought the rope, and they descended into the keep's ground floor. Originally this has been a stone basement, but some lord had put in a doorway opening onto the inner ward. Using her flashlight to find the door, she opened it slowly, while Edward stood ready with his sword.

Nothing, just a cold empty courtyard. Too bad they could not just go to the stables and reclaim their horses, but there was no chance they could bluff their way through the intricate gatehouse, with its multiple gates and double drawbridge. That meant they must go over the wall.

Finding a stair leading up to the wall walk, they mounted the southwest tower, dodging the few sentries keeping watch on a clear winter night. When they got to an embrasure overlooking the wedge-shaped buttress bracing the tower, she peered through, asking Edward for the rope. He handed it to her, saying, "Where did you get this?"

"Off a friendly stable boy." She took the rope and turned to face him, uncoiling one end.

Edward frowned as she unwound it, seeing the rope would not reach all the way down the tower. "Too bad it is not longer."

"It will be long enough." She tied one end around his waist. "Have you ever done this before?"

"Done what?" he asked as his lady pulled the knot tight, finally having him securely on a leash.

Robyn tied the other end of the rope around her own waist. "Climbing with a rope?"

Clearly Edward had not. He slung his shield and broadsword over his back, asking, "Is it hard?"

"Not really." Robyn pulled the last knot tight, wishing she were as confident as she sounded. Climbing with twenty-first-century Collin had been a lark; the closest thing to this escape was a moonlit descent of the Malibu cliffs to go skinny-dipping, half-drunk and half-dressed. This would not be near as much fun.

By belaying around a battlement, they lowered themselves to the top of the buttress, a great wedge of stone several stories tall that braced the outward side of the tower. Robyn went first, rappelling down to the buttress, then finding hand- and footholds on the sloping wedge. There she waited as Edward followed her down, then clung to the buttress top while they untied to release the rope. Knightly training ran more toward riding, prayer, and swordplay rather than rock climbing, but Edward easily mastered the technique, even by moonlight with his sword and shield slung across his back.

Edward anchored her from atop the buttress while she felt her way down the worn stone, letting gravity guide her feet. When she reached the limit of the rope, she stopped, clinging to the dark icy buttress, letting Edward climb down past her, keeping to the narrow trough between the sloping buttress and the curving tower wall. His foot slipped in the darkness above her. Dirt and stone chips rattled down on her. She closed her eyes and clung hard, imagining Edward coming down next.

Frantic scraping came from overhead. Followed by silence. Presently she heard the slow patient sound of someone picking their footholds, coming steadily closer. She opened her eyes, to look, and as Edward edged past her, he shot her a smile, saying, "Pardon, m'lady. I am kicking rocks on you."

"Just mind your footholds." Her fingers were numb by now, and she was hanging on by her toes, with the worst yet to come. Castle architects made the lowest part of the tower the hardest, blending the curved tower and triangular buttress into a flat vertical wall. Being lighter and more experienced, she should have led, but Edward was eager to go, while she could barely feel her hands.

Rapt concentration returned to her love's face as he reached out, searching for a secure hold on the molding of an arrow slit. Her fear for Edward was far greater than any she ever felt while climbing with Collin. Collin had been all cool expertise, confidently showing her the ropes, and she had not been nearly as much in love with Collin. With Edward, her whole life was on the line, literally.

Looking up, she saw the black battlements of Goodrich framed against cold bright stars. Good God, in a few more months she would be in no shape for this sort of thing. At least they were virtually invisible, wearing dark colors that blended with the aged stones. Deep shadow kept anyone above from seeing them, and there were no windows. If they did not break their necks, they were bound to get away easily.

Even as she thought that, she heard the clatter and bang of the outer drawbridge crashing down, followed by the hollow thunder of hoofbeats. At least a score of riders had burst out of the gatehouse barbican, headed hell-for-leather into the darkness. Holy Mary, their escape was discovered already. There was no other explanation for the mounted excursions on a freezing January night. How horribly unfair. Pinned to the stone wall, she could not even flee. Nothing could speed their descent, and when they got to the bottom, armed riders would be waiting. Robyn wanted to scream in fear and frustration.

Just when it seemed things could not get any worse, she heard a sickening scrape below her, followed by a jerk in the line that signaled Edward had fallen. Fear turned into outright terror. Bracing her feet, she knew she had no chance at all of holding on. In seconds, Edward's falling weight would tear her numbed fingers from the stone.

Suddenly the rope about her waist went taut, grabbing at her gut, and she was flung backward, her frozen fingers ripped from the wall. Robyn went sailing into blackness, arms spread, legs flailing, doing her best not to scream. With nothing to hold on to, and no way of slowing her fall, she gave herself up to Hecate.

And landed in Edward's arms. He was waiting in the darkness at the foot of the wall, arms out, having landed on his feet and knowing she was right behind him. Rope and gravity brought her straight to him, and she gave a surprised gasp at the sudden soft impact. "Hush," he hissed, "we have been discovered."

Really? She could hear more hoofbeats on the drawbridge, and soon searchers would be coming their way. Edward set her down without letting go, making sure she stayed on her feet, asking, "Are you unhurt?"

She nodded swiftly, hardly believing it herself.

"And the baby?"

How should she know? Men acted like motherhood came with a manual. For all she knew, the baby was sleeping happily through it all, cushioned from fear and chaos by layers of flesh. "Doing just great."

Edward grinned with relief. "Come, before they think to get dogs." They scrambled across the dry moat and descended the spur of rock that Goodrich sat on. When they paused for breath, Robyn forced fur-lined gloves over her frozen fingers. She could see torches moving in the darkness above as searchers fanned out from Goodrich. With mounted pursuers already ahead of them, the local Wye crossings would all be watched. So they headed in the opposite direction, west towards Wales, still roped together so as not to lose each other in the inky shadows.

Electric-blue moonlight lit up the Wye Valley, reflecting off the winding river, while the castle squatted black and sinister on the heights behind them. Splashing through a cold stream in her heavy boots, Robyn let Edward lead her north, along a low ridge trail that would become A4137, headed toward Owen's Cross. She followed the footpath for miles through the moonlight, cold and frightened, with no feeling in her fingers, happy that every step she took put distance between her and the Wydvilles. Bands of horsemen in Talbot livery came pounding up the path from behind them, but each time, she heard them first, and pulled on the rope to give Edward silent warning; then they hid in the brush as their pursuers sped past.

Lights showed at Owen's Cross, and they heard dogs barking. Talbots and Wydvilles could already be in the town, so they made for the farmstead below Hoarwithy that they had visited the day before. Dogs greeted them here, as well, but the people knew them at once, amazed to see the Lord and Lady of the March returning bedraggled and afoot. They took her in immediately, warming her hands by the fire and covering her boots and hose with a blanket, indignant to see a lady so mistreated. They would have fainted if they had seen her French jeans.

"Lady Stafford is not so frail as she seems," Edward declared. "Last night she bested the Duchess of Bedford's daughter in close combat."

Men smirked, and a boy nudged his brother, saying, "Armed with sharpened spindles and surly looks."

"With hand-and-a-half broadswords at barriers," Edward boasted. "Beat her with one shrewd stroke."

Men and boys cheered the Wydville's defeat. "Serves the bitch of Bedford right, for siding with the French."

Males were all willing to believe the worst of Wydvilles, who were deeply in league with the despised French queen. Women were more skeptical, asking, "Is that so, m'lady?"

Happy just to have the feeling back in her fingers, Robyn had all the notoriety she needed, directing their questions back to Edward. "My Lord of March would know, since he was my squire."

Laughing aloud, the women said that explained her strange ensemble. "M'lady looks like she was dressed by a man."

"And in the dark," added a giggling girl. English children learned early to laugh at the aristocracy, knowing there was no way they would ever be rid of them. Though this Herefordshire farm family did manage to swiftly dispose of the lord and lady who had come tromping out of the night. Robyn was given a pack mare to ride, and the Lord of the Marches was mounted on a plain bay plow horse. He had only his broadsword, shield, and a borrowed sallet and mail coat worn by a bowman in the French wars. Folks swore the rusty visorless sallet helm had been at Agincourt.

Boys led both of their mounts, while their older brothers went ahead to check the Wye crossing at Hoarwithy, to see this pair of noble lovers safely across the Wye. Night riders were on the loose, and this sleepy western shire was suddenly the scene of high adventure, even a French invasion, complete with fine wine and Parisian whores. What boy in his right mind would not be excited? Best of all, these boys could go home when it was done, to boast about their exploits, while Edward would be the one to suit up in plate armor and face the frog-eating French. Medievals firmly believed that heroics were best left to trained professionals.

Men returned to say Talbot retainers were in Hoarwithy, so they crossed the Wye at a shallow ford known only to locals. Here the young pages turned back, having gotten their noble charges safely over the Wye. Cold from the wet crossing, Robyn wondered how long it would be before they found safety, hoping they would not have to go as far as Gloucester. She was not looking forward to a Witches Night in the saddle and surrounded by armed men.

Beneath a bright winter moon, they headed north and east, making for a stretch of Roman road ten or so miles away. She let her mare follow Edward's big plodding bay, while she relaxed, closing her eyes and flexing her fingers, trying to keep them from freezing up again. Somehow she had to center herself. Back in Montana when she was only nine, she went with some Crow kids to see an old medicine man named Plenty Coups. The medicine man beat on a drum, chanted, and taught her signs, tickled to have a little white girl so eager to learn the old ways. He should see her now. Something the old man told her still stuck with her, "The Earth is your grandmother, and every step should be a prayer."

By now Robyn realized those sessions with Plenty Coups were the beginning of her education. Certainly nothing else she learned in the fourth grade was nearly so vital to her today, not even long division and mastering the hula hoop. She relied on her mount to step lightly, relaxing her grip on the reins and sinking down into herself, letting the mare have her head. Closing her eyes, she said a private prayer to Grandmother Hecate, whose season this was, the crone goddess who ruled over death and winter. And to Diana, whose month it was, the virgin goddess who ruled over birth and New Year's. Death crone and holy virgin, the two most taboo aspects of the goddess, while she herself represented the third aspect, Mary the mother, with a child growing beneath her belly.

This being the final Friday in January, she especially thanked Diana for getting her and the baby safely through their first month together. Her child had been conceived in a Sherwood Forest cave under a full moon, a most miraculous conception, considering the circumstances. Now the moon was full again, and they were both safely reunited with Edward. Reason enough to rejoice, no matter what else happened this night.

Sinking deeper into herself, Robyn let go, allowing her mind to drift. Though her eyes were closed, she could still picture the weird photonegative landscape, with black gaunt trees silhouetted against the bright moonlit sky, and white frosty grass. Stars shone like diamonds in the blazing night above, but she and her mare were a black void. Ahead of her, she saw a small hill of some twenty or so acres rearing up in her path. As she drew closer, white mist seemed to issue from the ground, much like the mist that enveloped her in the Stiperstones, only this time she knew it was not at all natural, but called up by Duchess Wydville to confuse her.

Soon the frigid ground was totally carpeted with fog, and the small humped hill loomed like an island in the sea of mist, flanked by the bell tower of a tiny chapel. Light appeared in the blackness, starting out in a small point, a fallen star embedded in the dark hill. The star grew in magnitude until it outshone the moon, lengthening as it grew, becoming a vertical slit that split the hill in half. As the slit widened and the hill opened up, tall tapers burning inside let her see into Faerie, the Land Under the Hill, home of ghosts and shadows.

Fairy huntresses emerged from the shining rift in the hill, wearing shimmering spider-silk gowns and riding great horned owls whose broad wings beat in utter silence. Each lady huntress had a snowy white hawk on her red-gloved hand. By the brilliant light from Faerie, she could see the huntresses' faces, recognizing the marriageable Wydville sisters—Anne, Margaret, Mary, and Jacquetta. Maiden huntresses, indeed, flying out to prey on men. Seeing them off was Duchess Wydville herself, dressed as a fairy queen in a rainbow gown that glistened like spun stained glass. Surrounded by a pool of light, Duchess Wydville shimmered with energy, drawing on all the powers of the night. Looking straight at Robyn, the witch-priestess blew her a kiss.

Blond elves wearing Wydville colors burst out of the hole in the hill, riding on white Talbot hounds and headed straight for her. She instinctively reached out to warn Edward, riding ahead of her, forgetting that this was all a witches' dream. Since it was a dream, her hand found him easily, clasping onto his shoulder and turning him about in the saddle. As she pulled him toward her, she heard Duchess Wydville's laugh ringing in her head, just as it had on Halloween, when the witch-priestess tricked her into committing treason.

Edward changed instantly, becoming a white gyrfalcon tiercel and immediately taking flight. Startled, she lost her grip on him, but luckily Edward had a fetterlock around one leg, and she managed to grab the chain. Pulled up short, the gyrfalcon fluttered frantically, then settled down onto her gloved wrist. She straightened in the saddle, feeling like an unmaidenly huntress herself, with her love securely chained to her. The Wydville maidens all had hawks on their wrists, while hers was a tiercel. But not for long, the gyrfalcon grew and changed, his feathers turning to fur, becoming the white lion of March—which she was holding hard to by a rear leg. Even for Miss Rodeo Montana, managing a lion on horseback is no mean feat, especially in your sleep. Worse than having a tiger by the tail. Edward snarled and roared, snapping at the night air, yet she would not let go, sure the flailing lion would not harm her.

She was right. Instead of slashing her open or biting off her head, the white lion transformed himself again, turning into a sprig sprinkled with yellow flowers, trembling softly in her gloved hand. Relieved not to be fighting a lion, Lady Robyn immediately recognized the *planta genesta*, the 'plant of life,' the ancient badge of the counts of Anjou, which gave Edward's family its name, Plantagenet. White rosebuds sprouted on the *planta genesta,* bursting into bloom as the yellow flowers vanished, replaced by big white blossoms. With the roses came the thorns, long sharp needles that penetrated her leather glove, pricking her mercilessly. Crying out in agony, she let the rose fall from her hand.

✦ ✦ ✦

Robyn awoke in an icy sweat, wincing in pain. She was back, plodding along through the moonlit night behind her knight on a plow horse. Hoarfrost shone on bare black trees. Faerie was gone, along with the miraculous hill and the Wydville witches, but that did not mean they were not watching. Her hand hurt horribly. Letting go of the reins, Robyn found she had big sharp rose thorns embedded in her glove.

Using her teeth, she tore the glove off her good hand, then plucked the bloody thorns out, one at a time. Gingerly she stripped off the punctured glove, finding the fur lining soaked with blood. Cold air numbed her hand, and the bleeding had stopped, but her wounds were real. She was under magical attack. So was Edward, and Robyn spurred her pack mare, getting close enough to grab at his cloak, saying, "I have had a warning."

Her good hand was on the reins, and numb fingers missed their hold on his cloak, but Edward got the message, turning in his saddle. "What warning?"

"Wydvilles are after us." That part took no seeress. "And they know where we are."

He reined in, asking, "Are you sure?"

She nodded, then asked, "Where are we?" Wydvilles might know, but Lady Robyn did not. All she saw was patches of bare frozen fields, showing between even darker trees.

"Almost to the road." He tried to sound encouraging, afraid she was flagging. "Ledbury is less than five miles off. And we have good friends in Eastnor."

North of the Wye, they were in thoroughly friendly country, and she felt ashamed for being so fearful—but the stinging in her palm had returned, hurting more than ever. "Then we should head for Eastnor at once," she suggested, "for I fear our enemies are nearby."

Edward told the two men closest to him to find the road ahead and send word if it was safe. They vanished into the night. Presently one returned to say the way was clear. Riding side by side with Edward, she emerged from the trees and onto the Roman road, running straight and level in the moonlight—either north into Herefordshire, or south toward Gloucester. Robyn whispered, "Which way?"

Edward held up his gloved hand for silence. "Listen."

Robyn listened, hearing a distant tinkling, the unmistakable ring of steel on steel, growing louder and clearer. Only one thing made that sound, mounted men in armor riding hard toward you. Staring north into the blackness, she saw flashes in the dark, moonlight glistening on plate armor and lance points. Edward saw them, too, saying, "They are coming out of Herefordshire, and might be friends."

Herefordshire was friendly to Edward, and this could be the welcoming committee, coming to meet them in full armor, without warning, on a deserted road, in the dead of night. Her hand hurt even more, and she shook her head. "Only the Wydvilles know where we are."

Edward rolled his eyes, showing why even the most patient of men were tempted to burn witches. Here he was safe among his own people, and he still had to fear enemies conjured up by magic. And he had to face them, mounted on a plow horse—all thanks to the Wydville witches. He pointed to the black trees on the far side of the road, saying, "Into the woods."

Robyn followed him in, knowing they had no chance of escaping in a flat-out chase, not mounted on a plow horse and pack nag, when their enemies were riding hardened warhorses and guided by spellcraft. Trying to lose their pursuers in the woods might be just as futile, but at least the disparity in mounts meant less on dark, narrow forest paths, where everyone must pick their way. They crossed one stream at a bridge, then splashed through another at a ford. Edward reined in on the far side, saying, "Ahead is a gap in the trees that leads straight to Eastnor."

"Really?" None of this looked the least familiar to her, though she had been in Ledbury only last summer, staying in the most delightful little inn, with clean linen and a clever pair of cats who kept the vermin at bay. Too bad they were not there now, brewing tea by the bedroom fire. Luckily Edward had grown up in the next shire, and he knew his way about, even in the dark. Plunging back into the trees, where narrow shadowy trails ran in several directions, Robyn kept close to Edward, having at best a vague idea where they were headed. Suddenly she saw more armored riders appear, cutting them off from Eastnor. More pursuers, or maybe the same ones? Or phantoms conjured up to keep them from their friends?

No sense waiting around to see. Edward drew his sword, telling her to go ahead. "Make for the Hereford road, my lady, on the far side of the trees."

She took her love's advice, pausing only to be sure he was right behind her; then they were off together, black bracken whipping at her legs, and his bare blade shining in the moonlight. Robyn hardly knew where they were going, dodging between dark tree trunks with her head down, praying not to be brained by a low bough. She splashed through another shallow stream, sending thin shards of ice flying into the night. Moonlight appeared ahead, and she made for it, hoping it would be the Hereford road.

And it was. She reined in beside a lonely pair of frozen wagon ruts, which cut across hilly pasture that climbed toward a gap in the lower Malverns—what would one day be A438 west of Tewkesbury. Edward halted beside her, waiting for the other riders to catch up. None did; the two of them were alone beneath a brilliant full moon ringed by an icy halo. Afraid to break the silence, she whispered, "Which way should we go?"

"Ledbury is but a few miles that way," he pointed west, "on the far side of Eastnor."

By now she very much wanted to be in that clean little Ledbury inn, but there were likely to be enemy riders between here and Eastnor. "What about Tewkesbury?"

Edward did not sound eager to head east. "Tewkesbury is too far. We might as well make for Gloucester."

She looked back down the road toward Ledbury, seeing more lights in Eastnor. Someone was awake. All this galloping about had set dogs to barking, and the countryside was coming alive. Amid the distant barking, she heard another sound, growing louder, the tinkling ring of steel on steel. She told Edward, "They are coming."

Edward nodded tersely. He could hear them, too. "We cannot outrun them," he told her, "so we must take to the hills."

Crossing the frozen lane, they climbed a narrow track through the tree line toward the heights overlooking the road. These were the lowermost of the Malverns, Midsummer and Hollybush hills, wooded knolls where the straight north–south line of the Malverns came to an abrupt end. Near the top, the steep wooded track turned into a footpath, then broke out onto bare tops, furrowed by Iron Age earthworks. Edward led her straight across the top toward an even higher summit, Herefordshire Beacon just to the north. Here the horses gave out, refusing to mount yet another hill. Dismounting, Edward helped her down, then released the horses, who immediately bounded off down the hill, headed back home to Hoarwithy. Horses had sense enough to seek shelter on a cold winter night, even when their riders did not.

"What now?" she asked, her breath misting before her. They were alone and afoot on a freezing night, beset by enemies who could find them through magic.

Edward slid his arm into his shield and drew his sword, saying, "This is Herefordshire Beacon. I played here as boy, and I know where you can hide."

"Where is that?" she asked warily, doubting anywhere would be safe from Wydville magic.

"I will show you." He led her up the footpath past earthen ramparts covered with frozen heather, entering the huge ancient hill fort sitting atop Herefordshire Beacon. Ringed by multiple walls and ditches, this fort was said to be where the ancient Britons under Caractacus made their last stand against the advancing Roman legions. Its center was a flat abandoned castle mound topped by a tall tangle of brushwood and tree trunks and used as a signal fire in case of Marcher uprisings or a Welsh invasion. But there had been no battles here since Glendower's day, and the frozen pile of logs looked much neglected. Anyone trying to set it alight would have to bring their own dry tinder, and lots of it.

Leading her to the southeast side of the hill, Edward showed her a cave entrance hacked from volcanic rock, what might once have been a hermit's cell or a shepherd's rest. She stared inside, not much liking the look of this hole in the earth, asking, "Where does it lead?"

"Nowhere," Edward admitted. "But you will be safe inside, so long as I hold the door."

He meant it, too. Edward had only an old coat of mail, and his White Lion of March shield—looking more like a knight from Arthur's time than a "modern" man-at-arms. But this was the land where he was raised, land given to him by Mad King Henry to defend. Caractacus had made his stand here, with all of Rome arrayed against him. Why should Edward of March fear a few Wydville night riders? His love and his child would be safe, so long as he had his sword and the strength to swing it. She was the one who was not so sure.

9

⚬═◦ Mortimer's Cross ◦═⚬

Forcing on a smile, she kissed her love for luck, terribly afraid it would be for the last time. Then she retreated into the tiny cave, which was only a few paces deep, with just enough headroom for her to stand—bleak quarters for a lady accustomed to being lodged in castles and manor halls. And only temporary. She realized that she could never lose the Wydvilles, not on this Witches Night, at least. They had any number of things to track her by: clothes she had worn, hairs from her head, the bed she last made love in. Running had been natural, but pointless. Edward had come to the same conclusion, and he did not intend to retreat another step. He stood with his sword grounded and his shallow, visorless sallet helm tipped back, peering into the darkness, waiting for his enemies to show themselves.

And the Wydvilles would be here in no time. Determined to fight magic with magic, Robyn knelt on the floor of the cave and cast her circle. This was still Witches Night, and if spellcraft could bring her enemies to her, the right charm could just as swiftly send them packing. She had only to find it. Using her lighter flame as a candle, she started to chant, praying to Diana whose month this was, the witch-goddess of new beginnings, who bore her coven name and protected pregnant women.

Kneeling in her rocky womb, she begged for guidance, sinking down into herself, letting her soul go. Next Monday would be Candlemas, like May Day and Halloween, a cross-quarter day. In the same way that Halloween was the gateway to winter, Candlemas was the doorway to spring, exactly halfway between the winter solstice and the spring equinox. Like a spring seedling, she was enclosed in the earth, with new life nestled inside her, yearning to burst forth.

Without taking her eyes from the cool blue flame, she felt herself rising up through the layers of rock and volcanic soil, pushing aside the grassroots and frosted heather. Still staring into the flame, she could see the whole sweep of surrounding landscape, looking out over half of Herefordshire and into several neighboring shires. Since she was not really seeing, everything shone in clear relief, hills crowned with moonlight, while towns and farmsteads stood out like points of light. Little Malvern lay to the north, nestled against Worcester Beacon, which overlooked Great Malvern. To the west was Ledbury and Hereford, and to the south Gloucester, with its cathedral, while in the east lay Tewkesbury and the low Vale of Evesham. Bonfires lit atop Herefordshire Beacon would be seen from Wales to the Cotswolds.

Concentrating on the blue-gold arc of flame, she let it grow to fill her vision, while she took both herself and the fire deep into the dry heart of the woodpile atop Herefordshire Beacon. Here the wood had been hidden from the rains and freeze-dried, its last ounce of moisture wrung out by the cold. She sank deeper into the flame, which expanded to envelop her, becoming a burning center to the beacon pile. Frost sizzled on the wood around her. First came smoke, then sparks, then little spurts of flame, growing into red greedy tongues, enclosing her in a cage of fire. Heat beat at her as the flames shot higher, and her hand hurt horribly, each rose prick feeling like a point of fire. When she could stand it no longer, she let go of the lighter and collapsed onto the cold cave floor.

She lay on the hard rock, listening to her heartbeat, knowing there was a second heart beating inside her, one she could not hear. That tiny presence comforted her, like having a "constant companion." Which was what Edward had promised he would be when they first met—though it had not turned out that way.

Slowly regaining her senses, she heard hoofbeats mixed with her heartbeats, faint at first, but growing louder as they got closer. Horsemen were mounting the footpath. Someone was coming, most likely wearing Wydville red-and-white. Damn, just when she thought she might lie down, if only for a second or two. Lady Robyn whispered a quick closing prayer, profusely thanking Diana for her continued protection. Then she picked herself up off the cave floor, hurriedly dusting off her wool hose and leather jacket, preparing to meet this latest test.

Edward stood with his mailed back to her, shield in front of him and sword bared, facing the oncoming cavalry. He had vowed on the day they met that she would meet no harm as long as he was with her, and so far, the thorn pricks on her hand were the worst she had suffered while under his protection. That and the soreness that came from too much riding, both in the saddle and bareback.

While she watched, the first Wydville man-at-arms galloped up, reining in before Edward. Though he had raced to get here in full armor, he plainly did not want to take on Edward alone, settling for a few tentative jabs with his lance, which Edward's shield easily turned aside. Edward was quick and strong, and if he got past the lance point, even plate armor was vulnerable to a shrewd sword thrust.

She stepped out of the cave, hoping to stop things before the game got deadly. As she did, flame burst from the heart of the woodpile atop the ancient castle mound, flaring up into the night. Yellow light washed over the startled face of the man-at-arms, who was wearing an old-fashioned open-faced basinet, far more useful at night, when visored helmets were like a blindfold.

With each step she took, the fire behind her burned brighter, throwing sparks high into the winter night. Edward's opponent backed his mount, awaiting reinforcements. Loath as this man-at-arms was to face Edward alone, he was even less willing to face Lord March's witch. Church bells rang below, breaking the dark stillness, sounding out an alarm. Herefordshire Beacon was blazing out its time-honored warning of Welsh invasion, something not seen since Glendower's day. For more than forty years, Herefordshire Beacon had lain waiting, used for lesser purposes and patiently restocked. Now the Welsh were about to come pouring over the border again in a full-fledged invasion, backed by the French and Irish—every Englishman's nightmare had come true. Answering points of light broke out below, signal fires, and moving torches that converged on them, borne by concerned men coming to see who had lit the beacon.

First to arrive were more Wydvilles, reining in beside their fellow, their worried faces clearly illuminated by the light from the giant bonfire. Sir Anthony came next, wearing a gold surcoat decorated with white scallops, and an open basinet. He was followed by a squire who carried his great helm, which had a double crest of white flags, with red Wydville squares. Lance in hand, the new Lord Scales looked down at them, knowing he now had faint hope of taking Edward alive and getting him back to Goodrich. The only way Lord Scales could serve Queen Margaret was to attempt murder here on Herefordshire Beacon, then try to escape as best he could through an aroused countryside—not at all Sir Anthony's style. Nor would murder be easy to commit when Edward was armed and armored.

Lest there be any doubt, Sir Anthony always had the example of the last Lord Scales to consider, his late father-in-law, who was pardoned by Edward, only to be beaten to death by London boatmen. Commoners often took an uncompromising view toward crimes committed by the nobility, expecting better behavior from those who got the best of everything. Sir Anthony saluted politely, saying, "Finding Your Grace missing, we feared mischance, thinking m'lord might be lost."

Without lowering his shield, Edward asked innocently, "Is this not Herefordshire Beacon?"

"Indeed it is," Sir Anthony replied ruefully. Herefordshire Beacon was blazing before him, drawing unfriendly attention from all directions. If Sir Anthony did not leave soon, roles would reverse, and he would be Edward's prisoner for the second time in a year.

"Then I know right well where I am," Edward declared.

"Excellent." Sir Anthony seemed genuinely pleased to be going. "Since we cannot serve Your Grace, my men and I would as soon withdraw—"

"By all means," Edward agreed amiably. "The hour is late."

"And the night most cold," Robyn added. She, for one, was tired of fleeing blindly through the frigid night: chasing after her could not be much better.

Sir Anthony nodded to Edward, saying, "With Your Grace's permission?"

"May we meet again in happier times." Edward plainly liked Sir Anthony, despite being enemies.

Lady Robyn could not resist a parting shot at the Wydville witches. "Give my regrets to your sisters."

"And mine, as well," Edward added, not meaning to seem ungrateful for all the blond attention lavished on him.

Lord Scales turned his armored back to them and retired in good order with his men, light from the flaming beacon glistening off his polished steel and golden surcoat. Sir Anthony never craved power the way the Wydville women did, much preferring the finer things. Good living and a good reputation meant more to him than running the country. If it was so terribly important to ensnare Edward, then his sisters needed do it, for Sir Anthony would far rather be a friend to the world.

Edward turned to her, grinning in triumph. "Thank Heaven for the beacon fire. Who could possibly have lit it?"

She smiled archly. "Who do you think?"

"You?" Edward's grin turned to amazement. She did a demure curtsy in her men's hose and hip boots, happy to have a spell work so well. Witchcraft was by no means an exact science. "How could you?" he marveled, mightily impressed.

She gave an offhand shrug. "Magic."

Well, duh. Edward rolled his eyes. "Is this going to be another woman's secret?"

"Afraid so." Lady Robyn did not make the rules; she just broke them occasionally for him—but not tonight, which had seen way too much excitement already. She was not the least tempted to defy the powers-that-be just to amuse her boyfriend. All she wanted was for people to come and take them somewhere warm and safe, like that little inn in Ledbury where she and Sir Collin stayed last May.

Villagers arrived from Little Malvern, less than a mile away, carrying bows, bills, hayforks, and torches, anxious to find out who had lit the beacon. Edward started crisply issuing orders, barely giving them time to bow and catch their breath. Welsh were coming over the border, and the French and Irish, as well—but not to worry, their government had the situation well in hand and meant to meet the enemy on the morrow, or Monday at the latest. All they must do was arouse the countryside. He sent some to Great Malvern to light Worcestershire Beacon, as well, while others were dispatched to raise the Beauchamps at Eastnor and alert authorities in Ledbury. Edward never liked to waste a minute, unless it was with his lady. Full of energy now that he was free, he told her, "I must go on to Gloucester, by first light at the latest, but I can see you safely lodged at Eastnor."

She did not want to stay at some strange estate, saying, "What I want most right now is to stay in a little inn in Ledbury."

"Then you shall." Glad to have her so easily pleased, Edward would have happily deeded the whole town over to her.

Ledbury was alive by the time she got there, with lights showing in Saint Katherine's Hospital and the bells still tolling at All Angels. Though the town was swiftly filling up with armed men, they found the little inn empty on the last day of a dismal January, in the midst of the Dead Month, when the minuscule medieval economy shrank down to nothing. Lady Robyn discovered that the poor alewife not only remembered her, but was also delighted to have her back. "Who could forget such a pretty young lady, escorted by Lord de Ruthyn's nephew."

On the run really, though the old woman was too polite to say so. And now Lady Robyn was back, with an even more noble "protector," going in a matter of months from lady on the lam to Lady of the Marches. Her hostess gave Robyn her old room, and put on a pot of fennel tea. Edward lay down to a short sleep, leaving word to have a fresh horse saddled and ready to take him on to Gloucester at first light, while Lady Robyn got to sleep in for once, relying on her love's promise to be back before vespers.

Drinkers in the common room woke her, boasting loudly over their breakfast beer about the drubbing they would give the French. Breakfasting in bed on fresh baked bread and honey, she watched out the window as more recruits came in from the countryside, mostly yeomen in bows and brigandines, followed by the first bits of Edward's little army, Welsh men-at-arms, Herberts, Morgans, and Gwyns, Cymry and Saxon riding side by side to defend their native Marches. As she watched, a black-and-white bird settled on the sill and tapped on the dark leaded glass, calling, "Hela!"

Instantly, Robyn opened the widow, saying to the magpie, "Hela, how happy to see you."

"Hela," replied the talkative bird, hopping inside and then flying to the breakfast table to search for scraps. Hela had a sweet tooth and doted on breakfast pastries.

"What are you doing here?" Hela was a Grey family familiar, usually watching over Joanna Grey's daughter, Joy—but known to shadow members of the family in danger.

"Hela hee-r-ee!" whistled the magpie proudly, still absorbed with her grand entrance. Robyn decided to see for herself whom Hela had come with, dressing hurriedly, using a big borrowed skirt to cover her jeans. Hela came flapping after her. Sir Collingwood Grey sat in the common room, along with a pair of younger cousins, plus armed valets, and mailed bowmen from Greystone. When she and Heidi called on twenty-first-century Collin, he had acted scared and guilty, faced with nothing worse than unexpected female guests. What a difference five hundred years made. Here was the same Collin, with the same curly dark hair, trim beard, and cool, alert gaze; only the medieval Collin looked totally at ease, sitting in half-armor in some old woman's common room, knowing that in a day or two he might be in mortal combat—just happy it was not today.

Seeing her, Sir Collin immediately went down on one knee, saying with earnest satisfaction, "M'lady, I came as soon as I knew you were in peril."

Actually she had been lolling in bed, eating sweets and thinking of ordering a bath, but it was the thought that counted. Sir Collingwood Grey was her champion, even before she was Edward's betrothed. She held out her hand for Collin to kiss, saying, "Have my heartfelt thanks, for I am sorely alone here in Ledbury, with armed felons all about."

Collin kissed her hand (always a bit of a thrill). Having strong sexy men, skilled in both bed and battle, kneel humbly at her feet was one of the main perks of life in the Middle Ages. Modern men had utterly lost the knack. As Collin rose, he asked, "And French invaders, as well?"

"Not yet." But soon. War was coming, and there was naught she could do to stop it. "Pembroke, Wiltshire, and Owen Tudor are marching through Powys backed by thousands of French and Irish. And worst of all, the Welsh are coming out, too, mostly Gwynedd spearmen, Carmarthenshire bowmen, and Tudor retainers."

"Fools, one and all." Collin had lived his whole life alongside Wales, and fallen in love with a Welsh witch, while watching the Tudors rise from bandit rebels to became a national menace.

"Hee-haw," Hela agreed, fluttering down onto the table.

Until Edward took the helm, King Henry's government had lurched from one disaster to the next, and Collin risked his life in losing battles at home and abroad, while the Tudors were promoted over him, given lands, castles, and seats in the House of Lords. Now they were using the wealth and position lavished on them to finance a foreign invasion.

Sir Collin made a place for her at the head of the table, ordering cousins and bowmen to stand while she was seated. He enjoyed his ambiguous position of being the "champion" of the heir apparent's betrothed. As did she. What lady would not want the most re-nowned lance in western England as her champion? Edward was man enough for any woman, but Edward was also Lord of the Marches and head of the House of York, not to mention heir to the throne. His time was not always his own—much less hers. While Sir Collin was her champion, sworn to protect her and fight in her stead in any trial-by-combat. Out of all the heavily armed thou-sands streaming toward Hereford, only Collin was solely concerned with her safety. Which meant Sir Collin and his young cousins could hang about the little Ledbury inn, eating sausage and drink-ing hard cider at Edward's expense, showing what a lark war could be, for the lucky.

Old Martha, the alewife, kept the warm spiced cider flowing, delighted by Lady Robyn's ability to attract frivolous young gentle-men who paid in silver, and never minded the price. Edward arrived in the late afternoon, happy to find his love in good hands. William Hastings was with him, along with Hastings's felonious brothers Ralph and Thomas—poor relations of the Plantagenets, but big folks back in Burton Hastings, Warwickshire. Half the town had come along, including tenants, retainers, friends, and relations. When it came time to go, a squire held her reins while Edward helped her mount. Martha kissed her good-bye, saying, "God go with you, m'lady."

"And may He abide here with you," Robyn replied. Martha's pious spirit infused the place, making it a safe haven and travelers' rest. Twice Lady Robyn had come here in times of peril, and both times she'd left refreshed and hopeful.

Martha gave her a final squeeze, saying, "Come back if you can."

"I will," she promised. This was the only inn where she ever felt at home, maybe the only such place in medieval England. Castles, manors, and convents always felt exotic—that was their charm— and the less said about dungeons, the better, but this little nameless public house in Ledbury was her private sanctuary, and its proprietress was living proof that people were the same, no matter what century. Here alone Robyn felt like she was happily in the present, just like everyone else. Even Edward liked the place.

All the way to Hereford, they had to work their way past bands of steel-clad men with bills and pikes slung over their shoulders, headed the same way they were. Ambling along at their own speed, the troops presented a hedge of steel points to any horseman coming up from behind. So Ralph Hastings had to ride ahead, saying, "Make way for the Earl of March."

He got ribald replies and grudging assent, but when she and Edward arrived, jeers turned to cheers. Men who objected to being turned off the road by the officious brother of a Midlands squire were happy to see Edward trot by. He was the boy who would get them through the coming days alive. Edward had been leading armies when he was ten, and so far had never been beaten. Moreover, he knew many of them by name, and he constantly called out greetings to the troops, happily showing off his pretty lady. Night had fallen by the time they reached Hereford, where more armored men greeted them, bearing torches and chanting.

"March! March! March! . . ."

Bells rang in All Saints, and the Cathedral Church of Saint Mary, as well as Saint John's Hospital, so all of Hereford might know that the hero of the Marches had arrived.

Having taken a night and a day to turn his small army about in its tracks, Edward collapsed in exhaustion, and for once Robyn got a restful, unexciting sleep at his side, courtesy of the Knights of Saint John. Established to protect travelers, the Order of the Hospital of Saint John of Jerusalem, later called the Knights of Rhodes and other things, was a most worldly order of warrior monks who thought nothing of giving her and Edward connecting apartments.

Sunday morning Mass officially ended the month of mourning for Edward's father and the other dead at Wakefield. Edward traded his black armor and black plumes for polished steel and a surcoat of murrey-and-blue sprinkled with white satin roses. William Herbert was there, along with Ralph of Raglan, who had survived the Tudor ambush at Lake Llangorse. Robyn congratulated him on his escape and asked if he had seen Heidi. Ralph of Raglan said he was sorry, but he feared the Tudors had her. "But the Vaughans have found a young lady lost and alone in the hills north of Hay. They are bringing her here."

Heartening news. Hopefully that would be Heidi. Whoever she was, no sane lady wanted to wander about the Welsh hills alone in midwinter—as Lady Robyn so recently confirmed.

Edward breakfasted his men on bread and cider west of town, at King's Acre, where two Roman roads diverged, one headed west up the Wye towards Hay-on-Wye and Wales, while the other ran north along the border, toward the old Mortimer stronghold at Wigmore. By concentrating at Hereford, Edward covered the southern exits to the hills, which spread in a wide arc to the south, west, and north. This forced the Tudors to come straight at him or try to slip through the hills to the north around Ludlow, Edward's boyhood home, where he knew every ford and footpath. "We have people watching every crossing of the Lugg," Edward explained. "The Tudors must meet us here at Hereford or try to get through my own lands, without my knowing." An obvious impossibility.

As she and Edward shared a cup of morning coffee, Vaughans and Baskervilles came riding down the western road, wearing freshly polished armor, with the Vaughans' Boy's Head banner flying overhead. With them was the woman whom Ralph of Raglan mentioned, wearing a Welsh cloak and mud-spattered gown, making Lady Robyn feel grateful for her freshly washed riding dress and clean underwear. As the travel-stained lady got closer, Robyn saw it was Cybelle.

Lord Audley rode out to meet his lady love, happily bringing her to Edward to report. Lady Cybelle dismounted and went down on her knees before Edward, knowing this was her moment, with knights, nobles, and massed men-at-arms looking on, and the fate of England in the balance. Heady stuff for a young French poetess, who kept silent until Edward gave her leave, her long black hair hanging loose about her pensive face. Then she rose slowly and replied with a flood of French, warning "Prince" Edward that his enemies were at hand, black-hearted earls and robber knights, aiming to despoil his ancestral lands. "They are camped a couple of days from here, beside this very same river, where there is a Saint Mary's church and water that reeks of brimstone."

There had to be dozens of Saint Mary's churches strung along the Wye, but a young Vaughan who spoke French tried to translate her story into practical geography. "Best I can tell they were camped at Builth when she left them, headed down the Wye on her own. We found her at Three Cocks and brought her in to Eardisley. From what she says, they are making for Radnor, then heading down the Lugg towards Combe Moor."

"That was two days ago," Edward declared, ordering horses saddled and trumpets sounded, fretting that the enemy might move too fast for him. "They could be in Combe Moor already, getting between us and Ludlow." He meant to march north and meet the invaders at the border. More troops were tramping up the road from Gloucester to join them, but Edward would not wait—and miss a chance to stop the Tudors on his home turf.

Robyn could feel the crisis coming. Good as it was to see Cybelle, this travel-stained French poetess was a storm petrel, the first bedraggled bird warning that the two armies were close, and about to collide. Despite this dismal news, Robyn gladly shared the last of her breakfast with Cybelle, coffee and jam pastries. "Oh, my lady, thank you." Lady Cybelle gave a low curtsy. "I have been living on offal for days."

Amazing the French would choose to invade a place where the food was so relentlessly lowbrow. Boiled mutton and field peas were high cuisine hereabouts. Robyn asked, "Have you seen Heidi?"

"Your blond companion?" Cybelle looked perplexed at the name, then shook her head vigorously. "Not since leaving camp."

"So she was with the Tudors?" Robyn had hoped Cybelle would be Heidi; still it was good to hear Heidi was alive.

"Umm, more brown witches' brew." Cybelle had taken an instant liking to sugared caffeine.

Lady Robyn gave Cybelle another pastry to go with it, asking again, "But she is with them?"

"With them? She is Lord Owen's constant companion." Cybelle sounded jealous that a blond nobody from the future should beat out a raven-haired poetess and a bevy of French courtesans. "Lord Owen does not mean to lose her a second time."

They would see about that. Lord Owen's days of riding about the country collecting young women were nearing their end, unless he had a sudden fit of good sense and retreated into Wales. Squires brought up saddled horses, a pair of speckled gray palfreys, and offered to help them mount. Cybelle protested that she had just gotten off a horse, but Edward had made it plain that he was moving, and ladies who could not keep up would be left behind. Cybelle asked if that was really so bad. "We could rest and bathe, then catch up with them on the morrow."

"Tomorrow may be too late." Lady Robyn sympathized with the desire to wash and rest, but she had spent yesterday afternoon pressing past thousands of armed men, and she did not mean to do it again. "Come," she coaxed the exhausted Cybelle, "I have good food and clean water, and I will see you have a bath and a bed tonight."

Cybelle made a face, but she mounted up anyway, not wanting to be left at the mercy of Herefordshire hospitality. Going from spy to martyr, Cybelle moaned most of the way, when not being cheered by male attention. Lord Audley lent Cybelle his scarlet cloak and jacket, ordering up a troubadour to serenade them. When this minstrel tired, the lead riders passed the lute between them, playing and singing, glad to keep the ladies happy, so long as it did not impede the march.

As always, Edward buoyed Robyn up, getting happier as he neared his boyhood home, reeling off familiar landmarks, like Burghill and Tillington Common, telling how he had hawked and hunted in these hills. Plows had turned up rich red marl, and the weathered uplands showed great bare patches of Old Red Sandstone. At each village, people rushed out to greet them, giving Edward a hearty cheer, then gawking at the knights and ladies, while men armed themselves and joined the line of march. The Tudors were coming on winding Welsh tracks, but Edward had a straight paved Roman road and less ground to cover, making up for his foe's head start. How they ever hoped to surprise Edward here, among his own people, was totally beyond her, but more practical considerations probably prevailed. Having promised their allies loot in England, it made sense to start with Edward's land. Planning campaigns based on the likelihood of plunder was an old Lancastrian tradition, since that was how Good King Harry ended up at Agincourt.

At Stretford, the road crossed a frozen stream, and a couple of miles farther along, a stone bridge arched over the Arrow. On the far side of the Arrow, a knot of armored riders came trotting over the frigid heath. Edward recognized his old governor, Sir Richard Croft of Croft Castle. Sir Richard reported that, "Pembroke's foreriders are south of the Lugg, having been seen at Byton and Combe Moor."

Edward turned to her, saying gravely, "That is less than an hour's gallop away. I must take a look."

She went with him, wishing she were riding Lily instead of a strange palfrey. Collin and his cousins came along to give her an armed escort, letting Edward attend to business. Where the Roman road reached the Lugg, there was a small crossroads where the wagon track to Croft Castle crossed the Lugg and then the Roman road before heading on into Wales. Clustered around the crossroads at the head of Wig Marsh was a tiny hamlet taking its name from a nearby stone cross—Mortimer's Cross.

Tenants came out to kneel before their knight and lord, and Lady Robyn dismounted amid dogs and children, pleased to be out of the saddle. Here Edward knew everyone by name, introducing her to the farm families, showing off Lady Robyn Stafford of Pontefract to the hometown folks, his exotic acquisition from far-off Yorkshire.

Sir Richard pointed out the importance of the hamlet, saying, "Four roads crossing two bridges come together here. Hold fast to this place, and we may block movement in all directions." Here was where the low Vale of the Arrow met the first line of Welsh hills, wooded tops rising to the north. Between the Roman road and the Lugg was a stretch of frozen waste called Wig Marsh. Anyone wanting to avoid the hills and marsh had to follow the Roman road north or south, or cross the stone bridge and head eastward toward Croft Castle. Edward's former "governor" was gracious and respectful with his suggestions, even though Edward had given the poor knight hell as a boy. Like any true teenager, Edward had rebelled against his governor, his father, and his king—in fact much of his current happiness came from having no one left to overthrow.

William Herbert's riders were sent ahead to secure another bridge a mile to the north, where the Roman road crossed the Lugg. Edward told them that when the Welsh spearmen arrived, they, too, should fall out along the road north of town. "We will be dining here."

By now Cybelle was slumped over in the saddle, nearly asleep. Robyn got some warm cider, spiking it with cinnamon to revive her, saying, "Wake up—we are here."

"We are, m'lady?" Cybelle looked about in surprise at the thatched hovels. "Where is here?"

She handed Cybelle the hot cider. "It is called Mortimer's Cross."

Cybelle thanked her and took a sip, saying, "We cannot be staying here. I can tell by the smell, there is not a bathtub or a clean bed for miles."

Robyn pointed to the stone bridge. "Croft Castle is across the Lugg, and a mile or so up the hill."

"God be praised." Cybelle took another sip, happy to be mistaken. "So what are we doing here?"

Lady Robyn indicated the lords and knights surveying the landscape and the armored horsemen settling in north of town. "This is a strategic crossroads."

"My God. Men." Cybelle shook her head and took a sip. "With a castle less than a mile away? That is what fortresses are for."

Lady Robyn agreed, being beyond arguing battle tactics with a poetess. Men shouted out that they had seen Lord Pembroke's riders. It was true, standing by the stone cross, Robyn could see over the fields sloping away to the west, to where horsemen were gathering, wearing Tudor green-and-white. Not many, but enough to know they were there for real.

Folks fell silent at the sight. Talk of invaders was one thing, seeing them at the far end of the fallow was another. Two armies, which a week ago had all of Wales between them, were now within sight of each other. To emphasize that, the first of Edward's Welsh infantry came marching up the Roman road, Usk spearmen in armored jackets, and archers from Glamorgan bearing bows taller than they were. Both sides were leading with their Welsh, since they knew the country best and would see the enemy first; while if left in the rear, the Welsh were also the most likely to melt away into the woods. Most of these men's fathers had risen with Glendower against Mad King Henry's father, and now their sons prepared to fight each other. Welsh were turning out to stop a Welsh invasion, since the split in the English royal family had split the Welsh, as well. Fratricide could be contagious.

With miles of empty moor and bare winter fields between the two armies, it seemed grossly unfair that knights and lords had to fight amid these families' homes. Children scattered to bring in pets and farm animals, while Robyn commandeered a sumpter wagon to carry the tenants' goods. When the wagon was loaded, the villagers of Mortimer's Cross headed over the Lugg bridge, and up the hill toward Croft Castle, herding their animals before them. Lady Robyn rode in the lead with a small boy seated on her saddle bow and two girls riding behind her, clinging to her cloth-of-gold waist. Collin and his cousins escorted the makeshift cavalcade.

Croft Castle smelled of baking bread. Owned by the Croft family since the days of William the Conqueror, the place was a handsome private keep with round pink-stone towers at each corner of the curtain walls. Sir Richard's wife, Eleanor, greeted them at the gate, sheltering the villagers in the bailey stables and sheds, and then making good on Lady Robyn's promise to Cybelle of a bath and a bed. Young, quick, and alert, with dark elfin features, "Laura" Croft had been Edward's governess when he was a boy, and had a wealth of horror stories about the having to oversee a headstrong, sexy "child" just a few years her junior, who outranked her from birth. "He went from debauching the serving girls to insisting on being 'lord' of the manor when my husband was away."

Robyn sympathized. There was only one real way to deal with Edward. Perhaps Lady Croft had even tried it, since there was a certain wistfulness to the woman's complaints, as if buxom, dark-haired Lady Laura wanted a second chance at being Edward's governess, just to get it right. And Edward certainly appreciated "older" women, as Robyn herself had discovered.

Changing into a clean riding dress, Robyn watched Lady Laura load the sumpter wagon with fresh loaves for the troops. Croft Castle's ovens had been baking nonstop since the first word of danger arrived. Facing either a battle or a siege, Lady Croft figured fresh bread would defend them better than spears and arrows. In a rare bit of medieval irony, peasant families would sit safe in the walled castle while knights and lords defended their cottages from the French. And though no one mentioned it, the Rape of Ludlow was on every woman's mind. Two years before, Mad King Henry, backed by Wiltshire, the Tabots, and Tudors, and most of the House of Lords, had taken Ludlow, some ten miles away. They looted the town and castle, and gave up women and girls to rape— no one expected this return visit to be much different.

When the wagon was full of bread and bacon, Robyn and Collin escorted it back down the hill, accompanied by meat on the hoof. These were Edward's home lands, and people anticipated Edward's needs, hoping to get paid for being helpful, while they treated the Tudors like the French pox, hiding animals and locking away women. At the bridge over the Lugg, Robyn saw Edward's little army laid out in the fading light, settling down around horse lines and cook fires, with the William Herbert's Welsh stretched along the Roman road to the north and Edward's own tenants and retainers camped in front of the bridge. Herefordshire troops were still arriving, along with the Gloucester militia and levies from Avon and Dorset, settling in along the road to the south, with Wig Marsh at their backs.

Lady Robyn wished it were in front of them instead. The safe thing would be for Edward to place his men on the east bank of the Lugg, with the river and Wigg Marsh between him and the enemy.

She asked Collin, "Why the west bank? Would it not be safer to fight on this bank, with the river in front of you?"

Lifting his sallet visor, Sir Collin surveyed Edward's position on the far bank. "Safer, yes, but it would not stop the Tudors. They could just block the bridge with a few spearmen, then turn south toward Leominster or Hereford. By forming up on the west bank, we can keep Pembroke from using the bridges over the Lugg or the Roman road south."

But it meant fighting with a river at his back, and by now Robyn knew that could be a death trap. She had seen Mad King Henry's army at Northampton, trapped in a bend in the rain-swollen Nene. And harpers told how Simon de Montfort and Llewellyn's Welsh were massacred at Evesham, caught in a loop of the Avon by a royal army under Edward Longshanks. As the chronicler said, "That was the murder at Evesham, for battle there was none."

Across the fields, she could see Tudor campfires spreading out on both sides of the wagon track leading into Wales. Pembroke's army was leaving the hills at last, coming down onto the flats, only to discover Edward awaiting them. Crossing the bridge, Robyn found that fences and ditches had been turned into barricades, with pointed stakes planted in the gaps to keep out cavalry. Both sides moved too fast to haul cannon around with them, so this battle would be fought the old-fashioned way, armored knights against bows and pikes. Edward's camp was like a class reunion, containing half the young men she had met since coming to medieval England. Hastings and his brothers were there, as well as Lord Audley and others from that tiny few who came over from Calais last summer, in that first burst of enthusiasm that won them London and the king. Her reins were taken by Henry Mountfort, a bowman who had been with her at Northampton. Only Matt Davye was conspicuously absent.

Edward helped her down while eager hands unloaded the wagon and led animals off to slaughter—the meatless season lay ahead, for those who lived to see it. Dinner that evening was bread, bacon, boiled beans and onions, washed down with beer and cider. Aside from some trail mix and peanut M&M's supplied by Robyn, Edward and Lord Audley ate the same as their bowmen, something Somerset or Queen Margaret would never do.

By the time her pregnant stomach felt full, night had fallen, and Edward ordered up a snug bed for both of them in one of the cottages. Though the night outside was icy cold, she lay curled in furs and body heat, while Edward fed the hearth fire. With Edward's long nude body beside her, she doubted the home owners were near as comfortable in Croft Castle. Warming herself against her love, she whispered, "This was to be our wedding eve."

"That is so." Edward gave her a kiss in remembrance. "Are you disappointed?"

"What? To be sleeping in a hovel and facing a battle in the morning?" She snorted in contempt. "I would much rather be married."

"As would I," Edward agreed, "so long as it was to you. Though it is lucky we are not."

"How so?" She felt crushed that her wedding day had been turned into a bloodletting, afraid tomorrow would cost her everything, leaving her bereft and alone, without even Heidi to help her.

His hand slid inside her silk chemise, stroking her full belly, soothing and comforting her. "Because then it would be unlucky to see you. Especially like this."

Clearly Edward meant to make the most of their luck. Reaching down and taking firm hold of her rear, he pushed them together, pulling her snug against his strong, broad chest. Even if there was no wedding, Edward wanted a wedding night. She tried to relax into his embrace, but she could not shake her fear of the morrow, and of what might happen to him. Edward whispered in her ear, "Are you worried about something?"

"Something? Everything." My God, the man was about to go into battle, which might not worry Edward, but had her pretty well petrified—so much that she felt herself pulling back, striving to protect herself.

He asked huskily, "Do you trust me?"

"Of course." With most things.

He grinned at her. "But not in battle?"

Sinking back into his grip, she confessed, "How could you tell?"

Edward laughed, running his rough, hard hands up and down her naked torso, boasting softly, "By now I well know how you feel. With eyes closed, I can sense the joy when you are pleased, the wantonness when you are aroused, and the tension when you are worried. However needlessly."

She squirmed a bit, snuggling closer. "Needlessly?"

"*Oui,*" he whispered as he kissed her ear. Edward liked to use French in bed, something he could never have learned from his mother, Proud Cis. Robyn suspected the influence of a French wet nurse, which led him to associate the language with a strange breast. He tightened his hold on her. "I have you now, and will not let go. You are mine, to have and to hold, and to keep safe. It would take more than the Tudors to pry us apart."

"*Vraiment?*" She liked having his hands on her, enjoying how his naked, insistent body engulfed her, pinning her to him, giving her no choice. Very much a blessing at the moment. No choice meant no worry.

"*Absolument.*" He kissed her breasts, then whispered, "Besides, battle is what I do best."

How true. So far, he had never been beaten in real combat, not even close. It was nice to know that this brawny young boy with his hands on her tits could indeed make everything right. He could find Heidi, set her up in London, even pay off the Italians. How lucky was she to have him for her feudal lord? "Maybe second best," she suggested, moving her hips in time to his. "Though most men would rather face a cavalry charge than a lifetime of pleasing one woman."

He laughed, fearless even in the face of matrimony. "If that is your worry, we can still be wedded tomorrow, right here in Croft Castle." With Sir Collin as best man, and Lady Cybelle and Laura Croft as bridesmaids. "Together we can do anything at all, even the impossible."

"As we have already," she reminded him.

"More than once," Edward agreed, gently massaging her, sliding his fingers over erect nipples, artfully catching them between his middle fingers, with a gentle rolling sensation she could feel in her groin.

"And that was just the two of us." She rubbed her bare body against his, saying, "Now we are three." From Edward's enthusiastic response, it was clear they would not remain three for long. Give him his way, and they would quickly be four, or more.

◆ ◆ ◆

She awoke in darkness and lay listening to Edward breathing beside her. Today she would have to leave him. This miserable hovel and these poor men were going to be engulfed in battle; she shuddered to think of the rain of arrows and the clash of steel. What a nightmare. She had been shaky enough in Goodrich hall fighting at barriers, but this would be frighteningly for real. Reaching over, she caressed her sleeping love, feeling his warm, unbroken flesh, praying to Hecate not to take him. To make doubly sure, she felt about until she found her lighter in the dark and lit a candle to Mary, as well, the first candle of Candlemas. This was Groundhog's Day, a cross-quarter day, like May Day, Lamas, and Halloween, halfway between solstice and equinox, halfway between winter and spring. And that was how she felt, suspended halfway between this terrible winter and the glorious spring she prayed they would live to see.

Edward stirred, slowly waking up to her touch. When his eyes opened, he smiled to see her staring at him by the light of Mary's candle. For once, he did not want to start where they left off last night, but took her hand instead, lacing their fingers together. She kissed their twined fingers and then asked, "Will there be a fight today?"

"Most probably," Edward admitted. "Though only if Pembroke wants one. I will not attack." Through hard marching and knowing the county, Edward had put himself securely across the enemy's path. Now he won just by refusing to move, since his forces would grow stronger each day as more reinforcements arrived. Neither Pembroke nor Wiltshire were overly bold, but Robyn guessed they would fight; otherwise, their mercenaries could not be fed and paid. Only a chance to loot the public treasury could cover the costs of this ghastly war. "Do not worry. We cannot fail." He brought his hand around to stroke her cheek. "We are at our hearths and homes, fighting for all the good that God gives man to fight for."

"That is what worries me." A war fought for "good" reasons was almost worse than a bad one, since a bad war was easy to oppose, easy to rally people against—but a war for good reasons was a prime stumper. She was still opposed to fighting, but had nothing to offer in its place. Lay down arms and let the Tudors have their way? Not likely. Next thing you knew, guys would have six wives, and the right to behead the bad ones.

Edward tried to soothe her, sounding supremely confident, saying combat was not near as dangerous as advertised. Amazingly safe, actually. He and his fellows would stand together in plate armor, with weapons at hand, blocking the approach to the bridge. "Anyone meaning to kill us will have no easy task, for it must be head-on in a fair fight."

To hear him tell it, he had little to worry about beyond an unlucky hit by a stray arrow, but that could happen in hunting— witness poor William Rufus, who succumbed to a royal deer hunt.

Unconvinced, Robyn got up, breaking the thin scum of ice on her water bucket and treating herself to a bracing icewater facial. Then she put water on for tea and dressed in a borrowed red riding gown that belonged to Laura Croft. She helped Edward arm himself, just as he had helped her at Goodrich on the night she beat the Wydvilles at barriers. There was a certain reassuring quality to encasing your love in steel, seeing each seam was tight, kissing the plates as they went in place, praying, "Keep my love safe through the hurricane of steel. Bring him back to me whole and alive."

"My squire does not normally do that," Edward pointed out. "A prayer or two, perhaps, but he does not actually kiss my armor."

" 'Tis a wonder you have survived so long." She kissed his lips, as well, showing there were other things his regular squire could not do. Then she served him ginger tea so he could face his fate halfway sober, fortified inside and out. Someone scratched on the door, and Edward clanked over to see who it was. Master Hastings, of Burton Hastings, stuck his head in the door, saying, "My lord, Pembroke is up and seems ready to fight."

Edward grinned, saying, "We will see how ready he is."

"Well, dawn will not wait," Hastings observed. Lest Hastings think she were holding him back, Lady Robyn brought her lord his helmet and candle, then followed him out into the icy gray predawn.

Edward's principal lords and retainers were gathered in the town churchyard, candles in hand, before an outdoor altar, waiting in armor for the Lord of the March. This was Candlemas, the feast of the Purification of the Blessed Virgin, which came forty days after Christmas, celebrating renewal and rebirth in the dead of winter, and the divine light shining in the darkness of human sin. They

were not about to miss Candlemas just because a battle loomed, figuring that was all the more reason to pray. She lit Edward's candle
with hers. He then lit Audley's, and Lord Grey de Wilton's, while
Audley lit William Herbert's who then lit his brothers' candles, and
so on, as the flame passed from man to man, spreading flickering
points of light throughout the army. Each candle represented
Jesus—his body, soul, and divinity. Mass began with a blessing of
the candles, followed by singing the Forty-seventh Psalm. "We have
received your mercy, O God, in the midst of your temple . . ."

Groundhog Day dawned cold and clear, just the sort of day to
drive any wise woodchuck back underground for six more weeks of
winter sleep. There would be no spring until her birthday. Robyn
shivered as she received Communion. Despite Edward's easy assurance, death was stalking his family—in the last couple of months,
he had lost a father and brother in battle, plus an uncle and several
cousins, all of whom went confidently to their destruction. Crossing herself, Robyn rose and returned to the cottage where they had
slept, collecting her things and leaving a gold ring hidden where the
family would find it.

Outside, she saw low, bright sunlight glistening on long lines of
sharpened steel across the plowed fields, shining almost straight in
the eyes of the Tudors—an advantage for Edward. Pembroke's men
were still filing in, showing some had marched half the night, only to
be beaten to the vital crossroads. At the northern end of the Tudor
line, she made out Wiltshire's red-and-gold banners and the French
fleur-de-lis facing Herbert's Welsh. Directly across from the town,
Pembroke's Gold Horse banner flew alongside French and Breton
battle flags, while south of the road, masses of armored spearmen
in Tudor green-and-white stood clumped beneath snaking red
dragon banners, with big wedges of bowmen thrust forward on
their flanks. She found Edward at the high point of the village,
where he could see all his men and they could see him. Collin and
his cousins were mounted and waiting, ready to escort her back to
the castle. Kneeling before Edward, she begged God's blessing on
him; then her lord bade her rise and helped her to mount. As she
settled into the saddle, a cry went up from the troops, "The suns!
The suns!"

Looking east above the bridge, she saw there were three suns in the sky, low and in a line, hanging over the high woods south of Croft Castle. They were not all the same, the "real" sun was in the middle and bigger than the other two, but the two smaller suns were still bright shining disks, almost impossible to look at. Frantically, Robyn tried to remember what Jo said to her that day in the Cotswolds, five hundred years in the future—"Here is a gift from Hecate. If you see three suns in the sky, do not fear for Edward."

She had thought three suns was a bit much, even for the Middle Ages—but here they were, shining down on her. Ice crystals in the upper atmosphere, no doubt, or mass hallucination. Certainly not swamp gas or weather balloons. Whatever the reason, she felt her heart lift. Her love was saved—she had history's assurance on that. Jo had read it in a book, so it must be true; science and witchcraft agreed. She called down to Edward, "You are safe. Three suns means you will not die today."

Edward smiled back at her, then turned to his men, saying, "Be of good cheer and dread not. By this sign we will win. These three suns stand for the Father, Son, and Holy Ghost, all arrayed behind us." He took her witch's promise of protection and broadened it to include the whole army, dragging in the Holy Trinity, as well; the troops loved it, cheering lustily, glad Lord Edward knew what was going on above. When the cheers subsided, he reminded them, "We fight in the name of the Almighty. Do not kill common soldiers if you can, only esquires, knights, and lords."

Edward did not consider ordinary soldiers his enemies, and talked them into surrendering whenever he could. Robyn wondered what effect this light show was having on the Tudors, first Candlemas, then this heavenly trio hanging over Edward's army—it had to be a daunting sight. Mayhap it would make them think thrice.

Slowly the three suns merged into one, and the troops again roared their approval, happy to have the heavens back the way they should be. They had only Edward's word that this was a godly thing. Edward himself was ecstatic, totally confident in her prediction, calling on one of his sergeants, Henry Mountfort, to help escort her back to Croft Castle, telling him and Collin, "You take care of Lady Stafford, and I will take care of the Tudors."

Collin tipped his lance, saying, "Thank you, Your Grace. Mine is much the happier task." How true. Collin was a Westminster champion with a long history of armed service to Mad King Henry, but he never thought politics was worth killing over. Robyn steered her borrowed mount toward the bridge over the Lugg, equally glad to be turning her back on the battle.

Medieval war and politics were incredibly personal—without mass armies or mass elections, political disputes must be settled in person, and hand to hand. Only bowmen dealt out anonymous death, and in Edward's army, at least, soldiers were punished for attacking innocents. Every man was here for a reason, from mercenaries fighting for pay and plunder to Herefordshire levies defending their homes. Lords and gentlemen, with the most to win and lose, fought in the front rank.

As she crossed the stone bridge, Robyn heard shouts behind her, and she turned to look. So far, it had been more like an armored camp meeting than a battle—but now Wiltshire's men were in motion north of the town, men-at-arms and French knights marching over the frozen furrows behind a hedge of spear points. Archers came with them, opening fire on Herbert's Welsh. Turning back toward Croft Castle, she paused again when she heard another shout behind them. Collin caught up with her, saying, "Sounds like Pembroke is advancing against Edward."

That could be the crisis of the battle, when the two centers met, and Pembroke tried to push Edward back into the Lugg. Robyn hesitated, fearing for her love despite all the heavenly portents. She asked Collin, "Can we send someone to see?"

Neither of them looked forward to sitting around Croft Castle, waiting to see who won. Arrows arched back and forth on the far side of the bridge as bowmen in the center exchanged volleys, but trees in between blocked their view. Sir Collin told one of his young cousins, "Take a look, but come right back and tell us what you see."

Without even acknowledging the command, the younger Grey wheeled his horse about and went clattering back to the bridge, meaning to see what was happening beyond the town. Robyn waited, fidgeting in the saddle—not worried for herself, with Edward's army between her and the Tudors, but sickened by the whole business, wishing it would soon be over. She had seen two battles since coming to the Middle Ages, both blessedly short.

"Who are they?" asked Henry Mountfort, pointing to some men to the north and west emerging from the trees along the river, and headed their way. They were all on foot and running hard, with even more men behind them, pouring out of the woods.

"Welsh," Collin declared, adding, "A lot of them."

"Which Welsh?" Robyn could not even tell their nationality, much less their politics. "Theirs or ours?"

"Ours," Collin reassured her. "They are wearing Herbert colors."

"Could they be reinforcements? Some of Herbert's men, coming late?" That did not seem likely, since Herbert's strength lay far south of the Lugg, and these men were coming from the northwest. Nor did they look like reinforcements, running toward the road in scattered groups, keeping no sort of order.

"Most of them do not have weapons," Collin observed. "They are fleeing. Herbert's men have broken, and these fellows forded the Lugg or fled over the bridge to the north."

Robyn could see he was right. Edward's northern wing was being routed by Wiltshire's mercenaries, and parts of it were in full retreat, throwing down their weapons and trying to save themselves. She glanced back down the road toward Mortimer's Cross, trying to see through the skeletal screen of trees. All she saw were gaunt limbs clutching at the cold winter sky. As she sat waiting on her gray palfrey, William Herbert's Welsh came streaming past them, some taking the road to Croft Castle, others headed home to the south. Collin called out, "What has happened? Where are your captains?"

They shouted back in Welsh, which Sir Collin did not speak, aside from pillow talk, but Lady Robyn heard them perfectly as they ran past crying, "Lord Herbert is dead! Lord Edward is dead! All is lost!"

PART 3

Sun in Splendor

Love not me for comely grace,
For my pleasing eye or face,
Nor for any outward part:
No, nor for my constant heart. . . .
            —Anonymous

10

❖ Groundhog Day ❖

What do they say?" Collin asked, still baffled by the fugitives' Welsh.

"That we are beaten already." Robyn left out the part about Edward and Herbert being dead. Just hearing those words made her feel hollow, and she could not bear to repeat them. Or believe them either, especially the part about Edward being slain. These Welsh might have seen William Herbert die, but they could not have seen Edward killed, who was half a mile away, by the crossroads at the head of Wig Marsh. She was closer to Edward than where they were coming from.

Collin was also skeptical, shaking his and saying, "Impossible."

Robyn nodded slowly, fighting her fear, reminding herself to breathe. She had seen the royal army at Northampton beaten in less time, but that was with Mad King Henry in command. Edward could not be beaten that quickly, much less killed, yet frightened Welsh continued to stream past, throwing aside weapons and armor, headed south for Hereford. William Herbert was surely beaten, if not dead. Looking cautiously to the north, with lance in hand, Collin reminded her, "Wiltshire's people may pursue."

For all she knew, Wiltshire's men were already over the Lugg, and the wise course was to retire to Croft Castle, putting several feet of stone between her and trouble. Though Sir Richard was with Edward, Laura Croft would certainly put up a smashing defense. Yet the words "Lord Edward is dead" echoed in her head. It was impossible to think of just holing up in Croft Castle, hoping to hear Edward was well. She must see for herself, and the road back to the bridge lay clear and empty. No Welsh were headed that way, and Collin's young cousin had not reappeared. She nodded at the empty road and the screen of skeletal trees. "I want to get word of Edward."

Collin tipped his lance toward the north, where Wiltshire's riders might easily burst from the woods at the heels of the Welsh. "What if we get cut off from Croft Castle?"

How badly did she want to stand a siege with Lady Laura? Not a lot. "Then I would rather be with Edward."

Collin obliged, sending a sergeant down the road to see what happened to his cousin. Best thing about having a champion was that you got to make the decisions, while he merely saved you from mishaps and reckless mistakes. Before the sergeant got halfway to the trees, Collin's cousin come pounding back up the road, calling out, "Dire news, sir!"

"What news?" Collin demanded. Robyn's throat tightened, fearing Edward had been harmed after all.

Reining in, his cousin reported gravely, "Herbert's Welsh are routed."

Collin waved his lance at the fleeing infantry. "That much we can see."

Disappointed that the disaster had gotten ahead of the news, the young fellow added, "Lord Pembroke is assaulting our men by the bridge."

"And Lord Edward?" Robyn asked, hoping this witless young Grey knew something that they did not.

"Alive and well, and fighting hard to hold the crossroads." He sounded much more cheerful than the situation warranted, pointing at some high ground overlooking Wig Marsh. "You can see his banner from that break in the trees."

Robyn decided to see for herself, urging her mare off the road and onto the high ground along the Lugg, where she could get a wide view to the south and west. As she approached the break in the trees, she heard shouts and the clanging of axes and war hammers on plate armor, sounding like a continuous multicar crash happening close at hand. Boys from the village lay on the hilltop, sneaking a peek at the battle. Dismounting, Lady Robyn joined them, judging the knoll to be well out of arrow range, with a river and a swamp between them and the action. "Luckily," she told the boys, "neither side has cannon."

"How absolutely rotten!" complained an older boy, hoping to see real firepower. The troops nearby were not even fighting, all the combat was at the crossroads, where Edward was engaged.

"What are cannon?" asked a younger companion.

"Giant iron-hooped barrels that belch fire and hurl huge stones," his elder explained, "filled with fire demons that explode in air. One of them blew up the King of Scots last Lamastide."

Young eyes went wide with wonder. "Outstandingly awful!"

"Huge black metal barrels," another boy elaborated, "so big they must be hauled in wagons. They shake the earth, rolling over men and beasts, blasting everything in their path." Youthful enthusiasm turned primitive medieval cannon into tanks, showing that any imaginative peasant boy could easily foretell the future of armored warfare.

"Where are they?" Younger boys leaped up, straining to see.

"Luckily, they do not have them," the first boy reminded them sarcastically.

"How rotten!" chorused his companions.

Sorry, no cannon. These lads would have to wait to see the age of gunpowder. On the far side of Wig Marsh, Robyn could make out the armored backs of Herefordshire billmen, with archers thrust out on their flanks. Mounted knights and men-at-arms were massed under the banner of Lord Grey de Wilton, another of Collin's many relations. Facing them across the furrows were Tudor pikemen clumped beneath red dragon banners, flanked by Carmarthenshire archers. Saxon and Cymry faced each other across the furrows, neither showing much inclination to attack. All the fighting was farther north, where masses of pikemen headed by French and Breton men-at-arms tried to push onto the stone bridge, fighting for hedges and ditches. Amid the men facing them, Robyn could make out Edward's murrey and blue banner, emblazoned with the White Lion of March and sprinkled with white roses. So long as that flag flew, his men knew he was alive and fighting. And so did she.

Collin rode up and reined in, much to the delight of the excited peasant boys, who got to inspect a knight up close. His cousins, squire, and mounted valet joined him, followed by Henry Mountfort and the bowmen. Collin pointed with his lance, saying, "Wiltshire is holding back."

Robyn saw what he meant: north of Edward's position, a solid block of armored infantry sat astride the Roman road, bearing red-and-gold banners and the lilies of France. Those were Wiltshire's victorious troops, having beaten the Herberts, but making no attempt to aid Pembroke, who was having a hard time of it. In fact, as she watched, Pembroke's troops began to fall back, scrambling through ditches under a rain of Yorkist arrows, leaving a trail of armored bodies behind.

Happily Edward made no attempt to follow, and the battle subsided. With no movement on the field below, Collin and his men dismounted, loosening their armor. So long as Edward's white lion banner snapped in the frigid breeze above the vital crossroads, there seemed small chance the Tudors would come crashing across the Lugg. Pembroke had failed to move him, and Wiltshire had not even tried. Nor did the Welsh on the far side off the fallow way show much sign of assaulting their Saxon neighbors. This seemed an excellent time to stop, and maybe open negotiations. "Now the French are wishing they had brought some cannon," Collin observed. "At Formigny they galled us with their fire until we came out from behind our trenches. Here they have no way of forcing Edward out."

Direct attack had proved fruitless, and Robyn could feel the momentum shift. The Tudors had led a successful march from France and Brittany, through Pembroke and Powys, gathering recruits as they went, always growing, always moving—right up to Mortimer's Cross, where they had been stopped. Now events hung in the balance. Collin summed up the odds, confidently acting as her military adviser. "Without the Herberts, Edward is likely outnumbered, but Pembroke has little chance of moving him, even if Wiltshire will help."

"So what will the Tudors do?" It seemed awfully late to hope for something sensible.

Her champion considered. "They could turn about and return to Wales, where they have good hope of eluding Edward, since his own Welsh are in disarray."

"Or they could sit down and talk peace." By far the best suggestion.

Collin smirked at her optimism. "Wiltshire, for one, will be wondering if it is time to run."

Or they could do something totally unexpected. As she and Collin stood watching, the Welsh on the far bank started to move, not heading straight across the furrows at the armored Hereford-shire infantry, but shifting southward, staying out of arrow range, aiming to cross the Roman road south of Wig Marsh. She asked her champion, "What are they doing?"

"My lady might well ask." Collin clearly did not think much of the maneuver. "Mayhap they hope to wrinkle Grey de Wilton out of his trenches by putting themselves across the roads to Hereford and Leominster." South of Mortimer's Cross lay the Herefordshire farmlands, low rolling country filled with poorly defended towns and villages, since most of Herefordshire's readily available armed men were here with Edward, arrayed right in front of Robyn, beneath the banner of Grey de Wilton. "Edward has archers cover-ing the fords of the Lugg," Collin observed, "and his people are defending Kingsland, but beyond that, there is nothing. If the Tudors could get across the roads south, Edward and Grey de Wilton must come out and attack them."

When learning to be a witch, the first rule Jo drummed into her was "Be very, very wary what you wish for."

As she watched the Welsh move sideways, a break opened in the Tudor lines—between Pembroke's beaten troops, and the Welsh headed south—with nothing but a screen of bowmen and skirmish-ers thrust forward to cover the hole. This screen got thinner, and thinner, as the archers fanned out to fill the widening gap.

Without warning, a shiver went though the English line, as Grey de Wilton's cavalry lowered their lances and then charged. His armored infantry came right behind them, scrambling over their own trenches, headed straight at the bowmen screening the gap. These archers only got off a couple of quick vollies before mounted knights and ax-swinging infantry plowed into them, scattering the lightly armed bowmen. Edward's attack had come, but instead of Grey de Wilton dashing himself against Dyfed spearmen, the blow fell on the weak spot in the Tudor line, bursting through with dev-astating effect.

Rout proved instantly contagious. Without bowmen to cover their flank, the Welsh spearmen came under a withering fire from advancing Herefordshire archers. Unwilling to face fire they could not return, Tudor infantry began to throw down their pikes, streaming southward down the roads they had hoped to hold. Then for the first time Robyn saw Edward's white lion banner start to move, as her love led a great armored charge against Pembroke's shaken center, which was also flanked and under fire. "They are done," Sir Collin declared, having been beaten enough times to know the signs. "Wiltshire could save them, but he will not."

Robyn pictured the pretty, cynical face of James Butler, Earl of Wiltshire and Ormond, a man concerned only with himself. If Wiltshire launched a spirited counterattack, Pembroke might be saved. In fact, an alert, talented commander could even have taken Edward's attack in the flank, rolling it right up—but by holding the last unshaken Lancastrian troops out of the fight, Wiltshire ensured the rout would be complete. Before Edward even made contact, Pembroke's troops broke and fled.

"What now?" Robyn asked. Being in the winning camp was a novelty to her, as well. This was the first battle that did not end with her fleeing for her life or sitting defenseless in a tent, waiting for some armed stranger to lift the flap. War was so much more tolerable when you were winning.

"Whatever my lady wishes." Collin was literally at her command. Another nice novelty.

"Where would the Tudor camp be?" she asked. "I have a friend I need to free."

Collin surveyed the fields to the west. "Somewhere between here and Combe Moor."

Heidi was out there somewhere, and her protector, Owen Tudor, was dead or fleeing. Anything could happen, and probably would, knowing Heidi. She asked her champion, "Can you get me there?"

Collin gauged their chances, having a dozen armed and mounted men with him. "We can try, my lady."

"Good, for I fear we may be needed." Ironically, they avoided the worst of the carnage by riding straight back the way they'd come, over the bridge on the Lugg. It was not until they passed the crossroads that Robyn started to see armored bodies, where Pembroke's attack had been turned back, and Herbert's Welsh overrun. She tried not to look, but could not always avoid it, even recognizing one, Ralph of Raglan, lying faceup in a frozen ditch, his helmet shorn off by the blow that killed him.

Most of the pursuit was to the south, so the road into Wales was relatively free of such horrors, though littered with spent arrows and dropped pikes. Wiltshire's men were getting away northward in good order, while the rest of the fugitives fled south over the fields and into the woods, avoiding the roads, which were swarming with Edward's horsemen.

They found the Tudor camp being looted by Devon knights, local militia, and Shropshire bowmen. Sumpter carts were upended, and baggage lay torn open and strewn about, while dogs and archers picked through the wreckage. French knights in full armor stood defiant guard over a single tent backed against some trees, lances leveled and refusing to budge. Hopelessly outnumbered, the dozen or so mercenaries were afoot and unable to flee, with only their armor and lance points to keep off the enemy. Archers faced the French with bent bows, calling out in Shropshire to surrender, though the French knights could make nothing out of, "Put down your pig-stickers, you goddamn peacock-buggering bastards."

Seeing a massacre in the making, Collin rode forward with raised visor, ordering the archers not to fire. Easing back, the bowmen obeyed, and Collin turned to the French commander, tipping his lance to say, "Sir Collingwood Grey of Greystone, at your service."

Raising his visor, a rugged-faced forty-something Frenchman replied, "Sir Louis de Coutes, banneret to Jasper Tudor, Earl of Pembroke. How do you mean to serve me?"

Sir Louis's companions laughed through their visor slits, glad their leader knew how to answer an Englishman. "Serve us wine, if you would," someone shouted in a Breton accent, "this day has been a thirsty one."

Collin joined in the laughter, then explained, "I was hoping to take your surrender."

"You? To take all of us?" Sir Louis thought it was bad enough to be beaten, without suffering insult, as well.

"*Moi?* Heavens no," Collin assured him. This was not Sir Collin's fight, being here solely as her champion and having no particular quarrel with Sir Louis de Coutes. "But I would be happy to accept your surrender in the name of my Lady Robyn Stafford of Pontefract."

"Lady Pontefract?" Sir Louis looked hopefully at her.

She urged her mount forward, acutely aware that bows were bent and she was the only one not in armor. Stopping in front of Collin, she told Sir Louis de Coutes, "I am she, Lady Robyn of Pontefract. Will you surrender to me?"

Unable to believe his luck, Sir Louis de Coutes grounded his lance and went down on one armored knee. "Lady Pontefract, it would be my pleasure."

Shropshire archers and vagabond knights were not good enough to yield to, but give Sir Louis a lady, and he happily laid down his lance. She asked sweetly, "And your men, as well?"

"Of course, my lady." What else were they to do?

Money-minded archers stepped up, claiming the prisoners were theirs, along with any ransoms due. Collin calmed them with a promise to see they got half. "For you may have captured them, but it was Lady Robyn who disarmed them."

"Our arrows would have disarmed them soon enough," objected a truculent archer. Victory had made him grasping.

"In which case, you would have gotten nothing," Collin retorted, noting that the covetous French were loath to give good Louis d'Or for punctured corpses. "My lady got them to surrender alive, and that is where the money lies."

Knowing they would get nowhere arguing with a knight, the bowmen grudgingly accepted half, able to walk away richer on a day that had left many men dead. Dropping their lances, the French surrendered, and archers swarmed over them, giving gleeful insult, while snatching away swords and knives. Even the suits of plate armor the Frenchmen wore were worth more than a plowman made in a year, while ransom payments might easily make a bowman wealthy for life. When an archer tried to enter the bulging tent, Collin stopped him with his lance, saying, "See to your prisoners. What is in this tent falls solely to Lady Pontefract."

"Why so?" demanded the bowman, not liking the tone of this pushy Cotswold knight.

"Because my Lord Edward of March would have it," Sir Collin assured the belligerent bowman. "If you doubt me, feel free to ask His Grace."

Rather than take his complaints to the earl, the archer stepped aside, and Collin dismounted. Seizing the tent flap, he said to Robyn, "If my lady will permit?"

She nodded, and Collin lifted the flap, peering inside. Squeals of feminine protest came from within, causing Sir Collin to step back, smiling, and let the flap fall. Someone inside called out, "Collin? Was that you?"

Heidi stuck her blond head out, staring hard at Sir Collingwood Grey, who had never seen her before. Heidi grinned broadly, saying, "Collin, it *is* you! Hallelujah!"

Dropping the flap, Heidi disappeared back into the tent, and Robyn heard her shout in medieval French, "Put away your rosaries, ladies. Sir Collin has come to save us."

Confused conversation came from within as Heidi coaxed the mademoiselles to come out. It was somewhat endearing to know that what French mercenaries chose to protect with their lives was not the pay chests or the Earl of Pembroke, but the camp followers. No self-respecting Frenchman could stomach the thought of pretty females falling into English hands. Where they would surely be misused by ham-fisted clods, brutes who could not even kiss right until the French taught them how.

Heidi reappeared, stepping out this time, dressed in Tudor colors—a long, green, low-cut gown embroidered with white hounds and trimmed with red velvet roses. She curtsied low to Collin, showing off her cleavage and getting hoots and applause from the looters and bowmen.

Reassured by Heidi's enthusiasm, women emerged from the tent, which was jammed beyond capacity. Most were knight's mistresses and serving women, though there were Welsh, as well, and soldiers' wives, and their children. Smiling shyly at the bowmen, a few of the French women recognized Robyn and waved, happy to see someone they knew, now that they were in enemy hands. And with good reason. Every man hereabouts had heard of the rape of Ludlow, a tale that grew ever more lurid in the telling. At Ludlow an invading royal army raped English farm wives and teenage virgins, so taking revenge on French whores was practically a national duty.

Heidi only had eyes for Collin, staying on one knee, gushing out thanks for, "your heroic and thrilling rescue, coming to our aid like a knight from a fairy tale. You have my eternal, heartfelt appreciation." Ecstatic to have her knight in armor appear out of nowhere, Heidi made it plain she would do anything to show her appreciation.

Some men might have been embarrassed by having a strange blonde practically proposition him in front of giggling foreigners and jeering bowmen, but chivalrous Sir Collin acted like it happened every day. Taking Heidi by the hand, he lifted her up, graciously accepting her thanks, saying that saving damsels was just a sideline at the moment, "I am here escorting Lady Robyn Stafford."

Luckily for Heidi, Collin was on the clock, since battle has its own rules—and any woman that brazen risked ending up in the tent and on her back, to the cheers of the assembled bowmen. Bryn or no Bryn. Looking up, Heidi saw her sitting on her horse, and she shouted, "Robyn!"

Dismounting, Lady Robyn hugged her long-lost production assistant, provoking another round of cheers from the armed mob around them. She could see the French women were thrilled by the friendly reception Owen's girlfriend got. For all they knew, the "Goddamns" meant to kill them all—just as their mothers vowed. Heidi herself was almost in tears, saying, "I thought I had lost you for good. When I saw Collin, I should have known—"

"Makes two you owe me." She had not only freed Heidi, but also brought along Sir Collingwood Grey, the man Heidi had lusted after across the ages. Few bosses took such diligent care of wayward employees.

"How did you ever manage?" Heidi wiped her eyes. "Was it magic?"

"Some." Robyn was in no mood to recount everything that had happened since she lost Heidi at Llangorse Lake. Her rescue by Edward, their stay at Goodrich Castle, and their escape was a story that had to wait. "There was a battle, and the Tudors lost—"

"No shit!" Heidi nodded at an arrow-studded corpse lying in the center of the sacked camp.

"Edward is chasing what is left of them halfway to Hereford." So far, Jo's prophecy of the three suns seemed to be holding, but she wished Edward were here at her side. "Wiltshire's people got clean away, along with some of Pembroke's cavalry. Everyone else is scattered—or dead."

Slowly Heidi absorbed what had happened while they'd huddled in that crowded tent. "Is Owen dead?"

"I do not know." Robyn shook her head, then winced, adding, "but Ralph of Raglan is."

Her friend looked aghast. "That nice guy who led us to the lake?"

She nodded grimly. "Lying in a ditch just down the road."

Heidi blanched, without even having seen it. "God, that makes me sick."

"Me, too." She gave her friend a squeeze. "Which is why we need to get out of here." In less than a week, this whole mad invasion had gone from absurd to awful. Six months ago at Northampton, the troops had all been English, and not very eager to fight—a third of the royal army went over to Edward before a blow was struck. Mortimer's Cross was infinitely worse. Despite Edward's plea to spare common soldiers, this battle had become a horrific slaughter, spurred by ancient antagonisms, pitting Welsh against Saxon, and English against French and Irish—leaving Lady Robyn with two dozen women and children to see to safety.

She got her escort to right one of the sumpter wagons and hitch up a pair of horses; then Sir Collin invited the women aboard, offering safe escort to Croft Castle. All of them cheerfully accepted, not wanting to hang out in a war zone when their own men were dead or missing. Smiling bowmen hastened to help them board, handing up children and possessions, along with freshly looted presents. Edward of March ran a godly army, and he would not let women be abused if he could help it. Anyone wondering how the French did it had to find out the old-fashioned way, by convincing some young female adrift in a strange land that what mademoiselle needed most was a stalwart Shropshire bowman.

Sir Louis de Coutes presented himself to her, going down on one knee, giving his parole, promising her proper ransom, and that he would not attempt escape, saying, "My lady warned me it would come to this."

"I did?" She did not remember meeting Sir Louis before.

Her prisoner nodded. "I was at the table when you told the Earl of Pembroke that Edward would meet us at the border, and there would be hell to pay. Never was there a truer seeress."

She shrugged off that bit of prophecy, saying, "I knew Edward—that is all."

Sir Louis added, "And you have my thanks for giving these women protection, for I fear for them, and would they were not here."

"Then you should not have brought them." Robyn had scant sympathy for the men who had made this mess.

"My lady, that was none of my doing," Sir Louis protested, "for I was a page of Joan the Maid, who would never allow women with the army."

Robyn smiled to think that this fellow had known Joan of Arc. "Except for Joan."

Her prisoner smiled back. "The Maid was a most exceptional woman."

No doubt. Lady Robyn bade him rise, meaning to talk to Sir Louis some more—but since he was her captive, there was ample time for that. Her champion helped her mount; then she led everyone back down the road toward Mortimer's Cross and Croft Castle. Sir Louis de Coutes and his companions walked in armor behind her, escorted by Collin's cousins on horseback, as much for the prisoners' protection as for dramatic effect. Behind them came the wagon, piled with women and children, while Henry Mountfort and his horse bowmen happily brought up the rear. Riding pillion behind her, on the "maiden's seat" atop the crupper, Heidi asked, "How are you doing?"

"Wonderful, now that I have found you." It felt good to have Heidi on the horse with her, someone solidly on her side, with whom she could be utterly honest. Heidi was the only nonmedieval she knew nowadays. The only other person in the whole world who had ever heard a jazz CD or chipped in for feta-and-pineapple pizza at 3 a.m.

Since she found Edward, Heidi had been the person most conspicuously missing. Suddenly, Lady Robyn's world was more or less coming together. Deidre and Matt, her maid and horse master, awaited her at Greystone. All she lacked for the moment was Edward, and she meant to find him before sundown. Until then, she trusted in Jo's prophecy. Heidi reached around and patted her belly. "And how's the kid?"

"Fine, I suppose." She felt relaxed and thankful, and had to assume the baby did, too.

"Just do not keep putting off that initial prenatal appointment," Heidi advised.

"Right, first thing in the morning." God, she was going to have to start shopping for a midwife—what a trip that would be. "How about you?"

"Me? Never better." Heidi shrugged off her recent captivity. "Owen was mad at me for running off, but much more manageable after I fucked him."

What man was not? "It was not totally rape," Heidi told her. "By the time they dragged me back to camp, I was ready for bed, and if it had to be Owen's, so be it."

Heidi never used to say things like "so be it." Robyn smiled at the medievalism, squeezing her friend's hand. "Wiltshire's bed would have been softer."

Heidi gagged audibly. "Gawk, if you like sleeping with one eye open. Wiltshire gives me the creeps."

Robyn agreed, along with half the kingdom. Too bad, actually, since the former treasurer and chief tax collector was otherwise rich and handsome. Also cautious—Wiltshire had been first to flee, taking the last intact troops and leaving his companions to face Edward alone. Lying along the road were men Wiltshire had deserted, Breton mercenaries and Pembroke's Welsh, who died trying to force the English to live under a mad king and a French queen. Seeing them so stiff and still was sobering, and it took the joy out of having Heidi with her.

Cheers and jeers greeted them at the bridge over the Lugg. Sir Collin Grey was notorious for his reluctance to kill and for his ill luck in battle, so having him come riding in behind Robyn and Heidi, followed by a dozen prisoners and a cart full of fallen women, provoked hoots and applause from the Gloucester billmen guarding the bridge. Ralph Hastings was there, bearing messages from his brother, who was with Edward. "Pursuit continues, and I expect Lord Edward will pass the night in Hereford."

Which meant that once her prisoners were safely lodged in Croft Castle she must head for Hereford. When Lady Robyn's small parade got to the castle gate, tenant women were coming out, headed home, now that the invaders were routed—their places about to be taken by French women who must be kept safe from their men. Mademoiselles waved and smiled, while tenant wives looked straight ahead, sternly ignoring them. One would have thought Mortimer's Cross was a major French victory. English daughters hanging on their mothers' hands looked back, wide-eyed and curious, gaping at the grinning foreign women in outlandish costumes.

Cybelle was there to greet them, along with Lady Croft. Cries of recognition came from the cart, and Cybelle insisted on kissing everyone as they got off. Heidi slid down, and Robyn dismounted, finding herself in an astonishing reunion of the women from last week's wayside meeting on the Roman road north of the Afon Tywi. Since that day, they had been through an icy hell of forced marches across frozen roads, ending in a ghastly battle, where the army they had been with was roundly beaten. Yet they were all miraculously alive and together, if only for the moment. Before she could think of heading south, Robyn needed a meal, a bath, and a bit of a rest. Heidi had not felt hot water in days, nor had any of the women from the wagon, making for a crowded bathhouse. Cybelle was there, as well, offering to pour and towel, just to be a part of the party. Adding hot water to Heidi's tub, Cybelle noted, "There is writing on your rear."

Heidi laughed, looking back at her butt. "Do not worry—it won't wash off."

"Where did you get it?" Clearly the young French poetess had never seen the like.

"Don't know," Heidi admitted. "Totally comatose at the time."

"Is it in English?" Cybelle puzzled over the inscription, which was high up on the left cheek. "What does it say?"

"This end up." Written in neat, red block letters.

Cybelle straightened, asking, "What does that mean?"

"Means you been to a party." Heidi smiled at Cybelle's surprise. "You know you have been to a damn good party when you wake up with 'this end up' tattooed to your butt."

Warmed, bathed, and fed, Lady Robyn headed south, having Laura Croft's promise to care for her prisoners—anyone who had been Edward's governess could certainly handle a few dozen French invaders. Heidi came with her, and Cybelle, all escorted by Sir

Collin and Henry Mountfort's bowmen. This was the same road she had ridden up on Sunday, and the difference was disheartening. Ditches that had been frozen and empty were littered with dead bodies and discarded weapons. As usual, the Welsh on both sides suffered worst, having the least armor and the fewest friends. No one needed spellcraft to see that coming. From the moment Pembroke and Wiltshire disembarked their hoodlums-for-hire, Lady Robyn knew things would end badly for the Welsh.

Hereford was small to begin with, and now it overflowed with armed men. She met Edward by the market cross, and he led her through cheering troops to the pink sandstone Saint Mary's cathedral, where they gave thanks together. Kneeling in Mary's own house, Robyn thanked the Mother of God for keeping Edward safe and whole, and she prayed for the souls of those who died on both sides. Which side they died on mattered not to Mary, whose sole concerns were forgiveness and mercy.

Edward gave earnest thanks, as well. She could feel him kneeling at her side, as he had during their Sherwood miracle, when Mary saved them with a breath of spring. Strange how she once meant to cure Edward of his medievalism, and instead ended up deepening his mysticism, introducing him to paganism and spellcraft. All with the best intentions.

When they were done, Edward led her out a side door in the nave, into the cloisters, to the cathedral library—where suddenly they were alone, for the first time since Hastings scratched at the cottage door that morning at Mortimer's Cross. Just them and the Mappa Mundi, a rare vellum map of the world already a hundred years out of date. What they must do just to get a little time alone, sleeping in hovels and now necking in the library—served her right for dating a teenager. Edward stripped off his leather gloves and pulled her against his armored body, saying, "It is so incredibly wonderful to have you safe beside me."

And it was wonderful to be safe, to feel his steel-clad arms enclosing her, even in a church library. She whispered, "I was terribly worried for you."

"For me?" He sounded surprised, and touched. Why should she worry for him, encased as he was in armor and surrounded by men-at-arms? Edward always acted like battle was not very dangerous, and certainly not enjoyable—all his hot-blooded lust was for her. "You feared I might be hurt?"

"Yes." Despite Jo's prophecy and his bland assurance, she had been terrified—it would take way more than three suns in the sky to quiet her quaking heart. "I could not bear to sit in Croft Castle and wait. So long as you were in danger, I kept having to tell myself to breathe."

"How sweet." Sticking his gloves in his hip boots, he pulled her closer still, pinning her against the bright shining scars on his breastplate as he kissed her hard on the lips. Shocked and thrilled by what he did to her mouth, she could feel the scrapes and dents in the metal she kissed that morning. Metal that had kept her love alive.

Breaking off the kiss, he whispered, "I was in absolutely no danger. Pembroke could not break our line, and Wiltshire was afraid to even try." Edward never feared his enemies. He feared doing wrong or he feared losing her, or having his family harmed—but he did not fear his foes. "Fools and cowards cannot hurt me. You alone could do that."

"How so?" Despite all her fears and tears, he seemed impervious to harm right now, holding her tight against his armor. Even the sun in heaven heralded his successes.

"By being so overbold and taking too many risks." One hand tenderly stroked her cheek, while the other kept her pressed against him. "Ralph Hastings says you captured a score of French knights."

"Oh, that!" As usual, she totally forgot her own escapades. "Young Master Hastings exaggerates."

"Undoubtedly," Edward murmured, sliding his free hand inside her riding gown, stroking her through the thin silk underneath.

"Only a dozen, and they were not all knights," she protested, knowing full well he had her. "Several were armored squires, and one a mere grosse valet."

His hand dropped down to her hip. "Nonetheless, most impressive for a damsel with child."

"I had help." Obviously. Collin and his cousins, Henry Mountfort, several dozen archers—that did not even count the baby, who was a constant inspiration to her.

"And a wagonload of French harlots," Edward added.

"Again, young Ralph exaggerates," she informed him primly. "Not all were French, or whores; the wagon held Welsh wives and small boys, as well."

Edward shook his head at her protests, saying, "No one is going to remember that."

He was right, of course. And to show it, he kissed her again, taking total possession of her mouth. When their tongues untied, he asked, "So why did you do it?"

"Come, I will show you." She lifted his hand off her rear and took him to meet Heidi.

Curious monks were waiting outside the library door, but Edward explained that "Lady Stafford is a student of languages, and had to see your library, which is justly famous throughout the Marches."

Lady Robyn agreed, saying the visit was most uplifting. "You have a wonderous library, and if ever I am staying in Hereford, I shall surely apply for a card." She saw by their knowing smiles, the monks even half believed her, courtesans being notoriously brainy and educated, promiscuous in mind as well as body.

Another cheering mob of armed men awaited outside the cloisters, applauding her and praising Edward. Suddenly she was thrust back onto center stage, sharing her love with all of England. Living at the eye of the storm meant they could barely go out in public without provoking applause, and every serious political question facing the kingdom had to be thrashed out by them in bed before it could be presented to the people, making for a most exhausting relationship. More people were waiting at the nearby hall of the Knights of Saint John, including Heidi, Collin, Cybelle and Lord Audley, the Hastings brothers, Henry Mountfort, and even William Herbert, amazingly back from the dead—though nothing would bring back Ralph of Raglan.

Still wearing Tudor white-and-green, Heidi knelt solemnly before Edward, symbolizing his total victory. Looking weary and travel worn, Owen Tudor's sometime lady, Heidi of Harlech, begged the Earl of March's protection—her former lord being a fugitive from the law. Edward happily granted her wish, saying, "Lady Robyn has told me from the very beginning that you favored my suit. You have my warmest thanks."

Heidi smiled sweetly up from her knees. "If Your Grace is half as wonderful as Lady Robyn claims, she would be daft to turn you down."

Edward said he would try not to disappoint her. "We are rude and simple folk, not what you are used to in Holy Wood."

Heidi assured him that folks in Hollywood were pretty rude and simple, too. "You have all made me feel much at home."

Having given thanks and seen Hereford safe, Edward got back in the saddle, planning to secure the upriver crossings on the Wye. He said his good-bye in armor, leaning down to kiss Robyn while she balanced on the mounting block, holding on to his stirrup. She whispered up to him, "Please do not follow them into Wales." She thought of the farmstead in Powys where she and Heidi got such a fairy-tale greeting, while girls harped and children sang. Thousands of these thatched farms from Powys to Pembroke would soon be mourning their dead—they did not need another Saxon invasion, as well. "It will just make things worse."

"I vow not to pursue them into Wales." Edward had seen the havoc wreaked on the Welsh, and he had no desire to hammer them further.

"Will you sleep here tonight?" she asked. Otherwise, she would have come through frozen hell to Hereford for nothing.

Edward smiled at her insistence. "I will be back by vespers."

Then he was gone, taking most of his troops with him. War and politics went away, and Hereford returned to being a sleepy county town locked in winter. Snow crowned the high walls and the crooked spire of All Saints' Church, while Robyn's apartment by the hall of the Knights of Saint John had both fireplaces blazing. She and Heidi sat warm and snug, enjoying broiled sea bream, slivered almonds, cooked carrots, and Spanish sherry, feeling free at last. For the first time since Wiltshire's men assaulted them on the way to Harlech, they were not on the run, not menaced by the law or having to put out for some lord. Pouring Heidi more sherry, Robyn asked, "What do you think of him?"

Heidi took the goblet, asking innocently, "Who? Edward?"

Lady Robyn poured some for herself, as well. "Of course Edward. How many incredibly rich and attractive boyfriends do you think I have?"

"Six or eight," Heidi estimated, "from the way you were busting your panties to get back here."

She shook her head. "Sorry, just Edward."

Heidi shrugged. "He's okay, if you like that type."

"What type is that?" She'd never met a man even remotely like Edward.

"You know." Heidi yawned. "Handsome, heroic, rich, charming, and sexy—"

Before Heidi could finish with first impressions, there was a rap on the door and a sweet voice saying, *"Excusez-moi."*

"Entrez," Robyn called out, "we are decent."

"Mostly." Heidi took a slow sip of sherry.

Cybelle stepped silently inside, shutting the door behind her, then standing with her back to it, holding the latch down with her hand. With unruly black hair half-covering her face, Cybelle whispered conspiratorially, "They have Owen."

"Oh, my God!" Heidi's face went white. Her former lord was the last person Heidi wanted to see in Hereford.

"Owen Tudor?" Robyn sat bolt upright, spilling her sherry. "How did it happen?"

"Some local peasants." Cybelle said it like she could not believe it. "They caught him and brought him to Hereford."

"What will they do to him?" Heidi looked horribly worried.

Lady Robyn was at a loss. "I do not know."

Her anguished friend asked, "Will you talk to Edward? Please? I do not love him or anything, but I cannot bear to see him hurt. He was good to me, most of the time."

"I'll talk to Edward." What she would say was something else. Everyone assumed she had the power to sway Edward, which in some ways she did. She had wheedled a promise to spare the Duke of Somerset out of Edward, but no one knew that, not even Somerset.

Heidi had to see Owen at once, just to be sure he was all right. He was held in Hereford Castle, a great double-walled keep, as big as Windsor, but falling into ruin. Lady Robyn easily convinced Lord Grey de Wilton's men to let them in, especially since she brought the sherry. Few medieval Englishmen could resist a trio of pretty foreign "ladies" of dubious repute. Add alcohol, and duty became a distant memory.

Owen Tudor was overjoyed to see them. He sat on an oak stool in a closely guarded presence chamber, no longer in armor, but wearing instead a stylish, high-collared red doublet over white-and-green hose. Nonetheless, he looked haggard, like he had aged ten years in the last week, and his voice nearly broke when he called out, "Heidi, my sweet love, how happy to have you here."

Heidi could hardly say the same—still she hugged him and asked if he was hurt, acting more like a solicitous daughter than a former kidnap victim-cum-girlfriend. Owen told how he had been captured, saying that after Pembroke and Wiltshire failed to break Edward's grip on the crossroads, there was talk of a parlay—but only talk. "With nothing much to offer Edward of March, we decided on one more attack, though no one stepped up to make the assault—so it fell to me, since my men had not been bloodied."

And they were bloodied, with disastrous results. Owen's Welsh had been the first to break, and they bore the brunt of the rout. Now Lady Robyn had to pick up the pieces, trying to save the Tudors from their own folly.

When Edward returned, Robyn went to see him at once, leaving Heidi with Owen. Edward was famous for his clemency: Somerset had beat Edward's father in battle and driven the Yorkists from their ancient family home in the north, yet he spared him. Owen's ineffectual invasion of England was a pinprick compared to that. She met her love back in their private apartments and was instantly in his arms, thanking him for returning as promised. She added, "I hate to be a burden to—"

Edward kissed her before she could finish, taking a long leisurely moment to explore her mouth. Out of armor for the evening and wearing a fetching silk tailored jacket over murrey and blue hose, Edward assured her, "You are never a burden, never in the least. You are the single soul who gives me what I most dearly need."

"Sometimes." There were other times, too, when she made third-millennium demands on his medieval conscience. "Right now I must beg a favor. Not for myself, but for—"

He stopped her again, this time with a fingertip. "Please, no. Pray do not even say it."

"Say what?" She watched his look turn serious.

His hands fell to her hips, taking firm hold of her. "You are going to ask me to spare Owen Tudor, and I cannot."

"Why?" She could not believe he was so abrupt and uncompromising, so unwilling to hear her arguments.

His hold on her hips tightened. "I am weary of seeing decent plowmen and brave knights dying for nothing. No one wanted this but Wiltshire and the Tudors, so why should they be spared? Better to spare the common soldiers and put an end to those who led them into treason."

She slid her arms around his neck, trying to entice him into mercy. "Owen Tudor treated me well when I was in his hands, saving me from abuse by Wiltshire's men."

"Were it not for the Tudors, the Earl of Wiltshire's men would not have been there to abuse you." He was right, of course; left to his cowardly self, Wiltshire would have stayed safe in France.

"Nonetheless, he protected me." She was doing this for herself as much as for Heidi. Owen had been an obnoxious oversexed bore, but that was not a capital offense, especially in 1461, and Owen would always have her heartfelt thanks for taking her out of Wiltshire's hands. That he did not flat-out rape her afterward was an added bonus.

"You are well worth protecting." Edward gently stroked her hips, letting her feel his concern. "All that shows is that he is a man of sense, at least when it comes to women."

"Then why cut off his head?" Or anybody's, for that matter? Third-millennium England got on amazingly well without hangings, beheadings, or even the odd impaling, proving Brits could behave themselves without the threat of gruesome execution.

"It is no more than what they did to Salisbury and my brother." Edward had strong personal reasons for discarding his usual clemency; his father's head currently adorned Micklegate Bar, the main gate to York, topped by a paper crown.

"Which is no reason to emulate them." The men who committed those murders were Gilbert FitzHolland and Lord Clifford, villains who gave even the Middle Ages a bad name.

Edward grimly refused to budge, saying, "My brother Edmund was not a warrior, and he had harmed no one. My uncle Salisbury was protected by the Christmas truce and Somerset's pardon. Owen Tudor could have made his peace with me at anytime, keeping his titles and castles—instead he wanted killing, and that is what he will get."

Tears welled up as she asked, "What about fair trials?" That was a promise she wrung from him when they first left Calais to liberate England, that no one would be executed except for real crimes, after proper trials. "You swore to abide by the law."

Edward sighed, saying, "That was when we were rebels. Now we are the law. If a Herefordshire judge and jury condemn Owen Tudor, it will be to please me. Better that it should be on my head alone."

He had her there too. People hated how lords corrupted the courts, intimidating judges and juries. Hereford still seethed at the Herberts for marching out of Wales five years ago, occupying the town, and forcing an inquest and quarter sessions to convict their enemies, killing under guise of law. Edward meant to act "in person" as Earl of the March, answering for his actions to Mad King Henry and the House of Lords. Nor would it do Owen any favor to have him hear his death sentence from a Saxon judge, like some Welshman caught with a pilfered pig. Seeing her tears, he softened, lifting his hand to caress her wet cheek. "I value your well-being above all else, but women throughout the Marches will weep over dead sons and lost husbands who would be with them were it not for Owen Tudor."

Wiping aside tears, she asked, "When will it happen?"

"A priest and headsman are already waiting." Edward was not one to dawdle over unpleasant tasks. "Why do you cry for him? Was he that good to you?"

She shook her head. "I am not crying for Owen. I am crying for you." Robyn had been proud that her noble boyfriend did not stoop to taking revenge, and now however good his reasons, things would not be the same.

When she got back, Heidi knew the bad news just by looking at her boss lady's face. Owen, on the other hand, was in rare spirits, swigging sherry with two pretty women, forgetting for a moment the ghastly mess he had made of the morning. Knowing what was coming, Lady Robyn had brought more sherry, and she had no intention of dampening the party. While Owen was recounting his exploits to Cybelle, Heidi whispered, "How bad was it?"

She grimaced. "Really bad."

Heidi kept the smile stuck to her face, but Robyn saw her eyes go sad, starting to tear up. Something horrible was happening, and there was naught they could do but uncork the second bottle of sherry, sipping it over ice before a roaring fire. Heidi smiled wistfully at her sometime boyfriend, saying, "Do not feel bad about being beaten—your descendants will be ruling this place."

Owen looked drunk and puzzled. "My descendants?"

"Yes," Lady Robyn backed Heidi up. "Your great-grandchildren will be kings and queens of England."

"Truly?" Owen hardly knew what to make of the statement.

"They are witches," Cybelle declared eagerly, "so they would know."

"Then let us drink to my royal progeny." Owen happily lifted a glass. Cybelle was spilling coven secrets, but it barely mattered, since they were talking to the dead.

Vaughans arrived, bearing Edward's order, and Heidi began to cry. Owen told her, "Weep not—it will all come out well."

So you say. Lady Robyn followed them to the market square, hanging on Heidi's arm. Cybelle brought up the rear. There was already a big crowd waiting. So as not to show favorites, Owen's captains were being executed with him, including her old dinner companion, Sir John Throckmorton. She had warned Sir John it would likely come to this, but he, too, had not listened.

Owen was not unduly alarmed, trusting in Edward's notorious clemency, assuming he would be given the choice of submitting to the new order. Even seeing the stock and the ax did not faze him, though it reminded Robyn horribly of Salisbury's death at Pontefract. Trumpets sounded, and a herald read the indictments, accusing the men of having broken the king's peace, and of waging war against their sovereign lord, which was the only blatant untruth, since they had waged war on Edward and the Royal Council, not on Mad King Henry—but everything good or bad these days was done in Henry's name.

When the herald finished, Roger Vaughan ripped the high crimson collar off Owen's satin doublet. Their willingness to ruin such a rich doublet finally convinced the former Master of the Queen's Wardrobe. No one cared about his beautiful doublet, because he was about to die in it. Luckily it was red. Even imminent death did not totally dampen Owen's spirits, and he said his good-byes, apologizing for so suddenly leaving the party, adding, "That head shall lie on the stock that was wont to lie on Queen Catherine's lap."

Robyn did not mean to see that, or have Heidi see it. So as soon as Owen was led off to the priest for last rites, she hustled her sobbing production assistant into the nearest church. There they knelt before the altar, surrounded the hundreds of candles left over from Candlemas that morning, and Robyn prayed for Owen, Throckmorton, and for Edward, who knew not what he did.

Heidi was never very religious, but right now she was pouring out her soul in heartfelt prayer, eyes closed, hands clasped. Tears rolled down her smooth, soft cheeks. This morning's emotional roller coaster had been hard enough on Robyn, and her ex-boyfriend was not the one being beheaded.

When the cheering outside ceased, Lady Robyn knew it was over, but Heidi kept crying and praying, her slim blond body shaking with sobs. What had she gotten this poor girl into? Heidi had come here with the best intentions, to help out Robyn and help herself to Collin—but her "make love not war" philosophy had gotten her assaulted, nearly raped, then dragged about the Welsh countryside by armed gangs. Now the one man who had shown consistent friendly interest in her was having his head cut off; anyone new to medieval England found such unfairness horrifying.

Reaching over, Robyn put her arm around her friend, hugging Heidi to her. Heidi nestled in, but did not stop crying. Vespers bells began to toll, and parishioners filed in, ignoring the two fine ladies sobbing on their knees. Normal folks with any sense knew to keep their distance from the nobility, even ladies in distress. This latest disaster began when Owen Tudor landed in the lap of a sad young queen.

Pulling herself together, Heidi wiped her eyes, muttering, "Poor, poor Gwyn. This will totally kill her. She really loved the big fat jerk."

And cute Little Owen no longer had a father. Heidi must have thought the same thing, because her tears returned, followed by more big wrenching sobs. Hoping not to make too much of a scene, Lady Robyn lifted Heidi up and led her out, whispering, "These people want to pray."

Big mistake. Heidi went willingly enough, still bawling her eyes out and hanging on to Robyn, stumbling out of the church and entering the market square, which Lady Robyn instantly regretted. Perched atop the market cross was Owen's bloody head.

Robyn froze, another mistake, because Heidi immediately looked up, opening her eyes for the first time since they left the church. Seeing Owen staring back at her, Heidi screamed hysterically.

Clamping a hand over her friend's mouth, Lady Robyn retreated into the church, letting go only when Heidi went back to sobbing. Slowly the crying subsided, though they continued to get curious stares, as Heidi fell to her knees. Robyn wondered if she would have to carry her friend back to the apartment, but instead of just lying there, Heidi began gathering up the Candlemas candles, which covered nearly every surface and parts of the floor. Robyn whispered, "What are you doing?"

Heidi did not answer, but she kept on collecting candles, filling the white lace apron on her Tudor green gown. Then Heidi turned and trudged resolutely out into the cold market square, head down with blond hair falling in her face. Without looking at the head, Heidi walked up to the market cross and dumped the candles on the ground, then arranged them in concentric circles around the cross. People in the square stopped to stare. When Heidi ran out of candles, she rose slowly and walked over to Robyn, asking, "Got a lighter?"

She handed one over, and Heidi reentered the church, emerging minutes later with more candles, and a hankie dipped in holy water. Dropping the candles at the base of the cross, Heidi stepped up onto the pedestal and began to wash the blood off Owen's dead face.

No one tried to stop her. Most of Hereford considered Owen Tudor a Welsh bandit turned traitor, and for every man he brought with him, two had risen up to oppose him—which was why he died. Yet even Owen's worst enemies let him confess, and saw he had last rites, before cutting off his head. Ultimate judgment was with God. Owen's head sat on the cross not to punish him, but as a warning to others—there would be peace in the Marches, and no one, high or low, could break it with impunity. If some daft woman wanted to wash the frozen blood from his face and set out candles for his soul, Hereford did not have the heart to stop her.

Done washing his face, Heidi went back for more candles, which she placed around the newly washed head, lighting them with her lighter. Then she went back for more. These candles were not mere throwaways; they were public offerings, hand-dipped by local families, brought to church with much ceremony and individually blessed by the priest. Yet Heidi was allowed to take them at will, burning them in honor of a dead rebel.

Folks certainly thought her mad, and assumed her travel-stained Tudor colors meant Heidi was one of Owen's many harlots—the fellow had, after all, seduced a queen. But medievals had a soft spot for harlots, especially crazy ones, and made a red-haired whore out of Mary Magdalen, who attended Jesus on the cross and at his tomb. Much as they loved the pure sinless Virgin, they had to give her a wanton sister, Mary the Whore, who knew sin yet willingly gave herself to God. Which made for a weirdly tolerant-intolerant society that would burn you alive for being a Baptist, but let some mad strumpet light public offerings for the soul of a beheaded criminal.

Hundreds of candles burned at the base of the market cross by the time Heidi was finished. Twilight slowly faded over the sea of twinkling candles as night finally fell on a day that began with three suns. Heidi dropped back to her knees to pray, her hair becoming a wild blond halo in the candlelight. Robyn waited patiently while Heidi prayed, then took her hand and helped her rise. Edward's strumpet and Owen's whore walked hand in hand back to their lodging, in a fitting end to the Groundhog Day from hell. Having ridden over thirty miles, and literally been through a battle, all Lady Robyn wanted was to sleep. Too bad really, since this was to have been her wedding night.

11

⊶ Friday the Thirteenth ⊷

*H*eidi poured medicinal brandy atop that afternoon's sherry, then passed out in Robyn's borrowed bed, just like old times. Back in Hollywood, Heidi customarily crashed at Robyn's place after being dumped—but having her boyfriend beheaded was an absolute first. Usually Heidi just wished them dead. Robyn undid the buttons on her friend's bodice and sleeves, then eased Heidi out of the stained Tudor gown, wrapping her in a warm soft coverlet. Heidi's tangled hair and tear-streaked face had to wait until morning.

Leaving Cybelle to watch over Heidi, Robyn went in search of Edward, finding him in the adjacent apartments, sitting in a massive carved wooden chair and wearing the crimson robe edged in gold she had sewn for him—proof he was thinking of her. Embers glowed dimly in the fireplace, and a captured Tudor battle flag hung behind his head, a red dragon breathing fire on a green field dotted with red roses—reminding her of the white rose ring on her finger. She was not just marrying a man, but a cause, a generational struggle for the heart and soul of England.

Edward did not move, silently eyeing her entry, his gaze following her as she moved about the room, busying herself by adding wood to the fire and lighting candles to go with the lamp. Finally he asked softly, "Do you hate me?"

She shook her head. "How could I?" Recrimination was pointless. Nothing could bring Owen back, so they would just have to go on without him. Any Welshman crazy enough to try to force a vindictive French queen and an infant king on the English throne had to expect the Saxons to take it badly—but she had hoped for better from Edward.

Walking over to his chair, she stood before her lord, not bowing or kneeling like the rest of the country must. At eighteen, Edward had no real superiors, and she alone was his equal, and until today, an equal who got her way, at least when it was life and death. In the past, they had quarreled over his family's insane ambitions—but in the last couple of months, those mad ambitions had cost him his father, uncle, and oldest brother, leaving no one to quarrel with but themselves, for they were now effectively ruling England, with the power of life and death over almost anyone—as Mad King Henry's stepfather just found out.

Edward reached over and took hold of her gown, drawing her to him. The sure, hard hands gripping her waist had been in battle that morning, wielding a steel ax that ripped through plate armor and linked mail, severing flesh and bone. Bards were already composing ballads about the havoc young Edward of March had wreaked. Her love was not just Lord of the Marches and heir to the throne, but also the most dangerous man on the field. Despite all the horrors of the day—or because of them—his hands felt exciting wrapped around her hips, arousing and sustaining at the same time. Many men had died today, but not hers. Still, there was no thrill at a victory so dearly won. Northampton had been an almost bloodless triumph that won them the kingdom. Mortimer's Cross was ten times worse. Here on Edward's home turf, his people had bled horribly just to stave off invasion. Instead of celebrating, they clung to each other for animal comfort. Edward whispered, "This was to be our wedding night."

Who could forget? She thought about their betrothal in the gilded chapel at Baynards Castle, saying their own vows, kneeling before a ruby-studded altar on Mary Magdalen's Day. That had been *très* romatic, all feasting, finery, sweet music, and secret fornication. She leaned in and kissed her love, saying "I want to be married in London."

Edward looked surprised, not expecting her reaction would be so specific. "In London?"

What were Jo's other two prophecies? Trust to London, and if her baby was a girl, name her Grace. Jo's most improbable prediction was the three suns, and that came incredibly true. So Lady Robyn would trust to London and hope for a girl. "At Baynards Castle. I want a safe place for our baby." If they were running England, they should start running it right. Much as she adored the

English countryside, London was the seat of power, the most populous city, and greatest port, England's window to the world.

"It will be a month or more before I can be there," Edward warned. "Wiltshire has gotten clean away, with most of his French knights, and Pembroke still holds his castles in Wales." Wiltshire and Pembroke's apparent escape made the disaster almost perfect. Owen was a better man than both of them, and he paid for it with his life, while they still lurked about, looking to do mischief. Edward sighed, saying, "I must make sure they do not just catch their breath in Brecon, then come stealing back over the border." Another reason Owen died was to leave the Tudors nothing to return for.

"You will not chase them into Wales?" The last thing Robyn wanted was Edward storming into Powys, leading a Saxon army.

He laughed at her concern. "Fear not, I would far rather be in London dancing with you than tramping about the Welsh hills with Wiltshire and Pembroke."

Pretty faint praise. What sensible young gallant would not rather be with her? After the morning's events at Mortimer's Cross, she refused to hang around in Hereford, passing Owen's head whenever she went to market while Edward rode hither and yon, on what was bound to be a snipe hunt. Pembroke would merely hole up in one of his Welsh castles, while Wiltshire would probably slip away to rejoin Queen Margaret. Lady Robyn, on the other hand, was going to London, the sooner the better, and she told her lord as much. "While you are seeing to the Marches, I'll be babyproofing Baynards Castle."

"Babyproofing?" Edward had trouble imagining the family castle under infant attack.

"Making sure it is safe for our child." She did not worry about exposed electrical outlets or the woeful lack of baby gates, but she did want a warm, sanitary birthing room that would double as a nursery.

"You will make a magnificent mother," Edward assured her, pushing up her skirt, planning to more closely inspect the baby-maker.

"I will?" She had her doubts, but it was way too late to act on them. Abortion was legal nowadays, but easily as dangerous as childbirth.

His hands found flesh, sliding under the uplifted gown, pulling her closer to him. "Our baby is not even here," he told her, "and you are already cradling and coddling."

"Pardon?" She reached down and pressed his warm hand against her smooth bare abdomen, saying, "Our baby is right here."

"Are you positive?" His hand slid down into her panties. "Mayhap we should make doubly sure."

Triply sure, from the way he grinned at her. Good. But he was not going to get his way with her, not tonight. She could not get that ghastly scene in the market square out of her head, or the morning's massacre at Mortimer's Cross. Easing his hand out of her pants, she told him, "If my lord wants me, he had best come to London."

"Why so?" Edward did not want to let go.

She spoke gravely, so he would not mistake her seriousness. "Because I would very much like to pass the night with my lord, but I cannot bring myself to make love in Hereford."

"Is Hereford really so bad?" Edward looked shocked. "It is a simple and pious town, practically choked with churches, though we are not presently on sacred ground," he added hastily, meaning they were free to fondle. "The place has a plain, rough-hewn charm."

"Not so long as the head of the man who sheltered me decorates the market cross." She used to pride herself on wildly imaginative excuses for disappointing a date, but she never expected to use this one.

Edward relaxed his grip, knowing no good would come of trying to force her. During her nine months in medieval England, she had been jailed, kidnapped, hounded (with real hounds) even racked in the Tower, but never successfully raped. And not for lack of trying, since she had been assaulted by everyone from a border bandit to a royal duke. Not that Edward was the type to try, getting laid being the least of his problems. What he really wanted was her, body and soul, in his heart and in his bed. He slowly shook his head, asking, "Were you put on earth just to throw obstacles in my path?"

"Probably." She leaned in and kissed him again. "Without me, your life would be way too easy."

"So I have discovered." Edward changed tactics, lifting her onto his lap while sliding his hand into hers, trying to cuddle and arouse her at the same time.

Good, but no go. She liked having his arms enfolding her and even enjoyed how his hand felt under her dress, she just could not bring herself to make love, not after all the misery she had seen. Resting her head against his shoulder, Robyn whispered, "Mary put me in your path."

"Mary Mother of God?" It said a lot about medieval men that Edward could skillfully run his finger between her legs while naming the Blessed Virgin.

"That very one." She tightened her thighs around his hand, secretly thanking Mary for sending her such a marvelous man. "I used to think it was Duchess Wydville that did it—or Joanna Grey. Now I know it was Mary, for without me, you would have things all your own way." In a matter of months, Edward had gone from titled teenager-in-exile to the most powerful lord in the land, fabulously rich and unbeatable in battle. Edward had no real restraints on him, except for heaven and Lady Robyn. "Mary wants you to yearn for something outside yourself."

"But I do," Edward protested. "I yearn for you."

"That is surely a start." She lifted his hand out from between her legs, kissed him tenderly on the fingertips, and then retired to her own apartments, to be there when Heidi awoke.

Lady Robyn left for Greystone next morning, knowing that Edward would come to London all the quicker if she were there, waiting. She rode at the head of a small cavalcade that included Heidi and Cybelle, Henry Mountfort, Collin and his two cousins, plus squires and attendants, and several of the French prisoners, a dozen-odd souls, showing how much her household was growing. Cybelle was coming to London because Audley's wife was arriving in Hereford, and her "friend" on the other side was hiding in the hills, or dead. When time came to divide the spoils with the Shropshire archers, all Lady Robyn wanted was Sir Louis de Coutes, who had been Joan of Arc's page—not that she needed a captive, but Robyn could not let go of such an interesting fellow. This turned out to be harder than it sounded, since two of the other prisoners were Sir Louis's valets, which he could not do without. Nor could Sir Louis hope to survive English cooking, so he needed one of the French women to cook for him. He selected a woman called Chantal, who had a young daughter named Marie, making four attendants for one prisoner, but Sir Louis de Coutes swore that he was worth the trouble and would bring a handsome ransom: "My lady will profit immensely from our association."

She would have to see. Edward also awarded her ninety gold nobles to cover her half-share in the captured armor. Suddenly Lady Robyn was in the money again. Temporarily. Her first payment to the Venetian bankers was due at the end of the month, fifty silver marks on Saint Porphyry's Day. Saint Poverty's Day. Fifty marks was most of the money she had. And there was another, bigger payment due on May Day.

Resigned to seeing her go, Edward immediately turned the trip to his advantage, assigning Henry Mountfort to be her sergeant-at-arms, charged with seeing that Baynards Castle was secure. He asked her to see that his mother and brothers were safe, until he could get to London, and he begged her to keep an eye on King Henry VI, "for His Royal Highness needs constant watching."

"As does the Earl of Warwick," she noted. Richard Neville Lord Warwick, "the Kingmaker," was Edward's first cousin, and the only great noble who had been with him from the beginning. Warwick currently had charge of London and King Henry, but Robyn had never trusted him. He was vain and cruel, and likely to turn on Edward. Warwick hated her, as well.

"Yes, by all means, keep watch on Warwick." The Nevilles had been Edward's allies since birth, but he trusted Robyn far more than all the earls in England. "And take good care of our child," he added, putting his hand on her belly. Moving his hand down to where the baby really was, she kissed him, remembering her Witches Night dream in Nest's little cottage, where she was transported to Baynards Castle, and surprised Edward in bed. Maybe it would come true. When the kiss was over, he vowed, "I will be in London for your birthday."

Then he helped her mount, and Lady Robyn set out down the Tewkesbury road, wearing her scarlet riding gown trimmed in cloth-of-gold, with her armored champion at her side, trailed by female companions, armed retainers, and prisoners of war. Most impressive, considering that three weeks ago, she and Heidi and been hiking south from Harlech with a single backpack and a couple of bottles of water. From female vagabond to the lady of Baynards Castle was not a shabby turn in the wheel of fortune.

Past Ledbury, she crossed the high sharp line of the Malvern Hills, descending onto the flat floodplain of the Severn. Herefordshire and the Marches were gone, and ahead lay the broad rolling Midlands, the rich heavy clay heart of England. Fording the Severn at Tewkesbury, she was back in thoroughly familiar territory, though Tewkesbury, with its stone abbey, wooded park, and water meadows, always made her uneasy, as if something unhappy had happened there, or would happen. Witches' warnings were often pretty unspecific.

Finally, she saw the high wooded line of the Cotswold Edge, rising above the Vale of Isbourne. Her first month in the Middle Ages had been spent in the Edge country, where the limestone ridge of the Cotswolds broke through the heavy clay of the Midlands plain. Greystone, Sir Collin's ancestral home, sat atop that ridge, overlooking Snowshill manor, flanked by pasture, parklands, and Littleworth Wood. Last time she saw Greystone had been in the third millennium, when she and Heidi came seeking Bryn—and found only Collin. Now the manor was again looking grim and medieval, though the new roof was finished, and the wooden floors were restored in the great hall. Fire marks from last summer's sack by witch hunters were still fresh. With time, the burn marks would fade, but they would still be faintly visible centuries later. Robyn remembered seeing them the day she first arrived in England. She had stood in Greystone's posh, modern, glassed-in entranceway, wondering idly what caused the fire, and what people's lives were like "back then." Now she knew.

Matt Davye and Deirdre met her at the bailey gate. Big, broad-shouldered Matt, conscious of his position as her horse master, remembered to bow, his crimson cap in hand. Deirdre, her teenage red-haired Welsh-Irish maid, just squealed with delight, climbing barefoot up the side of Robyn's high saddle, to hug and kiss her lady—one of the many reasons why most noble ladies avoided Irish chambermaids. Cybelle looked horrified, and the men laughed aloud, while Heidi smiled for the first time since Hereford. And once again, the medieval Bryn got to see Lady Robyn come riding up with Collin in tow—small wonder the Welsh witch was continually trying to send her to a distant millennium.

Tuesday, 3 February 1461, Saint Blaise's Day, Greystone, Gloucestershire

Hooray! I have my journal back. This little electronic bit of me has been missing since that foggy night in the Stiperstones. Well, now I am happily back from the future—with spare batteries! Lady Robyn has returned, ready and recharged.

This is certainly my most impressive descent on Greystone. Usually I arrive a step ahead of the law, fleeing witch hunters last April and returning in November, wanted for heresy and treason. But Edward has ordered all charges dropped, and I have prisoners of my own now—who are quite a hit at Greystone. Jo and Joy were both raised on French cooking, while Collin and Louis are delighted to swill brandy and refight the Hundred Years' War—a family feud among French aristocrats, some of whom happened to rule England.

Heidi, Deirdre, and I are all jammed into a third-floor room, clean and smelling of new-cut timber—but none too spacious. Heidi, on the other hand, is still a wreck, and being here is not helping. Bryn is in residence, and having a depressed Heidi living under the same patched roof as Collin and his beautiful wife is driving me nuts. Nor is Bryn the type not to notice. Witches Night could turn into a real nightmare. I need to get to London, if only to have a room of my own.

Robyn was delighted to have Deirdre back with her, especially with Heidi in the dumps. And brave, steady Matt was a most welcome addition now that she had three French prisoners to watch. Lily, her white Arab mare was here, as well. All in all, Greystone should have been a grand reunion—but without Edward, it was just a stop on the London road.

Robyn was not the only one who heard London calling. Ten-year-old Joy besieged her mother with requests to go, alternating tears and tantrums, until Jo could no longer stand it, saying, "Take the ghastly little changeling with you. See how much she brings on Cheapside."

Joy looped her arms around her mother's neck, saying between kisses, "Thank you, thank you."

Jo accepted the thanks and kissed her back, saying, "Now be gone, my difficult, sweet bastard."

Her black-haired bastard daughter beamed. Medievals thought nothing of sending children off to live in other households, believing they could learn from strangers better than from their own parents. Robyn readily accepted, though this medieval Joy was just as much a handful as the future girl.

So Joy came along, while Collin stayed. Lady Robyn's champion was also lord of a manor, and if the Tudor invasion was over, then there was work to be done. Plowing and lambing were already under way, while beans, peas, and mustard waited to be planted when the weather was right. Amiable Sir Louis became the ranking gentleman, riding at Robyn's side, disarmed but not the least defeated, wearing his white beret at a jaunty angle atop long graying hair. Old enough and French enough to thoroughly enjoy being the prisoner of pretty women half his age, Sir Louis de Coutes already counted his ransom well spent, making the most of this godsend. Their concerns were his concerns. As they rode south and east from Greystone over bare frozen fields, passing Lower Swell and Upper Slaughter, he asked, "Why is your sweet blond companion so sad?"

Without delving too deeply into Heidi's personal life, Lady Robyn told her captive, "She regrets the men killed on both sides, and the execution of Owen Tudor. As do I," Robyn added, lest Sir Louis get the wrong idea.

Sensing sympathy from his captor, Sir Louis asked. "Lord Edward's lady grieves for the men her lord conquered?"

"*Certainement.*" Her eyes were dry at the moment, but the deaths weighed heavy on her, especially Owen's. Until now, she had been proud of everything she and Edward had done together. Now that sense of innocence and mercy could never be recaptured. "Heidi just does not hide her heart as well."

Sir Louis smiled, saying, "You remind me of Joan the Maid."

"Really?" What a rare compliment.

"Joan, too, wept for the dead, even the English, since they died with their sins still upon them." All Frenchmen assumed the English had sins aplenty to confess. The French nickname for them, the "Goddamns," came from an Englishman's favorite expletive. "She cried at wounds, too, unless they were her own."

That Joan could weep for people who vowed to burn her matched all Robyn had heard about the teenage saint. Others could well take note. She thought of Edward's coldheartedness after Mortimer's Cross. "Men seem able to turn off that emotion, saying, 'If it is not me, or mine, it does not matter.'"

"Too true, my lady." Sir Louis de Coutes seemed genuinely sad, but it might have just been polite agreement.

For a while they rode in silence; then Robyn asked, "How did you become Joan's page?"

Sir Louis de Coutes stared off over the frosty landscape, remembering a distant spring. "When the Maid came to Chion to meet the king, she was lodged in a tower of Couldray Castle, and my lord made me her page. I was fourteen or fifteen, and the Maid was a few years older, a bright-faced farm girl, smart, pious, and gentle. I lived with her all day in the tower, seeing to her needs, and at night she liked to sleep with young women. And like my lady, Joan was graceful on horseback, so perfectly poised, you would think her born in the saddle."

"I was Miss Rodeo Montana," Robyn replied modestly.

"At Orleans, Joan had to ride about, showing herself to the people, or they would have broken down the door to her house. They never tired of seeing her ride."

That reminded Robyn of those heady July days when Edward and Warwick first liberated London and it looked like England was theirs for the asking. Crowds followed her and Edward wherever they went, happy just to watch them ride by. She asked, "Were you hopelessly in love with her, as well?"

"Of course." Sir Louis sounded wistful. "We all loved her. Not as men love women, though. Mine was the selfless love of a boy for something holy, pure, and brave that was also a girl, with ripe young breasts and a ready smile. Truth, beauty, and valor, all embodied in a grown girl eager to do good—who led you into battle, then sat and sang you children's songs afterward, while sewing a rip in your shirt. Such a love is something men feel only when they are young and the world is new. When we see honor and valor for the very first time and think it will last forever."

That was how Edward made her feel last summer, when this mad adventure first began—when he risked his life for her, wanting only a kiss, and for her to be his lady. "Like love for the Virgin?" she suggested. "Chaste but impassioned."

"Precisement." He nodded, then looked seriously at her, saying, "Joan was not a witch. At least not like my lady."

Robyn could see Joan's burning still angered him thirty years later. Small surprise—some hurts were so painfully deep, they never went away. She asked innocently, "What makes you say that?"

Louis de Coutes seemed a bit embarrassed, saying, "I was told Lady Pontefract was a white witch."

"Mayhap." Among friends, Robyn did not mind being called a witch. And though he was technically a captive enemy, Robyn liked Sir Louis enough to be honest. As honest as she could be with a man, at least, since there was much about witchcraft not meant for male ears. She decided to let Joan be her guide. "Did Joan tell you about her voices?"

He considered for a moment, as if he, too, was searching for trust. "Only that they guided and comforted her, and that they came from God."

Robyn nodded smugly. "Then you do not know for sure what sort of witch Joan was."

Sir Louis de Coutes looked unconvinced. "Do your visions and voices come from God?"

"Absolutely," she assured him piously. "Everything does."

"My lady is most right." Old Sir Louis knew better than to argue with his spirited young jailer, especially when she was in such a forgiving and merciful mood.

Wednesday, 4 February 1461, Saint Agatha's Eve,
Littlemore Nunnery, Oxfordshire

It is fun to be back here at Littlemore. Last time through, I was being hustled into exile by the Hastings brothers, homeless and on the run—and tremendously popular. Nothing excites a nun like a fallen strumpet, down on her luck and ripe for the picking. They get a vicarious look at the wicked world outside, and a potential pretty recruit. Now I feel like the harlot who made good, with a purse full of gold and a castle for lodging, fine inspiration to any wayward nun.

When I get to London, I need to make more inquiries about a printing press. Nothing ever came of the Venetian promises to find one, but the Hanse merchants swore they could get a good working press in Cologne, complete with type for less than twenty marks. Worth looking into.

Lady Robyn arrived in London at dusk on a cold Witches Night, riding down Oxford Street past Saint Giles in the Fields, then taking Drury Lane to Wych Street. At the Temple, she turned east on Fleet Street, following it to Ludgate, where Henry Mountfort announced her to the guards; then she was home, riding through her own gatehouse and into the small irregular inner ward. Stable hands took the horses, and Robyn ordered torches lit in the main hall and fires kindled in the keep, finding herself for the first time totally in command of a castle. At Pontefract she was indulged by the Duke of Somerset, who held the real power, but here she was completely in charge until Edward arrived.

In a short ceremony, Edward's steward and bailiff were confirmed in their posts, while Henry Mountfort was made castellan and Matt Davye made marshal of the stables. Then she told Deirdre to show Heidi and Cybelle to rooms in the keep, while she and Joy went to fetch Beth Lambert, for this was Witches Night. Matt's first task as marshal was to saddle fresh mounts, then ride with them through the dark icy streets to the Mercery in West Cheap, the commercial heart of the city. There they stopped at the black-and-white timbered town house of John Lambert, Sheriff of London. Which showed how much Lady Robyn's fortunes had changed. Having fled London under indictment for necromancy and treason, she was now returning to borrow the sheriff's little blond daughter for a witches' Sabbath. Such was the power of Lord Edward, even at a distance.

While servants saw to their horses, Lady Robyn paid her respects to Sheriff Lambert, easily one of the richest and most powerful men in London, a master merchant and former alderman. Someday men like John Lambert would be running England, with scant help from the "weaker" sex—but right now Sheriff Lambert must be polite to smooth-talking foreign women on dubious errands in the dead of night. Even offering up his firstborn daughter. Why? Because Lady Robyn of Pontefract was boinking the Earl of March. That simple, pleasant sweaty act made her more powerful than almost any man in the land. Edward of March had defied his royal father for her, and it was generally assumed he would cheerfully break any lesser man whom Robyn cared to name. Running the country based on who was doing whom did seem weird and anarchic—but medievals absolutely swore by it. Attractive foreigners, like Owen Tudor and Duchess Wydville, routinely fucked their way to the top levels of English society. Which, if you thought about it, made a good deal of sense—what better import was there than sexy strangers?

Glad that all Lady Robyn wanted was his daughter, the sheriff turned her over to his wife, Amy, who waited with daughter Beth in an upstairs bedchamber. As soon as Robyn and Joy entered, the two little girls ran and grabbed each other, hugging and kissing, neither having seen the other since November. Which left Lady Robyn alone for the moment with Amy Lambert, a slim lady in her thirties with big blue eyes and a heart-shaped face, the daughter of a rich grocer from Cripplegate. This always felt a bit awkward, since Robyn wanted to ask, "Do you know I am training your little girl to be a witch?"

There just was no polite way of phrasing it. Amy knew Lady Robyn was a white witch, and must have heard all about how London constables found her little blond Beth in the Baynards Castle presence chamber on Halloween night, kneeling in a black smock on a chalk pentagram point—along with the rest of the coven. Yet Amy Lambert happily turned her daughter over to Robyn again. Seeming to sense her concern, Amy told her, "We feel so very honored, having our Beth in Your Ladyship's household, and hope she serves you well."

"That is comforting," Robyn confessed, "for often I fear we expose her to unnecessary peril." Besides the disastrous Halloween bust, Beth also helped thwart a royal kidnapping at Greenwich.

Amy sympathized. "These are perilous times, even for children."

How true. Robyn wondered, was this woman a witch? Amy and her sisters were very tight, and the Lamberts were dedicated Yorkists, both signs of a secret coven—but covens were secret for a reason. So long as Amy never admitted what her daughter was doing, it could not be held against her, a sort of spiritual "don't ask, don't tell." Having lain on the rack in the Tower basement, Robyn knew the fewer secrets you had to spill, the better. Under torture, every fact, every name you knew, became precious burdens paid for in pain. Robyn promised, "I will strive to look out for her."

Amy nodded absently, saying, "My lady is too kind." Medievals often talked about their children as if they belonged to someone else. "Beth says you do not beat her, not even with a bare hand."

"Yes," Robyn confessed, admitting she had small talent for child abuse.

Amy Lambert rolled her eyes, "Heaven knows how you make her behave."

"Just lucky, I guess." Italians accused the English of hating their offspring, not for beating their children, but because they gave them to strangers to raise. But back home, Beth and Joy would be going into junior high school, three years of fenced-in boredom, being teased by older girls and getting felt up by preteen boys. Here they were entering the heir apparent's household, learning proper manners and bedroom politics, maturing into Court ladies under the eyes of the young men who ran England—if this invaluable entrée into the corridors of power included lessons in spellcraft, so be it.

"Must be magic," Amy concluded cheerfully. Witches or not, Amy and her sisters backed Edward's cause even when he was a titled outlaw, sentenced to die, with his supporters' heads adorning London Bridge. The penalties for Yorkist politics could be as horrendous as those for witchcraft, and it would take something far more frightening than Lady Robyn of Pontefract to make these women abandon Edward.

For safety and convenience, Lady Robyn turned the castle keep into a women's quarters, leaving the main hall for the men and servants, and for state use when Edward arrived. Baynards Castle's high-towered keep was a mini-fortress, built around a central light well, with iron-bound doors and its own cistern and storerooms, able to hold out for weeks even if the rest of the castle were in enemy hands. She took over Edward's sumptuous bedchamber, with its private garderobe and attached presence chamber. Cybelle got the smaller keep bedchamber, while Chantal lodged with her daughter on the floor below, between the chapel and the kitchen. Deirdre had a bed in the presence chamber, just outside her lady's door, and Joy and Beth were free to share any friendly bed or to make little nests of their own, sleeping with the castle cats.

Heidi, she took to her old tower room alongside the keep, with its thick warm carpet and canopy bed, the room she dreamed about that night in Nest's cottage. Now Lady Robyn was here for real, and so was Heidi. Heavy tapestries covered the arrow slits, which were filled with tall wooden blocks to keep out the night. "This used to be mine," she told Heidi, "the most private room in the place."

Heidi sat down on the bed, wearing a high-waisted gown in Robyn's colors, admiring the hand-carved woodwork. Black winter witches' shifts were laid out on the bed for both of them. "Regular old hobbit hole."

"More like Merlin's tower. When the arrow slits are open, sun comes in, and you get tall bright views of London and the river, bordered in stone." Robyn tried to make it sound inviting. "You can have whatever room you want, but I was hoping you would like this one."

"Feels like home." To prove it, Heidi got out her baggie and started to roll. "So what's bugging my boss lady?"

"Nothing," Lady Robyn lied, "I just thought we ought to talk."

"Why?" Heidi finished rolling, licking the joint to seal it. "Because your boyfriend killed my boyfriend?"

Robyn winced at how that sounded. "I have to know how you feel after what happened at Hereford." Since that awful vespers, they had barely been alone, traveling at the center of Lady Robyn's growing household, constantly surrounded by Frenchwomen, men-at-arms, and children. Not ideal company for close personal conversation.

"Okay." Heidi held out the joint. "Here, let's clear the air."

"Maybe you should just blow smoke my way," Robyn suggested, not really wanting to get the baby stoned.

"Forgot you were breathing for two." Heidi took a long drag, savoring her first joint in days. Slowly expelling the smoke, Heidi stood up, looping her arms around Robyn's neck. "Here, I will give you a taste, and you won't have to inhale."

Leaning in, Heidi gave her a leisurely kiss with an open mouth, letting Robyn taste the smoke on her tongue. When their lips parted, Heidi asked, "Answer your question?"

That was a shock. Robyn stared at her friend, wondering where this was headed. "Sort of."

Heidi smiled mischievously, her arms staying around Robyn's neck. "I love you way more than I ever loved Owen. Not even close. He was way not my type, and I only slept with him to keep him off of you."

"Thanks." Robyn definitely owed her for that. Owen Tudor was not her ideal either.

"Sure thing." Heidi was perfectly at ease prostituting herself for a friend. "And if Edward gives you too much shit, I will sleep with him, too. Give you a good reason to dump him."

Robyn promised to keep that in mind, asking, "Do you hate Edward?"

"Well, duh." Heidi rolled her eyes. "I just offered to help you dump him." Then Heidi turned serious, saying, "No, I do not hate your idiot boyfriend, but I hate what he did. I kept telling Owen that invading England was suicidal, pleading with him to pick on someone smaller and weaker, and with better weather, like Monaco or the Bahamas. Still, I would have given Owen a second chance."

"Me, too." Robyn could never shake the feeling that she ought to forgive her enemies.

"I know." Heidi kissed her again. "That's why I love you."

That kiss had been with a closed mouth, but Robyn was not sure she liked being tit to tit with Heidi, not with her friend in this mood. "I thought you came here to sleep with Collin?"

Heidi shrugged without letting go. "Shows how much you know."

"You do want to go home?" After all that had happened, she feared Heidi would be hysterically demanding to return to a sane millennium—not making unexpected passes at her.

"Absolutely," Heidi assured her. "Got tons of unfinished business back in the City of Angels." Heidi reached around and began unlacing Robyn's bodice. "But there is no rush."

"Getting to like it here?" Her frisky friend had not even really seen London, just Ludgate and Saint Andrews Hill.

"It grows on you." Heidi loosened the last lace and started on the buttons. "Best of all, since I am going back to the future, this is free time, when I can do whatever I want. Anything here and now is going to be buried five hundred years in the past. No records. No rap sheets. No one will even remember it but me."

And me. Robyn watched patiently as her gown sagged, then fell to the floor, leaving her standing in her silk slip and tall leather Northampton riding boots. "I thought we had a platonic relationship?"

"Probably." Heidi began undoing her own gown, letting it slide off her shoulders and loosening the high waist. "Unless one of us magically grows a penis, we are going to have to be just good friends."

"Don't look at me," Robyn replied, patting her abdomen proudly. "I'm having a baby."

"So you say." Heidi stepped out of her red-and-gold gown and reached down, resting her hand on Robyn's womb. "I can hardly tell."

"It will get real obvious." She could feel the changes inside her, getting greater each day. Robyn already feared her body would never be the same.

"That I gotta see." Heidi laughed, grabbing the hem of her own slip and pulling it over her head. Throwing it aside, Heidi looked down and admired her naked body, which was an eyeful, curvy yet compact, so perfectly proportioned it could be the entry under *female.* "I mean there is no rush, literally. If you sent me back, it would be to the time I left from, right? Even if I stayed here for months."

"More or less." Robyn was not even sure she could send Heidi home, but felt she had to try. Exact scheduling was hopeless.

Heidi scooped up one of the black shifts from the bed, shaking it out and holding it up against her naked body. "What do you think? Will I make a wicked witch?"

Blond, happy Heidi, half nude and grinning suggestively from behind a black shift, was not Robyn's image of a witch—though siren and succubus certainly came to mind. "I hope not."

"We are going to be witches tonight?" Heidi asked. "That was what Joy promised." Heidi pulled on the shift, then offered its mate to her. "What did you think this strip tease was all about?"

Thank Goddess it's Friday. Heidi was just in a witchy mood, not attempting to seduce her. "I thought you were trying to get into my panties."

"Heavens no," Heidi laughed, adjusting her shift, getting it to hang just so. "When that happens, you will know."

Comforting thought. Lady Robyn bent down and unlaced her leather boots, which really did not go with the evening. Witches tried to be barefoot. Heidi asked her, "So it does not matter when I leave here? Just so I am ready to go."

"Exactly." Lady Robyn kicked off her boots. "You have a real feel for magic."

"Told you so." Heidi beamed and preened, saying, "Come, put on your shift."

Robyn slid out of her slip and took the black witch's shift she had worn since Saint January's Day. Witches changed back to white summer shifts on Robyn's birthday, the first day of spring. "I meant what I said. You have the knack for spellcraft."

"So I could be a good witch?" Heidi sounded pleased.

"Scary good." Heidi had more natural aptitude for witchcraft than any woman Robyn knew. Opening herself to the cosmos was the hardest part of being a witch, trusting her powers, surrendering to the strength within. Heidi was easily the most open person Robyn knew, eager to follow the good wherever it went. If Heidi ever took spellcraft halfway seriously, watch out Duchess Wydville, there's a new witch in town. "You must be totally ready before anything can happen."

"Just like making love." Heidi ran her hand over Robyn's bare flank, something Heidi never used to do as a mere production assistant. Having been Lady of Harlech had plainly gone to her head. "I have way more love for you than Collin and Owen combined, but that does not mean we positively have to fuck."

"Happy to hear that." Robyn wriggled into her witch's shift. Marrying Edward was nerve-racking enough without throwing in some wild fling with her best friend.

"Do not get me wrong," Heidi hastened to assure her, "I love to fuck, love it a lot. When I was a kid, I actually thought for a while I had invented it. But sometimes you love someone just for who they are, not for what they do for you."

Noble sentiments. Heidi helped straighten the shift, giving her boss lady a final pat down, adding, "And it is not like there's any shortage of guys. These Middle Ages are as macho as advertised. But there's no AIDS, and I cannot get pregnant for months, so what is the worst that could happen?"

"We could both be burned at the stake," Robyn reminded her.

"My point exactly," Heidi declared, pleased Robyn saw it her way. "If that is the best they can do, we have totally got them beat." That was the spirit Robyn sensed: Heidi had that raw, Joan of Arc edginess, the need to do right no matter what, even if it meant washing blood from Owen Tudor's face and ringing his severed head with candles while his killers watched in embarrassed silence.

For their ritual, Robyn chose the same presence chamber that she used on Halloween, wanting to reclaim the place profaned by London constables and a busybody member of Parliament. This was her and Edward's castle, where they had first made love and been betrothed, and she wanted the chamber next to their bedroom to be a sacred space. She rolled back the carpet and chalked a big six-pointed star on the floor, the Mogen David, two sacred triangles, one atop the other. All the witches and witch wannabes gathered around it, dressed in their black shifts. Ten-year-old Joy Grey was technically the senior member of the coven, while Robyn and Beth were the junior members, and Deirdre, Heidi, and Cybelle were novices—but witches' covens have a loose hierarchy, and Robyn was the natural leader. Which did not stop Joy from reveling in her status as senior witch.

Robyn arranged them around the star points in reverse order of age, starting with Beth and ending with herself. A single tall green candle burned in the center of the star, and beside it lay a sharpened knife, its razor-keen blade gleaming in the candlelight. She had them all kneel, and led them in a keening chant taught to her by Jo Grey during her first week in the Middle Ages, this soothing centering chant moved easily around the circle, cycling faster and faster as the tempo rose, until a whirlwind of voices whipped around the candle flame.

Flaring upward, the flame swelled and brightened, filling the room with light. Not a voice faltered, even Heidi, who had heard it only a couple of times, kept perfect time. Another sign of how naturally all this came to the late Lady of Harlech. And thanks to the Displacement spell, Heidi knew every nuance of the language, hearing the chant as clearly as Robyn.

Suddenly Jo Grey appeared at the heart of the light, standing where the candle had stood, holding a pomegranate in each hand—brought all the way from Greystone by the spell. Though she was far off in the Cotswolds, Jo joined in the chant, setting a new tone and pace, turning their chorus into a beckoning call.

Rising in response, Heidi and Deirdre stood up at their star points. Robyn had decided they should be sister-initiates, since both were on the verge of making the Witches Flight, though for completely opposite reasons. Deirdre had practiced diligently, but with limited success. Heidi, on the other hand, had come literally out of nowhere, having already made the Witches Flight involuntarily just getting to the Middle Ages, showing more innate ability than any of the novices. So it seemed natural to promote the most practiced and the most talented together. Despite coming from different continents and different centuries, they each had what the other lacked.

Joy rose, as well, being the senior witch, stepping solemnly toward the center of the star, keeping up the chant, drawing the two older novices forward with her. When they reached the center, Joy presented them to Jo, bidding them both kneel before her mother. Jo held out the pomegranates, and Joy cut into them, first Deirdre's, then Heidi's. Handing Deirdre her slice, Jo told her, "Your coven name is Pyrrha."

Good choice. *Pyrrha* meant "fiery red," matching Deirdre's hair, and it was one of Robyn's favorite goddess names. Pyrrha was the daughter of Mother Earth and Epimetheus, "afterthought"—pretty fitting for Deirdre. Pyrrha was also a survivor, which balanced out her given name, Deirdre of the Sorrows. Heidi, too, got a coven name that matched her hair, Chryse, which meant "golden"—and which was the name of a priestess, a nymph, and an island. Both young women picked seeds from their pomegranates, eating greedily, with red juice running down their chins.

Chanting rose to fill the presence chamber with light and sound, women's and girl's voices reverberating off stone walls and the hand-carved wooden ceiling. Robyn felt the same thrilling release as she did at her own initiation nine months ago. Nine months and a new life. She was being initiated into motherhood each and every day. Chanting crescendoed, flowing around and through her, rising up from her deep in her diaphragm and streaming out her throat, melding into the other voices.

Then the candle went out, plunging the presence chamber into blackness. Chanting sank in volume, with Jo's voice no longer there to drive the tempo. Robyn slowly brought down the chant, softening the beat, letting it fade naturally. Witches Night was over. It was much more sedate than her initiation, which ended with witches dancing naked round a bonfire, but still a night to remember. When Robyn relit the candle, Jo was gone. Heidi, Deirdre, and Joy stood in the center of the star, their hands and lips red with pomegranate juice—all that remained of Jo's midnight visit. And strangest of all, the thorn pricks on her hand healed, vanishing as swiftly as they appeared.

Saturday, 7 February 1461, Saint Amand's Day, Baynards Castle, London

Nothing like coming back to London with a bang. Last night was such a huge success, it feels like all London is rejoicing. Saint Amand is the patron of innkeepers, and with Lent less than two weeks away, folks are celebrating religiously. I suspect innkeepers got their feast day put in February just to drum up business during the Dead Month. Even beggars at the gate are glad to see me back.

To prove what a wonderful daughter-in-law I will make, I plan to call on Proud Cis next Monday, with tidings of her son and presents for George and Richard. But not till Monday, since with Duchess Cecily, it is definitely never on Sunday. Warwick is avoiding his pious aunt, as well, getting himself made a Knight of the Garter instead, dubbed by Mad King Henry himself. Shows they do not care who they let in these days.

It feels so good and natural to be here in London, which has by far the best shopping in the land. Fresh fish, meat-on-the-hoof, eggs, milk, and what vegetables are to be had—all very welcome now that I have more than a dozen mouths to feed, not counting my inner child. Days of getting by on tea, toast, and prayer are long gone. Plus the place is an antique addict's heaven, where the finest local work mixes with loot from half the known world, sort of like a swap meet of the rich and infamous held in a port of entry. Good thing I am broke.

Baynards Castle's keep became her tight little fortress against the Middle Ages. It had a clean kitchen, daily baths, and some haughty castle cats that kept down the rats. Her public feasts were in the main hall, for Edward's retainers and supporters, but her private suppers in the keep were reserved for special guests, usually women she wanted to know better, like Dame Agnes, the prison reformer, and Elizabeth Poynings, whose family were Edward's landlords, letting him house his mother and brothers at Falstaff's Place in Southwark. That last earned Robyn's eternal thanks, since otherwise Proud Cis would be back in Baynards Castle. Visits from Edward's mother, Duchess Cecily of York, were among the many potential assaults Lady Robyn must defend against. She meant to have Amy Lambert over when she had the time and nerve.

Naturally men were dying to crash these parties, and a sort of a reverse snobbery reigned whereby Matt the marshal and Robyn's French prisoners were regulars, while rich mercers and titled nobles waited for invitations. Indeed, the French often insisted on preparing the meal, which Lady Robyn allowed so long as they washed their hands and did not boss Chantal and Marie. Fear of trading such pleasant captivity for English prison fare turned even the French into perfect gentlemen.

Alas, the same could not be said for some of the knights and lords who made it to her table, hoping to curry favor with Edward's lady or just enjoy the pleasures of her household. Guests included John Mowbray, a sullen, complaining teenager with a pretty wife, tolerated only because he would one day be the Duke of Norfolk. Another dubious guest was Lord Clinton, Deirdre's old master, who was always looking for a free meal served up by pretty females. Sometimes he got one, since Clinton was witty and charming, and Deirdre still had a soft spot for the master who introduced her to older men and French frills. An aging Casanova with excellent politics, Clinton was one of the few lords to side with the commoners from the very start, almost the only one outside of Edward's close family. While his politics were genuine, Clinton was clearly delighted to lift his lance for a cause favored by adventurous young women. And in London, at least, the Yorkists plainly had the women's vote—if women had been allowed to cast them. Edward's program of peace, reconciliation, and prosperity appealed far more than Queen Margaret's grim vows of fighting to the bitter end. How much more romantic it was to be ruled by a handsome young knight-errant than by a bitter foreign queen.

Monday, 9 February 1461, Saint Apollonia's Day,
Baynards Castle, London

Being broke has not stopped me from ordering a printing press from the Hansa merchants in the Steelyard. They claimed they could lay hold of one in Cologne, bringing it down the Rhine to Bruges, and then to London. They vow the press is in excellent condition, or at least it was last November, and only want twenty marks, saying I must make my own bargain with the printer. No one asked why I needed a printing press, but being Germans, they naturally assumed I could never operate it on my own, so they are getting me a printer, as well. London needs a new voice, so I parted with ten of my gold nobles, promising to pay the rest when the press arrives.

Saint Apollonia is the patroness of dentists and anyone suffering from tooth pain, making her day perfect for visiting my mother-in-law-to-be. Cybelle, Heidi, the girls, and I are going to call on her this afternoon. Pray for us.

Robyn decided to ride to Southwark, not wanting to put herself at the mercy of London boatmen, when she had Cybelle, Heidi, and two little girls in tow. Any worries about how ordinary Londoners would react to seeing Lady Robin again were instantly dispelled. People shouted greetings, and seemed to take Lady Robyn's return as a welcome omen, like the first robin of spring, a sign Edward of March was on his way. Riding down Thames Street, past huge dock cranes and fishmongers' mansions, they turned right on Fish Street, where workday traffic on London Bridge forced them to wait while horse drays and beer hand carts lumbered past; with no bobbies to direct traffic, disputes were settled by shoves, catcalls, and curses in Cockney, "Ow! Look wh' yer gowin, ye-oo stumbl'n slugs."

"Aw rawt, aw rawt, stand aside f' m'Lady Staff'ard."

"Wooze staff'ard?"

"Lawd Edward's." That line always got a laugh. "I now she makes mine stand." Sometimes it was no help to know what everyone was saying. Shouldering carts aside, porters let them up onto the bridge in return for smiles and waves. London Bridge was a medieval marvel, a city street carried on arches across the Thames, connecting London and Southwark, forming a proud little parish atop the river, lined with homes, shops, inns, pedestrian overpasses, and a stone chapel dedicated to the Saint Thomas à Becket, the London-born archbishop murdered by his king. This shrine to a martyred rebel set in the middle of this marvelous bridge showed London's bold, defiant heart.

Southwark would not exist without the bridge, since the suburb's main function was to serve the traffic headed for London Bridge from the south, with taverns, churches, bathhouses, and breweries. Wealthy homes naturally sprang up in a town dedicated to pleasure, towering over shops and taverns. One of the finest was Falstaff's Place, built with loot from the French wars and belonging to the late Sir John Falstaff, a knight much maligned by Shakespeare, who left a huge estate, currently being devoured by lawyers.

These same lawyers had leased the mansion to Edward until Michaelmas, and his stately widowed mother held court there, dressed in elegant black, while raising Edward's two remaining brothers, George and Richard, who were nearly the same age as Joy and Beth. Duchess Cecily had Edward's height, but she was fairer, with white-gold hair, and seemed to have aged alarmingly. Robyn had last seen Proud Cis in October, and since then, Duchess Cecily had lost her husband, her second son, and her oldest brother. These blows had left their mark, but there was plenty of fight left in Proud Cis, sitting at the head of Falstaff's table, with a son on either side of her.

Tall, good-looking George was Edward's oldest surviving brother, smart and athletic, but a little too full of himself even for an eleven-year-old. Edward had sent him a French knight's sword taken in battle, which George eagerly accepted from Robyn, making immediate swipes at imaginary enemies. Fortunately, Falstaff's hall was big enough to play handball in, so no one was hurt. Richard was smaller, younger, and far more serious. Edward had sent him a Breton banner, which had a white boar on it, one of Richard's favorite badges. Richard wanted to know all about the banner, asking when and where it was taken. Lady Robyn had the story ready, "Your brother Edward took it when the Bretons tried to break his line and seize the bridge over the Lugg."

Small, dark Richard nodded gravely, taking the battle flag.

Of all the brothers, eight-year-old Richard was the most like Edward, and so far, he was the only person in London to treat Mortimer's Cross like an agonizing sacrifice instead of a smashing success. Whenever Robyn looked on Edward's brothers, she kept wondering which one she would want for king, since they were the only ready alternative to Edward. Her hopes had been set on his second brother, Edmund, who was gentle and helpful, and might have made a kind and generous king, but he was murdered after the battle of Wakefield, stabbed to death by Lord Clifford, while Robyn stood and watched, one of her more horrible moments in the Middle Ages. That left George and Richard.

Tall, vain George was belligerent and grasping, making him the perfect medieval king—but Lady Robyn had her doubts. England dearly needed a king who cared more for the country than for himself, and George showed scant signs of caring for anyone. He wanted what his oldest brother had, without even seeing the sacrifice—not a good sign. Little Richard had the potential to do it all, being strong and just, while hopefully knowing his own limits. Too bad he was the runt of the litter.

Showing the absolute idiocy of hereditary monarchy. If her baby was a boy, then he already outranked everyone in the room, for he was Edward's true son, second in line for the throne. That they were unwed was a mere formality, one marriage would easily solve. Literally any boy could grow up to be king, so long as he came from her womb. Not only was the system utterly lacking in quality control, but it was grossly invasive. She felt like someone was staking out a future for her unborn child that hardly included her. Mad King Henry was taken from his young mother as an infant, doing little to improve his morbid fear of women.

"And is my son well?" asked Duchess Cecily, as if speaking to a servant. Her usual frosty familiarity, made even more bitter by widowhood. Lady Robyn had gone from being a mild irritant to an outright threat.

"Passing well, Your Grace." Robyn went down on her silk knees before Proud Cis, assuring her that Edward was doing wonderfully. "He survived the battle with hardly a scratch."

"Thanks to you?" asked the duchess, whose job Robyn was slated to get. Behind the digs and cold disdain lay the stark fact that Duchess Cecily's power was slipping. Edward was swiftly deposing the old nobility, including his mother. He would marry whomever he wished, and that woman would be the new Duchess of York, no matter how patently unsuitable.

"Thanks to Mary," Robyn replied, even though her own prayers must have helped.

Henry Mountfort hastened to agree, " 'Twas a miracle, m'lady. Right before the battle, three suns appeared in the sky."

"So I have heard," Duchess Cecily observed. Though the miracle Proud Cis hoped to see was her son coming to his senses and dumping his girlfriend from the future. The clause in the Act of Accord aimed directly at Robyn—denying Edward's right to marry without consent—was now a dead letter, with Duke Richard of York no longer alive to enforce it.

Seeing Joy and Beth smiling to each other while sneaking glances at George made Robyn feel the burden of royalty. Joy and Beth were free to find their way in the world, to think what they willed and love whom they wanted, even to be witches if they dared. If her child was a girl, she could easily join them. If he was a boy, then legal or bastard, he would always be his father's son, always a potential king under the Act of Accord—whether she willed it or not. Kings could erase bastardy with a wave of the scepter, but they needed a woman to make an heir. And right now, she was that woman.

Wednesday, 11 February 1461, Baynards Castle, London
Warwick's elevation to the Garter has gone to his head, for he now aims to march out and fight Queen Margaret in the Midlands. Not my first choice, by any means, but the dead hand of Owen Tudor hangs over Richard Neville, Earl of Warwick. Were

it not for the Tudors, Edward would be here already—as it is, Warwick must fend for himself, not an appealing proposition.

Having a baby to protect, my impulse is to cower behind the walls of London, but Warwick cannot do that. He has raised an army, thousands of men from Kent and the nearby counties, even importing Burgundian handgunners. That many men cannot sit in one place in late winter, eating up the food supply and soiling the drinking water—that is asking for an epidemic. Word from the north is that Queen Margaret's army is practically starving, forced to subsist on thievery and plunder, eating its way south. Margaret's campaigning style is more like a cry for help than a coherent strategy. Margaret "won" at Wakefield by violating a Xmas truce, and now she is bringing her "victorious" army south because she cannot feed it, hoping people will accept her as queen again out of sheer exhaustion.

Warwick's army must move, too, so he plans to march straight into the Midlands, gathering more men as he goes. He is taking King Henry with him, along with almost every lord he could lay hands on, including the indolent young Duke of Suffolk and the dying Duke of Norfolk, also the Earl of Arundel, Viscount Bourcher, and Lords Bonville, Berners, de la Warr, and Montagu, plus the papal legate to excommunicate the enemy army. At Mortimer's Cross, Edward had only two lords with him; but Warwick plans to confront the queen with overwhelming moral and military force, armed with everything from crude firearms to Catholic dogma. Seems logical enough, but I have utter faith in Warwick's ability to totally screw things up. He has already trashed my plans completely. I was supposed to keep watch on the king, and now Warwick is whisking him away. Without Warwick and King Henry here, Edward may not even come to London.

But I am not about to leave Baynards Castle, and go riding off into the Midlands, chasing after Warwick and the king. Everyone in London just hopes Edward arrives soon—especially me. Meanwhile it is two days until the thirteenth, and I've got to get ready. Witches' work is never done.

Warwick rode out of London the next day, backed by knights and retainers, taking his king and army with him. Robyn would have liked to say good riddance, but she suspected something far worse would come of this. Whatever happened, she had a coven to run, and tomorrow was Friday the thirteenth, one of the biggest dates in a witch's calendar. This one fell on the end of the Dead Month surrounding Candlemas, making the night doubly significant, since the world now teetered between winter and spring, and everyone looked eagerly for the end of winter and the return of warmth and light. This was where witches got in trouble, for honoring each season in its turn, treating night, winter, and death as part of life, instead of Satan's playthings.

Under the ancient lunar calendar, the second Friday of each twenty-eight-day month was always Friday the thirteenth, the Friday of the full moon, the most orgiastic night of the month, with the big brilliant moon overhead. Before the Romans, when witches reigned throughout Europe, this was a night to give in to wildness and magic, when nude women danced beneath the huge shining moon and men worshipped Our Lady of the Beasts, tearing off their tanned animal hides to run naked with the wolves. It was all part of the great pattern, where the Goddess claimed those odd difficult numbers as her own, three, seven, nine, thirteen . . .

When the Romans brought Christianity and the Egyptian solar year, Friday the thirteenth went from being a monthly night of moon madness to an occasional fluke of the calendar—but witches still celebrated those few lucky Fridays when the two calendars came together. Since Friday the thirteenth no longer meant a full moon, communal moon madness gave way to mass flights and midnight bonfires, except on those triple witching nights, when the full moon actually fell on Friday the thirteenth. Magic and tradition held together a community in hiding that used to live in easy harmony with the heavens.

Friday the thirteenth had last come in June, when Robyn was exiled to the Continent and cut off from the coven, casting her circle alone on the carpeted floor of a palace bedroom in Bruges, while Jo and Joy were prisoners in the Tower of London. Her feeble attempts to reach out to Jo were easily blocked by Duchess Wydville. Now the tables were totally turned: London was in their hands, including the Tower, and she had a fledgling coven around her. Tonight was the night when the coven would take flight, or so Lady Robyn devoutly hoped.

She had left the Star of David chalked on the presence chamber floor, discreetly covering it with a carpet. Knights and lords had supped atop it, sipping spiked wine while women and girls sang to them, suffering no harm to their souls—it was merely what men must expect when dining with a witch. Lord Clinton couldn't have cared less. At the witching hour, the coven rolled back the carpet, and Robyn cast the circle; then everyone knelt in black shifts on their star points, chanting together to the candle flame. This time there were no midnight visitations planned, and their energy was totally focused on the Witches Flight, which Deirdre and Cybelle had never done, and Heidi had only done inadvertently. Half of them had never done the flight voluntarily, and the only member who had done the mass flight was Joy Grey, senior witch present. An interesting evening awaited.

First rule of being a witch was go with the flow, casting aside all doubts and fears, knowing you were doing the impossible, and never worrying about how. When you have nothing holding you down, flight itself is a snap. But no matter how many flights a witch had made, each one was a personal challenge, to give up will and purpose and let the miracle happen, to gain power by letting go of control. So Lady Robyn let herself go into the night, rising with the chant, not worrying if anyone would follow. Besides, it was a child who led them. Joy was senior witch, and she had done mass flights before, plus the girl was headed for the arms of her mother, always a powerful impulse. Robyn was literally along for the ride.

As the chant grew and broadened, the chamber vanished around her, walls and ceiling fading into darkness, replaced by a black rush of air. Then stillness. Lady Robyn could no longer feel the chalked presence chamber planks beneath her, but found she was now kneeling on rough, uneven ground. Cold winter constellations shone down through gaunt limbs, and what had been a candle flame was now a witches' bonfire, ringed by wildly dancing women. Cutting across the night sky overhead was a huge bridge supported by soaring stone arches.

Half her coven was with her, the smaller half—Joy and Beth knelt right where their star points had been, still chanting away, knowing better than to break the rhythm. All the grown women, Heidi, Deirdre, and Cybelle, were gone. Too bad. Heidi was not as talented as she thought. Though it was still winter, there was a dreamlike warmth to everything, and the chant echoed off the arches overhead, sounding louder even than in the presence chamber. Slowly she brought the chant down, and when it ceased, she motioned for the girls to rise, saying, "Stay close, for we are far from home."

How far Robyn did not know, having never seen this place before. Taking the girls' hands, she led them toward the double ring of women spinning around the bonfire. As she approached the whirling wall of women, Robyn saw a familiar figure coming toward them, a slim raven-haired woman wearing a witch's shift and a wide smile. It was Jo.

Joy's hand tightened in hers, but the girl did not bound into her mother's arms as she used to; since turning ten last Christmas, Joy had learned decorum. Jo bent down and kissed her daughter, the senior witch. Then Jo kissed Robyn on the lips, saying, "Welcome to Avignon."

As usual, Jo had what was needed. However much Robyn wanted to just let things happen, in the back of her brain was the nagging question, "Where am I?" And now she knew, Avignon, French capital of the papacy. Popes had lived and ruled in this fortress city by the Rhone, during the "Babalonian Captivity" when the French hijacked the papacy. Antipopes had reigned here, as well, during the last schism. Now witches danced around the arches of the great stone bridge over the Rhône, singing the old witches' song:

"Sous le pont d'Avignon, on y danse tout en rond . . ."

Women and girls of all shapes and sizes danced in counterotating circles around the bonfire, the inner circle facing the outer one, spinning to the music of flutes, lutes, and bagpipes. Aged crones, little girls, milkmaids, alewives, shepherdesses and seamstresses, whores, nuns, Jewesses and Gypsies, all whirled hand in hand, smiling ecstatically at having survived another winter, thrilled to be alive and free, an international women's conspiracy to celebrate life, hope, and holiness at the end of the Dead Month.

Jo and Joy dragged her into the dance, pulling Beth behind her.

One moment she was watching in amazement; the next she was in the dance, with grinning women whirling past her. At first all she saw were smiling faces, but then she began to recognize some of them. First came Bryn and Nest, faces she could hardly forget. Then Elizabeth Wydville whipped by, winking at her, followed by the big blond-braided woman she met at Robin Hood's Well on her first day in Barnsdale. Lady Robyn had been welcomed into her Honour of Pontefract by a witch, and she had not even known it. She was even more shocked to see men dancing, too. Thinking she must be mistaken, Robyn was not sure until one came by naked, with antlers in his long blond hair, a man for sure, and enjoying himself immensely. Not surprising, because he was holding hands with Heidi and Deirdre, who flashed by next, stark naked.

More women whirled past. Witches Night had not lost its ability to surprise. Letting go even further, Robyn lost herself in the dance, not caring whom she was dancing with or how long it lasted. As the witches' stamina faded, the dance slowed, and singing turned to long mournful dog howls. Not howling at the moon, which was not up this late, but to Hecate, the bitch-goddess.

When the new moon rose, it would be the last moon of winter, and the next would be the first moon of spring, but that was all the more reason to give Hecate her due. Much as everyone might yearn for spring, witches knew it was dangerous to slight the winter or turn death into something evil. Dancing slowed to a stop, howling ceased, and they all stood hand in hand around the bonfire, the two rings still facing each other, saying a closing prayer to the goddess of death and winter:

> Come holy Hecate,
> Lady of the crossroads,
> Queen of the night,
> Foe of the sun,
> Friend of the darkness,
> Bloodthirsty bitch-goddess,
> Accept our sacrifice.

Both rings sank to their knees, bowing their heads before the goddess. Like the moon madness, the "sacrifice" was no longer literal, at least not a physical object, much less a living being, though some women had torn off their shifts and added them to the bonfire. Tonight the sacrifice was spiritual, the willingness to live free and unafraid, the way they had when sowing and planting were women's secrets and there was no calendar but the moon. The laws against women's magic grew more gruesome every year. If need be, they were offering up their bodies and souls to the flames.

To close the ceremony, each witch kissed the witches beside her. Hands dropped, but not all the kissing stopped, and there were hushed giggles around the dying bonfire. Leaving the girls with Jo, Robyn went in search of Heidi, happy her friend had made it and brought Deirdre, as well. Knowing Heidi, Robyn headed to where the giggles were loudest.

English witches were loath to let men into their covens, not because they had anything against men, but they had been doing just fine without them, so why ruin a good thing? Besides, medieval Englishmen had cares and duties that regularly killed them well ahead of the women. Make them into warlocks, as well, and there would soon be none left. Obviously not all witches thought that way, and however few men had managed to get into this girls' night out, Heidi had found them.

Her former assistant was in the innermost ring by the fire, happily on her back, with the blond antlered warlock galloping atop her. Blond on blonde, and thoroughly enjoying it. Deirdre was there, too, delighting a painted warlock in a wolfskin, doggy-style, while grinning guys in goat horns waited their turns. So much for congratulating her new sister-initiates. Both had taken to the Witches Flight with a bang, and hardly needed her approval. From the grunts of enthusiasm and murmured endearments, she could tell the men were Finns and Estonians, and eager to give these newly fledged witches a memorable first flight.

Getting into the orgy by the fire was easier than getting out. She found herself facing a ring of witches in various states of undress, who had come to join in or just watch, and assumed she was part of the show. Some women were lining up to get at the men; others were not so picky. Without warning, a big buxom witch stepped up, wearing nothing but a friendly look, asking in Swedish, "Where are you from, lovely lady?"

Trying not to get the woman's hopes up, Robyn replied, "Montana, a little place called Roundup."

"Never heard of it," purred the husky Swede, who would not have minded if Robyn came from the moon. "How do you speak such sweet Swedish?"

"Displaced." You would think a witch would know. "Before here, I was in London."

"Then you are English." A tall dark-eyed Italian witch stepped up, wearing nothing but a veil of shining black hair that reached past her hips.

"Not necessarily." Robyn thanked heaven that she still had on her shift. Things going on by the bonfire made her wild, inebriated LPGA weekend in Palm Springs seem like a Girl Scout campout.

"Is it true what they say about English witches?" asked the Italian slyly.

"What do they say?" Robyn hoped it was something nice.

Smiling, the tall Italian patted the dark triangle between her legs. "They say English witches do not like letting men in."

"Some do—some don't." Robyn spread her hands, trying to show off Edward's ring, racking her brain for some casual way to bring up her noble boyfriend and impending marriage. "There is no real hard rule."

Everyone laughed at that. Robyn tried to turn it into an exit line, but as she backed away, a hand closed on her wrist, turning her about. Robyn found herself facing a familiar-looking witch, a narrow-faced young woman with a shaven head, who was saying, "Lady Robyn, how marvelous to see you here."

"I am called Diana." She tried to hide behind her coven name, having no idea who this shaved and naked witch might be.

Leaning closer, the witch kissed her, saying, "You probably will not know me without my wimple."

"Sister Perpetua?" Robyn could barely believe it, having last seen the wayward nun at the abbey of Saint Mary de Pratis, across the Nene from Northampton.

Sister Perpetua ran her slim white hand over Robyn's hip, saying, "I never thought you were a witch."

"Well, I never really meant to be one," Robyn explained. "It just happened."

That got another hearty laugh. "Neither did I," the Italian told her. "I took in witchcraft with my mother's milk."

Sister Perpetua pulled harder on her hand, determined to lead her away, insisting, "M'lady, please come, there is something I must tell you."

Robyn went reluctantly. When Sister Perpetua first felt her up in the abbey of Saint Mary de Pratis, Robyn had prayed the nun would find some suitable outlet for her sexual frustrations. This was not at all what Robyn had in mind. Yet Sister Perpetua commanded respect, even in an orgy. Her shorn hair marked her as a nun, making her almost as much in demand as the men. If you are set on serious sinning, there is something immensely satisfying about doing it with God's wife. If Sister Perpetua wanted to haul off pretty Diana, the new witch at the orgy, everyone took it as the nun's due—and Diana's, who had clearly hit the jackpot first time out.

Smiling women parted for them, wishing them well. It was not like Perpetua was taking a man away—that might have provoked a riot. Robyn found herself jerked free from the crowd of flesh around the fire, back out under the stars, with the older women, little girls, and the more spiritually minded. Jo, Joy, and Beth waved to her. Bryn was with them, and so was the Barnsdale woman with the blond braids, both of whom started toward her.

Great. All she needed was beautiful Bryn smugly watching her fend off an amorous nun. Turning to Perpetua, she tried to disengage, saying, "It is absolutely thrilling to see you here, I worried that you—"

Sister Perpetua would not be put off, leaning in and silencing her with another kiss, then saying, "I have something I truly must tell you."

Here it comes. She tried to sound utterly naïve, asking, "What is that?"

Perpetua turned grave, saying softly, "Queen Margaret is in Northampton."

Robyn stared in disbelief. Even at a witches' Sabbath beneath the bridge of Avignon, that came as a shock. "What do you mean?"

Sister Perpetua repeated herself patiently, "Queen Margaret is at Northampton, with her army. And plans to march on London."

That meant Margaret had beaten Warwick to the Midlands, and

the earl was headed for Northampton, not knowing it was already in the queen's hands. Before Robyn could say anything, Bryn stepped up and kissed her on the lips, then whispered, "And Edward is still in Hereford."

Staring into Bryn's big brown eyes, Robyn realized she was not being seduced, but warned. Queen Margaret's army was between Edward and Warwick, and neither man knew it. But these witches did. Women's eyes were following the armies as they moved, from London to the Marches. And it spoke volumes that they were far more worried for Edward than for Queen Margaret.

Next to step up was the blond-braided woman Robyn met at Robin Hood's Well. This woman was a Pontefract tenant, who owed Lady Robyn rent and dues, and who could be hauled before the manorial court for displeasing Her Ladyship. For a witch, any appearance in court could be fatal, but at this moment they were equals, two witches meeting at midnight beneath the bridge at Avignon. The peasant woman took her lady's face in her hands, smiled, and gave Robyn a stout kiss. Then the big blond woman turned serious, saying, "Servants at Pontefract say that Sir Henry Lovelace has been meeting with Queen Margaret and Duke Somerset, and he plans to betray Warwick and Lord Edward."

Sir Henry Lovelace was Warwick's trusted steward and vanguard commander. Three witches and three warnings. Now what would she do with them?

12

⊷⊷⊙ Fat Tuesday ⊙⊷⊷

That was one wild night, and it ended back on a chalked star-point in the Baynards Castle's presence chamber. Lady Robyn found herself kneeling in the dark before a burnt-down candle, surrounded by the rest of her coven. As soon as Robyn closed the circle and lit a lamp, Joy and Beth leaped up, thrilled by their midnight trip to Avignon, doing their own witches' dance around the candle stub. Heidi and Deirdre were stark naked, glassy-eyed, and smelling of sex—thoroughly happy with their "maiden" flight. The only coven member looking dissatisfied was the black-haired French poetess, who had been left behind. Cybelle flatly refused to believe anyone went anywhere, saying, "This is absurd—not one of you left this room. I heard your chanting the whole time."

No one deigned to argue, which only angered Cybelle, who turned to Heidi and Deirdre, demanding to know, "Why are you naked? What happened to your shifts?"

Coming slowly out of their trance, the kneeling sister-initiates stared at each other for a long moment; then Heidi began to giggle. Which got Deirdre started. Soon both were laughing uncontrollably, making Cybelle even more indignant. The poetess demanded proof, "If anyone has been somewhere, show me some sign of it."

Unable to stop laughing, Deirdre rose to her feet, raised her arms, and did a giggling nude pirouette. Her point was obvious: If they had not gone anywhere, then what had happened to their clothes?

Cybelle was not buying, asking, "Come, what did you do with your clothes?"

"We threw them in the fire," Deidre declared proudly.

Heidi corrected her. "Actually, the men did."

"What men?" Cybelle wanted to know. This was supposed to be a Witches Night.

"Oh, they were not men," Deirdre hastened to assure her. "They were werewolves."

"Really?" Heidi was both shocked and intrigued.

Cybelle rolled her eyes in disbelief. Heidi turned to her former boss, looking highly pleased with herself. "God, I've been a fan of witchcraft forever. Who knew I would be good at it?"

Robyn smiled at Heidi's excitement. "I did."

"Good at what?" Cybelle scoffed. "Nothing happened."

Totally drained, Robyn lacked the strength to set the French poetess straight. Cybelle was jealous; this was the second time she'd been left behind on a Witches Flight. Too bad, but Cybelle was never going to get beyond novice by being in denial; she had to believe wholly and completely in spellcraft, or give up on being a witch. And at the moment, Lady Robyn had far bigger problems than Cybelle's spiritual growth. The three witches' warnings echoed in her head. Queen Margaret's army was between Edward and Warwick, and Sir Henry Lovelace was set to betray them. Somehow she had to get word to Edward, since warning Warwick was worse than useless. Outside, the lauds bells rang at Saint Brides and were answered by Saint Mary le Bow, letting London know it was long past everyone's bedtime. She hustled the girls into bed and then collapsed herself, sleeping right through prime, and morning Mass, as well.

Saturday, 14 February 1461, Saint Valentine's Day,
Baynards Castle, London

Valentine's morning, and where is mine? A week ago, it felt right to head off to London. It certainly beat hanging about Hereford while Edward searched the hills for Pembroke and Wiltshire. And I desperately needed somewhere safe and secure to have the baby. I have that here; a walled and fortified keep, safe, sound, and all set to be babyproofed. Everything but Edward. But now Queen Margaret is coming between us. Enough of this fooling around in the Marches, hunting for noblemen who are not worth finding anyway. Edward needs to be here. I need him. London needs him. Unfortunately, I am the one who has to fetch him. Edward is three days away, at least, but that cannot be helped. If I leave tomorrow or the next day, I can be in Hereford by Wednesday. Ash Wednesday is the first day of Lent. So Edward and I will be reunited on the day we are supposed to give up the sins of the flesh. Fat chance.

London was in Mardi Gras mood, celebrating the end of winter and getting in as many sins of the flesh as possible. Fish Street taverns were wide open, and cook's boys peddled meats that would soon be forbidden, crying out, "Beef ribs!" and "Hot sheep's feet!" Lords and mercers dined in great style, giving leftovers to the poor, who stood patiently waiting in the street while whores wearing red Valentine's Day hearts on their sleeves offered up love for less than six pence.

Luckily Robyn was not that desperate. Her love was waiting in Hereford, and all she must do was get there with her witch's warning. Letting the girls sleep in, Robyn went about her errands with Heidi, getting ready to go. At the Steelyard, the Hansa merchants told her that the press she wanted was in Bruges, so she paid to have it brought over, promising to pay the balance due when she could inspect the press. Though she trusted the German merchants, they were still medievals, fully capable of presenting her with an olive press and a pile of used parchment, then calmly demanding payment. Truth in advertising was another futuristic concept.

Elizabeth Poynings gave her a letter to take to her husband, Robert, who Elizabeth said was in Dunstable with Warwick's advance guard. Elizabeth was a total wreck, terribly afraid for her husband. Knowing well what that was like, Robyn sought to reassure her, saying that her husband was brave and steadfast. "That is what sorely worries me," Elizabeth replied. "He needs to care for me, more than for his king."

Such talk was treason, but there were plenty of London women who felt that way. Robyn took Elizabeth's hand to comfort her, but the worried wife was at her wits' end, saying, "I have a child now, and I fear that if anything happens to my Robert, the Percys will take our lands, and I will have nowhere to go."

"What about your family in Norfolk?" Robyn asked. Elizabeth was born a Paston, the family that were Sir John Falstaff's lawyers and inherited the old hard-drinking knight's estate.

"Oh, God save me." Elizabeth was horrified by the idea of going home. "My mother beat me horribly before I was married, and would do it again if I come back with a fatherless child."

Having her own baby on the way, with no legal husband, Robyn could sympathize. Calmly she asked, "Boy or a girl?"

"A boy," Elizabeth replied proudly, "named Edward."

"Good name." Robyn squeezed the distraught wife's hand. "What about your brother John?"

Elizabeth shook her head hopelessly, knowing her ambitious brother would have small time for her. "Perhaps Lady Pole would take me in, though I have little to pay her with."

"If need be, you may stay at Baynards Castle," Robyn promised, taking the letter from the frightened woman. "For free." Both she and Elizabeth hoped it would not come to that, but there was little they could do. Wives throughout London were caught in a similar vise—wanting to see the city defended, but hoping it would not cost them their homes and husbands.

Lady Robyn rode out of London after Monday morning Mass, determined to travel fast, taking Heidi, Matt, and a handful of mounted bowmen. She left behind a city in an uneasy state. Tomorrow was Fat Tuesday, and most Londoners felt it was their religious duty to have plenty to repent on Ash Wednesday. Drinking, meat-eating, and fornication were building to a crescendo, and all the same while, Queen Margaret was bearing down on them with her starving army, eager to bring a violent end to the Mardi Gras mood. Thanks to her latest Witches Flight, Lady Robyn knew that the vengeful Queen was closer than anyone thought.

She halted at Saint Albans, twenty miles north of the city, to say a prayer for Joy's father, the former Duke of Somerset, who was killed during a battle in the quiet abbey town. His body was buried in the abbey vaults. Heidi wanted to know, "Which side was he on?"

"Queen Margaret's." Robyn had been to Saint Albans before, and always the sleepy town had belied its bloodthirsty history, but things were suddenly in rewind, and as she rode in, the market street, with its shops and inns, was filled with mailed bowmen. "His legitimate son is the current Duke Somerset, one of Margaret's main lords."

"So Joy's half brother is the duke who had you on your back at Pontefract?" Heidi found it easier to keep track of bedroom maneuvers than battles.

"Temporarily." Emboldened by his victory at Wakefield, young Somerset had tried taking her by main force, as well. A private interview that began with her pleading for the life of the Earl of Salisbury ended with her pinned to the bed, submitting to heavy petting for Lord Salisbury's sake. Somerset did not get into her panties, and Salisbury was executed despite Somerset's promise of protection. Which was how chivalry worked. Preserving your honor could easily cost some poor fool his life. "Young Somerset is King Henry's cousin, which makes him Edward's cousin, as well, and Pembroke's. He is also Wiltshire's brother-in-law and, thanks to Joy, the Greys are his bastard relations."

Heidi smiled at the mobs of armored bowmen who were cheering them down the street, happy to see Edward's lady and her cute friend. "Family feud gone berserk."

"Tell me about it." Lord Salisbury, whom she would not put out to protect, was Warwick's father.

Lord Warwick himself was waiting with his men in a fortified camp north of town, at the edge of Barnard's Heath. Warwick's camp was defended with all the latest and nastiest equipment, including cannon, handguns, incendiary grenades, nets studded with nails, and ghastly star-shaped steel caltrops scattered about to maim enemy horses. Pinch-faced, long-nosed Richard Neville, Earl of Warwick, was wearing his Garter ribbon, but he was hardly her image of a knight. For one, he was not wearing armor, and any man trying to strike a macho pose while wearing wool pantyhose and a purse has serious problems. Far from being a knight-errant, Warwick was a vain, vengeful pirate with a mean streak a mile wide. To finance his private fleet and army, Warwick would raid foreign shipping, usually Spaniards and Germans, seizing the ships and drowning the crews, killing men whose only crime was having something that Warwick coveted.

Yet even Warwick deserved a warning, which the noxious Neville totally ignored, saying, "We have had no word of Queen Margaret, so she cannot be as close as Northampton."

"Closer." Her news was three days old already, and Margaret was sure to be south of Northampton by now. "Somerset and the queen could be here by breakfast tomorrow."

"No matter when they arrive, we are ready," Warwick boasted. "You have seen my defenses."

Gruesome, for sure, but it would take more than nets and nails to stop Queen Margaret. "My advice is to stay behind them, until I return with Edward."

Warwick answered stiffly, "I have already sent word to Edward of March."

Word of what? Warwick did not even believe the queen was in the neighborhood. "Good. Then I will try to speed him along."

Warwick smirked. "I am sure young Edward will come quickly for you."

Warwick was clearly a lost cause. Lovelace was there, as well, commanding Warwick's Kentish contingent, but it was hopeless to accuse him based on hearsay from some nameless Yorkshire witch. Even if Robyn succeeded in convincing Warwick, all he would do was execute Lovelace, and Robyn did not want that on her conscience. If Edward arrived in time to face down Queen Margaret, Lovelace's treason might not even take place.

As they left, Heidi laughed, saying, "That was a fine waste of time."

"I had to give it a try." The interview reminded Robyn of her attempt to save Duke Richard of York from similar stupidity before the battle of Wakefield. Or trying to convince Owen Tudor that invading England might not be as easy as it seemed. Both ignored her, and ended up losing their heads. Some biological imperative kept males headed into battle from thinking clearly; otherwise, there would be no wars at all.

Ordinary troops cheered them out of camp. Those men would have listened to her. That was what made Joan such a great commander: she talked directly to the men, cutting out the blue-blooded leadership. But Lady Robyn could not see herself taking Warwick's army away from him, so a timely warning was the best the Neville could expect.

She rode back down Saint Peter's Street, turning west on Folly Lane, which led along the "back side" of the town, to Watling Street, the main road running west and north out of Saint Albans. Shadows grew longer, and the day got colder—and Robyn could smell snow in the air. Families were fleeing south ahead of the snow, and Lady Robyn stopped several of them, hearing their story of homes looted, and churches ransacked by northern barbarians speaking weird Northumberland accents, "which sound like English spoken backwards." Looters stole lambs from the field and chalices off the altars, killing anyone who complained. Queen Margaret's advance could be charted by the towns these people came from—Grantham, Stamford, Huntingdon, and Royston, which was only two dozen miles away.

Giving each family silver from her purse, Lady Robyn offered them shelter in Baynards Castle if they had nowhere else to go. Most of the folks fleeing south were young wives or families with teenage daughters, since Queen Margaret had made it plain at the Rape of Ludlow that men could offer up money and goods, but pretty girls must pay a higher price. Her Majesty's control over her killers-for-hire was marginal, and Margaret herself was once robbed and threatened by her own retainers. Luckily for the French Queen, chivalry was not dead, and a fourteen-year-old boy, John Coombe of Amesbury, took her and the Prince of Wales up on his horse and brought them to Pembroke in Harlech. Learning nothing from her experience, Margaret now sent farmwives and milkmaids fleeing before her. Another reason why Edward of March's "whore" was more popular than the Queen of England.

Arriving at Dunstable after dusk, Lady Robyn found shelter in an Augustinian priory, giving thanks in a fine old Norman church that she had a roof overhead and a warm bed, while other women were fleeing through the winter night. Dunstable sat on the northern slope of the Cheltons, where Watling Street met the Icknield Way, and Warwick had stationed two hundred mounted archers commanded by Robert Poynings in an inn at the northern end of the main street. She gave Poynings his wife's letter, and word that Queen Margaret's troops were in Royston.

Poynings took the warning seriously, sending word to Warwick at once. He was the thirty-something younger son of a noble family at feud with the Percys, and had been John-Amend-All's swordbearer ten years before, when Kent first rose up against the queen and Court. He, too, had once been a prisoner in the Tower, which made for an immediate bond, and Robyn told him, "Elizabeth is sorely worried for you, more than she will say in a letter."

Poynings laughed grimly, saying, "I am very worried for me." No one hereabouts liked this winter war. His mounted bowmen were local recruits, commanded by the town butcher, and many had family nearby, frightened that fighting had come so close. He asked what she thought of the queen's army, having seen it at Pontefract.

Robyn sighed, saying, "Some of them are scary good. You know what the Percys are like, and the Scots are even worse. But they are fighting for loot, not their lives; expect them to be treacherous and cruel, rather than courageous." In the north there was no law but the great lords, who fought one another when not harrying the southron. North of the Tweed, *ride* and *raid* was a single verb, and expecting them not to steal was like asking fish to fly. Poynings had prepared for a long cold night, inviting her and Heidi to share hot spiced wine by his fire. His men had already started their last binge before Lent, since who knew what Shrove Tuesday would actually bring?

She and Heidi returned to the priory feeling far happier than the freezing night warranted. After a day of riding and two goblets of spiced wine, Robyn went straight to sleep. She regretted having that second goblet, but she would spend most of Fat Tuesday on the road, and reminded herself to ask for bacon at breakfast, for she would not see meat again until Easter.

Matt woke her in the middle of the night, saying, "M'lady, the queen's men are in town."

Jerked out of her drugged sleep, she stared into darkness, having a hard time understanding what he was saying, "Queen's men here? Do you mean in the priory?"

"Not yet," Matt told her. He had been sleeping in the stables, to keep an eye on their horses. "But monks are hiding their chalices and vestments, for troops are in the town."

Robyn lit a candle, asking, "How many?"

"A lot." Matt's eyes looked hollow in the candlelight. She had never seen him so worried, and they had been through some harrowing times together, ever since he came to change the cess bucket in her Tower cell. "And more march in as we speak."

She shook Heidi, who was sharing their borrowed bed, asking Matt, "Does Poynings know?"

"He is dead," Matt told her solemnly.

"Dead?" She did not believe it. For God's sake, she had just been drinking cinnamon wine with him. Her head still swam from it.

"They are all dead, or taken." Matt sounded terse, but she could tell he was close to tears. He, too, could not believe it had happened, even though he was telling her. "Queen's men surrounded the inn and took them in their beds, killing them before they could put up much of a fight. Only the butcher escaped, because he snuck off to sleep with his wife."

Poor Elizabeth. The woman had been horribly right to fear for her husband. Robyn felt sick and helpless, thinking of how casually the men of Dunstable were slaughtered, all those homesick lads and worried husbands. How ghastly.

Heidi sat up beside her, asking, "What has happened?"

"Something terrible," Robyn told her, "and we must dress."

Heidi threw off the coverlet and leaped out of bed, having the ability to go instantly into emergency mode, waking up sober and efficient, a talent picked up during her harrowing childhood, where her worst emergencies began with her in bed and asleep. Having no time for modesty, they both dressed hurriedly while Matt watched the door. Then he drew his sword and led them to the stables. Her bowmen were waiting with the horses, and as Matt had said, the street outside was filled with mounted men, so they had to slip out a postern through the priory garden, using one of Robyn's flashlights to find their way across the dark churchyard. After their bloody night's work, none of Queen Margaret's men wanted to follow a will-o'-the-wisp across a graveyard and onto sacred ground.

Fleeing into frigid moonless night, Robyn took the one route she knew to be safe, back down Watling Street toward Saint Albans and London. Queen Margaret was between her and Edward, so his warning must wait for Witches Night. Warwick needed to know now that Queen Margaret would be on him before noon. It was twelve miles to Saint Albans, and Robyn doubted Margaret would tarry, not if Somerset had anything to say. Of all Queen Margaret's lords, Somerset moved fastest, both in bed and in battle. Riding a dozen miles through the freezing dark, when dead tired to begin with, was not Lady Robyn's favorite way to pass the night—only being tortured in the Tower was worse. By the time she heard the lauds bell tolling in Saint Albans, she was clinging to her mount, half-asleep, relying on Matt to find the way. Heidi was sound asleep, slumped forward and tied firmly into her tall saddle.

Finally they reached the bridge over the Ver, the same one she crossed yesterday afternoon. Bowmen hailed them at the bridge, where Shrove Tuesday drinking had already begun in earnest. By now Robyn was beyond worrying about Warwick's authority, telling them straight out to expect Queen Margaret's troops momentarily. "They have taken Dunstable, and will be here soon."

Matt made the warning more explicit. "Poynings and his men were murdered in their beds. See it does not happen to you."

That sobered up the bridge watch. Lighting torches, bowmen led them down Saint George Street past Black Cross Chase, and straight into town, shouting the warning ahead of them. By the time

Robyn reached the market cross, the sun was almost up, and she asked a sergeant in Neville livery where his lord might be. The sleepy archer replied, "On Barnard's Heath, north of town."

Naturally. With Somerset and Queen Margaret coming down from Dunstable, about to hit the southern end of the town, where would Warwick be? Several miles away, set to defend the wrong end of Saint Albans. There was nothing to do but ride off and find him, which she did.

Warwick was up, and he had his men up, as well, turning them out of their heavily fortified camp—not the best maneuver with the enemy bearing down on him. But Lord Warwick was not to be dissuaded, telling her blandly, "I sent out several scouts, but only one has come back, saying Margaret is nine miles off."

Whatever. There were more important things to discuss than Warwick's tactical fancies. The Earl of Warwick was immensely popular in some quarters, and known to history as the Kingmaker, having backed King Henry, Duke Richard of York, and now Edward. Always playing second fiddle made him touchy, and deaf to sound advice, since no matter who won, Warwick always came in second. He quarreled with his friends almost as much as with his enemies, secretly hoping they all might lose, so that somehow Warwick would win. Which resulted in almost suicidal carelessness at times. She curtsied to the irksome earl, asking politely, "Would Your Grace allow me to withdraw and take shelter with His Majesty, King Henry?"

Warwick smirked at her timidity. "My lady may do as she pleases. King Henry is in the charge of Lord Bonville and Sir Thomas Kyriell."

Which was Warwick's way of saying that he had already lost track of Mad King Henry. Losing the head of state was no way to start a battle, but Robyn thanked him and backed out, anxious to find the king. Five years before, Henry had been wounded by an arrow at the first battle of Saint Albans. With a second battle looming at the very same spot, Henry was likely to flip out completely. Or worse yet, get skewered again. She had to see he was safe, for if anything happened to Henry, Edward would be king—which she had to prevent at all costs.

Since Warwick was going into battle, she insisted on giving the earl a kiss for luck, whispering as she did, "Lovelace will betray you."

Then she was gone in search of her king, taking Heidi and Matt with her. Despite Warwick's insistence that the foe was miles away, arrows were flying when she got back to Saint Albans. Shrove Tuesday had already turned into a battle. Firing from behind barricades and garden walls, and from atop the Fleur-de-Lys and the Red Lion Inn, Warwick's archers had stopped Margaret's advance up Saint George Street. Robyn wished them luck, and went looking for the king, knowing Henry of Windsor would be far as possible from the fighting.

She spotted King Henry's banner rising from a pasture east of town and rode toward it, finding His Majesty sitting under a tree. Robyn recognized the man in armor holding the banner as William Gower, one of King Henry's banner bearers. Waiting with him was Lord Bonville and Sir Thomas Kyriell, along with their retinues, some royal grooms, several monks, and a small sharp-faced man wearing shabby black clothes and farmer's boots, sitting cross-legged against an oak.

Dismounting, Robyn did a deep curtsy before the thin pale fellow in the frayed black farmer's jacket. This was Henry of Windsor, Henry VI, king of England, Ireland, and France, and the head of the House of Lancaster. Lady Robyn did not look up, until her liege lord gave her leave. "Lady Stafford," he declared, "how delightful. It seems like weeks since we were together."

"Months, Your Majesty." Henry looked like he had aged ten years, with gaunt hollow eyes, and long white streaks in his hair. He acted even more distracted, as well. Small wonder, since in the last six months he had been beaten in battle, captured, held against his will, kept apart from his wife, and forced to disinherit his son— it was amazing that he had any wits left at all. "We were last together at Greenwich, in October."

Henry looked puzzled. "When the Nevilles attacked me?"

That was in August. And they were not really Nevilles, but she had learned that with Henry it was best to go with the flow. "When Your Majesty hunted the royal deer."

"Of course." That was just before Parliament stripped him of everything but the crown. "Have you seen my queen?"

"Yes, Your Highness, in York, at Christmastime." Right now Queen Margaret was probably just across the Ver, almost within sight, but no one wanted to bring that up. Lady Robyn would have suggested that Henry should be hustled back to London for safe-keeping, but Margaret and Somerset were already between them and London.

Henry brightened visibly. "Did she speak of me?"

"With much love." As Edward's lady, she was one of the few people in England who passed easily between Margaret and Henry, since no one else was so well trusted by both them and Edward. King Henry had come to rely on her to send messages to his wife and his cousin Edward. "Indeed, she hardly spoke of anything else."

His Highness was overjoyed, not even asking about his son, whom Robyn had not seen anyway. Henry was about as good a father as he was a king. Getting his wife pregnant put him in a coma for a year and a half, during which King Henry sat and stared at the wall, not even acknowledging his son until the boy was a year old. Sadly, the country did much better when Henry was catatonic, so much that many folks remembered his coma with fondness, like the calm before the storm. Stolen away from his own mother, Henry had no training for life, much less fatherhood, and he treated Margaret as his long-lost mother, turning his kingdom over to her.

Lady Robyn took this happy moment to introduce Heidi, always a chancy proposition with a monarch who was terrified of women, but she had never seen a man flee from Heidi. Her gamble worked, as Heidi and Mad King Henry hit it off perfectly, chatting about her trip here and the remarkable weather in Maui, which she swore was "blazing hot when I left. So hot you could hardly bear a bikini."

"In February?" Even Mad King Henry was astonished.

"Something to do with the hurricane season," Heidi explained airily. "One day you are burned to a crisp, the next you are blown flat on your back."

"That is utterly unlike winters here in Hertfordshire." Where hurricanes hardly ever happened. Mad King Henry was completely captivated by the artless blonde, who could out-daffy him any day. Heidi offered him some trail mix with big chocolate chunks in it, and soon she had him eating out of her hand. This seemed some-what odd during a desperate battle to decide the fate of the kingdom, but Mad King Henry had clearly lost faith in battles. He was wounded at his first one, and his troops betrayed him at his second. This third one did not interest Henry in the least. Heidi, on the other hand, he found fascinating—at last, a pretty, nonthreatening woman, who was in absolutely no danger of talking down to him.

Lady Robyn was not too keen on battles either, this being her second in a month, but Lord Bonville asked what she had seen of the fighting. "Not much," she admitted, "mostly I sought to avoid it." Describing the fight in the market, around the big stone Eleanor's Cross, she estimated that, "Warwick's archers were winning, forcing Margaret's men back toward Saint Michael's Mill."

"What about my Lord Warwick?" Lord Bonville had recently changed sides—and was now looking like he regretted it.

"He was still on Barnard's Heath." Far from the action, though Robyn did not say so.

As the sun rose higher, the fighting heated up. Queen Margaret's men made another attack on the bowmen by the market cross; then Robyn saw troops wearing Somerset's colors suddenly burst out of Folly Lane, attacking the north end of town. Lord Bonville saw them, too, saying, "We need Warwick now."

Robyn nodded silently. She had seen enough fighting by now to know that without help from Warwick, the archers would never hold. The Neville earl needed to arrive now, with all his strength, or the men holding Saint Albans would be overwhelmed.

While the battle hung in the balance, Heidi and King Henry compared musical tastes. Heidi said that she absolutely adored Old English music. "The Beatles totally rock. And the Stones are okay, considering their age. I even like some of Elton John."

Mad King Henry confessed he had never heard of these groups, familiar as they might be to his subjects. "Court musicians played at Kenilworth, and now I hear only monks and choir music."

"Your Majesty must get out more," Heidi advised, though Henry's latest day trip from London had brought on a battle.

Henry protested that he actually liked religious music, adding shyly that he had composed a Gloria and Sanctus of his own. Heidi was ecstatic. "Really? A royal songwriter! Way to go, Your Highness. A Sanctus and a Gloria!"

Heidi absolutely insisted on hearing them, so King Henry hap-

pily obliged, proving to be a ho-hum composer, but a far better
singer than he was a king. Having a natural ear herself, Heidi easily
picked up the melody, accompanying him a cappella in medieval
Latin, singing the high parts to compliment His Majesty's plain-
chant. When they had exhausted Mad King Henry's original com-
positions, they went on to ballads and nursery rhymes, singing
every song Heidi and that nutty monarch knew. Which included old
favorites like the lullaby that ends with

> A cherry, when it's blooming, it has no stone,
> A chicken when it's peeping, it has no bone,
> A ring when it's rolling, it has no end,
> A baby when it's sleeping, has no cryin'.

And some lesser known ditties sung to still-familiar tunes:

> He won't come home till Easter,
> To see what he did see, to see what he did see:
> He won't come home till Easter,
> Or else at Trinity, or else at Trinity, or else at Trinity.

This impromptu Mardi Gras concert did not bother the armed
men standing about, who were entranced by Heidi's singing. Soldiers in battle were seldom serenaded by beautiful young blondes,
but when it happened, they liked it.

Henry had been king since he was nine months old, and by now
the English nobility was thoroughly accustomed to serving a
monarch who giggled and sang in moments of crisis—if he did not
go flat-out catatonic on them. They worked around him. In fact, an
insane head of state typified the medieval notion of aiding the hand-
icapped. It was the same sort of logic that made the King of France
pick King John the Blind of Bohemia as his vanguard commander:
the guy was a king, why would he need to see? Here and now, the
insane were treated like any other members of society, free to get
married, father children, even rule nations if they wished.

What did worry Lord Bonville was the battle. Warwick's archers
still held the town, but Somerset's attack out of Folly Lane had cut
the Yorkist army in half. Lord Warwick was fighting for his life on

Barnard's Heath north of town, cut off from Saint Albans, and from his king. Suddenly Lord Bonville, who had only just joined the Yorkist cause, was the lord in charge of Mad King Henry. Not an enviable position.

Wisest and safest would be to whisk Mad King Henry back to London, but Henry was a hard man to move. Ever since he was two, Henry had refused to go anywhere on Sundays, except to church. Even on weekdays, he tended to lag and complain, and being a king, he could not just be tossed on a horse and told to ride. Smart commanders like Edward no longer tried to take Henry with them on campaign, since he slowed them horribly, probably what His Majesty intended. Warwick had got Henry no more than a day's march out of London. Still, Robyn had to try, and told Bonville, "It would be far better for everyone if His Highness were in London."

Lord Bonville looked pained, saying, "I am here only to protect my king. Such matters are beyond my station."

And this was a member of the House of Lords speaking—a newly made Knight of the Garter, for God's sake—yet he was not qualified to act in a moment of national crisis. No wonder a clear-headed French peasant girl with a borrowed sword could thrash the English nobility so easily. After decades of mad rule, seeing the good punished and the bad promoted, they no longer dared think for themselves—but folks were still amazed that Edward won his victories with so few noblemen at his side.

"My lord, His Majesty would need far less protecting behind the walls of London." Lady Robyn felt horribly exposed here, with Henry singing under a tree. Anyone could come along, and she did not feel like giving the king to just anyone.

Bonville would not be budged, mumbling rather lamely, "The Earl of Warwick may soon prevail, and return to succor His Majesty."

They both knew how unlikely that was, with Somerset's troops between them and Barnard's Heath, battering at both ends of the town. King Henry must either stay here and be taken, or head off overland for London. "And if he does not?

Lord Bonville had no good answer, and precious moments were being wasted. But Bonville outranked her, being both male and a titled lord, so they must do whatever he willed, no matter how use-less. Medievalism at its most mindless.

Of course she could leave, but where could she go? Back to London made the most sense, but she hated to go without King Henry, who meant so much to so many. Just separating His Highness from Heidi would be a task in itself. Lady Robyn did nothing to spoil the Mardi Gras mood, hoping that things would break her way. Reinforcements might come from London, or some lord might show up who outranked Bonville and would listen to her. She said a prayer and waited, putting them all in the hands of Mary.

Warwick did not come, and there were no London reinforcements; instead, the outnumbered Yorkist archers in the town gave up the fight, falling back from the market cross, then breaking completely, streaming out Shropshire Street and Cock Lane, climbing over garden walls and hedges, scrambling through ditches to seek shelter in the woods and fields. Seeing Warwick's archers scatter, Lady Robyn told the bowmen who had escorted her from London that they, too, had best flee, for she could not save them if they were taken. They thanked her, and then they were gone. Matt she kept with her, since he wore her colors and was technically a noncombatant.

Lord Bonville saw that he had been beaten, and he knelt before his king, saying, "Your Majesty, fortune has favored Queen Margaret—"

"It has?" His Highness stopped playing with Heidi, shocked to hear that his queen had won. "Are you sure?"

"Indeed, there is no doubt." Even Bonville had given up on Warwick, nor did Sir Thomas Kyriell or Gower, the banner bearer, contradict him.

"This is absolutely marvelous, a Shrove Tuesday miracle." Henry was so used to losing battles by now, first in France, then at home, that he just naturally assumed whoever he favored would be beaten. "We must give thanks at once."

Which they all did, since giving thanks never hurt. Besides, Lord Bonville seemed about to change camps once again, saying to King Henry when they finished praying, "If Your Majesty will grant me pardon and safe conduct, I will take Your Highness to Queen Margaret."

"Could Her Majesty not come here to us?" Henry liked his spot under a tree, and he did not much fancy going into Saint Albans, where he had been wounded once before.

Bonville assured him it was perfectly safe, with the town in Margaret's hands, saying, "We are the ones in need of royal protection."

"Which you have, all of you." King Henry wanted nothing to mar this happy moment, and his favorite part of kingship was granting requests, giving titles to his relations, and pardons to perfect strangers. "Our royal protection, and most merciful pardon."

Meaning to see King Henry safely delivered into enemy hands, Robyn mounted up and rode into Saint Albans with Heidi and Matt at her side, dismounting when they got to a prosperous two-story black-timbered town house. Looting had already begun, and the startled home owner who answered Lord Bonville's knock was shocked and delighted to confront a royal visit rather than armed robbery. His family and servants fell to the floor before King Henry, begging his royal pardon for having the temerity to be living on a battlefield. Once again, Henry immediately dismissed their fears, grandly declaring their goods were safe, and their lives spared.

Robyn saw how royalty could be addictive. No wonder Henry liked being king, despite its many drawbacks. Literally everyone Mad King Henry met was overjoyed to see him, falling to their knees to give heartfelt thanks, and he was able to immediately grant their fondest wish—not to be robbed and murdered in the mayhem around them. With King Henry safely lodged in town, Bonville found a fellow named Thomas Hoo, directing him to find Queen Margaret and tell her where her husband was staying.

Hoo did not find Queen Margaret, but he did find Henry Percy, Earl of Nothumberland, because bowmen wearing the Percy crescent came to the door, escorting a delegation of lords sent to fetch their king. And only the king. Lord Bonville was immediately arrested, along with Sir Thomas Kyriell, and Gower, the banner bearer. They protested that they had King Henry's protection, but were promptly hauled away, without a word from His Majesty. Not a good sign. Robyn was determined to stick close to Henry, to see him delivered safely to Queen Margaret, since His frail Majesty was the only life between Edward and the throne.

Luckily, they did have King Henry's protection, and though His Highness had not even blinked at seeing Bonville, Kyriell, and Gower led off, she doubted Henry would part with her and Heidi so easily. Mad King Henry figured things differently from other men—and other monarchs, for that matter. Bonville, Kyriell, and Gower were men-at-arms, the bane of King Henry's reign. Strong, forceful men like them had bullied Henry all his life, and His Highness did not miss them much. But she and Heidi were another matter. Henry thought women were weak, sinful creatures, inherently promiscuous and put in man's path to test his purity, which made it all the more a triumph to drag two such tempting specimens through an excited mass of armed men.

Saint Peter's Street reeked of blood and wine. Armored bodies littered the road, and Margaret's troops had emptied the inn wine cellars, toasting their success with claret and Spanish sherry. Mardi Gras was back in full swing. Drunken bowmen bowed and gave their king a great "Hurrah" as he passed, before returning to robbing and abusing his subjects. Nor did King Henry make a move to stop the looting, proudly leading her and Heidi through the press. Amazingly, it was no one's business to see that the troops did not destroy the town they had spent all day trying to take. Lords who fought to rule all of England could not properly command Saint Albans.

This procession ended at a large tent topped with Lord Clifford's checkerboard banner. Not a cheery omen, since it was Clifford who murdered Edward's younger brother Edmund, after the battle of Wakefield. However, once inside the tent, it was all joyous celebration as Henry and Margaret were reunited after months of separation. Lady Robyn felt hugely out of place, like the ghost at the banquet, but at worst, they suspected her of enjoying loose relations with Edward of March, which was a sin though not a crime. Not a few of these men hoped she might also have loose relations with them, as well. So she could stand there with a smile pasted on her face, watching all her work being undone, and folks would only think she was coming to her political senses.

Though the battle was still being fought, King Henry began to pass out honors, something he found far safer and more satisfying.

First to be honored was his young son, the seven-year-old Prince of Wales, who wore pricey child's armor, a purple velvet brigandine trimmed with gold. In case the kid did not feel important enough, every man in the army was wearing his black ostrich feather badge—the same one Edward had worn while in disguise. After another round of prayer, Mad King Henry knighted his son, and then the young prince knighted practically anyone who stepped up.

Or even limped up. First to be honored was Andrew Trollope, who had stepped on a steel caltrap—which went through his boot and pierced his foot. Having betrayed both the Plantagenets and the Nevilles, Trollope hobbled up to claim his reward, confessing to the young prince that he did not deserve knighthood, "for I slew but fifteen men, since I had to stand in one place while they came at me."

Everyone laughed at his sally, and the awards ceremony went on, alternating prayers and one-liners. Besides the two-time traitor Trollope, thirty others stepped up to be knighted, including the Lord Roos, and the young Earl of Shrewsbury, who owned Goodrich Castle, and John Grey, Elizabeth's husband, who had already styled himself a knight and now was one for real. Everyone from supporters in Parliament to Queen Margaret's Wardrobe Master was raised to knighthood. Having won their second battle in as many months, the Lancastrian lords were positively giddy, and as soon as they got King Henry back, they had to use him to bump everyone up a notch on the feudal hierarchy, in an awards-ceremony-cum-tent-meeting. Before the battle was even won. There was still the off chance that Warwick would come blazing back from Barnard's Heath, with his handguns and flamethrowers. Highly unlikely, 'tis true, but Robyn knew Edward would never stop in midbattle to have an infant hand out awards to noncombatants and walking wounded. None of these thirty new knights did anything to stop the looting in Saint Albans. Lancastrians lost so often because they refused to take even war seriously.

Last to kneel before the prince was a stab from the past, literally, a man-at-arms whose mere presence made her wince, Gilbert FitzHolland. He had shaved off his blond beard for the ceremony, but she easily recognized his cruel lip and crafty eyes, and he had spotted her, as well, smirking her way as he stepped up to be honored. FitzHolland had hated her since the first day she arrived in the Middle Ages. Without knowing where she came from, he sensed that behind her pert answers and transparent evasions, she did not give a damn for him, or his king, or his one-size-fits-all religion. In Mad King Henry's England such opinions were capital offenses, and as a king's sergeant-at-law, FitzHolland had been striving to see justice done to her since day one. After so many dubbings, the little prince had to be tired, and Robyn hoped he would slip, beheading FitzHolland by mistake.

No such luck, the knighting went off without a hitch, and now her nemesis was Sir Gilbert FitzHolland, while she had become Lady Robyn of Pontefract. Since that fateful Saint George's Day when they first met, the two of them had been rising up the social ladder, for all the wrong reasons. She was now sleeping with a royal duke, and Sir Gilbert had recently cut the head off an earl. Medieval England was plainly the land of opportunity for energetic folks with few scruples. She nudged Heidi and nodded, whispering, "That's the FitzHolland I warned you about."

"Darth Vader himself." Heidi had heard hideous FitzHolland stories from the coven members hounded by him—tales of torture, kidnapping, and offhand murder.

"Just about." Robyn surveyed the men crowding the big tent, seeing none of FitzHolland's usual accomplices. "Luckily, he is alone. No sign of his bastard brothers, or Le Boeuf, his pet executioner."

Sir Gilbert was bad enough. So long as she was close to King Henry, Robyn felt reasonably safe—but that could not last. Oddly, the two people best disposed toward her were also the most power-ful, Henry and Margaret, which showed she had not wasted her nine months in the Middle Ages. She told Heidi, "All we can do is stay close to the royals and play ladies in distress."

Heidi rolled her eyes. "Too totally medieval."

"Just do not flub your lines," Robyn reminded her, though by now Heidi was a veteran lady in distress, with a proven track record in handling medieval men. Not to mention werewolves.

This family reunion and tent revival ended with another prayer; then the newly minted knights trooped out to smite Warwick's min-ions out on Barnard's Heath. Mad King Henry instinctively went

the other way, headed for shelter in Saint Albans abbey. Lady
Robyn mounted up and followed her sovereign, with Heidi and
Matt riding behind her.

Only to be blocked by Sir Gilbert FitzHolland, now mounted
and backed by armed retainers in Holland livery. "What ho, whore!
Who said you could trail after your betters?"

"We have His Majesty's protection." For what that was worth.

"Let me see it, strumpet." FitzHolland had her there, since she
had not gotten the safe-conduct in writing.

"His Majesty will remember me." She hoped.

"His Highness will not even know you are missing." FitzHolland
leaned over and seized her reins in his steel gauntlet. Matt tried to
come to her aid, but FitzHolland's men deftly cut him off. Violence
hung in the air—indeed dead bodies and weeping women lined
Saint Peter's Street—and FitzHolland must have figured that a couple more would hardly be noticed.

"Good, Sir Gilbert," a confident voice called out, "I will take
charge of these women."

"What ape in hell are you?" FitzHolland turned in the saddle to
see who was interfering with his abduction.

"Her Majesty's ape," the armored horseman replied. It was the
newly knighted Sir John Grey, Margaret's cavalry commander. Sir
John Grey was plainly in a gay mood, having his knighthood confirmed and his king freed, all in the same morning.

FitzHolland had a similarly excellent morning, yet was in his
usual sour humor. Lady Robyn knew from grim experience that it
took someone else's pain or humiliation to put a smile on FitzHolland's face. Her captor demanded to know, "Why is it your business
what I do with this woman?"

"Not my business," Sir John replied jauntily, "Queen Margaret's. Her Majesty wants both these women in Saint Albans
abbey, under the care of old Abbot Whethamstede."

By now Robyn was not the least surprised to see Queen Margaret's commanders nearly coming to blows in the midst of victory.
Barely a battle went by when Margaret's men did not change sides,
disobey orders, or fight private quarrels—it was partly Margaret's
loose command style and partly straight out looter mentality. Every-

one was here for what they could gain, and since it was all illegal, arguments abounded. Right now they were fighting over her.

FitzHolland fumed aloud, but he finally backed down, dropping her reins and moving his charger aside. Both men were newly made knights, but young Sir John Grey was Queen Margaret's cavalry commander and married to a Wydville, while FitzHolland was a bastard relation to an insane branch of the royal family. So instead of being hauled off to who-knew where, Lady Robyn found herself escorted down Saint Peter's Street to Saint Albans abbey by Sir John Grey. By now it was near to noon, and though the day was warming, snow had started to fall, whitening and softening the steel-clad bodies. At close range, heavy yard-long arrows had gone right through plate armor, puncturing the knights inside. And all around them victorious troops were breaking into the breweries and emptying the shops, robbing everyone, right down to the beggars.

Sir John saw them safely to the abbey gate, easily earning the knight-errant award on this dismal Shrove Tuesday. He told Robyn, "Abbot Whethamstede will see you are safe for the night, and my wife is arriving on the morrow from Goodrich. This is not a good time for women to be out and abroad on their own."

Or witches either. Sir John was born into a ranking witch family, and he had a witch-wife, giving him connections to Queen Margaret's inner circle that FitzHolland could only envy, and fear. Robyn thanked him for his service, saying, "Without you, Queen Margaret's protection would have done us little good."

Sir John laughed, saying, "Queen Margaret does not care for you. I lied about that to cheat FitzHolland. You have no protection, so be on your guard until my wife arrives."

Good to know that. She should have learned by now never to believe a Wydville—or any of their in-laws. He still got a kiss goodbye from her and Heidi, because he had come to their aid, and because he was riding off into harm's way. Heidi sighed as he cantered away, "How come the best ones are married?"

"Or gay," Robyn pointed out.

"Or married and gay." Heidi was beginning to get how the Middle Ages worked. In 1461, adultery and closet marriages were already a cottage industry—witness Sister Perpetua, married to God but still certainly getting around.

Once inside the abbey, it was plain the royals could protect no one. Abbot Whethamstede was beside himself, pleading with King Henry to save the abbey, but all the old man got was the bland reassurance Henry gave everyone. Of course the abbey was safe, this was sacred ground, and a king's first duty was to be God's steward. "Not a stone of this abbey will be touched."

Oddly enough, Mad King Henry's prediction came to pass, since the abbey stones were left standing, though everything else of value was looted by His Majesty's troops. Food, wine, furniture, tapestries, vestments, crosses, chalices, and Abbot Whethamstede's silverware, all vanished in an orgy of armed robbery. Locals were too frightened to object, and no one in the army cared enough to stop it. Almost all Queen Margaret's troops were northerners, recruited with the promise of plunder. FitzHolland was one of the few southerners in Queen Margaret's army, and one look at him told you their quality was not the best. Anyone who gave a groat for what the folks in Saint Albans thought was already fighting for the other side.

Matt took the horses, saying he would find a place to hide them, while Lady Robyn spent the night barricaded in an upper-floor room with Heidi and a dozen frightened nuns who sat on the floor praying and telling their beads, terrified that armed men would break in and drag them out into the Mardi Gras party, this being one Fat Tuesday Saint Albans would not soon forget.

As the nuns nodded off, Robyn complimented Heidi on her singing. "You did great—that extended duet was just what Henry needed to keep from totally flipping out. You have learned to handle royalty well."

"King Henry? He was a snap." Heidi arched an eyebrow, "I seduced the man who seduced his mother. Remember?" Heidi was, in fact, getting on famously with the royal family, especially the male members.

Robyn smiled ruefully. "Well, he is with his wife now."

"Aren't they all?" Heidi leaned back against a nun and tried to get some sleep.

Whatever happened next, Robyn meant to get a T-shirt stitched that said, I SURVIVED THE SACK OF SAINT ALBANS.

She awoke in predawn chill to the sound of men pounding on the door, demanding entry in the king's name. Nuns moaned in dismay, but the men outside sounded sober, and there was no real way to keep them out. Reluctantly they tore down the barricade, and the oldest and bravest nun unbarred the door, asking, "Who dares disturb a house of God?"

"Sir Gilbert FitzHolland," was the chilling reply, "coming to do the king's business." It was indeed FitzHolland, looking mean and miserable, wearing boots and half-armor at a truly wretched hour in the morning.

"Not with us," the old nun protested, "this is sacred ground."

"No, not with nuns," FitzHolland scoffed at that suggestion, "with the two witches you are harboring,"

Robyn rose to face him, feeling rather rumpled wearing her slept-in riding gown, saying, "We are under the protection of Sir John Grey and Queen Margaret."

FitzHolland sneered at her protests. "Queen Margaret is not here. And Sir John Grey is dead, killed by your friend Warwick. You and your accomplice are under arrest for witchcraft and treason."

13

⋯⇒ Ash Wednesday ⇐⋯

Warwick was no friend of hers. Having botched the battle of Saint Albans—and lost King Henry to boot—he succeeded in killing the one enemy commander giving her some protection. Thank you, Lord Warwick. She did not even want to believe it. Sir John had been so happy and matter-of-fact, magnanimous in victory and concerned with her safety. Now he was gone, dead. Hardly fair. Not to him, or to her. And poor Elizabeth Grey was another widow. Half the women she knew had lost husbands or lovers in this national catastrophe—Heidi, Jo, Gwyn, Proud Cis, Elizabeth

Grey and Elizabeth Poynings, old Countess Alice. What a list, and here was FitzHolland, sword in hand, eager to add more names.

Luckily this was the Middle Ages, and women had an immediate recourse when confronted by villains like this. Dropping to her knees, Lady Robyn crossed herself, and addressed the Almighty in his own tongue, praying in Latin for the soul of Sir John Grey, father of Thomas and Richard, husband of Elizabeth Grey, née Wydville. At times Sir John had been her enemy, and at times her protector—either way, she missed him mightily. Lest the Lord assume that Sir John Grey was the only one with problems, Lady Robyn suggested the Almighty ought to also look in on his abbey at Saint Albans, where unchristian things had been happening for the better part of a day now, with small sign of abating. Heidi joined her, and it did not take much to get a bunch of scared nuns praying—not in a looted abbey on Ash Wednesday.

Faced with a room packed full of praying women in a house of God, lesser villains would have gone looking for easier prey, but FitzHolland was determined to have his prize. Stepping through the doorway, he seized her arm, jerking Robyn to her feet. "My lady will go with me. There will be time for plenty of prayer."

FitzHolland was wearing gauntlets, and the frigid steel bit through her dress fabric, bringing back the day a month ago when Wiltshire's men beat her to her knees. They had only wanted to pummel and rape her, while FitzHolland was ten times worse. Her sole hope was that he would just take her and spare Heidi, whom FitzHolland had never seen before yesterday.

Heidi took it out of his hands, standing up beside her and seizing her cloak, saying, "Stop. This is a house of God. She has these sisters' protection."

Horrified nuns stared up at her. How Heidi thought they could help anyone was beyond them, since half the sisters had taken their vows just to escape situations like this. FitzHolland glared at this unwelcome intrusion, asking, "Who are you?"

Heidi tried to be cooperative, without letting go of the cloak. "A friend."

FitzHolland grinned to hear that. "Which makes you a witch as well." Guilt by association was a hallowed principle of medieval jurisprudence. "Come with us."

Tightening his steel grip until it hurt, FitzHolland dragged her out of the room and into a bare abbey hallway stripped to the stone walls and smelling of smoke. Heidi came with her, refusing to let go of the cloak. FitzHolland's men closed around them, and she was hustled down the hallway, with Heidi hanging on to her. None of the nuns objected.

Outside under gloomy skies, Ash Wednesday lived up to its name. Fires had filled the air with soot. As they passed a scorched outbuilding, Lady Robyn rubbed her hand on a burnt timber, then put a palm smudge of ash on her forehead. Heidi did the same. Whatever happened, this was a holy day, the first day of Lent, when Christ suffered in the wilderness. People were supposed to suffer with him, giving up the sins of the flesh, and the smear of ash on her forehead was the traditional sign of sorrow for Christ's suffering.

Queen Margaret had gone them one better, turning Saint Albans itself into a howling wilderness. Losing was so ingrained in Margaret by now, that the queen had to turn her latest victory into a loss by destroying what she won. After Mortimer's Cross and Owen Tudor's execution, Hereford had an unsettling normalcy to it. Any victory celebration was muted by the long list of dead, as people strived to recover and forget, getting ready for market Wednesday, trying to block out the bloodshed with work. Only Heidi had insisted on making a scene, washing Owen's face and lighting all those candles. Here in Saint Albans, no one was allowed to have a life. Everyone was robbed of everything worth taking, and what was not burnt was left abandoned, with doors thrown open and shutters swinging in the winter wind. Bodies had been carted off to mass graves, but broken belongings still littered the street. And women were not safe, not even in Saint Albans abbey, amid a room full of nuns. FitzHolland led them to a half-timbered town house, filled with Duke Holland's men. Robyn saw no sign of the original owners as she was shuffled into a dark second-floor bedchamber, with a heavy door bar and the window shutters nailed shut for the winter. FitzHolland bade them be comfortable, and then he left. Lady Robyn lit a candle stub with her lighter, seeing a washstand and a single bed with a chamber pot beneath it, and no other furniture. Heat came from a low fire in a fireplace far too small to crawl out through. Hearing the heavy bar slide into place, she told Heidi, "Make yourself at home."

Heidi flopped down on the bed, while Lady Robyn took the candle stub over to the window and examined the shutters. They were nailed shut with big hand-forged spikes, which were actually easier to get out than modern finishing nails. One of the hinges was loose as well. Luckily, everything in the Middle Ages was handmade, and what hands could make, hands could take apart. She had a sturdy nail file in her purse. Finding it, she started to attack the loose hinge. Heidi asked from the bed, "What's going to happen?"

"If I get this shutter open, we are going out the window." One advantage of a ridiculously adventurous life was that it prepped you for dire emergencies. When you have escaped from a besieged tower on knotted bedsheets and rappelled down Goodrich Castle on a rope, you think nothing about going out some second-story window in a Saint Albans town house, even in calf-length boots and a scarlet riding dress.

"What happens if we do not get the window open?" Heidi clearly had her doubts about digging their way out of this second-floor bedchamber with a nail file.

"Nothing good," Robyn replied, grimly working on the hand-forged iron hinge with her tempered-steel file. This could work, if she kept at it. Heidi had not seen her get out of Berkeley dungeon with her VISA card. "FitzHolland is as bad as they come. He's the one who tortured me in the Tower."

Hence her frantic attempt to take apart the window. Her stay in the Tower of London had been the most terrible thing that had ever happened to her, bar none. FitzHolland had kept her in a black windowless cell, coming in only to gloat and wring lurid confessions from her on the rack his father built. She would do anything to see that never happened again.

"What's FitzHolland's problem?" Heidi had just met the man, but already knew there was something seriously wrong.

"Hereditary insanity." You could see it in FitzHolland's eyes, the way they bulged in anger when he did not get his way.

Heidi came over to help her with the window, worried by what she was hearing. "Thought that was King Henry's problem?"

"They are cousins." She handed Heidi a nail that she had prized out of the hinge.

Heidi used the heavy nail to dig at another one, still buried in the shutter. "Isn't Edward Henry's cousin?"

"Different branch of the family." By now Robyn knew the bloodlines by heart. "King Henry and the Hollands are directly descended from princesses in the French royal family, and the insanity is sex-linked, like hemophilia or color blindness—it only shows in the men, though women carry it, too. Edward's mother is a Neville, and his maternal grandmother was a Mortimer. His dad was nuts, but no more than most old guys with too much money and a short temper."

"But the royal side of the family keeps marrying tainted French princesses." Heidi had caught on to how hereditary monarchy could become a family curse.

Robyn nodded, prying at a nail with her file. "To preserve their claim to France." That mad claim was literally driving the family nuts. "But a lot of the old families have this problem—failure in the male line. Inbreeding seems to hurt men the most." Another reason why widows and teenagers were starting to rule England.

"Figures." Heidi shook her blond head sadly. "Guys got to be free to fuck, otherwise what use are they?"

Lady Robyn nodded. "If you want a big crop of healthy babies, marry some ambitious squire like Lord Rivers."

"Or Owen." Heidi went back to working away at her nail. "What are the symptoms?"

Robyn pried another nail out of the loose hinge. "You met Henry. He is a pretty mild case, and Pembroke barely shows it at all, though they had the same mother. Henry's grandfather, on the other hand, went completely psychotic. Mostly it's paranoia, erratic instability, excessive cruelty, and a dash of good looks. King Philip the Fair of France was supposed to be a handsome recluse who hated to talk in public, tortured and murdered the Templars, and drove the Jews out of France. FitzHolland's grandfather was a torturer and murderer, and his father supposedly invented the rack."

"Shit!" Heidi pried harder. "You make him sound like the Marquis de Sade."

"You wish." De Sade was way too subtle for the Hollands and, like most Frenchmen, was more hung up on sex than death. Which could not be said of Gilbert FitzHolland—the whole time he was hurting her in the Tower, he never even tried to see her naked.

Leaving her loose hinge hanging by a single nail, in case FitzHolland came to check on them, she attacked one of the nails in the sill, tearing her own flesh with the steel file. Tears welled up, as she and Heidi worked side by side in silence. She could hardly believe how horribly Warwick had screwed up. That idiot Neville had thousands of men in armor, armed with cannon, handguns, and those deadly long bows, and he had London solidly behind him—all Warwick had to do was hold out until Edward arrived. Instead, Warwick had lost everything—her, Heidi, Mad King Henry, Saint Albans, thousands of lives, all those guns and cannon. There were a lot of folks worse off than her, like wounded fugitives slowly freezing in the snowy fields—it was too much to hope that Warwick was one of them.

"Matt's free." Heidi tried to sound hopeful.

"Maybe he will have the sense to find Edward." When FitzHolland had her in the Tower, Matt had been her sole hope, the only guard who seemed on her side. She had told him then to go to Edward, and she guessed Matt would know to do that now. "But it will take time."

"Would the Wydvilles spring us?" Heidi plainly did not care who saved her.

"Maybe." She did not want to get her friend's hopes up. "For a price."

"What do the Wydvilles want?" Heidi had gotten her nail half out, and she was pulling on it with both hands, trying to get out of the room by main force.

"Power, mainly. Wealth, too." She watched her friend pull, realizing the candle had almost burned out.

"Pretty typical." Heidi pulled harder on the nail.

"Perhaps." Edward did not need wealth, since he had that in spades, but he certainly planned to run England. And after Warwick's latest fiasco, who could blame him? "Some folks figure it is better to win the consent of the people—while the Wydvilles just want to win."

Heidi ripped the nail free, grinning triumphantly. "And they think you can help them?"

"Let's hope so." She felt perfectly willing to sell herself to the Wydvilles if it got her away from FitzHolland. No one came to check on them or bring them food, or water. Robyn knew from past experience that FitzHolland was lax about feeding prisoners. Twice they snacked on the water and trail mix in her bag. But each time she returned to the task more frayed and tired than before.

When they had an inch of candle left, Robyn gave her bleeding fingers a rest. They had one hinge loosened and two nails pulled from the frame—not much to show for hours of work—with another hinge and a dozen nails left to go. Pretty hopeless. By now it was Ash Wednesday afternoon, though so cold and dark you could barely know it; gray light came through the shutters, and the frigid air had the vibrance of day, not the stillness of night.

Heidi was hungry, asking, "What do you think room service is like?"

Robyn rolled her eyes. Blowing out the candle, she put more wood on the fire, and huddled with Heidi for warmth on the narrow bed, rubbing arnica and ointment on their raw hands. Then Heidi insisted on rubbing her neck and shoulders, as well, which actually relaxed her, letting her forget for a moment all the weight she carried. Turning the neck massage into a full out backrub, Heidi got behind her on the bed, working her way down Robyn's back and buttocks, stripping off her boots to get at her calves and feet. Medievals had a lot to learn about massage. Heidi's hands were so soothing that Robyn sank facedown into the bed, giving her body to the lice and vermin that lurked in the linen—if the worst she got out of this was bug bites, that would be way better than her stay in the Tower.

When Heidi was done, the ex-Lady of Harlech lay down alongside Robyn, hips to buttocks, one hand cupping her former boss's breast, taking full advantage of the fact that they were not going anywhere. By now Robyn had learned not to be too alarmed. Heidi had to be physical with her affection; whatever Heidi liked, Heidi had to touch—even fondle if possible. Leaning over, Heidi kissed her ear, whispering, "What are the ashes for?"

"What ashes?" With eyes closed, all she could feel was the bed beneath her and Heidi's body half atop her.

"On our foreheads." Heidi stroked her brow.

Heidi felt good lying on her—good, but way too small. She wanted Edward's firm weight enveloping her, protecting her, ready to spring into action, pummeling any dozen villains who dared come through the door. She thought for a while, then smiled in the dark, whispering, "For you."

"For me?" Heidi squeezed her breast in excitement. "Really?"

"Women like you anyway." Was anyone else she knew "like" Heidi? Hardly.

Giggling with delight, Heidi did not mind sharing the honor. "So what do you mean? About the ashes."

"It's a long story, literally."

"We got time," Heidi assured her.

"Hopefully." Robyn wished they had gotten more done on the window. "FitzHolland could haul us out anytime, and do Heaven knows what."

"Then I absolutely have to hear the story." Her uncertain childhood had taught Heidi to treat each moment as her last.

"Okay, but first we must free ourselves, for it is a holy story." Robyn badly needed to be centered, and to cast out her fear.

"You mean like do a ritual?"

"A horizontal ritual." She felt much too relaxed to get up and cast a circle.

Heidi giggled. "My favorite kind."

Obviously, but Robyn meant this seriously. Rolling over to face Heidi, she took her hands, saying, "We have to admit we put ourselves here."

Heidi rolled her eyes. "Really? I thought FitzHolland picked this place."

"FitzHolland picked the spot, but we chose to oppose him. And to do it on his own turf, in his time and place."

Heidi looked levelly back at her, eyes twinkling in the firelight. "This is true."

Lady Robyn had to absolve the Earl of Warwick, as well. Sure the noxious Neville had screwed up—but it was Warwick, what else would he do? She had insisted on undoing Warwick's mistakes,

despite the obvious dangers. Squeezing Heidi's hands, she whispered, "I wanted to come back here, and I wanted you with me. But
you wanted to come as well, or I would never have been able to
bring you."

Heidi nodded. "I wanted to be with you."

And here they were, locked in a second-floor bedchamber, waiting to see what FitzHolland had planned for them. "Just so you
know you asked for it. Now you must not molest me while I tell
you the story, because it is a holy one, and a women's secret."

Heidi vowed to behave, settling back to listen, still holding
Robyn's hands in hers.

"What follows is not just a women's secret," Robyn warned,
"but a crime, as well. If you tell this to a man, or to the wrong
woman, you risk being tortured, hanged, or burned. So are you
sure you want to hear it?"

"More than ever." Heidi squeezed her hands.

Her friend's reckless disregard for consequences could be infectious—since they were out to burn you no matter what, why not
go the whole way? "Ash Wednesday is the first day of Lent, the
forty days of fasting before Easter, and in Christian terms, the
ashes are a sign of sorrow for Christ's suffering, in the wilderness
and on the cross. And that is half of why I wear them." Lady
Robyn was by now medieval enough to fully believe that Christ
was God come to earth, but that Mary who bore him was the
Goddess—it was the only explanation that even remotely made
sense.

"Witches tell an older story, saying that Easter was celebrated
with eggs and bunnies, long before Christ. Easter is the spring rite
sacred to the Mother Goddess, called Oster by the Germans, Ishtar
by the Babylonians, Isis by the Egyptians, and Esther in the Old
Testament. This female half of the Easter story was edited out of
the Bible. It is Ishtar's story, and Mary's story, and it tells about a
virgin girl who grows in the summertime, dies in winter, then is
reawakened in spring by love's first kiss—it is the story of Snow
White, Rose Red, Sleeping Beauty, Cinderella, Thumbelina, and all
the other heroines sent into the woods, to find love and death. It is
the story behind the virgin sacrifice. Actually, it is every woman's
story, though I never knew it until I came here."

Heidi just lay there, looking back at her, smiling slightly. Robyn asked, "Afraid you are in bed with a religious fanatic?"

Heidi's smile widened. "At least she is a pretty one."

Lady Robyn went on with her tale, saying, "I never understood Disney until I came to the Middle Ages. All those weird Snow White, Sleeping Beauty, wicked-witch stories are actually folk legends about a girl who conquers death through the act of love, who gives of her body so that people may go on living. For some obscure reason, having to do with his mother, this was the story Walt wanted to tell, over and over again. Each time the heroine's opponent is the Death Crone, death in her various guises—the wicked witch, the bad fairy godmother, the Snow Queen, the Old Toad, and the Mother Mole. Our only triumph over death is new life, born from the prince's kiss."

"At least in the PG version." Heidi had long ago discovered what the cartoons left out.

"But each heroine has to go through hell to find her love." No surprise there. "She must literally or symbolically endure a winter's death, either sleeping like Snow White and Sleeping Beauty, or living underground like Thumbelina. Or like Cinderella, a maiden can partake symbolically by putting funeral ashes on her face."

"And that is me?" Letting go of Robyn's hand, Heidi touched the ash on her forehead.

Robyn nodded. "You lie between winter and spring, death and life, and FitzHolland is as much a devil as you are ever likely to meet. Yet you have inside you the power to make new life."

"Waiting for my prince to come?" Heidi asked slyly.

"Something like that." Robyn's prince had come and gone.

Heidi read her mind. "How about you?"

Lady Robyn laughed. "My ashes are Christian symbolism. I am already a mother." For better or ill, the seed of life was growing inside her, just like in the frozen fields outside, where seeds were stirring beneath the snow. "You are the maiden; I am the mother."

Dinner was bread and wine, and since it was Lent, there was not even cheese to go with it, much less sausage. All of Christendom was finishing the winter on reduced rations, and the prisoners were properly thankful for their wine and bread, making it into an Ash

Wednesday feast. Heidi asked, "And what about Esther in the Bible?"

"Esther 'went down' literally, becoming a concubine to the King of Persia. Worse than death to a good Jewish virgin. But she rose again and got the king to marry her, showering favor upon the Jews—which is why all good Hebrews celebrate Purim sometime soon. None of this made sense until I came to the Middle Ages."

"Fancy that?" Heidi smirked.

After prying four more nails out of the window, they called it a night, halfway to getting the window open. "If we get a burst of energy, we might even break out by morning."

Sleep did not come easy on a narrow bed with Heidi lying beside her, complaining at every flea bite. And as soon as sleep arrived, it was immediately whisked away by the sound of the bar being drawn back. Heidi shook her, saying, "Someone is coming in."

No shit. She immediately thought of that horrible Saturday night in the Tower, when FitzHolland, Le Boeuf, and the old Lord Scales burst into her cell, determined to wring every bit of useful information out of her before Sunday morning put an end to the grim festivities. Being wakened in the middle of the night would never be the same. For Heidi it was old hat, and Robyn could feel her friend crouched over her, waiting for the door to open. Lying there, Robyn realized that Heidi was braced to defend her, half-covering her, with one hand between her and the door.

Light flooded the room, and Robyn saw that Heidi was holding one of the big hand-beaten nails in her hand, for all the good that would do against men in armor. But there were no men in armor, only two great ladies backed by nuns bearing torches. At first Robyn thought she was dreaming, or at least hallucinating, seeing two Court ladies in heraldic gowns enter the room; Jacquetta Wydville, Duchess of Bedford, and old Lady Scales, Sir Anthony Wydville's mother-in-law. Medieval England never lacked for the surreal, even in the middle of the night.

Heidi palmed her nail, leaped out of bed, and had the good sense to go down on her knee before Duchess Wydville. Lady Robyn did the same, happy that they had worn underclothes to bed for warmth. She had on a long silk chemise, and Heidi wore a linen shift, both of which paled in comparison to the satin, velvet, and clouds of lace worn by their noble visitors. Wydville white-and-scarlet contrasted with the nuns' dark habits, and Lady Scales's black widow gown. Duchess Wydville declared in a thick middle European accent, "It is vonderful to see you, Lady Stafford."

Wonderful to see you under lock and key was what the witch-duchess meant. Lady Robyn replied evenly, "How good to see, Your Grace."

Duchess Wydville turned to Heidi. "And who is your fair young bedmate?"

"Her name is Heidi, Your Grace."

"Pretty name, for a pretty maiden," purred the duchess. "Are you, too, from the future?"

Heidi tried to make it sound less like a curse. "Afraid so, Your Worship."

"*Nein, nein,* do not apologize, sweet child." Duchess Wydville herself was born in Luxemburg. "You are pretty and well-spoken, and will go far—unless we have to burn you."

"Oh, I am totally not worth burning." Heidi tried to sound as insignificant as possible, her existence in this millennium being merely a cosmic oversight.

"We would be happy to give you protection." Duchess Wydville spoke not only for herself and Lady Scales, but for individuals too powerful to be named. "Yet you have continually rejected our hospitality, last month at Codnor, and more recently at Goodrich, both times fleeing in the company of known outlaws and rebels."

Robyn felt like an incorrigible runaway, shamelessly chasing after thoroughly bad boys. "Pray forgive my silly ingratitude."

Duchess Wydville arched an eyebrow. "And your pert replies?"

Robyn nodded obediently. "Those, too, if it pleases Your Grace."

"All would be forgiven if you would only see reason," Duchess Wydville reminded her. "You know that our true interests coincide. You want peace—so do we. You want Edward of March excluded from the throne—so do we. There was even a time when we were on the same side."

That would be before the Duchess had Gilbert FitzHolland burn Greystone and kidnap Jo and Joy, sending Robyn fleeing for the

Welsh hills. Being allies with the Wydvilles was like living with a wolf pack, with Duchess Wydville as the alpha bitch; you lived and breathed by their rules, and even then they might turn on you. Though compared with the Hollands and FitzHollands, the Wydvilles came off like the Brady Bunch.

"If Edward of March will recognize the rights of the Prince of Wales, the nation might end its strife." With Queen Margaret in power and Edward in their pocket, witches would be running England, not totally a bad thing. Spellcraft would get some protection, and witches were not very war-minded.

Lady Robyn could have a big part of that, if she played her hand right. "What makes you think I can convince Edward to support the prince?"

Duchess Wydville's smile turned to a knowing smirk, as if to say there were nuns present. "So long as you want it with all your heart, then we will easily sway young Edward."

Duchess Wydville was right, of course. They were witches, after all, and love magic was the most reliable—far easier than changing the weather. Together they could whip up a love spell that would have Edward never wanting to be king, if it meant losing her. So long as the spell was heartfelt, anything was possible. Almost. Edward in love was still Edward of March, not just a man but a cause. If Edward reversed himself at whim, particularly at her whim, she would become the most hated woman in England. Or maybe second to Queen Margaret. "Even for love of me, Edward would never betray his followers."

"Nonsense," the duchess snorted at the notion. "Even now London is coming over to the queen's side. With the king, queen, Edward, and London all together, supported by the best lords, as well, everyone will line up to obey. He would not be betraying his people, but leading them."

Warwick would be odd man out, but after this second battle of Saint Albans, Warwick's stock was at rock bottom. In the last week, the city fathers had lent Warwick two thousand pounds, equal to an earl's income, and that, too, was gone. What really mattered now was what London did. "Will the city open her gates for Her Majesty?"

"Archbishop Bourchier and the chancellor have fled, along with Warwick, leaving London in the hands of commoners." Duchess

Wydville's disdain made it plain she thought the commons had scant hope of running the city on their own. "Mayor Richard Lee and his aldermen have asked us to negotiate the city's surrender to Queen Margaret."

London was lost. With Queen Margaret's army less than a day away, the city's fate was being decided by the witch-duchess and the French queen. Unbelievable. Without Warwick, the city fathers folded right up. Some were secretly on Queen Margaret's side from the start, yearning for a return to the glory days when her lavish spending put tax money in their silk purses. Ordinary Londoners would be aghast, but no one consulted commoners—not in moments of crisis. This was when the country could use a mentally competent king. As it was, Queen Margaret would have King Henry and the capital, and most of the House of Lords, making Edward once again a rebel against the crown.

Duchess Wydville's smile widened. "Whatever men say, we know there is nothing really worth fighting over. All that matters is that we, and those we love, are safe. You can have life and happiness with Edward as Duke and Duchess of York, or Lord and Lady of the March."

Or she could burn at the stake. Duchess Wydville was anything but subtle. Her son-in-law, Sir John Grey, was dead, killed the day before in what must have been a grotesque mischance in the midst of victory—a supreme family tragedy inflicted on her oldest child, and only grandchildren. Yet here was the duchess, wheeling and dealing, and intimidating prisoners, as if it were just another Ash Wednesday. Robyn sighed, asking, "What does Your Grace desire?"

"We can see that London returns easily and peacefully into the king's hands. My Lady Stafford is well loved in the city, and she could sway the turbulent commons. Her Majesty has dispatched Sir Baldwin Fulford to Barnet with four hundred men, but the city itself has not opened its gates."

That was good news. London was holding out against Queen Margaret, even though the chancellor and the archbishop had fled, and the mayor was in league with the Wydvilles. Edward had a hope, even if she did not.

"So we require a way into the city, and safe lodging within the walls."

Which meant Baynards Castle. That was what lay behind this late-night call. Duchess Wydville was not taking a moment to gloat or even trying to recruit Robyn to the cause. Despite the smashing victory at Saint Albans, Queen Margaret was still desperate to get into London. Four hundred men in Barnet did not amount to much, but four hundred men in Baynards Castle was a power base, and the beginnings of a city garrison.

"I can do nothing to help from here," Lady Robyn pointed out, hinting that Duchess Wydville might spring her if Her Grace wanted real cooperation.

Her Grace was not buying. "And here you shall stay, unless you swear to surrender Baynards Castle into King Henry's hands."

"No one will surrender Baynards Castle on my word," Robyn protested.

Duchess Wydville replied with a patient smile, "If you give your parole and vow to surrender the castle, you will be escorted there at once."

"Pray give me time to think on this," Robyn pleaded. She could not just give Baynards Castle to the queen, but it did not seem healthy to say that to Her Grace.

"Do not take too long," Duchess Wydville warned. "Gilbert FitzHolland is eager to see you burn. There are more prominent executions scheduled ahead of yours, but the list is short."

With that, Duchess Wydville left, trailed by the nuns and Lady Scales, who had not said a word. When the door closed, they were back to kneeling in the blackness. Heidi exhaled softly, saying, "Her Grace is sure the cheery sort."

Robyn grimaced. "You should see her dancing naked round a bonfire."

"I did," Heidi replied, "at Avignon. I just did not know her. Who was the other lady, the one in the black widow gown."

"That was old Lady Scales, widow of the late Lord Scales." Mother-in-law to Sir Anthony Wydville, whom Heidi had not met.

"Lady Scales did not say much," Heidi observed.

"Her Ladyship probably just wanted a good look at the woman who helped kill her husband." Lady Robyn did not have a lot of friends in Queen Margaret's camp. She heaved a long, slow sigh, saying, "I cannot go along with her."

"Along with who?" Heidi asked. "Lady Scales? I hope not—she looked like death done up for a holiday. I would not go with her if they had a gun to my head."

"You should have seen her husband." She shivered at the thought of old Lord Scales. "He was as ghastly as they come."

"And you killed him?" Heidi asked, more awed by that than by being introduced to Duchess Wydville.

"I had a hand in it," Robyn admitted, not proud of being involved in anyone's death, though she had only been trying to get away from men who had abused her. "It was him or me."

"I am sure it was." Heidi gave her hand a squeeze.

Robyn said a prayer and returned to bed, trying to get some of that sleep she promised herself. And she succeeded, not waking until gray light filtered through the shutters. Heidi was already awake and working on the window nails—but to no avail, since before she had gotten another one out, nuns were scratching at the door. They brought bread, beer, and fried smelt, which tasted delicious, crisp and salty, the first protein Lady Robyn had eaten since Fat Tuesday. With the food came clean gowns in Wydville red-and-white for both of them, hints toward where their true interests lay. Before they could even get started on the window again, armed guards came to fetch them. Reluctantly, Robyn realized they would never go through the window. Too bad. Now they would have to face whatever FitzHolland had in store for them.

Which started with nothing more sinister than morning Mass back at the abbey, where King Henry and Queen Margaret were still in residence. This was a good sign. When they held her in the Tower, they did not let her out for anything, treating her like she was already dead. Now she was allowed to hear Mass at the abbey with the Wydville women, and afterward she and Heidi were taken to a big hall on Saint Peter's Street, where Queen Margaret's Court was assembled, with King Henry in the middle, dressed in black and looking horribly uncomfortable amid his glittering lords and lackeys in their livery colors.

What came next was not nearly so pretty. Her companions from the day before were brought in—Lord Bonville, Sir Thomas Kyreill, and William Gower, who still had King Henry's safe conduct. Everyone expected them to pledge loyalty to the restored regime, which they had all served; indeed, so far as the three were concerned, they had never left King Henry's service. His Highness had merely changed hands. Before King Henry could say anything good or ill about them, Queen Margaret announced they would be put on trial for treason, with her seven-year-old son as the judge. This was followed by a travesty of a trial, at the end of which, Queen Margaret asked her second grader, "Fair son, what deaths do they deserve?"

"Let them have their heads taken off," declared the tyke in royal purple.

Appalled silence greeted the boy's eager announcement. Horrified to hear his death sentence pronounced by a gleeful child, Bonville looked straight at Queen Margaret, saying, "May God destroy those who taught thee this manner of speech."

God might well destroy Queen Margaret, but Her Highness was determined to see Bonville, Kyriell, and Gower dead. Robyn prayed that Mad King Henry might object, having gratefully promised them protection when they guarded him during the battle. But his fear and awe of women kept him from contradicting his more forceful wife, nor did any of the assembled nobility dare speak out. You did not need to be a seeress to know that this demonstration of naked power over the noblest men in the land would come back to haunt Queen Margaret. In the meantime, it supplied a splendid mother-and-son moment, as Margaret and the prince led everyone outside to witness the executions. FitzHolland was there, to see that Robyn and Heidi got a good view of the block. This was only the second time Lady Robyn had been forced to endure a medieval execution; the only other time had been on her first day in the Middle Ages. Once was more than enough. She had avoided them ever since, most recently at Hereford, where she had hustled Heidi away before the ax fell.

Now she had no choice, and she stood there holding Heidi's hand while the condemned confessed their sins and were given last rites on a cold misty morning, with snow on the ground. Aside from Margaret and her son, no one felt very good about this. Edward had Owen Tudor executed for leading a foreign invasion, but these men only served their king. Mercifully they were gentlemen and would just be beheaded. Had they been commoners, they would have been tortured and mutilated first.

Heidi whispered in horrified Welsh, "Why is the queen doing this?"

"Part savagery, part revenge," Robyn whispered back in the same language. Nuns who talked to priests in the burial parties said Warwick had lost a couple of thousand men, but no leaders of note. "Sir John Grey was the most important man killed, and he was on the queen's side. This is Margaret's way of evening the score."

Warwick and the real leaders got away, so Her Majesty would take out her wrath on those fool enough to surrender, proving the absolute futility of trying to make peace with Queen Margaret. Robyn had begged Lord Bonville to make off with King Henry, and they could all have been back in London, laughing about their escape, but instead Bonville was going to pay for ignoring her warning. Ordinary bowmen assigned to him had known better, taking off as soon as the white witch told them to flee.

To make the horror complete, Le Boeuf was back, FitzHolland's pet executioner. He wore his hood, but Robyn recognized him by his short, powerful build and his cocky style. Strutting up to the block, wearing greasy leather, he made a great show of honing his double-headed ax, drawing cheers from the unruly troops, who were happy to see southern knights and lords humbled. "Hey, Lay Beef," someone shouted, "show them how to hold their heads."

Le Boeuf preened for his audience. Since his victims were gentlemen, he could not play with them like commoners, hanging them until they were half-dead and then cutting them down for more torture. Yet he flaunted his power over them with little flourishes, drawing out their hopeless humiliation before he cut off their heads. Rank has its advantages, and Bonville went first, getting the fresh honed edge of the ax. Robyn closed her eyes as the blade fell, but she could still hear the blow and smell fresh blood. Worst of all, she knew these men. She had spent half the day with them, and even with her eyes closed she could picture their faces while hearing them die. There was no sound quite like the meaty thunk of a headsman's ax at work. And she had to hear it three times. Le Boeuf reversed his ax so Sir Thomas Kyriell got a clean sharp edge, as well. Gower was a mere bannerman, and he had to make do with a used blade.

Each blow seemed to take something from Robyn, just as Owen's death had, striking at the center of her being. She could feel them in her belly. And from what the good duchess said, each death moved her and Heidi's names up on the list.

When it was over, Duchess Wydville took charge, having FitzHolland's guards herd her and Heidi toward the side door of a George Street town house. As they entered a short alley, it all became too much for her—the midden stink and kitchen smells mixing with blood and horseshit from the street. She felt sick, faint, then dizzy and nauseated, unable to take another step. Heidi reached out and grabbed her.

Holding on to her friend, Lady Robyn leaned over and threw up against the side of the house. Bits of half-eaten smelt landed in the alley dirt, next to the side steps. Heidi had plenty of practice with this, and she helped keep Robyn's hair from falling in her face. When she straightened up, Heidi held out a handkerchief, asking, "Feel better?"

Robyn nodded shakily. "Lots."

Good would be a wild overstatement, after what she had seen this morning, but she did feel better. Proud not to have barfed on the borrowed Wydville gown, she wiped her mouth on Heidi's hankie, then mounted the steps, and entered a plush solar that had been badly looted, leaving nothing but a single clothes chest and the bare walls. Duchess Wydville awaited within, backed by her serving women and several of her daughters, all wearing Wydville white-and-red, except for her oldest daughter, Elizabeth, now in widow's black.

"Vell, vhat do you think now?" asked Duchess Wydville smugly. "Are you joining us?"

No. More than ever. Refusing to answer, Robyn stared back at the witch-duchess, thinking, Her Grace must be out of her mind. How could anyone think of foisting this type of government on London? Executing lords and knights for trivial offenses might sow terror among the ruling class—but was that really what Queen Margaret wanted? It was one thing for Edward to kill noblemen, since he had the commons behind him. For Margaret to turn against the nobility was suicidal lunacy, since aside from fellow foreigners, nobles were the French queen's sole support.

"*Gott im Himmel,*" Duchess Wydville shook her head, as amazed and disgusted with Robyn as Lady Robyn was with her. "You pair of pretty fools. Two stakes stand just down the street in unhallowed ground by Black Cross Close, also a good supply of wood. Your trials vill not be long, so start by taking off your gowns."

"Our gowns?" What did that have to do with their trials, short or lengthy? "I do not understand."

Duchess Wydville sniffed, "Since you are not joining us, you do not need the dresses. You are to be burned in just your shifts, but serving girls vill bring you cloaks to vear till then."

Heidi did not like the sound of that. "When is then?"

"This morning, in the half-hour." Her Grace looked surprised at Heidi's ignorance. "If you are not going to give up Baynards Castle, you must be burned, and it is best to do it soon. Her Majesty has much to do today."

While their day would end at Black Cross Close, which they had passed on the way into town. She and Heidi would get a couple of rude cloaks, some semblance of a trial; then they would be marched out the door to their deaths. Which meant this was the last room they would ever be in—no wonder the Wydvilles wanted their satin dresses back. All this was monstrously illegal. For one thing, she was pregnant and could not be burnt until the baby was born. But "pleading the belly" would not do Heidi any good, and this crew was clearly beyond such legal niceties—particularly when the baby to be burned might compete with their own bloodthirsty prince. Heidi looked over at her, and Lady Robyn told her production assistant in Welsh. "Maybe we ought to give up the castle?"

Heidi nodded solemnly. "No lie, boss lady."

Duchess Wydville did not speak a word of Welsh, but she had no trouble guessing what was said. "Make up your minds. Queen Margaret's army moves as soon as the morning fog lifts, and you must be burned by then."

Why the huge hurry? It had taken Queen Margaret and her army almost two months to get here from Wakefield, where they won their great victory over Edward's father—three days ride on a willing horse. Having taken weeks to reclaim her kingdom, Margaret meant to burn them before lunch. Incredibly unfair, but there was no one to appeal to. Duchess Wydville had very neatly called her bluff, proving Lady Robyn was not willing to die just to see London free. "If I give up Baynards Castle, will you let us go?"

Duchess Wydville grinned warmly. "Vhy should I need to keep you?"

Lots of reasons, but Lady Robyn had no desire to bring them up. Her only hope was to go along with the Wydville's mad schemes and pray that Matt got through to Edward. If Edward could get here, it would not matter who held Baynards Castle. "Then the castle is yours."

"Splendid," declared the Duchess of Bedford, happy to see things working out for the best. "You will not regret it."

Robyn already regretted it—but what could she do? She was just not Joan of Arc material. Martyrdom was for dummies—and besides, she was breathing for two. She might throw herself away, but Robyn meant to give her child a chance at life. Still she felt ashamed and degraded, betraying her friends and Edward's trust just to keep from being burned. Queen Margaret's reign of terror had become personal, a forced choice between cherished beliefs and continued existence. Plainly the French queen planned to do this throughout southern England, executing anyone showing signs of a conscience—and ruling over the rest. All that stood in her way was pesky old London Town, and Lady Robyn was about to give Margaret the keys to the city.

Duchess Wydville had damage to do elsewhere, and she left them in charge of her widowed daughter, who asked if they wished to eat before they rode. "Certainly," Robyn replied, feeling faint—and ravenously hungry, despite her horrible morning. Pregnancy just would not give up, demanding food even in the midst of death. "So long as it is not fried smelt."

Lady Elizabeth smiled thinly, saying, "We can do better than that." Sending women to fetch food and cider, the Widow Grey asked, "Is there anything else you need?"

She reached over and took Elizabeth's hand, saying, "Yes, I need to thank you."

Elizabeth looked startled but did not withdraw her hand. "Thank me?"

"Yes, very much." She squeezed Elizabeth's hand. How strange to think that this was the woman who first initiated her into witchcraft, that this same hand led her to the altar on her first Witches Flight. "For your husband's sake. On Tuesday, after he was knighted, he took us from FitzHolland and found us safe lodging with the nuns."

"He did?" Elizabeth stared in disbelief. Despite all the effort to "win" Lady Robyn over, the Wydvilles trusted her even less than she did them.

"My lady need only ask the nuns." If Elizabeth would not believe her, the widow could ask God's wives. "He was everyone's image of a knight."

"And then some," added Heidi, still impressed with the way Sir John swooped in to save them.

"You said good-bye to him at the abbey?" Elizabeth's doubt turned to realization that they must have been among the last to see her husband. "Then you saw him take leave. What did he say?"

She could honestly reply, "His last words were of you."

What every wife wanted to hear, though Elizabeth could barely believe it. "He spoke of me to you."

"He told us to wait in hope of your arrival." Heidi had a publicist's skill at padding a quote, making the irony even heavier. Neither of them mentioned the kisses good-bye, which might not have gone down so well. A wife wants the last lips to be hers.

"Sir John was wonderful." For once Robyn need not lie about the deceased. "Happy, triumphant, and merciful, all at once."

And of course he died—it might even be what killed him. Elizabeth shook her head sadly, saying, "It does not do to go into battle in love with all the world."

Maybe not. But hatred could kill you even easier, as Robyn had seen repeatedly. She gave Elizabeth's hand a final squeeze and then let go. Food arrived—fresh bread, dried figs and apples, smoked salmon, boiled crab, and eel pie chased with hot spiced cider. Even in Lent, the Wydvilles ate well. Lady Robyn could not complain, greedily gobbling up crab, conveniently shelled by semiclean hands, enjoying the soothing feel of food in her belly. Smoked salmon and apples went down especially well with the cider. Neither she nor Heidi would touch eel pie.

Her hearty appetite in the face of disaster amused Elizabeth. "How happy to see you put on flesh; it makes you seem healthier." She had put on weight since her sword-fighting days at Goodrich, but Elizabeth was the first to mention it. Did the Wydville guess the reason? Hopefully not, since while they might let a flighty witch slip away, they wouldn't allow a potential heir to the throne escape.

Horses arrived, and it was time for Lady Robyn to pay for breakfast by handing over Baynards Castle. Queen Margaret meant to be in London as soon as possible, since her army had made a complete shamble of Saint Albans and could no longer stay there. Duchess Wydville came to see them off, saying, "Foolish girls, do not fail, or FitzHolland will have you."

FitzHolland would probably have them anyway, after Robyn had been disgraced and humiliated by betraying her friends and was no more use to the Wydvilles. That was what the English did to Joan, forcing her to recant and submit to their authority. Then they burned her. Still, it felt good to be free of the witch-duchess, if only for a while. Elizabeth told them they were going first to Barnet, where Sir Baldwin Fulford was waiting to enter the city. "Queen Margaret plans to divide her army," Elizabeth explained. "Most will be kept back at Dunstable, while the best troops will go on to Barnet, to be closer to London."

Which meant the Wydvilles were among her best in the army, because that was their escort—but there were less than a dozen. There were hardly any southerners in the army, and most of them were newly recruited. Margaret was caught in a vicious cycle of raising huge mercenary armies that she could only pay with loot, which made her ever more unpopular, keeping her from borrowing money. London had voted the worthless Warwick two thousand pounds only last week, just in hope of keeping Margaret away. Lady Elizabeth filled out their escort with more French mercenaries, who could not desert, though they had not been paid since coming to England.

Mounting up, they rode off into the cold English mist in search of London. It was less than ten miles to Barnet, through South Mimms and past Dancer's Hill, rising above the fog. Despite being broke, the French knights were glad to escort women to London, where ladies were thought to be especially loose. Elizabeth teasingly agreed, saying, "By repute, young Edward of March has seduced half the good wives in the city."

"By repute," Robyn replied tartly.

"No, no, it was true," the French insisted, knowing nothing

about Edward, but absolutely sure that any young Norman with a fair head on his shoulders could have his will with the wives of London. "It comes from their husbands being so inept in bed."

That none of them had been to England before only made their stories all the better. They stopped at South Mimms and again at Gladmore Heath, just short of Barnet. Here they reined in at an alewife's house marked by a broom, to rest the horses and wet the men's throats. Lady Elizabeth felt suddenly indisposed, and since the widow had no women with her, Robyn and Heidi attended her. At the back of the house, they found a privy that was hardly up to Court standards. Mercifully, it was too cold to stink much. Before they could put it to use, Elizabeth pulled them toward the kitchen gate, whispering, "Come with me if you want to live."

No need to ask twice. Robyn pulled Heidi after her through the kitchen gate, where a narrow mews led to the stables. There, Lady Elizabeth helped them saddle their horses, who were not happy to be going again so soon. When the mounts were ready, Elizabeth gave her a leather bag full of provisions, saying, "Now be gone, into the fog. I will say you headed back toward Saint Albans."

"Why are you doing this?" Robyn hated to look two gift horses in the mouth, but Duchess Wydville's eldest daughter never struck her as particularly compassionate. Cunning, calculating, and if need be cruel, but her people skills were never better than polite.

"Because if I do not, you are dead," Elizabeth replied curtly. "Mother has promised you to FitzHolland as soon as London is ours, for a big public burning at Smithfield."

What Robyn more or less expected—the only real surprise was that Elizabeth would go against the duchess. Lady Elizabeth had always been the dutiful daughter, married to a lord's heir, lady-in-waiting to Margaret, and a witch-priestess as well, respectfully climbing the feudal ladder, while her younger sisters flaunted their tits before whoever might give them a title. Robyn was seeing a very different side to Elizabeth Wydville, a woman for whom Her Grace's word was not law, and who meant to someday surpass dear old mom.

"Mind you, Mother might well be lying to him, but I cannot count on it." Dangling victims before FitzHolland was one of the ways things got done in Mad King Henry's Court. Sometimes the victims fell, like the Earl of Salisbury, and other times they just got a good scare.

Robyn was glad to settle for any kind of fright, feeling a great weight lifting from her soul, knowing she could live without having to give up Baynards Castle, without making a mockery of everything she and Edward had stood for. She thanked Elizabeth Grey née Wydville immensely. Duchess Wydville's pretty blond daughter merely shrugged, saying, "I have seen far too much death of late."

Elizabeth was not the only one. After a moment's pause, the young widow added, "And I feel like I may need friends. You might one day be my friend. FitzHolland never will be one."

When all was said and done, they were both witches. This was the witch who welcomed her into the coven and now, once again, had given her a new life. She must be sure to use it well. Giving Elizabeth Wydville good-bye kisses, they got on their horses, and Robyn led Heidi out into the fog, trying to skirt Barnet by making for Dead Man's Bottom.

14

◆══ London Calling ══◆

Gladmore Heath was a high, open stretch of ground where the Saint Albans road approached Barnet from the north. By now the sun was up, and there was only a low mist along the road, but fog still pooled thickly in Dead Man's Bottom, and the low areas east of Barnet were a fluffy white sea. Lady Robyn had ridden the Saint Albans road enough that she found the fogscape thoroughly familiar; Barnet was but ten miles from the Thames, and the London fog was her old friend by now. Finding the bridle path lane that led down into Dead Man's Bottom, she followed it, letting the mist close in around her. Snow lay in the hollow, and soon Robyn had to get down and guide the horse, since all she could see was dirty path at her feet, cutting through a white-gray world. Heidi was an invisible presence behind her, asking, "Can you see through this?"

"Nope." But she could follow the slope of the ground downward, leading them away from the road and from any possible pursuit. By noon the fog would burn off, and they would be able to see their way home.

"Though you do know where we are going," Heidi called down, perched high on a pale horse, her head in the mist, unable to see a thing.

"Yep." Thank goodness. For the first time since that horrible Monday night in Dunstable, she felt totally safe and free. Since the moment Matt woke her to say that Margaret's men were in the town, she had been harassed, intimidated, threatened, and held prisoner, all for no good reason. Now she was free again, on her own turf, protected by a thick Thames fog. Free to speak her mind—and she had lots to say. All of London needed to know just how cruel and bloodthirsty Queen Margaret had become. So did Edward. And the world.

"So where are we going?" asked Heidi.

"Home, to Baynards Castle." No blundering bunch of Midlands bowmen and French hirelings could hope to stop her, showing the idiocy of invading parts of England that even Miss Rodeo Montana knew better than they did. The fools had expected her to not only hand over Baynards Castle, but show them the way there, as well.

Heidi giggled behind her. "I love it when you go all terse and cowgirl on me."

"We aim to entertain." Lady Robyn had plenty to say, but Heidi had been at Saint Albans with her, and she had seen it all.

"I mean it," Heidi called through the fog, "sometimes you are way sexier in the saddle than in bed."

"Just what every girl hopes to hear." Especially from her spacey production assistant. Heidi was a dear, but still had growing to do.

To show it, Heidi called out a short time later. "So when will we get there?"

"In time for dinner," Robyn promised.

"Goody," her former assistant declared. Coming to the Middle Ages had actually matured Heidi immensely, though you had to know her to notice.

When the fog finally lifted, Lady Robyn remounted, glad to see they were miles south and east of Barnet, guessing from the lay of the land that they must be somewhere near Tottenham. When she found an unkempt plowman to ask, he told "Yer lost Ladyship" she was nowhere near Tottenham. This was Canonbury Manor, owned by the priory of Saint Bartholomew at Smithfield. Tottenham was miles to the north and east, and London was off to the south.

"So how far is it?" Heidi demanded as they set out again.

"Five miles," Robyn guessed. "Maybe less."

"Cool!" Heidi exclaimed. "I am cold and hungry, and about done with this lady-in-distress bit."

"Me, too," Robyn agreed, untying the food bag that Elizabeth Wydville had given them, finding it contained figs, fresh buns, and a big slab of cheese, though this was the second day of Lent.

"Cheese!" Heidi liked the look of that. "Thought we could not have cheese until Easter?"

"You can if you are pregnant." Here was proof that Elizabeth had guessed her condition.

"What if your friend is pregnant?" Heidi asked hopefully, pulling up alongside her.

"Depends on how good friends you are." Church dogma was never her strong suit.

"I'll take that as a yes." Heidi leaned over and took the cheese, breaking off a bit and giving back the rest.

Lady Robyn stared at the hunk of cheese in her hand, given by her enemy to nourish her baby. "I cannot guess what possessed Elizabeth to let us go like that. Maybe her husband's death unhinged her, making her to act a bit human." One month back in the Middle Ages had her mooning over a bit of cheese. How touching that the newly widowed Elizabeth Wydville worried enough about her to defy Queen Margaret and Mama Wydville. England dearly needed such willingness to show mercy, no matter what faction you favored.

Happily chewing her cheese, Heidi chuckled, saying, "That was so totally about Edward."

Robyn turned in the saddle to look at her friend. "Edward?"

Heidi rolled her eyes at Lady Robyn's naïveté. "Well, duh? Elizabeth is minus a husband, and Edward's the number-one bachelor in the land. Do the math."

"Really?" It made some sense. If she were Elizabeth, she would certainly be wondering where her next man was coming from. They did not make widows wait for nothing. And the woman did like Edward, even from afar.

"This is all about Edward. Did she ever do anything for you while her husband was alive?"

"Not much," Robyn admitted, handing Heidi more cheese, "but wouldn't she want me out of the way?"

"Sure, if she's an idiot," Heidi snorted. "With you dead, Edward would just find someone else, and the Wydvilles would merely be a bad memory."

But with Lady Robyn saved by Elizabeth Wydville, the witch-duchess's daughter had instant entry into Edward's circle, and some claim to his sympathy. Having saved his girlfriend, the beautiful widow could not possibly be after Edward—the sort of challenge no man could resist. Heidi reminded her, "When you were with Collin, and I was absolutely mad for him, I still booked you into the most romantic bed-and-breakfasts, making sure they had a hot tub and a fireplace. Stupid girls snub Mr. Right's girlfriend; smart ones become her best friend."

No chance of that. Elizabeth Wydville would remain tolerable at most, so long as the good widow kept her hands off Edward. "And if I mention any of this to Edward, I would look incredibly catty."

"Another beauty of the ploy." Heidi enjoyed seeing a skilled siren at work. "Any complaint by you would just alert Edward that Elizabeth wanted him, without upsetting her demure young-widow act."

Making her doubly dangerous. Heidi was not bothered in the least by Edward and Elizabeth being on opposite sides in a desperate civil war, sure that sex easily trumped politics. This trip to the Middle Ages had convinced Heidi that in any millennium, human heads were ruled by hormones. Win or lose, Elizabeth Wydville would rather have Edward of March owing her a favor than a surrender of Baynards Castle to the queen. This was becoming the story of Margaret's life; the women of England just wanted Edward. Heidi added, "And so far as Elizabeth is concerned, you are the best sort of girlfriend for Edward."

"What sort is that?" Ditzy displaced time traveler?

Heidi rolled her eyes again. "One who has not married him."

For whatever reason—their last wedding date fell on a full-out battle. Certainly Elizabeth Wydville was now an active rival for Edward. What sane young gentlewoman was not? So let the best witch win.

Finally Robyn found the Fleet River, following it down to Smithfield, the outdoor stock market beneath the tall stone walls of London where she and Edward had starred in last summer's tourney. Today the scene of their former glory looked cold and desolate, covered with frost and frozen cow paddies. Bypassing Newgate and Ludgate— which were bound to be barred with armed enemies at Barnet—Lady Robyn went straight to one of her private gates, the kitchen postern, a little covered entry where the castle drew water from the Fleet River, which was cleaner than the Thames, though not by much.

She pounded on the wooden postern with her boot, and a surprised cook's boy in Edward's livery was flabbergasted to find the lady of the castle demanding entrance. Hurriedly, he flung open the gate, bowing as she and Heidi rode in, both wearing Wydville red-and-white, mounted on formerly borrowed, now stolen, horses.

Comforting stone walls closed in as the boy shut and barred the gate, securing her keep. She was safe—no one was coming in without Lady Robyn's leave, unless they brought a battering ram. Even if London surrendered, she could hold out here until Edward arrived. That was the great wonder of living in castles, the thrilling sense of high walls and fortified gates keeping the lawless medieval world at bay. Otherwise castles were cold, cramped, and drafty in winter, only romantic if you had a roaring fire, decent room service, and a brawny young warlord between clean sheets—at least in Lady Robyn's experience.

Liveried servants flocked around her, filling the small corner of the inner ward between the bathhouse and the stables, cheering the return of their wayward meal ticket. Hearing of Warwick's defeat, they feared the bad times were back, when Baynards Castle was in the "king's hands," and most of them were out on the streets, and no one was ordering up dances and dinner parties—a castle without a lady could be a dreary place. But Baynards Castle's lady was back, and Henry Mountfort helped her dismount, as Deirdre and Cybelle came running out of the keep, holding up their long skirts, with Joy and Beth close behind them. Robyn was mildly disappointed to see Matt Davye take charge of the horses, wishing he had gone straight to Edward. Still, it was good to see him safe. With typical Irish decorum, Deirdre tackled her mistress, lifting Lady Robyn off the ground, to the delight of the English, who would have done it if they dared. Scolding her in Gaelic, Deirdre declared, "This is the second time in two months that you have gotten totally lost. Do it a third time, and you are in serious trouble."

Too true. "This time I was not lost. I was merely at Saint Albans with Queen Margaret." And she never wanted to go back again.

Mention of Queen Margaret ended the merriment. Such was the French queen's magic; her mere name could shut up a crowd of happy Londoners. Edward's steward spoke up, saying, "My lady, we have heard that Saint Albans was sorely looted."

"To the bare walls," a bold stable boy added.

She had hoped to put off politics until after she had a bath, but plainly that was not possible—it went clean against custom to address your household from the stables, but Lady Robyn prided herself on being an unconventional lady. Stepping up onto the mounting block, she easily topped the crowd, since she was in riding boots and medievals tend to run small. "Yes," she announced, "Saint Albans is grievously sacked. Personal intervention by King Henry saved part of the abbey, but the town was given up to Scots and brigands for plunder."

Somber faces stared back at her, many with friends and relations in Warwick's army, and some with kin in Saint Albans. "Citizens of Saint Albans were mainly spared," she told them, knowing there was no need to make Margaret worse than she was, "but I saw Lord Bonville, Sir Thomas Kyriell, and William Gower executed this morning, though they never fought against the queen, and spent the battle protecting the king." Margaret had shown the whole county that no one was safe, not if knights and nobles were executed at the whim of a child. Everyone looking up at her had far fewer rights than Lord Bonville; in fact, they were risking their necks just by wearing Edward's murrey-and-blue.

And everyone knew that London was next on Queen Margaret's list. "Help is on the way," she vowed, "but we must hold out until it comes. We are under siege, and all gates must be locked and guarded. Those of you with families outside London can bring them in if you wish, and anyone wanting to go does it with my blessing, for that is one less mouth to feed. I am going into the city to fill our larders. Queen Margaret may have won the battle of Saint Albans, but the battle of London has just begun. Let's see she loses this time."

Everyone cheered, even the French prisoners, who were afraid of what could happen to them among the wild English if their fair captor disappeared. When the hoorays subsided, Edward's steward asked, "What if London lets the queen in?"

They all knew that the most likely outcome of the battle of London was a negotiated surrender. "We will try to keep the city gates shut, but if London gives in, we will hold Baynards Castle until help arrives."

Someone called out, "My lady, what of Lord Edward?"

"He is coming," she promised them, "and we must hold out until he is here." They all cheered that, too.

Having given her word, now she must make it good. She left the task of securing the castle to Matt Davye and Henry Mountfort, retiring to the keep and ordering up clean clothes and a hot bath for herself and Heidi. "We have to go into town and scrounge," she explained. "Sieges are fought with food."

Heidi glady shed her Wydville gown. "When the going gets tough, the tough go shopping."

Exactly. When they were both bathed, and dressed in Stafford scalet-and-gold, Robyn rode into town, finding that the beggars by the castle gate had grown in number during this hard winter. Homeless families had joined the old and crippled, all waiting patiently for handouts, happy to see Lady Robyn had returned. Her Ladyship passed out silver pennies, fearing she would have to feed these people, too. Lady Robyn might reluctantly give her life for the cause, but how many babies would she starve just to keep the queen out? Not a lot.

Down Thames Street at the Steelyard, she found the Germans forting up, too. Thames Street would put up a fight, even if the rest of London gave in—being the axis of trade and the international district, the riverfront street had more to lose by going back to rule-by-pillage. Lady Robyn confronted a stiff German in finely crafted half-armor, who would only offer up a few hundredweights of grain and some salted cod, "if you will pay the balance and take that printing press you requested."

"You have my printing press?" She had all but forgotten she had ordered it, a lot having happened since then.

Herr Hansa nodded eagerly. "We have the press and a pair of Cologne printers that we would rather not house and feed."

"Do you have paper?" Wild thoughts raced through her head. Here was the voice she had been wanting.

"Some could certainly be found," the German assured her, "for a price."

"What sort of price?" There were no proper paper mills in England yet, so people made do with imports and hand-produced paper.

"Four shillings a ream." That was merely high, not outrageous—ten pages of handmade paper for a penny.

"I will take ten reams." Her first payment to the Venetians was due next week, but bilking Italian bankers was the least of her worries. Lady Robyn had her latest extravagance hauled back to the castle, feeling particularly foolish, since she had gone looking for food, and come back with two more mouths to feed. Since Heidi started out in studio publicity and was the only one who spoke medieval German, Robyn put her in charge of the printing press. "Get it set up and working, and maybe we can put out a late edition."

"You want to do a newspaper?" Heidi sounded dubious.

"Wish we could," Lady Robyn shook her head with regret. "Just a simple broadsheet, maybe folded in the middle, hopefully with writing on both sides."

"Sounds possible," her production assistant ventured, though right now the "press" was a pile of parts and lumber.

"Get the girls to help," she suggested. Blond Beth was the only born Londoner among them, and at ten or so, she was the closest to their target audience in reading comprehension and literary taste. "And try to keep the French and Germans apart."

"Sure thing." Heidi was adept at international relations.

Lady Robyn went back into the city with Deirdre, looking for provisions, finding shops closed and market stalls emptied. Butchers had already closed down for Lent, and green grocers had scant to offer in mid-February, though she did lay hands on two score sacks of dried beans, which seemed like a godsend amid the mounting scarcity. Unable to do better, she stopped in at West Cheap to call on Amy Lambert, who happily received her in their tall black-and-white timbered town house. At street level, the house was stuffed with bolts of fabric and busy apprentices, but Amy made her guests comfortable in an upper chamber, beside a warm fire, where Beth's siblings served them mulled cider and almond rolls. Wearing a slinky scoop-necked blue gown beneath a white butterfly headdress, Amy asked about her daughter. "Does she strive hard and dutifully?"

"Absolutely." On the very night she left home, Beth had been dancing her little heart out around a witch's fire at Avignon.

Amy expressed delight, adding hopefully, "And is she learning to obey?"

"That might be a stretch," Lady Robyn confessed. Both Beth and Joy were eagerly learning which adult rules to obey and which to blithely ignore.

Amy well knew her daughter's willfulness. "But she does do her chores?"

"Enthusiastically," Robyn reported. "Right now she is hard at work as Heidi's editorial assistant."

Amy looked puzzled. "What is that?

"Nothing strenuous," she assured her sister-initiate's mother. "We are putting out a tabloid, actually a double-printed broadsheet, to tell what happened at Saint Albans and to keep Queen Margaret's army out of the city. Elizabeth is helping compose it, since the German printers do not speak English." And heaven knows what Heidi would come up with on her own.

"Germans, really?" Amy Lambert shook her head, saying, "I knew Beth would learn amazing things from you."

Spellcraft, paganism, and now an apprenticed printer's devil, while Beth's poor brothers were in school, being taught plain geometry and Latin grammar with a willow switch. Embarrassed, Robyn muttered to her sister-initiate's mother, "We try to do our best by Beth."

"Thank you ever so much," Amy replied smoothly. "And someone must keep Queen Margaret out. How delightful to find that it is my daughter."

Lady Robyn could see where Beth got her easy smiling attitude. Amy was utterly convinced that being fostered into Edward's household was the best thing for her little blond daughter—if this was how the ruling class behaved, so be it, that was what Beth needed to know. Those chronicles that show medievals as pious and impractical were not written by the likes of Amy Lambert. They were—*hello!*—written by monks.

Whatever her views were on child rearing and witchcraft, Amy was not eager to see Margaret's troops appear. Noblemen had all but fled the city, leaving no males above the rank of mayor—it was the women who had nowhere to run to. Duchess Cecily in Southwark. Lady Robyn in Baynards Castle. And that did not count the duchesses of Bedford and Buckingham, and Lady Scales, who had gone over to the queen. Amy told her, "Mayor Lee has sent aldermen to meet with Sir Baldwin Fulford at Barnet, promising him money and to admit some of Queen Margaret's troops if Her Majesty withdraws the rest."

"They are already withdrawing," Robyn warned, "to Dunstable." For once Margaret had done the right thing by backing off and trying to sweet-talk her way into London. But once within the gates, Her Majesty would surely order up a slew of executions, and after Saint Albans, no one could know for sure who was on the death list. Lady Robyn certainly, and perhaps John Lambert, the Yorkist sheriff with a witch-daughter. She told the sheriff's wife, "I am stocking Baynards Castle for a siege."

Amy nodded. "Everyone is laying in food. Mayor Lee and his men are gathering a wagon full of bread, beans, and Lenten stuff, to send to Barnet in the morning."

"By what gate?" Robyn asked, hating to see any food leave the city, especially to feed Margaret's men. "Every loaf that leaves London will be used against us."

"My husband will know which gate before morning," Amy promised, "and as soon as he does, I will send word."

"Thanks." She wanted to ask Amy's husband to keep his constables away from the gate when they tried to send out the wagon, but that might be too much. Settling for giving Beth's mother a kiss good-bye, Lady Robyn got a gift in return, a leather bag full of dried apples. This February the gift of food was the truest.

Returning to Baynards Castle, Robyn felt like Ali Baba, or Jane and the Beanstalk, with her forty sacks of beans piled on packhorses. The dried apples went to the beggars at the gate. Matt met her at the stables, saying the bundles of salted cod had already arrived, and he had sent the grain straight to the mill to be ground into flour. "Better stock up on the boiling oil, too," she warned. "Margaret's men may be in London by tomorrow."

"Unless we stop them." Matt grinned maliciously at the prospect of street fighting on the morrow. FitzHolland was going to have to take Baynards Castle the hard way. Heidi and Cybelle had the press set up in a chamber off the main hall, and they were getting set to cast type. Still, there was no hope of an afternoon edition. Composing and setting up a print run, working backward and in medieval English would take time, especially with the aid of two stolid Germans and an excitable French poet, none of whom spoke the language. Heidi had started with a three-inch headline:

Saint Albans Sacked!

Followed by suitably lurid text:

Savage Northumbrians and bloodthirsty Scots brigands fell on this helpless abbey town, lusting for murder and mayhem. . . .

"What do you think?" Heidi asked. "Too timid?"

"Sort of," Robyn agreed. "And way too old news."

"Not scary enough," was Beth's expert opinion, and Joy concurred.

"They're right," Robyn decided. "Though I do like the bloodthirsty Scots brigands—"

"Well, then—how about this?" Heidi changed the headline to:

London Attacked!!

"That's more like it." Robyn liked the way the words leaped out at her. "Only do it in red."

"But that has not happened yet," objected Matt, who lacked Hollywood training.

"It will," Robyn reminded him. "And when the attack comes, there will be no time to write about it."

"Tomorrow's news today," Heidi boasted.

"And make the text present tense," Robyn added. "That always bumps it up: 'Savage Northumbrians and bloodthirsty Scots brigands march on London, lusting for murder—' "

Beth approved. "Now *that's* scary."

Heidi liked the sound of it, as well, asking, "So what goes below the fold?"

"That is where we put the part about Edward coming to the rescue." Something else that had not happened, but London needed reasons for holding out against the queen. The more reasons, the better, so somewhat reluctantly Robyn added, "And Warwick, as well."

"First scare 'em, then spare 'em." Heidi admired the classic one-two punch. Subtlety was lost on most medievals. "How many men will Edward have with him?"

Robyn tried to estimate from what she had seen and from what Edward had said. "After Mortimer's Cross, maybe six thousand or so that are willing to come to London."

"What about Warwick?" Heidi asked, hoping to raise the numbers a bit.

Saint Albans had left Warwick's army in even worse shape. "A lot less, perhaps four thousand, if he's lucky."

Beth was not impressed. "That does not sound like a lot."

Heidi nodded soberly, saying, "The girl's right, those numbers need to be ten times as big, or no one's gonna believe them."

"So make it sixty thousand and forty thousand," Robyn suggested. Magically, Edward's and Warwick's armies became ten times larger, at least on paper.

Heidi approved. "That's more like it. So what about the back side?"

"Let's get the front sides printed," Robyn decided, "then we can worry about the backs."

It took nearly until midnight to get the type cast and the front sides printed—but they looked spectacular hanging to dry in the main hall, with their big red headlines and breathless text, telling of three armies converging on London. Matt was impressed, saying, "If that does not get men into the streets, nothing will."

Having gone this far, they could not stop, and they stayed up half the night, composing, casting, and printing the backsides, too, telling the whole story of Saint Albans and the executions of Bonville, Kyriell, and Gower. Along with whatever else anyone felt like complaining about—"Ladies ripped from sanctuary and nuns terrorized," and "Farm families stripped of stock and livelihood." They finished up with Edward's call for Peace, Justice, and Good

Lordship, which compared favorably to Margaret's knack for war, rapine, and plunder.

"How shall we sign it?" Heidi was not sure who should get the credit, or if they even wanted their names on the paper, since signing this list of complaints was like writing their own death warrants. Freedom of speech was centuries away, and London's first newspaper was a clear act of treason.

Robyn already knew what she wanted on the bottom. "We will sign it 'the White Rose.' "

"Outstanding." Heidi grinned and went to work, tossing off orders in three languages. With no standardized spellings, proofreading was an exercise in imagination. Less than half of London was considered "literate"—which meant being able to read Latin. No one kept track of how many people could read English. Amazingly, Beth could read the simple text backward as easily as forward, claiming the words looked the same to her either way.

After midnight, a London constable appeared at the castle gate with a message for Lady Robyn, never a welcome moment. This time it was neither a warrant nor indictment, but a carefully folded piece of vellum with a single word inked on it in a slim feminine hand—NEWGATE.

Lady Robyn was back in favor with the law, and London's unofficial defenses had silently drawn tighter. By the time the prime bell rang at Saint Brides, the main hall had two thousand copies of the White Rose ready to hit the streets of sleepy old London Town. Matt Davye and Henry Mountfort were in charge of distribution, assigning five hundred copies to Southwark, while the bulk of the print run went to points throughout the city—Saint Paul's, the Mercery, Cornhill, London Bridge, and East Cheap. Men took paste pots and brushes, to paste the broadsheets on buildings and market stalls, while loose piles were handed out to sympathetic innkeepers and parish priests, to pass on to customers and parishioners. As milkmen led in their cows and apprentices awoke for work along Cheapside, the *White Rose* was there to greet them.

Matt and the men came back waving fresh baked bread and two big barrels of pickled herrings. Asked to explain the loaves and fishes, they replied gleefully, "Newgate," sitting down to spread plundered herrings on their breakfast bread, triumphantly describ-

ing the scene at Newgate when the city fathers tried to send food to
Barnet. Men had converged on the gate from all over west London,
easily overpowering the wagoneers and emptying the wagon, to
hearty applause from thieves and felons behind the barred windows
of Newgate. "With not a constable in sight." Either because Sheriff
Lambert called off his men or because the constables decided not to
take a drubbing for Queen Margaret. "Sir John Wenlock's cook
made off with the wagon, but by then it was almost half empty."

"And the silver?" Robyn asked, knowing the mayor had been
collecting money for Margaret, as well.

"Someone knows where that silver went," Henry Mountfort
assured her, "but not us. All we got was herrings." They were calling it the Battle of the Herrings, after Falstaff's famous victory in
France, also fought during Lent.

Seeing her men back safe, Lady Robyn got some much belated
sleep, leaving word that she should be woken if danger approached.
All too soon Deirdre came in, carrying a hot mug of coffee, saying,
"Duchess Wydville is back."

"How do you know?" Lady Robyn gulped the coffee, glad to see
she was getting Deirdre half-trained; last summer she had been the
one who made the coffee, using it to coax her lady's maid out of bed.

"Her Grace just rode right past our walls, entering the city through
Ludgate, along with Lady Scales and the Duchess of Buckingham."
After this morning's ruckus, Newgate must have seemed unsafe.

Robyn dressed to ride. If she was going into the turbulent city, she
wanted Lily beneath her and armed men around her. At this moment
of crisis, with the fate of the capital hanging in the balance, the
absence of male nobility was astonishing. For God's sake, these guys
were supposed to be running the country. Up to last fall, they had
been. October's parliament was full of sound and fury, and the House
of Lords had passed the Act of Accord, making Edward heir to the
throne. Now parliament was long gone, and the fighting sparked by
the Act of Accord had decimated the nobility. Half the great families
were headed by widows, and most of the remaining nobles were
under Queen Margaret's thumb, so much that she put her advance
guard under a mere knight, Sir Baldwin Fulford. With Warwick and
Norfolk beaten, Edward was the only great lord in the field against
her, leaving the defense of London to women and commoners.

She rode out of Baynards Castle to the cheers of beggars, with Matt at her side and Henry Mountfort behind her, backed by a half-dozen bowmen. All the men wore mail and plate, and she had a chain-mail shirt hidden under her long heraldic tunic, the first time Lady Robyn had worn armor for real. As they neared Saint Paul's, apprentices and shopkeepers on Carter Lane cheered them on; with the city teetering on the brink, retailers were pleased to see heavily armed men commanded by one of their best customers. And apprenticed boys were ecstatic to get a wave and a smile from a pretty lady of dubious means. Pasted on the walls of their shops was the *White Rose,* with its bold red headline, LONDON ATTACKED!!

As she rode into Saint Paul's churchyard, Lady Robyn saw people reading the paper. Those who could not read had others read it to them. Heidi's breathless prose came from several sides at once, describing in lurid detail the sack of Saint Albans and the abject terror of the nuns. London could easily become addicted. Clerics clustered around Saint Paul's Cross claimed that the mayor was going to issue a proclamation, "since the Duchesses of Buckingham and Bedford are back."

Lady Robyn waited with them, anxious to hear what Mayor Lee and Duchess Wydville had to say. Presently a herald in city colors appeared, accompanied by red-robed aldermen and armed constables. Silence settled over the churchyard as the herald unrolled his parchment and cocked his head to cry out.

Loud clear words carried over the sea of heads, announcing that Good Gracious King Henry and his queen were returning to London. His Majesty's true subjects would be protected, and the city would be spared pillage, but evildoers would be punished. "And all loyal subjects should keep to their houses, so that His Majesty, King Henry, and the good king's men may enter the city in peace."

Swift angry shouts of, "Nay! Nay!" burst from the crowd, as people waved the *White Rose,* with its wild promise of tens of thousands coming to the city's defense. Cries of defiance turned to a swelling chant, "March! March! March!"

Robyn urged Lily toward Saint Paul's Cross, and the crowd parted for the lady on her white horse. She rode right up to the stone cross and then turned Lily about, so that her mount's broad white rear faced the herald and aldermen. Then she rose in her saddle, addressing the crowd in a plain London accent that always brought applause from the unwashed. "Edward is on his way, and we must keep the city safe until his arrival."

Coming from her, they believed it. Who would know Edward's comings and goings better? Cheers erupted all around her, drowning out the protests from the city fathers. She waited patiently as her public applauded, smiling her Miss Rodeo Montana smile. She had faced bigger and tougher crowds in Roundup.

When the Londoners quieted down, she warned them, "This city is under attack. Your enemies are asking you to drop your guard. I was at Saint Albans and heard Good King Henry vow that the town and abbey would be spared. We all know what came of that. Now they want to do the same to London. Will you let them?"

"Nay, nay!" the throng shouted back, waving clubs, blades, and rolled-up copies of the *Rose*. London was not about to huddle behind shutters while Mayor Lee and Duchess Wydville threw open the gates to the men who sacked Saint Albans. Refugees from Peterborough and Huntingdon had brought stories of rapes "that spared neither maid, wife, nor nun." No one was eager to test the truth of these rumors. Afraid to face the angry crowd, the herald and aldermen retreated, vacating Saint Paul's Cross. Men stepped up to speak in their place, starting with a popular brewer who sounded like he was running for mayor.

Robyn wished him well, urging Lily away from the cross, letting men take her place. She was ready to defend London, but the Brits were going to have to run it. Being Lady Robyn Stafford of Pontefract was all the challenge she needed.

As they let her through, hands tugged on her gold-trimmed gown and fingers reached up to touch hers. Teenage apprentices started a chant of their own, quickly taken up by some of the men, "Staff-hard! Staff-hard! Staff-hard!"

She was the living proof that Edward of March was the virile young leader that the country yearned for—not some confused sexual casualty, like the current king or Henry the Impotent of Spain. Smiling at the chant, she made her way to Matt's side, and her armed men closed around her, drawing a wall of horseflesh and steel between Lady Stafford and her enthusiastic fans—then they rode back to Baynards Castle. Queen Margaret's first attempt to take the city had been turned back, and Lady Robyn had not even needed her chain mail.

London became a city in arms, with watches in plate armor at every gate, captained by brewers and butchers. Though the taverns were open and violence hung in the air, everyone was on their best behavior. One prominent pro-Margaret prisoner had been hauled out of jail and beheaded, and even common criminals were wary of trying people's patience; no one wanted to be caught breaking the peace or doing anything that smacked of rapine or looting—not with the whole city determined to prevent another Saint Albans. Lest anyone forget how desperate things were, Heidi and Beth were hard at work on the next edition of the *White Rose,* laying out the front page beneath a banner headline:

Under Siege!!

The subheading read, QUEEN MARGARET DEMANDS THE CITY OPEN HER GATES! Heidi made it sound like a horrible idea, picturing armed brigands and Scots barbarians prowling the streets, killing who they willed and taking what they wished. This bleak picture led naturally to the return punch below the fold, LOCAL BREWER SAYS NO!

What could be more heroic? Or more British? By now Heidi had seen that large stretches of British history were best explained by a steady diet of beer and ale. Luckily Heidi had been raised in a six-pack-for-breakfast household herself, and she knew the words that brought beer-sodden blood to a boil, turning the pot-valiant bragart into a man of action. That's what a good Hollywood publicist did.

Days anyway. Nights were when a good publicist really puts out. And tonight was Witches Night, the night when Lady Robyn must make good on her promise to bring Edward to London. In the old tower room, that had been hers, she told Heidi, "Best if I do it by myself." Lady Robyn planned a swift solo out-of-body flight to the Cotswolds to find her man, alone and unencumbered. "This message is too vital to risk a mass flight."

Heidi sat hunched on the bed, staring thoughtfully back at her. "You do not have to do it all," Heidi reminded her, "leave something for us to screw up."

"This is personal," Robyn protested. Over the last couple of days, she had freely vowed that Edward would be here soon, in a week or so at the latest, bringing a huge Welsh army to liberate London. "I promised to produce Edward."

"Like I didn't?" Heidi had put that promise boldly in print—EDWARD IS COMING! In true journalistic tradition, this breathtaking scoop was based on naught but wishful thinking. Heidi had to make it happen.

"What about the girls?" Lady Robyn's visit to her young liege lord was not going to be PG. Just because King Henry was lost and England's fate hung in the balance did not make the trip all work, not on Witches Night. Without passion, spellcraft would never get her off the carpet.

Heidi practically breathed passion, making her a natural coven leader and something of a seeress—who never doubted for a moment that Lady Robyn would return to this tower room. Coolly Heidi peered into the coming Witches Night, making knowing the unknowable sound as easy as handicapping the Oscars. "Joy will want to go to her mom, taking Beth with her. Cybelle is still struggling to get off the ground, and it was smart to pair her with Deidre. I can see the girls get through to Greystone, and still be there for you."

"Stick to the kids." With Duchess Wydville running interference between her and Edward, Robyn mainly worried that innocents would get in the way.

Heidi smirked at her confidence, facing down a witch-duchess that had tricked her more than once. "You need me way more than they do."

"Too true," Robyn admitted ruefully, having usurped coven leadership from little girls with as much, or more, experience. "Mary looks out for silly young virgins in peril—but also for mothers-to-be."

"So even sinners get divine protection so long as we are preggies?" Heidi sounded disbelieving.

"Something like that." Though you would hardly know it from the appalling childbirth mortality rate. Lady Robyn still had private doubts about giving birth in the Dark Ages.

That evening, three girls and three women gathered in the Baynards Castle presence chamber, kneeling atop their star points. Like many covens, theirs was rather mixed, ranging from a titled lady and a French poetess to a bastard serving girl, since spellcraft had no regard for rank or station, and visted every known nation. Only Beth was a born Londoner, while two came from the future, and Joy, Deirdre, and Cybelle each came from one of the kingdoms Mad King Henry claimed to rule—England, Ireland, and France. The battle of London was not just being fought by knight's cooks and native Londoners, but by everyone who loved the city, from foreign sailors in the fleet to Germans in the Steelyard, and witches in their circle.

Robyn knelt between Beth and Heidi, facing the lit candle, surrounded and shielded by her coven's energy—if sincerity could defeat the Wydvilles, she would be totally safe. As the chant went round the kneeling circle, Lady Robyn let herself go, becoming another nameless soul sinking into the space between heartbeats, where her love lay waiting.

Black night engulfed her, but she focused on the candle flame, letting love be her guiding star, drawing her westward, back to the Cotswolds Edge, the far-off lip of the limestone country. Lying directly between London and Hereford, this was where an army had to pass to get out of the Marches and into the Midlands, and here Edward had old friends at Greystone and Broughton Castle, and ready reinforcement from the Nevilles and Hastings in Warwickshire.

Slowly the candle flame expanded, growing longer and brighter, becoming a lighted window in a manor hall, one Robyn immediately knew, though she had seen it only once before, and never stayed there. This was Ebrington Manor, a high, frowning manse surrounded by walled gardens and black yew groves. It belonged to Chief Justice Sir John Fortescue, the Greys' once-powerful neighbor, who had fled to join the queen, leaving Ebrington in "the king's hands." Which currently meant Edward's, who spoke for his royal cousin in these parts. Dogs barked in the darkness.

Lady Robyn alighted on a grassy walk leading toward the south wing of the manor house, knowing in her heart that the lighted window led to Edward. There was no moon, but light poured out of the high window, easily illuminating the path, which was bounded by a wall on one side and a thick thorn hedge on the other, making the manse look like Sleeping Beauty's castle. She was alone, except for the dogs, which continued to bark. Small surprise, since she was the one drawn to Edward. Joy and Beth had good reason to avoid Ebrington Manor, since Joy had been fostered out here last spring—with disastrous results. Joy Grey's resistance to discipline resulted in a raid on the Greystone coven and Joy's arrest, landing her in the dungeon at Berkeley Castle—until Robyn came to rescue her. Not something the witch-girl would want to revisit. And if Joy did not come here, Beth would not either.

Determined to reach that lighted room, where she could already feel Edward's presence, Robyn ran lightly down the path, her naked toes barely brushing the hard frosty ground—everything had a dreamlike ease about it. Passing through an open gate, she saw a gloomy ground-level entrance right beneath the lit window, and she made for it.

Dogs poured out of the open doorway, big white Welsh grey-hounds with sharp, vicious teeth and red-tipped ears. They bounded straight at her, leaping and snarling, completely blocking her path. White hounds were a Lancastrian badge, and the red ears meant they were spirit hounds, like the Talbot hounds from the Land Under the Hill that Duchess Wydville set on her, north of Goodrich. These dogs were also most likely sent by the Wydvilles, to keep her away from Edward.

Somehow she had to get through the horrid, snapping pack. Her for-tified nest at Baynards Castle was under attack, with little more than a week's worth of Lenten stuff to feed on and a victorious army at the gates. Edward could change all that. With Edward at her side and lead-ing the defense, London would never give in, turning it into a siege in reverse, with Margaret's army starving in the cold bare countryside—if Lady Robyn could only get past these bloody hounds.

But each time she tried, the spirit hounds beat her back, nipping at her face and hands, their claws raking her thin black shift. Frus-trated and frightened, she retreated down the frozen path, away from the panting dogs, still smarting from nips and scratches. Tears started to well up. This was absurd, being alone in the night with a horde of nasty hounds, when she should be with Edward. What an absolute fool she was, supposing Duchess Wydville would let her just waltz in unmolested, when so much hung on keeping her and Edward apart. Now she truly needed help.

"Hell-la! Hell-la!" As if in answer to her plea, a black-and-white magpie came winging through the dark gate, proudly announcing her name. "Hell-la!"

Robyn recognized the bird at once, as Joy's flighty familiar and the Grey family watchbird. Glad for any assistance, she asked, "Hela, what in heaven are you doing here?"

Robyn did not really expect the bird to answer, but the magpie replied loudly, "Kaw-lynn! Kaw-lynn, kum-ming!"

With that the hounds looked up, staring intently at the black open gate that Robyn and Hela entered through. Silence settled over the frigid pathway as Hela alighted on a rosebush and began to nervously preen herself. Lady Robyn listened intently, knowing by the way their bloodred ears had pricked up that the hounds had already heard something.

Hoofbeats sounded in the dark gate, soft and distant at first, rising into a swift, energetic canter, growing with each beat, coming up the road from the Chipping Campden—the direction of Greystone. Lady Robyn stood stock-still, staring at the empty gateway. Steadily getting nearer and clearer, the loud reverberating *clip-clop* drowned out the hounds' panting and her own ragged breathing, becoming the only sound filling the velvety blackness.

Slowly, a silver armored figure on horseback emerged from the gloom, with a blue-and-white pennant on his lance, and a kiwi-green Minnie Mouse kerchief tied to his steel sleeve. Sir Collingwood Grey, warlock and reigning Westminster Champion, came riding through the gate atop his gray charger, his sallet visor up, and his lance at rest. Sir Collin rode right up to where Lady Robyn stood, and he reined in, smiling broadly, saying, "I was informed my lady required assistance, and I have come to render it—if you so desire."

"I do indeed." Lady Robyn could barely believe her luck. "Who told you I was here?"

"This delightful blond sprite that came in the night." Collin turned in the saddle to reveal he had a companion riding on the "maiden's seat." Heidi flashed her boss a triumphant smile, and Sir Collin added, "This winsome visitor swore on her soul I would find you here, in need of succor."

Heidi slid off the mount's mailed crupper, wearing just a grin and her black witch's shift, saying, "So, are you thrilled to see us?"

"To my toes," Robyn admitted. "How did you know I would need you here?"

Heidi laughed at her surprise. "I'd be a pretty piss-poor seeress if I didn't."

"And I a sorry champion," added Collin, proud of being prompt with his lance. He nodded at the hounds, saying, "With my lady's permission."

Lady Robyn gave her leave, and her champion spurred his mount, lowering his lance to beat a path through the pack. Hounds parted angrily, snarling and complaining, but careful not to come within reach of the steel lance point. They had been happy to torment an unarmed woman, but wanted no part of an armed knight and his mailed mount. She and Heidi followed in his wake.

At the door, Collin did a clattering dismount, leaned his lance against the manse, and drew his sword. White dogs gave him a wary look, while Hela settled into his place on the high saddle. Sir Collin turned to her, indicating the dark open door that the hounds emerged from, saying, "If my lady will allow, I will lead the way."

"By all means." Happy to have his armored bulk ahead of her, she took Heidi's hand and entered the silent sleeping manse, leaving Hela in charge of the mailed warhorse. This ground floor stank of dog, and was clearly a kennel-cum-storeroom, arranged so the dogs could keep the rats down. Light came from a stairwell at the far end of the room, falling down the stone steps from the chamber above.

Picking though the litter and dog dung, Collin lead the way to the stairs, where he turned to her, arching an eyebrow. She nodded, and Sir Collin ascended the steps, with her and Heidi at his steel heels. They emerged into the corner of a spacious, high-roofed manor hall, lit by a flaring fireplace. Servants slept on benches and mattresses along the walls, making it seem more than ever like Sleeping Beauty's palace, but above the fireplace was the Fortescue coat-of-arms, and the family's punning Latin motto, *Forte Scutum Salus Ducum*. Fortescues were inordinately proud of having been the "strong shield"—*forte ecu*—of William the Conqueror, even claiming to have saved his life by stopping an arrow meant for him at Hastings. William, who gave England French manners and the Tower of London, was one of her most ghastly rulers, roundly hated by most of his subjects—though clearly not by the Fortescues. The family's bootlicking attitude led the current Chief Justice Fortescue to side with Queen Margaret. Justice Fortescue was supposed to have advanced ideas on a parliamentary monarchy and the rule of law, though he did not blink at an infant ordering the beheadings of Bonville, Kyriell, and Gower. Medievals liked to leave a healthy gap between theory and reality.

Most medievals anyway. Some meant to have their way, come hell or high water. While everyone else in the hall lay peacefully asleep, one person was painfully awake, the Duchess Wydville, standing by the fire wearing a goat-horned headdress and a black satin gown with crimson-silver flames stitched into the fabric, looking very much the witch-duchess, holding a tall three-branched candelabra that cast light only on her. This was not the "real" Duchess Wydville, no more than Robyn was "really" there—both of them were actually in London. Ebrington was just where they must do battle. Her Grace haughtily kept up pretenses, saying, "How happy to haff you here, Lady Stafford."

"Happy I got past the hounds?" Hardly. She knew that Duchess Wydville was backed against a wall. Edward was the difference between total victory and sure defeat. No negotiations could paper that over—not after Saint Albans II. Everyone must announce their final allegiance. Edward or Margaret? England's past was at war with her future.

"Sir Collingwood Grey, how excellent to see you, too." Duchess Wydville acknowledged the knight in armor who had made this meeting possible. Collin merely nodded, knowing a man who did not mind his words on Witches Night might wake up as a toad—or worse. Her Grace turned to Heidi, adding, "And the newest strumpet from tomorrow. Vhut a jolly reunion."

"No one invited you," Robyn reminded the witch-duchess. Her midnight tryst with Edward had become uncomfortably crowded.

"Ungrateful girl. You could haff had all you wanted," the duchess replied reproachfully, "had you but handed over Baynards Castle, as you promised."

Lady Robyn did not believe that for a heartbeat. She and Edward living happily ever after, bearing potential heirs to the throne, was never in the Wydville plans. "I will present your kind offer to the lord of Baynards Castle, when I see him next."

Her Grace asked slyly, "Will that be soon?"

"Were it up to me, I would be with him now," Robyn replied evenly.

"Truly?" Duchess Wydville sounded disbelieving.

Lady Robyn laughed. "Try to stop me."

"Only you can do that," observed the duchess tartly, looking more than ever like the witch in Sleeping Beauty, come early to the christening, with her gloating smile and goat-horn headdress. "That is why I am giving you the choice of going back to your own world. Here is my blessing for your new baby, may the child within you grow up healthy and happy, and in a place of safety—centuries from now. Any child of Edward's will be a potential heir to the throne, always a target for mayhem or abduction, so long as you remain here. In your own time, the child can grow up free of fear and safe from our rude diseases."

Give a few lectures on germ theory and hygiene, and some folks never forgive you. Robyn had gotten a reputation as the Lady Macbeth of London, always insisting that everyone wash their hands. "I do not want that choice," she insisted, "so take your blessing and go—"

"Nonetheless, you have it. *Nein?*" Her Grace was not about to budge, either, planting the tall candleholder firmly in front of her, resting on three iron feet shaped like dog's paws. "There are two doors behind me. One leads to Edward and misfortune. The other leads to your own time, where this manor still exists—though we are long gone. You, though, can be there, alive and happy, in your impossibly clean and healthy future. I freely warn you that if you choose to stay with Edward, you will be horribly disappointed, and you will very soon see how truly alone you are in our world. So go back, my darling, be with your own people—both you and your child will be so much better off." With that, the good duchess disappeared, leaving only the tall three-branched candelabra to illuminate the two doors, which were made of oak with identical iron latches.

There was no one left to argue with. Here was Duchess Wydville's final trap, using Robyn's own doubts and deepest misgivings to power the spell, forcing her to choose between being with Edward and succumbing to her fears for their child. She strode up to the doors and halted, getting no feeling from either one. Both seemed somewhat inviting, a sign they both hid things she needed.

Heidi spoke up behind her, asking, "Do you really want to stay here with Edward?"

"Sure." Most of her did, anyway. "But it is not that simple. So long as I have any doubts about staying, I cannot be sure of choosing the right door."

Feelings could be used to throw her back to the future against her will, so long as those feelings were genuine and she gave in to them. Some part of her wanted to go back, and have her baby in safety—that she could never deny or totally control. Duchess Wydville had succeeded in turning sure defeat into a fifty-fifty shot—two doors, today or tomorrow, take your pick—hoping Lady Robyn would get rid of herself.

"Well, I don't have any doubts," Heidi declared.

She looked over at her friend. "How does that help?"

"I will show you." Heidi turned to Collin, who had his visor up, revealing his serious chiseled face, which had led many an unwary lady into distress. Deftly loosening his bevor, Heidi kissed Collin on the lips—a long, involved kiss, so tender it made Robyn wonder, where was Bryn? No doubt having a witchy Sabbath with Jo and the kids. One drawback to being a sorceress was having to leave your man unwatched on Witches Night. Unless your man was in a high-walled manor, guarded by ghost hounds of hell. Then you were allowed to combine spellcraft with pleasure—provided you picked the right door.

Heidi regretfully unlocked lips, whispered a soft good-bye to Collin, and then stepped up to Robyn's side, facing the twin doors. "You are not sure if you want to stay, but I know that I want to go back. So let me pick a door—then you take the other."

"Are you sure you want to do this." Robyn was not even positive it would work.

"Absolutely," Heidi insisted. "Done all the damage I can around here. Got you back to the Middle Ages, and I was the lady of a castle with a boyfriend out of Shakespeare—for a little while, at least. Now I have a mom and a job to go back to, or rather your job, since you won't be there."

Which meant this was good-bye. Robyn felt shocked and dismayed, though it made sense, certainly more sense than her possibly landing in the future while Heidi stayed in the Middle Ages. This was one sure way for her to get to Edward, and for Heidi to get home. Heidi had nothing to keep her here, and she was bound to choose the door to the future—who knew when Heidi would get that chance again. "Tell the studio you have my vote."

"Like they care." Heidi rolled her eyes at how Hollywood rated the opinion of ex-employees, right up there with recommendations from the Audubon Society and the PTA. "But I am making you the female lead of a killer treatment; then it will be give me your office, or lose the story."

"I will miss you." And then some. She had come to rely on Heidi, more than she ever thought possible when the girl came pounding on her door back in the twenty-first-century Cotswolds, not awfully far from here.

"Me, too," Heidi admitted gravely. "Give my good-bye to the girls. I remember being on Maui, standing on a beach with a phone in my ear, asking what the Middle Ages were like."

Lady Robyn smiled to keep from crying. "Now you know."

Heidi lifted the latch on the door nearest her, at the same time leaning over to say, "And give this to Edward." Heidi French-kissed her good-bye, then added with a grin, "You are way better than he deserves."

Probably so. Lady Robyn seized the iron latch in front of her, knowing they must go through together, to get full advantage of the spell, ensuring they were each sent in different directions. As Heidi lifted her latch, Lady Robyn did the same. All she could see was blackness on the far side of the door. Giving Heidi one last smile, Robyn stepped through into darkness. There was no need to say good-bye to Collin, since she hoped to be seeing him soon.

Light from the hall did not pass the doorway, and she immediately bumped into a steep cramped staircase leading to the floor above. Feeling her way up worn narrow steps, she had no idea what millennium she was in, knowing Brits habitually took centuries to widen the back stairs. She prayed that Edward was at the top of these steps, but she might be about to pop in on the twenty-first century Fortescues, snugly asleep in the family manor, fancying themselves completely safe from nocturnal advances by deranged Americans mistaking them for medieval nobility.

Stairs ended abruptly, opening onto an upper bedchamber above the main hall. Though still totally in the dark, Robyn no longer doubted that she was in the Middle Ages, since the closed bedroom had that musty medieval mix of burnt incense, heavy spices, sweaty leather, and barnyard odors. Only medievals could give the master bedroom that dank dogs-in-the-basement smell without so much as a whiff of pine-scent deodorizer or stale tobacco. Modern homes were so much cleaner, and more polluted.

Heavy muffled breathing came from what had to be a curtained bed in the far corner, the deep male breathing of a man who had done his day's work and deserved a night's rest. She felt suddenly guilty to be adding London's problems to Edward's many cares. Hopefully, her presence would compensate, since she herself could barely wait to feel his flesh pressed hard against hers, comforting and exciting at the same time. Assuming this was Edward.

Slipping carefully across the black chamber, she found the curtained bed with her outstretched fingers. Medieval bedrooms seldom had sufficient furniture to trip over. Sliding between the dark curtains, she lifted the coverlet and felt about for Edward, finding a broad warm back that seemed familiar. Hoping to Heaven this was her love, she doffed her torn witch's shift, sliding in naked beside him, whispering, "Awake, my lord, you have a visitor."

Her sleepy companion rolled over, drowsily saying her name. "Robyn?"

Good sign—at least she was not molesting some absolute stranger. "Who else?"

"How wonderful," he whispered, enfolding her in his arms, enthusiastically pressing his warm body against her, already aroused. Even in the dark, Robyn recognized Edward's big muscled body, and the easy way they fit together. Gratefully, she gave herself up to his embrace, happy to be held and wanted, and protected from the world. Without Heidi to help her, she needed Edward more than ever—so did London. He sighed happily, " 'Tis so very exciting to have you here."

"In spirit, at least." Here lying at his side, the spell was strongest, and most intimate. "My body is in Baynards Castle."

Her boyfriend took that as a challenge, slipping a hand between her legs, laying forceful claim to her far-off body. At the same time, he leaned down and kissed her breast, slyly catching her left nipple between his lips and tongue, tugging gently. This warm, wet sensation sent thrills rippling through her abdomen, proving Baynards Castle was nearer to Ebrington than maps made out. She snuggled closer, determined to dispose of business first, getting the bad news out of the way. "Warwick has lost the king."

"So I have heard." Edward's voice turned somber. "And I was told you were taken at Saint Albans, but escaped, making me worry much for you—"

"Do not fear—that was nothing." She kissed him to quiet his concern. Just another "burn within the hour" brush with the stake, which every accomplished witch had on her résumé. Rubbing against him to show how alive she was and how little he need worry, Lady Robyn felt his broad hands wander over her naked body, pressing them closer together. Edward had let his mad cousin run the country and let his own father almost ruin their cause, but he had wanted her from day one, vowing to put aside the crown—if need be. So long as she was his, and his alone.

"I was heartstruck," he insisted, "to hear you were in peril, and vastly pleased to find you had been saved." To show his vast pleasure, Edward slid a brawny leg in between hers, gently prying her thighs apart. She reveled in the rough, hairy friction as his powerful young body slid into her, incredibly hard and insistent. His warm pulsing weight pressed her deep into the bed, engulfing her in a soft dark world made of flesh and feather mattress, totally shut off from the universe and utterly given over to pleasure. Even if it was "all in her head," she was enjoying this witch's dream immensely, as was Edward.

After what must have been a millennium, this dream within a dream wound down, replaced by sweaty exhaustion and labored breathing. Such rapturous moments of relapse were almost the best parts, lying still entwined, filled up with pleasure, yet set to start again. Being in bed out-of-body was next best to being there in person. But Lady Robyn desperately desired the real thing, a true loving lord in her castle. Stroking Edward's invisible features, she whispered, "We need you in London."

Her love whispered back, "But we are doing wonderfully right here. In truth, I have something amazingly delightful to show you—"

"No doubt." Edward was clearly ready to go again, but she first wanted his vow to come to her in the flesh. Real dangers had brought his dream girl here. "Mayor Lee and his merry aldermen want to turn the city over to Queen Margaret, but the commons will not have it. Naturally all the nobles have fled, while Duchess Wyville and Old Lady Scales are trying to charm the city into surrendering."

Edward laughed in the dark, amused by the mess women had made in his absence. "And I would make all the difference?" Pulling her cheerfully toward him, Edward sounded like he had heard it before, how England had no hope without him. Since only bold action by the boy wonder could save everyone, Edward decided to start at once, catching hold of her breasts, then running thumbs over her captive nipples, while his groin stirred and stiffened. "What about someone new? That might be intriguing, too. Me, you, and . . ."

Unable to see his face, she could not tell how seriously he took all this. Her visit was not mere midnight nookie; she had vital news for him, and she needed his reassurance. Reaching for the spot by the pillow where he usually kept a lighter, her hand closed on the bit of plastic as easily as if she had summoned it. Flicking it on, she told him, "Come, my love, London needs you, and I need you."

Her love looked rather shocked, as if this had all been a happy dream, suddenly made too real by the lighter flame. For a long moment Edward just stared in surprise, which turned slowly back to delight as he focused on the light playing on her naked curves. Then a sulky complaining voice from behind him broke the silence, saying, "You and London should learn to share."

Elizabeth Wydville's sleepy blond head appeared over Edward's shoulder, looking unduly satisfied for a woman who had just lost her husband. "My Lord of March has grown so great that there is more than enough of Edward for everyone."

Edward did not look the least surprised to find a second witch in his bed. Grinning guiltily, he did the unnecessary introductions. "My lady, you remember Lady Elizabeth, who was with us at Goodrich."

"And who tried to deliver you to the Tudors," Robyn noted

tartly, seeing no need for such formality, since they were all naked already. Not just naked, but intimate. "Anything we say with her here goes straight through her mother to Margaret."

"Lady Stafford." Elizabeth Wydville laughed, shaking out her long golden hair. "I hoped we were better friends."

Edward plainly hoped so, too—more than friends. From the look of things, Lady Elizabeth had been lying there in the dark—not in body, but in spirit—eavesdropping on their tryst, while Edward happily made love to two women, on the same night, and in the same bed. In his dreams. Men naturally assumed that if one woman was good, two would be better, and when better to find out than Witches Night? No wonder events in London were no news to Edward; Elizabeth had already given him her version. He pleaded, "You are the one who always wants peace."

Just not a piece of Elizabeth Wydville. There was a sort of wicked allure to sleeping with the enemy on Witches Night, in the chief justice's bed. How many laws would that be breaking? But you want your first woman to at least be a friend, not some black widow with designs on your boyfriend. If Edward wanted a ménage so much, he should not have beheaded Heidi's ex-boyfriend—that particular female friendship had "Welcome Edward" written all over it, until he sacrified feelings to politics. She shook her head hard. "Her or me. Make your choice."

But Edward was thoroughly hooked on bedroom politics by now, claiming, "We need whatever aid we can get."

"Her or me." Robyn refused even to argue. She felt scratched up, put upon, and chewed over by dogs, and in no mood to compete with the merry widow for Edward's affection. Even the Fortescues' great curtained bed was not big enough for both of them.

"I will make it easy." Elizabeth Wydville gave an exasperated sigh and rose up, showing more shapely ivory torso, without a single scratch or bite. Leaning over Edward, the blond widow rested her hand on Robyn's bare abdomen, saying, "May she live long, growing up strong and full of grace."

Lady Elizabeth turned and gave the disappointed Edward a good-bye kiss, then was gone, vanishing instantly from his bed, leaving the Lord of March asking vainly, "Where did she go?"

"London, most likely." That's where things were happening.

"Can you bring her back?" Edward did not ask if she wanted to do it.

"Not likely." She gave a witch's laugh without being the least amused. "Besides, I shall be back in London soon myself, and could look her up then." Edward was the one about to end up in a big empty bed. "We need you desperately. Not just me and your unborn child, but a whole city that loves you."

"And I will be there." He acted like that had already been accomplished, thanks to Lady Elizabeth's visit, so they could get back to the real business of the evening—even though it was only the two of them. He ran a firm hand up her calf, asking, "Are you really going to hold some witch's dream against me?"

"That is a woman's secret," she retorted, being in no mood to share innermost secrets, not with Edward. That feeling broke the link, and she was instantly gone from Ebrington, headed home to Baynards Castle.

15

⊷═ The Battle of London ═⊷

W*hen she opened* her eyes, she was back in Baynards Castle, and her only consolation was picturing Edward left alone in the dark atop the chief justice's big bed. Without a word to the coven, she led them in a final prayer, then closed the circle. Immediately they were on her, asking, "What's wrong? Where is Heidi? Did you not find Edward?"

She shook her head, saying, "Oh, no. I found Edward." And more.

They all knew that something was wrong, asking again, "What has happened to Heidi? Why are you naked? Where did you get all those scratches?"

"Heidi has gone home." She hated to admit it as much as the others hated to hear it. This had been a costly Witches Night. She'd said good-bye to Heidi, only to find Edward dallying with a phantom widow. The whole coven did not need to know how desperate things had become, so she tried to put the best face on events, saying, "Heidi has her home in L.A. and was only visiting here, but her love stays with us."

"Will she be back?" Beth asked plaintively, already missing her wild blond role model.

"If God wills it." Deftly passing the buck up to Heaven, Lady Robyn led them all in a prayer, wishing Heidi godspeed on her journey. She said nothing about coming back scratched and naked.

Deidre was not fooled. Her red-haired maid demanded to know what else troubled her. "What happened. Was it Duchess Wydville? Was it FitzHolland?"

Robyn resolutely refused to say, shaking her head, merely assuring them, "Edward knows our plight, and he is coming."

She pretended she had not seen Elizabeth Wydville with Edward, because that was how Elizabeth would play it, acting the prim and proper widow, destitute, submissive, and apologetic, having given Edward a haunting feel of the flesh beneath the black silk. Modesty made the best come on, so long as the man knew it was false.

At least Edward had his warning. Where was Alan ap Gruffydd when you really needed him? Lady Robyn thought of that gallant young Welshman who came without question to her aid, and whom she thoughtlessly left flat on his back in Llanthony, languishing with just a kiss to remember her by. That was a fellow who knew his chivalry. Yet she left him for Edward—so this is what she got. Which meant that for the moment, both she and London were very much on their own.

Making it all the more vital that citizens should awake to a new edition of the *White Rose*. As soon as the ink had dried, men headed into the city, handing copies out in the inns and posting them on market stalls from Saint Paul's to Billingsgate. The *White Rose* was such a hit in the taverns that Robyn was tempted to sell ad space—if the pace of news ever slackened. Her first payment to the Venetians was due next week, so she was facing not just battle, but bankruptcy, as well.

More news kept arriving. Amy Lambert called, ostensibly to see that her daughter was well settled at Baynards Castle, but bringing word that Mayor Lee had made a secret agreement with Duchess Wydville. "Four aldermen will be escorted by the two duchesses and Lady Scales to meet with Queen Margaret."

What a picture that was; three widows with the fate of London in their hands, and likely England's future, as well. By now the male nobility was nearly exhausted. Most of the old leaders, like York, Buckingham, and Salisbury, were dead. Margaret was surrounded by ne'er-do-wells like young Somerset, and thugs like Percy and Holland, too roundly hated to rule. And of course King Henry, nobleman number one, was mad as a March hare, sort of setting the tone for the rest. Lady Robyn asked, "What offer will they be taking to Margaret?"

Sitting in the presence chamber, wearing a scoop-necked gown and a butterfly headdress, her chair atop the carpet that hid the six-pointed chalk star, Amy Lambert primly explained, "They will bring four men from Queen Margaret to treat publicly for entrance into the city."

Eminently reasonable. The part about public negotiations showed the deft hand of Widow Wydville. Right now the *White Rose* was free to present Queen Margaret's demands in the worst possible light, forcing Her Highness into an open debate. Robyn asked Amy, "What will Margaret offer?"

"No looting—and only the king's most trusted lords will enter the city." Amy knew that seemingly mild offer was a death sentence for the Yorkist leaders. If Holland, Clifford, and Percy got loose in the city, no one would be safe from their vengeance. Still, it would be hard to argue against a truce and public debate. Margaret was so much easier to deal with when she was playing a parody of the Mad Queen, heading an army of cutthroats and border rabble, and screaming, "Off with his head!" whenever someone wore a white rose instead of a red one. This kinder, gentler Margaret was infinitely more scary.

Next came Elizabeth Poynings, asking about her husband, who commanded Warwick's doomed garrison at Dunstable. Robyn feared she was talking to another widow, since Matt had said the man was dead, but Robyn did not have the heart to pass on that grim bit of hearsay, instead promising to do her best, telling Elizabeth, "No matter what happens, you may shelter here."

Elizabeth thanked her, then asked hesitantly, "Has m'lady heard the grievous news about Edward of March?"

"What grievous news?" Robyn had to remind herself she had just seen Edward alive and doing all too well in the Cotswolds. Word of any real harm to him could not possibly have reached London so soon.

"That Queen Margaret has sent word that the city must proclaim him a traitor." Elizabeth Poynings looked anguished, though that threat to Edward hardly compared with losing a husband. Her concern merely showed how much the women of London feared Edward might not appear in time, or not arrive at all. If Edward ever dropped his troublesome finicky girlfriend, London would surely welcome him with open legs.

Alarm bells began to toll over the city roofs, and Lady Robyn extracted herself from her painful interview with yet another prospective widow to meet Henry Mountfort in the main hall, who reported that the alarm came from Aldgate, on the far side of the city. She told him, "Make ready to defend the castle. I will see what can be done at Aldgate."

Her sergeant-at-arms looked taken aback, asking, "M'lady, is it wise to take such risks?"

"Probably not," she admitted—but this was a crisis, and she had to be there. Lady Robyn tried to mollify her retainer, saying, "I will take Matt with me."

And not just Matt. When she got to the stables, Sir Louis de Coutes was waiting, along with his two valets, all wearing half-armor and hip boots. Sir Louis went down on one knee, vowing that he could not allow his fair captor to go out unprotected. "For the town will be full of armed and excited Englishmen, and all manner of mischief will happen."

She could guess what her French prisoner was thinking. He had lost Joan the Maid this way, when she'd been pulled off her horse in an armed brawl at a besieged town gate. Sir Louis meant to see that did not happen again. Lady Robyn pointed out, "You have given your parole not to fight."

Sir Louis politely corrected his captor, "I only vowed not to fight Lord Edward. Escorting his lady through danger could hardly be doing him harm."

In fact, chivalry practically demanded it. If you could not beat your enemy, the next best thing was to squire his girlfriend around when he was away—it made you look good, and you could always get lucky. Turning to Matt, she asked, "What do you think?"

Her horse master did not hesitate. "M'lady, we need every sword we can get."

She smirked at Matt Davye's enthusiasm for his former enemy. "Even if we must trust the French?"

Matt nodded sadly. "Times are that bad, m'lady." So she rode out the castle gate with chain mail under her gown, backed by French prisoners in plate armor, all wearing her red-and-gold. Bells tolled their warning overhead, and people cheered her, waving copies of the *White Rose* as she rode past Saint Paul's. On Watling Street, she met a troop of German panzenars, armored infantry from the Steelyard, marching to their post at Bishopsgate, one gate west of Aldgate. Apprentice boys with swords and staves fell in behind them.

At Threadneedle Street, the Germans turned off toward Bishopsgate, and Lady Robyn led the apprentice boys on through the stock market and up Cornhill to Aldgate, past the church of Saint Andrew Undershaft, named for the maypole that overtopped the steeple. Aldgate sat in a corner of the city wall, in the shadow of Holy Trinity Priory; from there the wall ran west to Bishopsgate and south to the Tower, while beyond the wall lay the impoverished ward of Portsoken. Her apprenticed boys were welcomed by the cheers of armed citizens gathered at the Saracen's Head inn on the south side of the street, while Mayor Lee and the city fathers were assembled at Holy Trinity, whose prior was also an alderman.

Robyn instantly sensed a stand-off. Mayor Lee would have gladly opened the gate to the queen's men, but he dared not anger the armed mob gathering beneath the Saracen's Head. John Lambert stood guard at the gate, and when she asked to have a look from atop the walls, Beth's father graciously agreed. Richard Lee might be mayor, but my Lord of March's girlfriend had the citizens behind her. Sir Louis de Coutes came with her to the ramparts and stood at her side with a shield ready while she leaned out an embrasure, looking down on poor outcast Portsoken.

She immediately recognized the banners of Sir Baldwin Fulford and Sir Alexander Hody, Queen Margaret's commanders at Barnet, backed by hundreds of armed men, mostly bowmen and moss-troopers, filling the shabby little suburb. Lady Robyn was instantly recognized, as well, as someone who had seen her at Saint Albans or London shouted, "Heigh-ho, look up, lads—it's March's whore!"

Sir Louis leaned out an embrasure to shout down in mocking French, "Go away, you silly English, with your silly *heigh-ho*. We will not let you in."

Trying to raise the level of discussion, she called down, "Sir Baldwin. Sir Alexander. Can you hear me?"

"We hear you, harlot. Give us something to see!" More jeers erupted from the troops below, who were mainly bored and just as happy to have a pretty face appear on the battlements, even if she was an enemy. By now Lady Robyn took the cheerful obscenities as a compliment—at least they knew who held London against them.

"What have you to say?" Sir Baldwin was just below, heading a squad of bowmen and some mounted men-at-arms.

"Only this," she called back. "London and Portsoken are under King Henry's protection, and their people are loved by God, do no harm, and I will speak for you later—if need be." It always paid to have friends on the other side.

Sir Baldwin did not think so, and he damned her as a rebel against the king, who was now safe in their hands. "Open this gate or your heads will decorate it!"

Archers took that as a signal to shoot, and arrows arched toward her from several angles. In all her months in the Middle Ages, this was the first time men had fired right at her, trying to kill her where she stood—the effect was frightening. She saw one shaft grow alarmingly large as it winged straight at her. Two others came at an angle from outside her field of vision.

Sir Louis's shield shot up, catching the arrows coming in at an angle. As they thudded into the shield, she shied away from the one coming head-on. Years of dodging flying clouds told her just which way to duck. Had she ducked the other way, she would have been dead.

Men below laughed at the near miss, like it was the funniest thing they had seen so far. Shaken, she stayed behind the shield, giving up trying to talk sense into Sir Baldwin Fulford. Sir Louis stuck his head back out to shout down, "Go away, you silly English. Or I taunt you again."

Catcalls answered him, along with cries of, "Bugger yer way back to France, you frog-eating fool."

Sir Louis had the last laugh when a city herald repeated the Frenchman's message, saying the gate would stay shut. Mayor Lee had seen the sense in siding with his citizens. Sir Louis shouted down, "How was that *heigh-ho?*"

He was answered by another volley of arrows that bounced off the battlements and clanged against his armor, but hit nothing vital. More business-minded bowmen began to rob and loot Portsoken, producing piteous wails from old women and families too poor to take shelter inside the city walls. Now they must watch their few belongings being pawed through by men determined not to come all the way to London for nothing. Smoke rose from shops and tenements outside the walls.

That finally opened the city gates. Archers mounted the wall walk, driving Fulford and Hody's men back from the gate with a storm of arrows. Then the angry crowd around the Saracen's Head came pouring out of Aldgate behind a hedge of pikes. Pillagers barely had time to drop their loot before the enraged citizens were on them, wielding their pikes and huge two-handed axes that cleaved through plate and mail. Not the greeting that Fulford and Hody expected, having foreseen either an easy entry to the city or a leisurely sack of the suburbs. Instead they found themselves fighting for their lives, something not the least to their liking. Queen Margaret's mounted scouts and border riders scattered over the fields, and Sir Baldwin Fulford led the rout downriver, fleeing ahead of his bowmen.

Dazed by the carnage, and the sight of that arrow coming right at her, Robyn descended, finding that Sheriff Lambert had taken charge of Aldgate, and citizens were demanding that the gate keys and city watches be turned over to them. Though a city herald had sworn that Margaret's army would never enter London, no one trusted Mayor Lee. That left only one entrance not in the citizen's hands, and when Matt had helped her remount Lily, Robyn called out to Sheriff Lambert, "I will secure the Tower."

Beth's father looked surprised by the offer, but she knew Lord Fitzwalter, the lord lieutenant of the Tower, having helped get him his job, by bringing down the previous lord lieutenant. So when she rode up to the Bulwark Gate, her presence carried some weight, and Fitzwalter invited her in, where she negotiated an agreement that allowed citizens to guard the Iron Gate while the lord lieutenant preserved the contents of the Tower for King Henry. "With one exception."

"What is that?" asked Fitzwalter, worried by what Edward's girlfriend might want from the keeper of the Crown jewels.

There was something she wanted more than the royal regalia. "I want the torture rack that is in the White Tower basement."

"The rack?" Just about the last thing the lord lieutenant expected from a fashionable young woman.

"That is right, the Duke of Exeter's Daughter." Which rather ironically made the rack Gilbert FitzHolland's half sister. "I want it hauled out the Bulwark Gate."

Fitzwalter's wariness turned to curiosity. "Whatever for?"

"That is my concern." Her motives were pure, but none of Fitzwalter's business.

Figuring he was getting off well, Fitzwalter agreed, and his men hauled the rack out into daylight, probably a first for the torture instrument. Just seeing the wooden bed and the windlass for tightening the chains made Lady Robyn's wrists and arms ache. Gathering evidence by torture was illegal in England without a warrant signed by King Henry—but the Hollands were notoriously lax about the letter of the law. Curious Londoners stared at the black ugly rack, having heard the stories—and sometimes even seen the victims—but never the thing itself. During her stay in the Tower, she slept on it to keep above the rats.

When the citizens' curiosity was satisfied, she had the Duke of Exeter's Daughter hauled to the top of Tower Hill, to the spot where witches and heretics were burned. There she ordered the hated rack piled atop dry wood and doused with oil, then lit the oil with her lighter. London was seeing the world turned upside down, with the crowd on Tower Hill cheering to see a witch burning an instrument of torture.

Saturday, 21 February 1461, Saint Margaret's Eve,
Baynards Castle, London

London has not seen a Saturday night like this since last summer, when we first took the city from Queen Margaret. And this time we have the Tower, too—without a great lord in sight. Last summer London opened its gates to the rebel earls, defying King

Henry and showing her favor. Tonight, London is governing herself. And I was here to see it happen.

Not everyone is pleased with the new anarchy. Since Southwark is outside of the walls, Proud Cis is packing the kids off to Flanders. I offered to lodge George and Richard in Baynards Castle, but having lost one son to me and another to the war, Duchess Cecily in not willing to risk her youngest. Too bad. Having boys in the castle would have been fun.

Margaret has made no new attempts to force the city gates. And tomorrow is not only the Lord's day, but Saint Margaret is the patron saint of whores. What could possibly go wrong?

Plenty. Edward's younger brothers went down to the docks, where they boarded a Dutch ship and were whisked away with the tide. Duchess Cecily dried her tears, then grimly announced, "Since Southwark is no longer safe, we will be taking up residence in Baynards Castle."

Ghastly news there. When she set up Baynards Castle as a women's shelter, Lady Robyn never thought proud Cecily of York would appear at the gate. She would far rather have put up Queen Margaret, since Her Majesty had at times been nice to her, and never suspected Robyn of molesting her son. Without warning, the enemy was suddenly inside her castle, and she did not even get to douse Duchess Cis with boiling oil. Luckily, Proud Cis insisted that she and her ladies must have the main hall, which left the keep in Lady Robyn's hands, her fortress of last resort.

She got a bit of her own back, by making Duchess Cecily share the main dining hall with the French prisoners, making for very lively table talk. Over codling and crayfish served with date compote, Duchess Cis declared that while living in Rouen, she had studied the case of Joan of Arc and concluded that the Maid could not be a considered a true mystic. "Forby she was convicted in court of witchcraft."

Sir Louis de Coutes merely smirked, saying, "In a French court."

Proud Cis sniffed. "Even a French court can give justice."

"Not this time," Sir Louis noted. "The court was reversed five years ago. I testified to the grievous errors in her previous trial."

Duchess Cecily was not going to get trapped into defending one

French court against another. "No doubt an English court would have convicted her properly."

"Alas," Sir Louis shook his head sadly, "that we shall never know."

"Why not?" Proud Cis did not think a French prisoner was in any position to judge an English court.

"Because you already burned her," Sir Louis pointed out. "Since we French readily admit we convicted her unfairly, Joan will remain forever innocent. Thanks to English eagerness to have her burned alive."

Lady Robyn made no comment, except to ask her server for some fried monkfish. It struck her as ironic the Edward had been born where Joan was burned. They had much in common, like youth, popularity, and a recklessly successful military record—in some ways Edward seemed to be Joan reborn as a man, just to further bedevil Mad King Henry. Seeing Robyn putting fried monkfish atop the codling and compote, Duchess Cis seemed to suspect she was eating for two. "Your appetite has improved, even as your morals have suffered."

Robyn merely asked for more monkfish, with mustard and herb sauce. Later, when it was time to bid each other a good Saint Margaret's Night, Edward's mother hissed, "If he marries you, I will swear he was my bastard."

"Was he?" Robyn wished to heaven Edward was illegitimate, and unfit for kingship. Proud Cis did not answer, shutting her door in disgust. If Robyn had thought for a moment that Duchess Cecily could get them barred from the throne, she would have married Edward months ago.

Monday, 23 February 1461, Baynards Castle, London

Ten months in the Middle Ages. Funny how it almost feels like home—all it needs is Edward. And money. Four more days, and I must pay off the Italians.

Word has come that Warwick was captured by Queen Margaret, but I doubt it. We could hardly be that lucky, even on my ten-month anniversary.

That night she dreamed of Heidi, finding herself back in her own glass-and-stucco West L.A. apartment, which now apparently belonged to Heidi, who was whipping up some minced-boar lasagna, showing unsuspected domestic skills. Heidi asked, "How did things go with Edward?"

Robyn winced in her sleep, "Would rather not say."

"That bad?" Heidi shredded a layer of mozzarella over the minced boar. "Who was she?"

"Who was who?" Lady Robyn played dumb and tried to help with the meal, but she kept finding medieval utensils and ended up pounding at the tomato-paste can with a mace.

Heidi rolled her eyes. "Who was Edward with?"

"Am I that obvious?" She set down the mace and started scraping tomato paste out of the battered can.

"You and Edward could not have gotten into this funk on your own, not in the middle of a Witches Night fuck, ergo, there was someone else there." Heidi never used to lapse into Latin and formal logic, using four-letter words like *ergo*—blame it on the Middle Ages. "I could list the most likely suspects, but that could take time, and malign the innocent."

"Elizabeth Wydville," Robyn admitted, knowing she could keep nothing from Heidi—though who Edward was doing was almost a state secret.

Heidi whistled. "Could have been worse."

How? Elizabeth was just the thin edge of the wedge, backed by the whole incredible weight of the Wydvilles, with their unbridled greed, overweening ambition, and wild unwed daughters. Elizabeth herself was one of the better ones, though that was not saying much, since everything Lady Elizabeth did was for herself. When Elizabeth blessed the baby in her belly, the witch-priestess added her own prayer for a girl—knowing the big winner was the woman who gave Edward sons. She woke up from the dream dearly missing Heidi.

Wednesday, 25 February 1461, Saint Porphyry's Eve,
Baynards Castle, London

Saint Poverty's Day tomorrow. I owe the Venetians fifty silver marks that I no longer have. Happily, I live in a castle, which are notoriously hard to repo. Help, Edward. Please come soon. Bring money. Your honey is in hock to the Italians, and they do not take VISA.

Lady Robyn awoke on Saint Porphyry's Day full of dread, not knowing how she would find the money, and afraid of what the Italians would do. Until today, the city had been her haven, her island of safety, surrounded by the war-torn winter countryside— now she was in trouble here, too. She lay in bed with her eyes closed, happy she lived in a house designed to keep creditors at bay, when she heard a bird rapping on the window. Throwing on a robe, she got up and opened the shutter.

"Hel-la!" The magpie came hopping into the room, looking about for crumbs, or anything that caught the eye. "Hel-la hee-re!"

Dressing at once, she had Matt ready the horses and organize an escort, saying, "Our prayers are answered. Edward is nearing the city." Nothing less could explain Hela's sudden arrival. Collin would be coming with Edward, along with God knew what other Greys. Ignoring creditors and misgivings, she rode out to meet her love, guided by the black-and-white bird, meeting him well beyond the city walls.

As expected, half the Marches had come with him, seeing their hero safely to London—though it was nowhere near the tens of thousands that the *White Rose* had promised. Not that her readers complained, since Edward was the only who mattered. Collin came with him, along with Hastings and his Midlands retainers. Even Warwick, riding alive and well at Edward's side, did not detract from the pleasure of having her love here at last. Edward was wearing his murrey-and-blue, with a new badge, celebrating his victory over the Tudors at Mortimer's Cross—it was a gold disk with rays, symbolizing the sun in splendor. Above him flew the White Lion of March, and the lions and lilies of England and France. There was a white silk rose sewn to his black cap.

Despite all that had happened, or because of it, his kiss of welcome was warmer, more urgent that she expected, and his mailed arm came around her back to bring them closer. He insisted on having the kiss linger, though they were in public, letting everyone know where his heart lay.

Did she have him worried? Hard to tell. Clearly he was happy to see her, but halfheartedness was never her worry with Edward. Lady Robyn rode through Ludgate with her love, past women gathered to sing a greeting to the city's hero. Now more than ever, what happened next was up to them. Queen Margaret was headed north with the remains of her starving army, and the Tudors were crushed, while Mad King Henry had been whisked away and Warwick, the so-called Kingmaker, was humbled. Edward was lord of the west, the beloved of London, and heir to the throne. And Lady Robyn was the only one he heeded, to the astonishment of nearly everyone and the envy of quite a few. She and her lord rode through the city side by side beneath a banner sprinkled with gold suns while Londoners sang:

> Let us walk in a new wine yard,
> And let us make a gay garden
> In the month of March
> With this fair white rose and herb, the Earl of March.

That week's Witches Night was the last in February, and Robyn treated herself to a private ritual while Beth and Joy led the coven. She retired to her old tower room, wanting a place that felt close and familiar, though she still could not cast her circle alone. She was never alone nowadays. This time she did not try for supernatural pyrotechnics, merely offering up her thanks to Mary, praying for guidance, for her and her child, now that she was on the verge of motherhood. And she said thanks to Heidi, who had brought her back here, for better or worse.

She finished up kneeling on the Persian carpet in the little tower room that had been hers, then Heidi's, and now hers again. Cold night air, smelling of the river, raised goose bumps on her skin and made the candle flicker. Closing her circle, she got up and changed into a red-and-gold robe out of the cedar clothes chest, then took her candle and went looking for Edward. In all the hoopla of liberating London yet again, they never had a chance to talk, not about the future or even about last Witches Night. Waiting a week had not made her feel a whit better about finding him in bed with Elizabeth Wydville.

Baynards Castle was dark and quiet, after the loud events of the last week. With Edward in residence, the keep presence chamber was back to being their private bath, and the carpet no longer concealed a Star of David. Much as she reveled in having Edward back, she missed the bright energy that used to fill the room—when Deirdre and the girls used it by day, laughing and singing over their sewing, while the coven did magic there at night. Now their cheery little haven from the world was back to being the London headquarters of the House of York.

In the bedroom, Edward's stuff lay strewn about, boots and books, a lute, and several bits of armor, but no Edward. She considered waiting for him in bed, but decided to check the stairwell instead. An odd feeling of déjà vu made her think that if she went straight to the stairs, Edward would be there.

And he was. Boot steps rang on the stone stairs. Looking down, she saw it was Edward, carrying a single candle, his boyish brow furrowed in thought. She retreated to the bedchamber, and blew out her candle. First a careful check of the bed—finding no one there, not even in spirit. Then she crawled in to await him there, just to be doubly sure there were no new surprises.

Lying curled in the dark cold sheets, she listened to him enter and remove his boots, and then his hose and doublet. When his candle went out, she tensed in anticipation. They had not made love since Ebrington either, and she was aching to feel his warm flesh beside her, if not inside her.

Curtains parted, and the mattress sank with his naked weight. At last they were safe and together, secure in her walled city. Looping her arms about him, she whispered, "I missed you mightily."

"Me, too. That will never happen again." He made her feel he meant it, gripping her hard and covering her mouth with his own. His fierceness felt exciting, even though they had not talked, with his powerful body straining against her, eager to go further. Sometimes she wished Edward would just make her marry him—right now, on the spot. He was her feudal lord, for God's sake, and very likely to be her king someday. When their lips parted, he promised, "From now on, it is just the two of us."

"Truly?" She could not believe that, not after all that had happened.

"Who else is there?" He was now atop the feudal pile. His father was dead, and King Henry was trailing northward after Queen Margaret. Edward outranked everyone who remained.

She pushed his hand down, below her belly. "There is our child."

He smiled at her sense of priorities. "True."

"And Lady Elizabeth." She would not let Edward skip over her feelings to get to the dessert.

"Which Lady Elizabeth?" Edward actually sounded like he did not know. Heaven help him if there turned out to be more than one.

"The one you were with last Witches Night," she hissed, not liking that she had to say it.

He replied in hushed tones. "Was that not a woman's secret?"

"And I am a woman, you idiot," she reminded him, pressing his hand against her breasts. "Of course you can tell me."

He clearly liked the feel of her breast. "I had not thought of it that way."

"So, what happened between you and Lady Elizabeth?"

"My lady must be fair," he protested, catching her nipples between his fingers.

"Must I?" she whispered, enjoying his touch but trying not to show it.

"Hear me out, at least," he pleaded, drawing her nearer at the same time. "I lay dreaming in my bed when Lady Elizabeth entered my dreams, though I surely did nothing to call her. But being it was a dream—"

"You enjoyed yourself immensely." She could see Edward meant to pass off that Witches Night tryst with a Wydville as some witchy wet dream, with himself as the innocent young victim. Just another helpless teenager assaulted in his sleep by a sinful sorceress.

"Not near so much as when you came along." He kissed the hollow of her neck.

"And you had two women in your bed," she noted.

"In my dreams," he hastened to add, smiling to show his innocence. Mayhap he was innocent. Or just happy to have both her and Elizabeth Wydville in the same city—one pregnant, the other a newly made widow in waiting. Whatever the answer, Edward kept trying to defend his dream girl. "Lady Elizabeth said she set you free at Barnet. Is that so?"

Heidi had been so right. Elizabeth immediately cashed in on that good deed, making it an invitation to share Edward. Did the Wydvilles ever stoop to subtlety? Apparently not. "Yes, she freed me, and means to make the most of it."

"But she has changed sides," Edward protested, "in spirit, at least."

Robyn winced at that reminder. How like a man to think it less important, because it was soul to soul, instead of flesh to flesh. Once again she felt godawful glad to live in a castle with a tower gatehouse, a stout drawbridge, and a great portcullis gate—none of which would open to the beautiful blond widow Wydville, not anytime soon. Though Elizabeth Wydville was not the real problem; Edward was. Damn him. Medieval men loved to complain that women "threw everything away on a whim"—then did exactly that with women, defying law and religion for a lady's smile, treating their female side as a great big get-out-of-responsibility-free card. Even Mary's blessed mercy was mysteriously given, not earned by man. No wonder Heidi was such a hit here.

Nonetheless, Lady Robyn graciously forgave her lord and master, nestling closer to his warm hard body, happy just to have him home.

Collin was another knight-errant too loosely in touch with his female side, but he was always welcome. He called the next day, which was the final day of February, making it a perfect four-week month, starting on the Sunday before Mortimer's Cross, and ending on a simple Saturday. She gave her champion a private audience, thanking Collin for coming so promptly to her aid, and for not pretending that events at Ebrington had been a dream or anything but a desperate magical encounter. "I do not know how to properly reward you."

Collin laughed and shook his head. "Fear not, your friend has seen me most improperly rewarded."

"My friend?" It took Robyn a second to see who he meant. "You mean Heidi? How?"

" 'Tis a secret." Sir Collingwood Grey smiled and winked. "Entitled 'This End Up.' "

So Heidi had her way with Sir Collingwood Grey. Small surprise there. At least Sir Collin never pretended to be anything but a cad in armor. But happily that was Bryn's problem, since she was the one who kept marrying him. Whenever a witch made a fool of herself, it was almost always over a man.